The fact that he has begun to stock up on supplies makes her think he intends to keep her here for some time.

What seems like once every hour or so, he asks the same question, the same thing he's been asking since he brought her here.

"When is she coming?"

"I don't know who you mean," Lulu says.

"When is she coming?"

"Who?"

"The white girl. When is the white girl coming?"

After this happened a few times, Lulu figured out who he meant. Still, she hasn't let on to him that she knows, continues to play ignorant. At first she might have told him, but not now. Now she has had time to reconsider that idea. As long as he wants something from her, she judges, he will keep her alive. When he has the information he wants, then he will kill her like she believes he did the rest of her family . . .

MISSING WHITE GIRL

JEFFREY J. MARIOTTE

JOVE BOOKS, NEW YORK

THE BERKLEY PUBLISHING GROUP
Published by the Penguin Group
Penguin Group (USA) Inc.
375 Hudson Street, New York, New York 10014, USA

Penguin Group (Canada), 90 Eglinton Avenue East, Suite 700, Toronto, Ontario M4P 2Y3, Canada
(a division of Pearson Penguin Canada Inc.)
Penguin Books Ltd., 80 Strand, London WC2R 0RL, England
Penguin Group Ireland, 25 St. Stephen's Green, Dublin 2, Ireland (a division of Penguin Books Ltd.)
Penguin Group (Australia), 250 Camberwell Road, Camberwell, Victoria 3124, Australia
(a division of Pearson Australia Group Pty. Ltd.)
Penguin Books India Pvt. Ltd., 11 Community Centre, Panchsheel Park, New Delhi—110 017, India
Penguin Group (NZ), 67 Apollo Drive, Rosedale, North Shore 0745, Auckland, New Zealand
(a division of Pearson New Zealand Ltd.)
Penguin Books (South Africa) (Pty.) Ltd., 24 Sturdee Avenue, Rosebank, Johannesburg 2196, South Africa

Penguin Books Ltd., Registered Offices: 80 Strand, London WC2R 0RL, England

This is a work of fiction. Names, characters, places, and incidents either are the product of the author's imagination or are used fictitiously, and any resemblance to actual persons, living or dead, business establishments, events, or locales is entirely coincidental. The publisher does not have any control over and does not assume any responsibility for author or third-party websites or their content.

MISSING WHITE GIRL

A Jove Book / published by arrangement with the author

PRINTING HISTORY
Jove mass-market edition / June 2007

Copyright © 2007 by Jeffrey J. Mariotte.
Cover design by Rita Frangie.
Cover photograph of "Barbed wire" by Atli Mar/Nordic Photos/Getty; cover photograph of "Young woman standing behind net curtain" by Will Sanders/Stone/Getty.
Text design by Laura K. Corless.

ISBN: 978-0-515-14308-9

JOVE®
Jove Books are published by The Berkley Publishing Group,
a division of Penguin Group (USA) Inc.,
375 Hudson Street, New York, New York 10014.
JOVE is a registered trademark of Penguin Group (USA) Inc.
The "J" design is a trademark belonging to Penguin Group (USA) Inc.

PRINTED IN THE UNITED STATES OF AMERICA

10 9 8 7 6 5 4 3 2 1

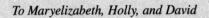

To Maryelizabeth, Holly, and David

Acknowledgments

A novel like this couldn't be written without the assistance of the many people who provide factual information, moral support, and generally good company. Of course, factual information can be twisted for fictional effect, so anything that's right in here can be credited to the following people, while anything that's wrong should be blamed solely on the author. That said, I'd like to thank Mario Escalante and Ulysses Duronslet of the U.S. Border Patrol; Carol Capas of the Cochise County Sheriff's Office; Xavier Zaragoza of the Douglas, Arizona, *Daily Dispatch*; Glenda, Curtis and the crew at the Douglas branch of the Cochise County Library; Robin Brekhus of the Gadsden Hotel; J. Carson Black; Cindy Chapman; Howard Morhaim; Ginjer Buchanan; and Maryelizabeth Hart for the contributions they made to this effort.

DAY ONE

1

The back of a van or a truck, she guesses, but hard, anyway,
and ridged. She rolls on the turns, slams into solid steel when
the vehicle brakes suddenly. A hump that keeps ramming into
her spine might be a wheel well. Head pounding, blindfolded.
Duct tape holds an awful rag stuffed in her mouth and straps
down her hair, bites her flesh.

No idea how long she's been riding, or who took her.

Or why.

No idea. . . .

2

Any other time, there would have been cameras there, a press corps. An American family murdered in their home—that was newsworthy, Patrol Lieutenant Buck Shelton knew, even in today's world.

Except this wasn't any other time. This was week two of the disappearance of Elayne Lippincott. Because she was sixteen, blond, popular in school and had two local modeling jobs under her belt, Elayne's kidnapping had drawn hundreds of reporters to Cochise County in Arizona's southeast corner. Buck had been out to the Lippincott estate and seen the satellite trucks corkscrewing the sky and the white vans emblazoned with network logos jammed together on the sweeping paved driveway, evidence of America's obsession with the case.

Victor Lippincott, Elayne's father, was a prominent banker in Sierra Vista. His wife Beatrice would likely have been referred to, in a more urban setting, as a "socialite." Their Santa Fe–style adobe mansion was surrounded by a broad expanse of lawn that summer's rains and a gardener's careful attention had left uniformly green. On that lawn a white tent had been erected to shield the press corps from Arizona's sun and the monsoon rains. Red ribbons tied to the guy lines fluttered pennantlike in the stiff wind, while beneath the tent's peaked roof, reporters and crews flocked together like too many ducks crowding a too small pond. Every time the Lippincotts showed themselves, the reporters waiting outside pelted them with questions. At night the crews thinned but didn't dissipate altogether, as the well known and well paid visited local restaurants and hotels, only to return in the morning, rested and fed, to continue their slow-motion stalking.

Buck (given name Hawthorn, God only knew why) had heard the term "media circus," seen some on TV surrounding the O. J. Simpson, Laci Peterson and Robert Blake cases, and others. But he had never imagined that sleepy Cochise County would host one.

So while papers from nearby Douglas and Bisbee would send reporters out, the national press was too consumed by the latest missing white girl to pay any attention to the wholesale slaughter of a black father and a Mexican mother and their mixed-race kids. Buck didn't know if race entered into the decision to ignore the murders, but it for sure owned responsibility for all the fuss over Elayne Lippincott. Nothing, he had observed, boosted news ratings like a story about a missing white girl.

Trouble was, law enforcement and local officials paid attention to where the media spotlight fell. Cochise County's sheriff, Ed Gatlin, had become a regular face on *The Today Show*, Wolf Blitzer's *Situation Room*, *Larry King Live* and half a dozen other news programs. As a result, he had marshaled the full resources of the Cochise County Sheriff's Office, as well as officers loaned by the Arizona Department of Public Safety, to find Elayne Lippincott.

Twelve days later, Elayne hadn't turned up. And Buck Shelton had a houseful of bodies on his hands.

The Lavender house was a single-story Territorial adobe, decades old and showing the years; not something that would ever grace the pages of *Su Casa* magazine, the way the Lippincotts' showpiece had. All it had in common with the Lippincott home, which nestled against the southeastern flank of the Huachuca Mountains with a view all the way across the San Pedro Valley, was that it was made of mud, as houses had been in this region for a thousand years, and flat-roofed, with wooden vigas and ceiling beams. It was a working ranch house squatting tentatively on a patch of high desert scrub, not an ornament at the end of a sweeping paved driveway. There wasn't a Kokopelli or a coyote wearing a bandanna or one of those fake pueblo-style ladders or a wagon wheel to be seen, but up against the corrugated metal barn was a tire that had come off a tractor sometime in the last decade.

Somehow, the house's plain facade almost made it worse that its interior held five dead bodies. These were not rich people who'd led charmed lives, but hardworking folks, and they'd ended up butchered just like their own stock.

Buck shook his head sadly. He had known the Lavenders since they'd moved into the area seven years before. They raised goats and geese, some swine, ran a few head of cattle. They had planted an orchard that threw a few apples their way, once in a while. Mesquite erupted from the grassy fields like the splashing drops of the devil's own rainstorm, and they cut some of it, selling it to El Real Mexican Fine Foods for stove wood.

He glanced at the vast blue bowl of the Arizona sky. Towering clouds marched in from the southeast, some shredding at their bottom edges, dumping rain down in Douglas, no doubt. The summer monsoon. The morning had been still and hot, but a wind was working itself up and those clouds would be here within the hour. They'd not only slice several degrees off the day's temperature, but also wash away any footprints or evidence that might have been left behind outside by the killer or killers. Buck longed for one of those professional crime scene teams you saw on TV, trained scientists with their flashlights and evidence kits. He had a kit of his own, but it wasn't one of the glossy, high-tech-looking things on the tube, and he didn't have any beautiful young people to examine the scene for him. He had himself and Scoot Brown, the young deputy who had been first on the scene, and neither was anyone's idea of a beauty queen.

Responding to a call from a UPS driver, Scoot had gone into the house, then stumbled back out and puked onto the ground, kicking dirt over it when he was finished. Now he sat inside his car looking green, and the delivery guy leaned against his brown truck with his arms folded over his chest and a bitter expression on his tanned face. Not much help there.

Nodding to Scoot, Buck approached the house. Scoot had

tacked a sign-in sheet by the front door, and Buck wrote his name on it. He'd rubbed on some apple-scented lip balm and touched a dab of it on his mustache, just below his nose—not enough to mask any evidentiary odors, but enough, he hoped, to lessen the impact of human bodies cut open and left to rot.

It wasn't.

Later on, Sheriff Gatlin might be able to kick loose a team of criminalists from Bisbee. But for now, Buck and Scoot Brown were the only resources the sheriff felt he could spare. They were two-fifths of the staff of the Elfrida substation. Buck was the senior officer and he wanted to check out the scene for himself. The coroner's people, if they came at all, would stand up numbered cards and take pictures and measurements. Finally they would haul out the bodies. Before all that happened, Buck wanted to form his own impressions of what had happened to the Lavender family. He knew these people. Someone had murdered them. He didn't want to leave to strangers the task of finding out who.

The front door opened into a living room. The Lavenders had a couple of dogs, as most everyone in these parts did, and the dogs tracked mud in, especially this time of year, but Manuela Morales Lavender followed behind them with a vacuum cleaner as best she could. The dogs, a yellow Lab and a mutt who was part shepherd with a lot of other parts mixed in, were tied to the fence now, and if they had seen anything, they weren't telling.

The furniture inside was old but clean. A brown cloth couch was worn on the seat cushions and frayed at the arms. An oak coffee table served as resting place for a coffee can that held remote controls for a TV, a DVD player and a boombox stereo system all arrayed against the opposite wall on a discount-store entertainment center made of pressboard and covered in wood-grain paper that peeled at the corners. Some of it, near the floor, looked as if it had been gnawed away, possibly by one of the dogs. The light brown carpet it all sat on had eroded in the high-traffic areas, like a field overgrazed by livestock, but under the entertainment center and the coffee table and near the walls it was still full and unfaded. Green leafy houseplants were scattered around the room, as if the foliage outdoors stole inside when no one was looking.

Pictures had been hung almost randomly on the white interior walls; most were the type you could buy, already framed, at Target or Kmart. The largest was an aerial photograph of the Waikiki coastline at dusk, with Diamond Head brooding in the background. Buck noticed a smear on the wall near the photo, which hung off to one side of the entertainment center, almost in the hallway. Too high up to be from a dog's paw, unless one of the mutts had stood on his hind legs to reach up the wall. And though it was turning brown, as if the wall had begun to rust, liquid red shone at its core. Someone with blood on his hand had touched there, steadying himself maybe. Buck turned away from the dining room and kitchen, which Scoot had already told him were empty, and forced himself into the hallway.

The smells that had assaulted him as soon as he passed through the door were worse. Lemon Pledge fought a losing battle with the slaughterhouse smells of blood and shit and raw meat. Nothing he hadn't encountered before, but rarely to such a degree and in such a confined space. This was no slaughterhouse, but a small ranch house. He let his mouth hang open, breathing through it.

A longer streak of blood marred the wall at the same height from the ground as the first one. He found another on a doorjamb. Clicking on a flashlight so he didn't have to touch light switches, Buck shone it through the door, revealing a bathroom. Dark stains on the sink faucet showed that the killer had washed his hands. The sink was wiped clean, but not the handle. On top of the toilet tank was a box of tissues with a minute stain near the perforated opening. Probably the killer had used those to swab out the sink, then flushed them. They could be recovered from the septic tank, if absolutely necessary, but the blood on them would be from the Lavenders, and any transfer from the killer would probably have been washed out by the flushing or contaminated beyond usefulness.

He skipped the next two doors. The kids' rooms, he was sure. He wasn't ready to face those. The door at the end of the hallway led into the master bedroom, and horrible as it would be, at least he would probably find adults in there.

The master bedroom had its own bath and a large closet. It was the kind of room that country-style decorators tried to emulate, but this one was the real deal. A quilt covered the brass-framed bed, and another one, in process, was draped over a wooden quilt rack near one wall. A big cedar chest crouched at the foot of the bed. A couple of paintings decorated the wall, landscapes that had probably been in the family for so long their subjects no longer had any particular meaning to anybody.

Buck found Manuela Lavender, wearing a nightgown, faceup on the floor. Her legs were splayed awkwardly and the nightgown had ridden up almost to her left hip. He wanted to pull it down, to allow her some modesty, but he knew the integrity of the scene had to be preserved until it could be photographed.

Her face was bruised, lips split, a couple of teeth knocked out. She'd been hit hard with something. That hadn't killed her though. The hole over her breast had probably done that. The cotton nightgown was singed at the hole's edges, and blood had infiltrated the cotton fibers like a battalion of tiny saboteurs. Two flies twitched lazily around the wound. Gently, Buck prodded with the toe of his boot, turning her just enough to see the fist-sized exit hole between her shoulder blades.

He moved on to Hugh, also on the floor, closer to their un-made double bed. Rolled over on his side, arms flopped out, legs bent, Hugh wore pajama bottoms with no shirt covering his muscular chest. He'd also been shot, in the back of the head. Most of the top half of his face was gone. Bits of brain and skull and flesh littered the quilt and clung wetly to the wall above the bed, shellacked there by a spray of red. Hugh's had been an old man's face, prematurely aged by sun and wind and work. His dark skin had taken on a grayish cast over the years. As with many ranchers, there had been a permanent ridge above his eyes where his hat rested every waking hour unless he was eating or in church. All gone now. Buck bit back a curse.

He couldn't stomach much more of this, but he forced himself to keep going.

The next room was the one he'd been most afraid of entering. The two younger kids, boys, shared it. He knew their names, Kevin and Neal, made himself say them out loud. They were eight and six. The room looked like a boys' room, with action figures and children's books and Scooby-Doo sheets on the bunk beds. The boys had been handsome kids, Buck had always thought, inheriting golden brown skin, their father's tightly curled hair, and their mother's almond-shaped eyes.

Those eyes were closed now, mercifully. Both had been stabbed in the chest and stomach, not shot—stabbed twice in Kevin's case, the older boy; three times in Neal's. Blood had soaked into the sheets beneath Kevin's body, and no doubt the mattress as well. Neal was on the floor near the lower bunk. His fingers were abraded, and Buck wondered if he had fought to protect his brother.

· One door remained. Buck remembered the last time he had seen Lulu Lavender, down in Douglas on the Fourth of July. She had been at the park for the fireworks display with a young man from Bisbee. They had been holding hands, kissing, laughing together. She was a beautiful girl, with coloring and eyes like her little brothers', but with a glow all her own. She was eighteen, slender, active in the community, always pushing a petition or putting up posters about some cause or other.

He swallowed hard, closed his eyes; tapped the flashlight anxiously against the outside of his thigh. He didn't want to go in there. He wanted to mount Casper, his white Arabian stallion, and ride high into the Mules where the air was clean and fresh and no dead teenagers waited for him.

Lulu wasn't a hard case like some teens, or a Goth or a punk or any of those other things kids got into these days. A good student at Cochise College, she worked part-time, babysitting and the like, but put most of her efforts into classes and her causes. She respected her parents. On the walls of her room she had posters of bands she liked, photos of animals she'd

raised during her 4-H days, more photos of herself with friends
and family from vacations, picnics, school trips. Her bedspread
was a quilt she and her mother had made together.

He was surprised to find the room empty. Her bed was un-
made, blankets and sheets snarled up like a twister had struck,
but he couldn't see any blood. Lulu hadn't been murdered in
the night, like the rest of her family. At least, not in her own
room.

He hurried through the rest of the house. The dining room
and kitchen he had ignored earlier. A walk-in pantry. A mudroom.

No Lulu.

The Lavenders had a barn, a corral, a little well house and
almost eighty acres of land. If Lulu's body was out there somewhere, he'd find it. But if it wasn't, only three other possibilities came to mind. She could have spent the night with that
boyfriend, up in Bisbee. She could be missing, like Elayne
Lippincott. Or she could have done all this. Buck didn't think
that was likely. It took a certain type of individual, cold and
empty, to kill her own family, and he couldn't see Lulu as that
type.

Anyway, her purse, wallet and cell phone had been in her
room. If she had gone someplace voluntarily, she would have
taken those.

Rage rose in his throat like bile. Someone had come into his
territory to kill these people. He took it personally. Unprofes-
sional, maybe, but he had become a cop in the days when trust-
ing gut instincts was more highly valued than science. He had
developed a cop's gut, and he continued to rely on it, maybe
more than he should.

Buck exited through the mudroom door. Scoot Brown had
emerged from his car and paced outside. "The girl's missing,"
Buck said. "Lulu's not in there."

"I haven't seen anything out here," Scoot offered.

"Call it in, then check the barn. You don't find her in there,
I want you to walk every square foot of this property."

"Right," Scoot said.

Buck saw footprints in the dirt around the house, but he'd

have to check the feet of the family members, rule them out before he knew if they meant anything, and he'd have to make casts of the tracks before the rains came. Same with the tire tracks in the dirt drive and the unpaved road that led off Davis Road. Follow Davis about six miles till the pavement started, and it ran straight into Douglas, another ten miles south. In the other direction it hit McNeal at Highway 191, which ran through Elfrida and on up the Sulphur Springs Valley.

At the other edge of Douglas was the Mexican border. If Lulu had been taken there, she would be outside the reach of American law enforcement. He just had to pray that wasn't the case.

He glanced down Larrimore Trail, away from the backdrop of the Pedregosa Mountains and the Swisshelms toward Davis Road. Another house nestled in a little hollow there, surrounded by scrub. He jabbed his thumb toward it. "That's where the new folks live, right? The old Martin place?"

The young deputy nodded, chewing on his lower lip. He hadn't started for the barn yet. "That's it."

"Know their name?"

"Mailbox says 'Bowles.'"

"How long since they moved in?"

"Late winter, early spring, seems like," the kid said.

"So maybe six, eight months," Buck said, mostly to himself. "He teaches at the college?"

"What I hear," the kid said. His eyes were big, liquid. *Probably his first murder scene,* Buck thought. Different than car accidents or UDAs freezing or dying of thirst in the desert. Harder to take, even for him.

Going to have to have a look at the professor, Buck thought. He had no particular reason to do so but proximity, and that gut of his. The Lavenders weren't wealthy; no one would mistake their house for someplace where a lot of cash or high-end electronics would be found. Anyway, the brutality, the savagery on display here indicated something more personal, some emotional component, which meant the murders had likely been committed by someone who knew them. *A neighbor, maybe.*

Scoot stood beside the house, as if the order to leave it had given his feet roots. Buck would check the barn himself, then. He needed to make a more thorough pass through the house with his kit, collecting whatever evidence he could find, but first he wanted to make sure Lulu was no longer on the property. Reminding Scoot to call Sheriff Gatlin's office in Bisbee and then to cast those shoe and tire tracks, Buck headed toward the barn, silently promising the Lavenders that he would find Lulu, and discover who had violated them in such a horrific way.

3

" ... **Jessica Drake reporting from Sierra Vista, Arizona. Jessica?**"

"Thanks, Martin. I'm here at the Lippincott house, where we've just learned of a potential breakthrough in the abduction of Elayne Lippincott. Authorities today say that they've received a tip from what is described as a reliable source, which they believe might lead them to the present whereabouts of Ms. Lippincott. As you know, Elayne Lippincott was abducted twelve nights ago from the house you can see behind me, here in southeastern Arizona. At the time, police found some evidence in the house but not enough to point them in any specific direction. With this new tip, however, police may well be able to locate and rescue Elayne Lippincott and return her to the family that misses her so deeply. Martin, back to you."

4

Six miles from the Lavender house, Barry Drexler sat in the cramped office of Rojelio Chavez, his employer, with his fists clenched so tightly that his fingernails dug into the flesh of his palms.

"You know sales have been down," Chavez was saying. He sat in his rocking desk chair, tilting back toward shelves full of catalogs, phone books and cartons of inventory. The rest of the tiny office was similarly cluttered, so much so that Barry had often wondered how Chavez managed to find anything he really needed. "I've been putting my own money back into the business, trying to stay solvent. But I just can't afford to keep doing that."

It wasn't much of a job, working at Redi-Market. But since Barry had wrecked up his back five years before, he hadn't been able to keep ranching. Years of drought had made ranching a questionable business anyway, especially at his small scale. He had tried auto mechanics, but things had changed in that field so much since his younger days, he hadn't been able to make a go of it. His one mechanic's job had been lost to a Mexican kid a third his age, and he'd been lucky that Chavez had been willing to take him on, at fifty-nine, even part-time.

Two years later, he sat behind the register in the little market four nights a week, selling liquor, smokes, packaged foods and sundries to the people in McNeal. He had met folks there who had lived in the area as long as he had but with whom he'd never had contact before. The job had opened up a new social world to him, as well as providing a paycheck and getting him out of his empty house.

"So when's it happen?" he asked.

"Last day will be Friday," Chavez said. "I'll put up a sign today, let everyone know what's happening. If anyone asks for details, just have them see me."

"Right," Barry said.

"Barry, I'm really sorry about this. If there was anything else I could do, I would. I know the community counts on this store, and I know you like that regular check." Rojelio Chavez appeared genuinely pained. His smooth forehead furrowed like a freshly plowed field, and the lower tips of his drooping black mustache were wet from him chewing on it while he talked.

Barry relaxed his fists and rubbed the gnarled surface of his left thumbnail. "You got that right."

"I can't do much by way of a severance package. I'll cut you a check for a couple of weeks."

"Anything you can do, I'd appreciate." Barry couldn't quite believe he was being so deferential. Chavez was forty, with plenty of money. His wife worked at the hospital down in Douglas. His family wouldn't go hungry no matter what. Barry didn't have any family, hadn't since his wife Clarice died eight years back. They'd had one son, killed in the first Gulf war, so Barry was effectively alone in the world. He had a brother named Stuart, eight years younger, who had moved to Ohio after his own army stint and gone to work for a big insurance company. That company had folded a few years back, and it turned out the pensions promised to its employees didn't really exist. Stuart had a wife and a kid still in college, so his financial straits were even worse than Barry's, but that didn't mean Barry could get by on his minimal savings. "Why do you think it is, business bein' off?"

"Could have to do with the Wal-Mart," Chavez said. Barry had expected that response, since his boss had been complaining about the giant chain ever since they'd expanded their superstore in Douglas, just blocks from the Mexican border. "People are willing to drive all that way to save a few pennies, and then while they're down there they buy ten things they don't even need."

"That's right." Barry had been there a couple of times himself, but the size of the place had put him off. Aisle after aisle stacked high with junk, most of it plastic, some of it he couldn't even guess as to what it was used for. He'd never been able to find what he wanted in there, and looking for it disoriented him.

"You might think about applying there," Chavez said.

"At my age?"

"They hire older folks sometimes," Chavez replied. "As store greeters and such. I'll give you a good recommendation if you want to try it."

Barry quit worrying the nail. The stiff visitor chair across from Chavez's desk was getting uncomfortable. "I'll give it some thought, Rojelio. Thanks for the offer."

Chavez stood up, which Barry knew meant their cheery little get-together had come to a close. "Let me know if there's anything I can do."

For Barry to do that, he'd have to remember to copy down Rojelio Chavez's phone number from the store's emergency contact list. His employer had never given it to him, never invited him over or socialized with him in any way outside the shop.

He thought, for just a moment, about cleaning out the cash register before locking up tonight. He wouldn't get much out of it though; couple hundred bucks maybe, certainly not enough to risk jail over. Living on a fixed income would be hard, but at least his mortgage payments were low, and he had five rooms to wander around in. Spending the rest of his years in an eight-by-eight wouldn't do, not at all.

"Guess I'll get to work, then," Barry said.

His employer didn't answer.

5

She can't get comfortable. With her wrists bound behind her back, no position offers relief, and anytime she finds one better than another, the violent motion of the vehicle throws her out of it. Her shoulders burn with agony, her mouth aches to be free of the putrid rag filling it. The boxer shorts she was wearing when he came are soaked and soiled.

She wonders if the ride will ever end. Death would mean sweet release from the pain, the terror, but she can't will herself into its embrace and she doesn't have the ability or resources to take her own life. Instead, she prays for salvation, for rescue, but if her prayers are answered, it's not in the concrete, non-metaphorical way she needs at the moment.

Someone else, she tells herself, would have paid attention from the beginning, kept track of the twists and turns, the time elapsed, so that she might someday direct authorities back to wherever it was she was being taken. Not her, though. She was unconscious at the beginning, and when she woke up all she could think about was her family and her own physical discomfort. She heard gunshots, back at home, after the guy came into her room and slapped a wet rag over her face. Almost instantly she felt woozy, disoriented, and he tied a rope around her and carried her out of the house, into the truck. She tried to fight, to stay awake, especially when she heard the shots, but then she was out.

Her father owns a rifle, in case, he says, anything bothers the livestock. She only remembers it being loaded once during her lifetime, when she was eight or nine, which means that the shots she heard were almost certainly fired by her attacker.

She can't assume he had left anyone alive at home, although she hopes with all of her might that she's wrong.

Once she awakened, she had no idea how long they'd been driving and couldn't see outside to look for landmarks. She thinks about trying a couple of times, dismissing it each time as too late, then the bolts of pain shoot through her body and the humiliation of her circumstances sends shame rushing through her and she forgets all about it for another minute or hour.

By the time the vehicle stops, she has fallen asleep. She dreams of a bird, trying to fly, but its wings have been matted with thick oil and all it can manage is useless fluttering. When the rear door opens and light streams in, light she can't see but can only sense through the blindfold, for just a fraction of a second, she thinks she is home in her own bed.

But then she remembers.

6

With only morning classes on that Wednesday, Oliver Bowles left the campus of Cochise College shortly after noon. Rain had started a few minutes before he got out of the building, and by the time he reached his Subaru Outback it pelted him full force. As he drove east on Highway 80 and then north on 191, it sheeted down the front of the windshield, reducing visibility to almost nil. He fought to keep the car on an even keel, hydroplaning from time to time.

When he'd moved from San Diego to Arizona in late January, he had laughed at the signs that said DO NOT ENTER WHEN FLOODED. Monsoon season started in early July. Now that he'd lived through two months of it, he no longer laughed, and he understood the prevalence of high-clearance trucks and SUVs in the area. A four-foot dip didn't seem like much in dry weather, but when it filled with rushing water it could be treacherous.

He had learned to love the area, especially the border town of Douglas. Dinner in the El Conquistador dining room of Douglas's Gadsden Hotel had become an every-other-Friday-night ritual for him and Jeannie, always accompanied by a wonder-filled stroll around its gorgeous lobby, admiring the marble and gilt and huge Tiffany window and Tom, the taxidermied mountain lion who watched over it all from the landing of the sweeping staircase. He liked the small town atmosphere, the fact that people at shops and the post office and library all seemed to know one another and welcomed them like old friends after the first few visits. He'd never lived near such a little country town, never dreamed he would take to it, but he had.

Lightning daggered the dark sky. Thunder boomed from everywhere at once. The wind, blowing toward the west, slapped wet tumbleweed off Oliver's windshield.

By the time he turned off Davis Road onto Larrimore, almost an hour later, his shoulders ached from the tension and his hands felt frozen in place on the steering wheel. He stepped from the wagon into slick mud and opened the front gate to his property (which, he had discovered, really did need to be closed in order to keep stray cattle out of the yard). Standing outside the car he saw activity at the Lavenders' place, a couple hundred yards up the road. Big white SUVs, it looked like. Hard to tell through the driving rain, but they might have had light bars on top. Border Patrol or Cochise County sheriffs, he guessed. He knew only that he had never seen them there before. He didn't know what they might be doing at the neighbors' house, and given the absurd public fascination with that missing girl over in Sierra Vista, he would have been surprised to learn that there were any deputies available to come out into the boonies.

Maybe Jeannie would know. She'd started a job at a little art gallery in Bisbee, a few hours a week to begin with. Selling their expensive San Diego house and buying the little place here, even with a piece of land most Californians could only dream of owning, had left them with a financial buffer, so working, for her, was more about getting out of the house than economic necessity. Since she hadn't met many people in the area yet, most of her time was spent at home, trying to make their little ranch house into something they could live in. She had a knack for decorating, and she'd decided to veer away from the expected Western style, instead going for a French country look.

Having parked inside the corrugated steel garage, Oliver splashed though quarter-inch puddles to the covered front walk. The wagon had made it okay, but Jeannie still drove her old Camry. They would have to trade that in before she was stuck someplace or washed away in a flash flood.

"Are you soaked?" she called as he walked in the front door.

"Pretty much," he admitted. He toed off his leather shoes, not wanting his hands to touch the muck adhered there, and left them in the tiled entryway. "It's as bad out there as I've seen it. Everything okay here?"

"Fine," Jeannie said. She emerged from the spare bedroom, which she was turning into an office/library, with a paintbrush in her left hand, holding a can of sage paint under it with her right, to catch the drips. She wore splotches of the paint on her *Abbey Road* T-shirt. "The lights flickered a couple of times, but we never really lost power."

Oliver ran his fingers through wet hair. "Guess I know why people wear cowboy hats and boots around here," he said.

"Things like that don't become customary without a reason," she agreed. "Unless you maybe count parachute pants. And those oversized ball caps they wear cocked at that weird angle so the bill doesn't shade your eyes or your neck."

Jeannie was thin, with pale skin and straight hair the color of straw framing a narrow, high-cheekboned face. At thirty-six, she could pass for late twenties or so. The black T-shirt was cropped, lifted slightly by breasts that swelled beneath it, large for such a slender woman, and Oliver admired the stretch of flat stomach he could see extending down into the waistband of her faded jeans. Her grin illuminated her whole face, glowing from her cornflower blue eyes, crinkling the sides of her nose and making the freckles there stand out, and every time Oliver saw it he knew he was incredibly fortunate to have met her, luckier still that she'd stuck with him through everything.

"Those do look pretty ridiculous," he said. "As I'm sure I do."

She leaned in, kissed him hard on the lips. "Wet puppies turn me on," she said. "Especially that puppy-dog smell."

"All I smell is paint," he countered. "You've been busy."

"A little."

"You know what's going on at the Lavender place?"

"There've been cars there most of the morning," she said.

"From the sheriff's office. I saw one drive by. But I've been listening to the radio and haven't heard anything about it."

"I guess it wouldn't be the best time to walk down there," Oliver said. "But Lulu wasn't in class today. I just hope it's nothing serious."

"We could drive over if you're worried."

Oliver shook his head. "The road's like soup," he said. "I'll call instead."

Tugging his wet shirt away from his torso, he found the cordless and sat down at the dining room table. There was no such thing as cell phone service this far out, but at least the local phone company had run land lines a few years before. He knew the number well enough—since he and Jeannie had moved in, Lulu had been an incredible help, happy to teach them about all the aspects of rural life they had never experienced. Dealing with private wells and septic tanks and Gila monsters and rattlers had all been new and different to this pair of suburbanites, and there had been times they wondered how they would have survived it without Lulu's assistance.

A male voice he didn't recognize answered the phone. "Maybe I misdialed," he said. "I'm looking for Lulu Lavender."

"This is Lieutenant Shelton with the Cochise County Sheriff's Office," the voice informed him. "Who am I speaking with?"

"My name is Oliver Bowles. I'm Lulu's teacher, and her neighbor. Is everything okay?"

"You're the fellow lives down Larrimore Trail from the Lavenders?"

"That's right."

"I'd like to come and see you, if that's okay."

Oliver swallowed back his fear. This didn't sound good at all. "Sure. We'll be here."

He ended the call and looked at Jeannie, who watched him through narrowed eyes. "What's up?" she asked when he didn't speak right away.

"A sheriff's officer answered the phone. He's coming over to talk to us."

Jeannie's face blanched and she tugged at the lower hem of her Beatles shirt. Watching her chew her pale pink lower lip, Oliver couldn't shake the feeling that a bad day was about to become much, much worse.

7

The rain hit while Buck Shelton was walking the Lavenders' acreage looking for any sign of Lulu. The barn hadn't offered any clues. He checked the pigs and cows in case they'd been drawn to a body, but they scattered at his approach, revealing nothing.

As he wandered the brush-choked slopes, dodging the piercing thorns of mesquite, occasionally snagging his boots on long vines of desert gourds or clumps of thick grass, thunder roared overhead, lightning strobed the sky like paparazzi at a celebrity sighting, the wind picked up and the first heavy drops thudded into earth that had already dried and cracked since yesterday's storm.

He had left Scoot to take casts, photos and measurements, since the young man seemed incapable of moving more than about ten yards from his car, and gone on the walkabout himself. He hadn't really expected to find anything. There would have been no reason to kill everyone else inside the house and take Lulu away to kill her. If she had been killed here, she would be in her room like the rest of the family.

Buck tried to run down the sequence of events in his own mind. The killer or killers had entered through the front door. He hadn't seen any sign of forced entry, but many people around here never locked their doors at night. No way to tell how the dogs had reacted, if at all. Chances are they'd been away from the house, hunting rabbits or doing whatever it was country dogs did at night. The killer or killers entered the boys' room first, stabbing them quickly so as to not allow them to raise the alarm. From there he—Buck couldn't help feeling this had been a one-man job—went into the master bedroom, shooting Manuela and Hugh.

That noise must have awakened Lulu, unless she was asleep with an iPod plugged into her ears or something. Had she tried to run away, or hidden under her covers? The killer couldn't have waited long after shooting her parents before he charged into her room. The condition of her bed made it look as if she might have been there when he came in. He grabbed her and wrestled her out of bed, perhaps. Or he threw back the covers and showed her the gun.

Still, Buck believed the killer had taken the time to wash his hands in the bathroom. Had he taken Lulu out to a truck or van, bound her or worse, then gone back into the house to clean up? That would take a degree of coolness that few people possessed. But he couldn't have committed the murders while Lulu slumbered unknowingly in her room. So she was out of the house altogether, or the killer had restrained her outside somehow and gone back in.

When the rain hit, Buck ran for the house. By the time he reached it, his shirt was glued to his skin and water ran off the brim of his hat as if from a downspout. Scoot was nowhere to be seen, so Buck went inside.

"Scoot!"

"Right here, Buck!" Scoot came down the hallway carrying the department's digital camera, which recorded time, date and exposure information into its files so that they couldn't be manipulated on the computer without leaving evidence. "Find anything?"

"No sign of her," Buck admitted. "I'm calling Ed."

The Lavenders had a phone mounted on the wall in their kitchen, beneath a shelf of patron saint candles in tall glass containers. Buck's cell had no signal here, so he used his Motorola portable to call the sheriff. As he dialed, he reflected on the fact that none of the saints on that shelf had done the family much good in the long run. The coiled cord stretched long enough to reach a scarred pine dining table, so he drew back a chair and sat down.

After being transferred three times, he had Ed Gatlin on the line. "Sheriff Gatlin," he said. "It's Buck Shelton."

"Yes, Buck." Impatience in his voice. Patience had never been his long suit, and now that he had an emergency situation on his hands—and omnipresent media—he was even worse.

Buck got to the point. "We have a problem out here," he said. "Four people dead, murdered, out between McNeal and Douglas. Their teenage daughter is missing."

"Oh, Christ, don't tell me that," Ed said. "That's all I need right now."

"I'm going to need some help out here, Ed."

"I don't have it to give you," Ed said without hesitation. "I don't know if you've been keeping up, but we've got some major developments going on. We just found out there's a boyfriend no one knew about, and the Lippincott girl snuck out of the house to hook up with him. Which means the house isn't our crime scene after all. The boyfriend says she never showed up, so now we aren't sure where the hell she was snatched. Every fucking eyeball in the country is on us and suddenly we look like we've been walking around with our dicks in our hands for two weeks."

"I understand that's a priority, Ed. But I've got four bodies and another missing girl here. Could be the same guy took her too."

"Or it could be that she's out of town on a school trip. Or maybe there's a copycat, in which case we should try to keep the media away from that one. Once he realizes he's not drawing the attention the Lippincott snatcher is, maybe he'll give her up."

"Or kill her," Buck pointed out. "I'm just saying the five of us aren't really a full-fledged investigative unit. I need forensics, I need detectives, maybe even a full-on task force."

Ed gave a bitter laugh. "You mistaking me for someone with a budget? Some big city police force, maybe? You can have a forensics team. Until we can figure out where our real crime scene is I don't have any use for them. Beyond that, if I can free up any resources for you, I will. Don't hold your breath, though."

"Whatever you can do, Ed. Anything will help." Buck clicked off the radio, disappointment swamping him like the rain outside had. With twenty-two years on the job, he had at least twice as much experience as anyone else at the Elfrida substation. Scoot Brown had worked for the state prison for a couple of years and for the sheriff's department for three. Raul Bermudez had been around for nine, Carmela Lindo for five. Donna Gonzales ran dispatch, answered phones, made copies, but she was office help, not a real cop.

And they were supposed to solve a multiple homicide and kidnapping?

At least, he thought, if it could be confirmed that Lulu had been kidnapped, the FBI would take over. His feelings were mixed on that score—they were far more practiced at this sort of crime than he was. But he suspected they'd cut him out of the loop altogether, and that was the last thing he wanted. So far the feds had waited in the wings on the Lippincott case, because there had been no ransom demands or other evidence pointing to a kidnapping, which made her still just a missing person.

The phone rang before Buck could leave the kitchen. Ordinarily he'd let it go to voice mail or an answering machine, but he didn't see the latter and didn't know if the Lavenders had the former. Anyway, little about this case was ordinary, and if a ghost of a chance existed that whoever called could be helpful, he thought he needed to grab for it. He took a handkerchief from his pocket and draped it over the handset of the Lavenders' phone. Pinching the receiver near the top, trying not to obscure or smudge any prints that might have been left by the murderer who, he reasoned, would have held it toward the middle, he lifted it from the phone. "Lieutenant Shelton."

"Maybe I misdialed," a male voice said. "I'm looking for Lulu Lavender."

8

Having determined that the caller was the new neighbor, Buck told him to stay put. He would need to question them, and he might as well do it right away. One more thing he wanted to take care of first, though. He located an address/telephone book on the counter below the phone, and flipped pages until he recognized the name he was looking for: Jace Barwick, in Bisbee. Lulu's boyfriend.

He dialed the number, waited. After a couple of rings, he heard a click. "Hello?"

"This is Lieutenant Buck Shelton with the Cochise County Sheriff's Office. I'm calling for Jace Barwick."

Hesitation. "Umm, that's me."

"Mr. Barwick, are you Lulu Lavender's boyfriend?"

"We see each other," Jace said.

"Did she happen to spend last night with you? Or away from her home anywhere, to your knowledge?"

"No," Jace answered immediately. "I talked to her right about nine-thirty, and she was at home. Then I got an e-mail from her, sent a little after ten. And she posted an entry on her blog later than that. I think she was there all night."

"And you haven't heard from her today?"

"Not yet. Can you tell me what this is all about?"

"Please think very carefully, son. Is there anyplace else she might have stayed the night? A friend's house, something like that?"

Jace didn't consider for long. "Like I said, she posted on her blog, late. She wouldn't have gone out after that. Please, what's going on? I'm kind of freaking out here."

"I'm afraid I might have some bad news for you, Mr. Barwick. I'd prefer to tell you this in person, but I'm afraid that there isn't time for me to drive up to Bisbee right this minute. Lulu's not in her house. Her family has been killed—her mother, father and both boys, but there's no trace of Lulu, and—"

"Oh my God!" After the exclamation came a huffing noise that Buck took for labored breathing, or perhaps an attempt to hold back sobs.

"I'm sorry to have to tell you this, sir. There isn't necessarily any indication that Lulu's been hurt in any way. That's why I asked you if there's any other place she might have spent the night, because there's no sign of struggle in her room." He heard no response from the other end of the line, and wondered if Jace had hung up, or fainted. "Mr. Barwick?"

"I'm here." The voice was faint, unsteady. "She has some friends around there, but I don't know all their names. Sasha, I think, and Elenora. Becka. Paul. I . . . There are more, but . . . their numbers are programmed on her phone, I think."

"We'll do everything in our power to find Lulu, Mr. Barwick. I don't want you to have any doubts on that score."

"Do you . . . do you know who . . . killed her family? Kevin and Neal?"

"At this point we don't know much of anything, I'm afraid. But we'll find out, you can bank on that."

Jace sniffled a little before answering. "Okay. God, I can't believe . . . Nothing better have happened to her."

Buck was not at all surprised by the boy's quick switch between emotions. He was dealing with a lot, and it had all come from nowhere. Buck had seen the bodies, and Lulu's empty bedroom, all of which made the whole thing very real, very concrete. Jace didn't have that advantage. Very likely it wouldn't be real to him for a while yet.

After finishing up with the boyfriend, Buck left Scoot to mind the crime scene and drove through the downpour to the old Martin house, where Oliver Bowles lived now. The sand-colored stucco house occupied a five-acre parcel that had once been part of the same ranch the Lavenders owned now. A ten-thousand-acre spread had been whittled down to eighty-acre lots, then just under forty, and finally five. That kind of subdivision was common enough in these parts—Buck's own ranch had once been a larger cattle outfit, but it had been split between his father and three other siblings, then divided again when his father died. Most of the owners had sold out and moved on or passed away long ago, but Buck still owned some of his dad's portion, and ran some cattle on it with the help of a Salvadoran immigrant named Aurelio Santana.

Beside the house Buck couldn't stop thinking of as the Martin place—they had lived there for forty-eight years and both Nestor and Leticia were buried down in Douglas now—was a steel garage, and behind that a shed big enough for a riding lawnmower and some other garden implements but not much more. The rest of the land, except for a trimmed lawn immediately around the house, was the same combination of mesquite, creosote bush, yucca, rabbitbrush and other high desert scrub the Lavenders had.

Buck thought he'd seen Oliver around the area a couple of times but had never met him. When the door opened, he knew he had been right.

"Mr. Bowles?"

"That's right. Oliver Bowles. Come on in." Oliver Bowles extended a hand, and Buck took it. The man's grip was firm and he gave a friendly handshake. *Nothing sketchy there,* Buck thought. Oliver directed Buck through the dining room and into a living room, really an extension of the same area, defined by furniture more than walls.

Oliver looked to be in his late thirties. Lean but muscular, he appeared to be a guy who worked out some. Maybe he played tennis or soccer, not football or baseball. That was just a guess, but a cop had to learn to make quick judgments about people, sometimes instantaneous.

Oliver had short black hair, about a third of which had turned to gray; black wire-framed glasses, stylish, with small oval lenses; deep creases in his thin cheeks that probably acted as dimples when he smiled. He wasn't smiling now. He wore a black polo shirt, jeans and leather moccasins, with no socks or jewelry.

"Has something happened at the Lavenders'?" he asked. "Stupid question; you wouldn't be here if it hadn't. What's going on?"

"I'd like to be the one to ask the questions, if you don't mind," Buck said. "After I'm done, then you can have a turn, and I'll tell you what I can."

"Should my wife be here?"

"She home?"

"She's painting in the other room," Oliver said.

"Sure, fetch her too, please."

Oliver pointed to a leather armchair and left the living room. Buck sat down, examining the room. Nicely decorated with lots of floral fabrics on chairs and sofa—the leather chair was an anomaly, and Buck guessed Oliver had offered his own favorite seat. Cut flowers and live plants spilled from pots here and there, mostly copper with white china handles and ornamentation. The smell of fresh paint masked any aroma from the plants and flowers.

Buck heard murmured conversation, then both of them came into the room. The wife was a looker, a little younger than her husband and with a body on her that made Buck think of the calendar hanging on the wall at Hank's Auto Repair and Tires. The Arizona sun had tanned Oliver Bowles, but his wife kept out of it or slathered on the SPF 50. Only a spray of freckles across her nose showed that she had ever stepped outside the house.

"This is Jeannie," Oliver said.

"Pleased to meet you, Sheriff," she said. "I only wish it were under different circumstances."

"You can call me Lieutenant Shelton, ma'am," Buck said. He had taken off his hat and held it in his lap, in the leather chair Oliver had indicated. Holding his hat with his left hand, he half-stood and shook Jeannie's with his right. "Or Buck. Cochise County only has the one sheriff and he don't like us to forget it. You're doing some painting?"

"That's right," she said.

"You didn't just move in, did you?"

"We've been here since January, Lieutenant," Oliver answered coolly. He and Jeannie sat together on the couch across from Buck. "We didn't do a whole lot of work on the house right away, because we wanted to see how we liked it here, how my job would pan out, that kind of thing. We're feeling a little more settled now, so we're going ahead with some projects. Now, what is it we can we do for you?"

Buck had wanted to get a sense of both of them, but now that he had he wanted to question them separately. "I'm sorry, ma'am, but I'd like to talk to each of you in turn. All right if I take your husband outside for a few minutes? You can go back to your painting and we'll be right back."

Her smile wrinkled the skin around her nose. "Be my guest."

Oliver Bowles shrugged and led the way back outside. "Is this how it's usually done?"

"That's right," Buck said. "I like to hear from one person at a time."

They stood under an overhang just outside the front door. The lawn needed cutting. Buck knew how that was—during the monsoon season grass you had to coax out of the ground burst forth so fast you could hardly keep up with it. "What do you want to know?"

"You all know the Lavenders very well?"

"We've met the whole family a few times," Oliver said. "But we haven't really socialized much, I'm afraid. Been kind of busy. Really the only one we know well is Lulu."

"How did you come to know her?"

"She's been in a couple of the classes I teach at Cochise College. And she's been very helpful since we moved in here. She came over the day we moved in and introduced herself. Since then, anytime we've needed to know something like how to get cows out of the yard or what to do about tarantulas or centipedes, she's been the one we turn to."

"How often would you say you see her?"

"Monday, Wednesday, Friday," Oliver said. "Last quarter she was in a Tuesday/Thursday class. Sometimes she rides to school and back with me, but only if she's not doing something else before or after classes."

"And what about your wife?"

"She sees Lulu, I don't know, maybe once every week or two. We have her over for dinner sometimes. And she's watched our house a couple of times when we went out of town. Is Lulu okay, Lieutenant?"

"Like I said before, Mr. Bowles," Buck dodged, "you'll get your turn, but it's not here yet. Can you tell me when the last time either of you saw her was?"

"Monday," Oliver answered flatly. "I drove her to school, then saw her in class. She had an activity after school so she didn't need a ride home."

"What about the rest of the family?"

"When did we see them last?"

"That's right."

"I don't know. When I'm driving Lulu she usually comes over here and meets me. Has a cup of coffee with us, and then we take off. When I drop her off, sometimes there's somebody outside and other times there's not. I guess it's been a couple of weeks since I've seen them."

"Have you been in their house?"

"Yes," Oliver said. He watched a curve-billed thrasher hop from a soaptree yucca to the ground, no doubt chasing some tasty insect. "They had us over for dinner after we got settled in. We had them over once too. They're nice people and everything, but we really didn't have much common ground, so we didn't keep it up."

"How long since you've been inside there, would you say?"

"Probably four or five months," Oliver said, then corrected himself. "Or, no. Couple of months ago Lulu had a DVD she wanted to loan me, so when I dropped her off I went in the front door, stood there talking to Hugh for a couple of minutes while she found it. Nothing more extensive than that."

"You don't have any idea where Lulu spent last night, do you?"

"I would assume she spent it at home. She's a good girl,

gets along with her family. There's no tension there that I've seen, if that's what you're driving at."

So far Buck had no reason to suspect that he was lying or trying to cover anything. Time had come to drop the bomb, watch Oliver's reaction.

"Lulu's missing," he said. "And the rest of the family has been murdered. Hugh, Manuela, the boys, they're all dead."

Oliver's reaction was subdued. A narrowing of the eyes, parting lips, a slight blanching of the skin. "Are you serious?"

"Absolutely," Buck said. "I just came from there, as you know."

"But—someone *killed* them?"

"That's right. All except Lulu, who's nowhere to be found. I know this will be hard for you, since you seem close to the girl, but I have to ask: Do you think she's someone who could have killed her own family and run away?"

Oliver shook his head dramatically. "Definitely not. No. No. She isn't that kind at all. She's peace loving, gentle. She's a bit of a progressive activist, actually, certainly not a person with any violence in her."

"We've all got some violence inside us, Mr. Bowles," Buck corrected. "Sometimes it's just a matter of how far down you have to dig to turn it out."

"Not Lulu Lavender."

"I don't think so either, sir," Buck said. "If it's okay with you I'd like to talk to your wife now. You can wait out here until we're done."

"You say that like I have a choice."

Buck tossed him a smile. "Guess I'm peculiar that way."

He left Oliver on the covered walkway and found Jeannie inside, trying to resume her painting but obviously unable to focus on anything but her anxiety over what he and her husband were discussing. She invited him to sit in the same chair he'd used before, and he complied, again removing his hat. They talked for about ten minutes, covering much of the same ground, but she had nothing different to say about the Lavenders than her husband had.

Finally, he told her the same thing he'd told Oliver about

the murders and Lulu's disappearance. "Your husband doesn't believe that Lulu could kill her own family," he added.

"I agree," Jeannie said. "Lulu would never do anything like what you're suggesting. She didn't even want us to kill rattlesnakes."

"Good for her," Buck said. "It's against the law to kill them."

"That's what she told us," Jeannie said. "But more than that, she said, they're God's creatures too, and if we just left them alone they'd leave us alone. So far, she's been right." She paused a moment, then brought her hand up to her face, as if she could catch the escaping sobs. "Oh, God, she's got to be okay."

Buck let her plea hang in the air for a few moments, wanting to see how she would follow it up.

"Do you have any idea who might have done it, Lieutenant?" Jeannie asked, breaking the silence. "Or where she might be?"

Buck spread his hands. "I have nothing at all yet, except a houseful of bodies and a missing girl," he admitted. "But we'll find her, and we'll figure out what happened. You have my word on that."

9

Jeannie held her hands over her mouth like the speak-no-evil monkey, trying to digest what the lawman had told her. Anyone bearing news like his should look more distressed, she believed. This man just sat upright with his cowboy-style hat across his lap and his hands on its brim. There might have been sadness in his brown eyes, hooded by heavy lids and with a slight downturn at the outer corners, but she had never seen him before so that could have been his standard expression. His hair was dark brown, with a flattened ring where his hat usually rested. He had a prominent nose, a wide mouth with thin lips, a pronounced jaw. Exposure to sun and wind had leathered his skin, so that the wrinkles around his eyes and mouth resembled cracks or fissures in its surface. He was probably six-one or -two, and his tan uniform was clean but worn, with long sleeves snapped at the cuffs, black cowboy boots mostly hidden beneath the pants. He sat on the edge of the leather chair so his gun, handcuffs and whatever else dangled from his belt didn't mar its finish.

Nothing about him indicated that he had just come down the road from the neighbors' house, where he had looked at four dead bodies. Jeannie didn't even want to think about the fact that there had been a killer on their road—a road with only the two houses on it. Had the killer picked the Lavenders at random, driving right past their place to get to it? She couldn't imagine any reason why a struggling ranch family should be the target of such an act. But how did one rationalize the insane, or understand that which was inexplicable?

"Do you have any idea why someone would have . . . would

have done that?" she asked as he was leaving, her voice catching as she spoke.

"None at all, ma'am. That's what we have to figure out. Once we've done that, then I reckon we'll have a much better idea who did it."

Having joined them inside, Oliver said, "Solved a lot of mass murders, Lieutenant?" There was an edge to his voice that Jeannie didn't like, as if he were angry at the deputy and purposely baiting him. Not beyond the realm of possibility, she knew. Oliver had never cared much for authority figures to begin with, and after the last year that dislike had turned bitter.

The lieutenant let it roll off him. He spoke softly, casually, and if she hadn't become accustomed to the country accents of rural Arizonans, Jeannie would have assumed he'd been raised in the South. "Fortunately it doesn't come up that often in these parts," he said. "But don't you worry, we'll get it taken care of, all right."

"I hope you do," Oliver said, with less hostility this time. Which was good—the last thing they needed, Jeannie thought, was to make an enemy of local law enforcement.

"Well, I'll get out of your way now, let you go on with your day," Buck Shelton said. He fished a business card from his shirt pocket and put it down on the coffee table. "That's got my numbers on it, office and mobile. If you think of anything that might help, no matter how mundane it might seem, give me a call. Same thing if you feel nervous or threatened, like anyone's coming around here that oughtn't to be."

"Thanks, Lieutenant Shelton," Jeannie said quickly, before Oliver could answer. "We'll do that."

The lieutenant left, and Jeannie and Oliver stood in the doorway staring at each other. "My God," Oliver said after a few moments of uncomfortable silence. "Can you believe . . . the Lavenders?"

"And poor Lulu," Jeannie added. "She must be frightened out of her wits."

"Lulu's tough," Oliver said. "Of course she's scared. But if I know her, she's already looking for a way out, and a way to kick the ass of whoever's got her."

Thinking about Lulu choked Jeannie up again. She stepped forward, pressed herself against Oliver's wide chest. His arms wrapped around her, fingers pressing into her back. Even after everything they had been through, he remained her rock, her anchor, in a way that surprised her whenever she dared to think about it. She fancied herself an independent woman, and she knew she could get by without him.

But she would rather not have to. It always came down to that.

On his way out, Buck Shelton had asked them to keep what he'd said to themselves. He had referenced the media madness surrounding poor Elayne Lippincott's disappearance, and Jeannie had understood immediately. Rita Cosby had practically moved in with the Lippincotts, although rumor had it she was getting bored with Sierra Vista's nightlife and hoping for a quick end to the case. Jeannie would not have wanted Larrimore Trail to become the latest press encampment, especially since the only neighbors to interview or harass would be herself and Oliver.

The lieutenant had indicated also that it was a law enforcement decision, something to do with keeping Lulu's abductor off-balance by not letting news of his crime leak out. She was happy to go along with his request, and Oliver agreed.

After a few minutes, she returned to her painting. She had almost finished the two walls she was turning sage green, leaving the other two white for contrast. As she brushed up against the masking tape she had applied at the corner, her mind kept reeling back to the lieutenant's visit. He had never specifically said why he had come over. She had assumed, at first, it was because of the proximity of the houses. He hadn't seemed to know, until Oliver mentioned it, that Oliver and Lulu knew each other and sometimes drove to school together.

Then again, what if he had? What if there had been some clue—a diary entry, a note, something, he had found at the Lavender house that had sent him their way? Did he know something about Oliver and Lulu that she didn't? There had been a time when she wouldn't even have wondered, but the trust on which their marriage had been based had been broken, and although they had moved on together, reestablishing that trust had proven difficult.

Jeannie shook her head, embarrassed at herself for even thinking along such lines. What Shelton had described involved unspeakable violence. Oliver might have been capable of deception, dishonesty, but not murder or kidnapping. Such things weren't part of his makeup. *Just because you were burned once,* she told herself, *doesn't make the man you love a killer.*

She resolved to put such thoughts out of her head and returned her focus to her painting.

10

"I mostly came to the area because I wanted to serve at Fort Huachuca," Hugh Lavender had said. "It's the only military post still operational from the days of the Indian Wars, and it was the home base for the buffalo soldiers of the day."

"Buffalo soldiers?" Jeannie repeated. She passed a bowl of mashed potatoes to Manuela (real ones with crushed fresh garlic added, not the instant boxed kind she and Oliver usually ate). The boys, Kevin and Neal, were parked in front of the TV, watching *Toy Story 2*. "I've heard the phrase, but . . ."

Hugh rubbed the tightly curled hair on top of his head. "The Indians had never seen hair like black men have. They were used to long, straight hair. Maybe some natural waves, but nothing like this stuff. If you check out some of the pictures of the Apache warriors and their women, you'll see it looks like they spent time at the salon, used all the latest hair products, but it was just their own natural hair. They thought our hair looked like bison fur. So they called the black troopers 'buffalo soldiers,' and the name stuck."

"And how did you two meet?" Oliver asked.

Lulu giggled. "He thought she had great cans."

"And she does," Oliver said. "But I'm sure there was more to it than that."

Manuela laughed too. She had probably put on weight in the intervening years, but she was still a looker, Oliver thought, voluptuous and pretty, with some of the softest skin he had ever touched. "That was part of it, though," she said. "I had gone to a movie, with some girlfriends, over there in Sierra Vista. I was young, you know. When I left home, I had a school

sweatshirt on, but underneath it I had this tight top, cut down
to there, with a push-up bra underneath shoving everything I
had up and out."

"I still remember the way she looked," Hugh said, gazing
admiringly at his wife. "Caught my eye, that's for sure."

"He was at the theater with some of his army buddies, and
we saw each other and couldn't stop looking. I had never been
out with a black man, and my parents thought I was crazy
when I finally told them. He came up to me and started talking, and next thing I knew I told my friends to go to the movie
without me. We just went to a diner and got Cokes and yakked
for hours. I got in trouble for getting home late, but I didn't
care."

"That's basically all it took," Hugh added. "We were married eight months after that, and she"—he ticked his head toward Lulu—"was born ten months later. We went into debt
honeymooning in Honolulu, and she was conceived there, so
we called her Lulu."

Oliver had looked at Lulu then, who smiled almost shyly,
and saw the love with which her parents showered her reflected back at them.

"Oliver?"

"Yes?" Jeannie had been speaking, but he hadn't been
hearing anything she had said.

"Where were you?"

"Thinking about that time the Lavenders came to dinner
here," he said. "I can't stop thinking about them."

"I know what you mean." Jeannie had been quiet, contem-
plative, ever since Buck Shelton left. She had gone back to her
painting for a while, then come out and started dinner. They
were at the table now, eating without enthusiasm, cruising
through the evening on autopilot. Warren Zevon's *The Wind*
played softly in the background.

Back in San Diego, Jeannie had been a volunteer for two
different organizations, Habitat for Humanity, which worked

building housing for low-income people in Mexico, and the Nature Conservancy. She hadn't earned any money, but doing good work brought her an enormous amount of personal satisfaction, more than she had taken home in her previous career as a middle manager at an electronics company.

Since moving to Arizona, she hadn't found much, other than the part-time gallery work, to do with her days. Oliver worried about her, afraid she would get bored, restless. So far she seemed content to work on the house and be domestic in a way she never had before. Whether that could last, he didn't know.

"It's just . . . it's so awful I can't really process it," he said after a while. He put down his fork, done. Eating another bite just seemed like too much effort. "And I can't help wishing I could come up with something that would save Lulu. Something she told me that I'm not thinking of, maybe, that could be pertinent."

"You can't hold yourself responsible for the actions of a madman," Jeannie said. She folded her napkin and set it beside her plate, a sign that she had given up on dinner as well.

"I'm not," Oliver replied. "I'm just wondering . . . you know, if it was someone who knew her. Someone she knew, who maybe she mentioned at one time or another."

"If it comes to you, then that's great," Jeannie said. She rose, lifting her plate, reaching across the table for his. She had cooked, which meant it was his turn to do the dishes. "But you can't force it, I don't think."

He followed her into the kitchen, carrying glasses and silverware. By the time he got there, she had put the plates in the sink and was running water on them, but her shoulders were shaking. He put his hands on them, kissed a tear off her cheek. She pressed back into him, gripping his hands with hers.

"Forget the dishes," she said, her voice husky. She blinked back tears, turning her body into his arms. "You can do them after you do me."

"Right now?" he started to ask. But her mouth was on his, hungry, tongue probing, and he didn't bother to talk any more.

Jeannie's hands roamed down his back, cupping his ass, then moving forward to undo his belt with an urgency that was unusual but exciting.

He managed to turn off the running water before she pulled him onto the floor.

But just barely.

11

He had rented the mountain cabin ahead of time. Knowing what would likely transpire, what to expect, was only one of his gifts, but in this case it had been less an application of talent and more common sense, thinking through the plan, that had been responsible. He had known he'd be taking the girl away from the house. He would need a place to keep her. It would need to be secluded, private.

So he had spent a couple of days driving through Arizona's high country. He had settled on the Mogollon Rim area, where a natural escarpment two hundred miles long marked the edge of the Colorado Plateau. From the Rim, he could look down two thousand feet onto rolling, pine-covered mountains that slanted toward the deserts of southern Arizona somewhere out of sight. In the other direction, to the north, the plateau gave way to the ruddy arid land of the four corners region, the redrock deserts of Utah.

The cabin he found was a quarter mile from the rim's edge, screened by Douglas fir, ponderosa pine and aspen. Bare dirt, partially carpeted by pine needles, surrounded it. A long driveway led in from the Rim Road, passing only two other cabins on the way. The one nearest the road belonged to the owner of the property, a woman named Peggy Olsson.

Driving the Rim Road, he had opened his senses, listened to his pulse—another of his talents—and it had told him when to turn. He had pulled his truck to a stop outside Peggy Olsson's cabin and braved a fierce wind to knock on her door. A minute passed, then a woman pulled it open with a tentative, awkward motion. She was in her forties or early fifties, with red hair

showing strands of silver, glacial blue eyes, a hard mouth and a
voluptuous figure that a bulky sweatshirt tried hard to disguise.
"Can I help you?" she asked, her voice smooth as strained
honey. She did a better job than many at masking her distaste
for his appearance.

"I'd like to rent a cabin," he told her. "I understand you
might have something available."

She gave a surprised, nervous laugh and forced a smile.
The fingers of her right hand pinched a few strands of her coppery hair and fed them into the corner of her mouth. "Where'd
you hear that?' she asked. "I usually rent them in the summer
but close up after Labor Day."

"So you do have an empty cabin?" He already knew she
did, of course, and that she would agree to rent it to him. But
he had to go through the motions. Knowing the outcome didn't
allow one to skip the steps necessary to reach it.

"Well, yes . . ."

"I'd be happy to pay whatever your summer rate is. A little
more, maybe, for the inconvenience. You won't even know
I'm there. I'm working on a project, see, and I'm looking for a
private place where I won't be disturbed for a few weeks."

"Not much chance of that," Peggy said. "It gets quiet up
here after the season. Sometimes the road isn't even open.
You okay with that?"

He ticked his head over his shoulder toward the four-
wheel-drive truck parked there, an old green Ford full-sized
pickup with a tan Gem camper shell, bleached almost white
by the sun. Faded gold curtains covered every window. "Sure.
That thing'll go just about anywhere."

"I can't handle laundry or meals or anything like that. You'll
be on your own. There's a Laundromat and a grocery store over
in Show Low, and more choices down in Payson, of course."

"On my own's the way I like it," he said.

She gazed out toward a big pine, its branches swaying
in the wind. "Okay, then," she said. "I guess I could use the
money, so if you're okay with the terms then I guess we have
a deal."

"That's great," he said, favoring her with his best approximation of a smile. Sometimes that soured an agreement, but Peggy Olsson wasn't really looking at his face.

A week later, he returned and unloaded his cargo into the cabin, replacing the rope that bound the girl with shackles that he chained to a radiator in the second bedroom. He had moved all the furniture out of the room, leaving only a mattress on the floor, a metal bowl and a roll of toilet paper. He would bring her meals to her on a plastic tray and take them away when she was done. The whole ordeal wouldn't have to last long, he hoped. Just until she told him what he needed to know. Or until he had the girl—the one he really wanted, the precious one—in his hands.

He should already have known which it would be. But he couldn't see the outcome of all this, didn't know which way it would go.

That failure troubled him more than anything else.

12

When Gabriel Rodriguez Loreto had heard the Call, he was sitting between two stunning women sporting four of the biggest breasts he'd ever seen outside of a porn film. The one at his left hand was blond (not naturally, darkness at the hairline proved that, but her hair was frosted to near-platinum in spots, so he thought the roots just added to the overall look), wearing a shiny gold dress cut almost to her navel in front, with a hemline that barely cleared the tops of her thighs. Her spike-heeled shoes were made of a transparent plastic embedded with flecks of gold, and her jewelry—hoop earrings, a thin choker, a couple of rings and an ankle bracelet on her right leg—was also gold. Her right hand was on Gabriel's thigh, and not just sitting there but kneading, long fingernails sometimes digging painfully into the flesh through his silk pants. The pressure of her hand promised all manner of pleasures, once they left the club and went back to her place.

The woman on his right appeared, at a glance, to be more covered up. On closer inspection—and Gabriel had inspected very closely indeed—the top that pretended to disguise her abundant charms proved to be made of a thin black mesh, the holes in which showed everything in satisfying detail. The top met satiny black pants at her narrow waist, tight enough to show that she wore no underwear at all underneath them. She had on black strapped high heels, a sinuous silver threaded chain at the waist, drop earrings and, beneath the mesh but still visible, a small gold crucifix dangling deep in the canyon of cleavage.

This woman's name was Natalya, she had said. Her hair was black, her makeup heavily applied, with deep red lips surrounded by a thin black line, black around her eyes and rose on her cheeks, dusting over what looked like skin badly scarred by acne. She had told him her name immediately before describing a few of the things she planned to do with him. As she shouted these words into his ear, in order for him to hear over the thundering techno blaring from the club's speaker system, she had rubbed her breasts back and forth across his arm. She punctuated her pledge by shoving her tongue into his ear and swirling it around a couple of times, then leading him over to the low leather couch where the blonde, whose name Gabriel still didn't know, joined them.

Carolina, his wife, wouldn't approve of him doing any of the things Natalya had suggested—at least, not with Natalya. But there was much about Gabriel that Carolina didn't know, couldn't know. She knew he had taken a new job, working with his brother Enrique, and she knew it was a lucrative position, but she didn't know the details of the job. Being told would only put her in danger, and make her worry. She might guess, but Gabriel would never confirm or deny.

The club was a riot of loud music and sweaty bodies writhing in dance and other activities, flashing lights and the smells of perfume, tobacco, alcohol, sweat and sex. A low ceiling made the bass boom even louder than it might have, made the lights more blinding, the whole scene more intense. On the second floor of a downtown block in Sonoita, with a shoe store and a bakery below, the club held a hundred people comfortably, but half again that number had crammed inside. Two months before, Gabriel would never have been allowed through the door. That was before Enrique had arranged for him to become a soldier in the Sonora Cartel. With that position had come cash, nice clothes, respect and the opportunity to meet the kind of women he had only dreamed of. He was strapped, with a nine-mil tucked into a leather shoulder holster—just like James Bond's, according to the guy who had sold it to him. He had a buzz on, and a film of perspiration coated him, and he would end the night in the arms of one or both of the fine babes who were coming on to him.

Except then he had heard the Call. Or lived it, to be more

accurate. The club, the music, the smoke and noise and crush of the crowd, even the women, had all dropped away, vanished. He was transported (and for a few seconds he worried that some of the blow he had done that night was tainted, somehow, giving him hallucinations) deep into the jungles of central Mexico. He was behind the wheel of a small truck, and he was filled with a sense of well-being that nothing, not even his new, exalted position with the cartel, had ever given him.

A blink, two, and then he was back in the club. Natalya and the blonde stared at him, aware that he had, if only mentally, abandoned them for a moment. Gabriel gave them the easy grin he'd been practicing in the mirror for just such an occasion, but he knew the grin was shallow, barely scraping the surface. He couldn't genuinely smile, because with his return to the club and his real life had come an overwhelming sensation of aching emptiness.

"I shouldn't be here," he said.

"What?" the blonde asked. He looked deep into her brown eyes, blinking, vacuous. She had a body, no doubt some skills, but ultimately nothing to offer him that mattered. The same went for his fancy clothes, his expensive pistol, his shiny holster. It was all meaningless. He belonged out there in the jungle. The vision or whatever it had been had lasted only seconds, and he didn't know what it all meant, but he knew with absolute certainty where he had to be, and when.

He stood up with difficulty, brushing aside the hands of the two women trying to hold him back. He pushed through the bodies on the dance floor, looking for Enrique. A couple of minutes of searching turned him up, body pressed against yet another incredible-looking woman, their mouths locked on each other. Gabriel grabbed Enrique's shoulder, shaking it. "Enrique," he said, "I have to go. I need your truck."

"Buy your own, *ese*," Enrique said. He was wasted, his words slurred, his handsome face seeming close to collapsing in on itself.

"I don't want the new one, the Tahoe," Gabriel clarified. They shouted at each other. "Just the old Toyota. That's still in your garage, right?"

Enrique let go of the woman and turned to Gabriel. He nearly fell forward, catching himself on Gabriel's shoulders. His fingers squeezed hard, digging in uncomfortably around Gabriel's shoulder blades. "You're talking crazy, man," he said. "Sit down, let one of those fine *putas* blow you, you'll feel better."

"I'm not kidding, Enrique. I have to go tonight, right now."

"Arturo has a job for us later on," Enrique said. "You're going nowhere, *mi hermano*."

Arturo was their *jefe*, the boss, the highest-level cartel officer Gabriel had met. He lived in a mansion outside of town, surrounded by twelve-foot walls and guarded by men with machine guns. His pool, Enrique had said, always had women like Natalya and her friend in it, swimming naked. Behind the house was a caged enclosure in which two Bengal tigers paced, cared for by a man who had once been in charge of big cats for the San Diego Zoo. He had brought his own recipe for tiger food from the zoo, but Arturo occasionally supplemented their diet with the corpses of those who crossed him.

"Fuck Arturo," Gabriel said. "There's something important I have to do."

Enrique slapped a hand across Gabriel's mouth. In his inebriated condition, he smacked his brother harder than he intended. His eyes widened and he moved the hand away, kissed Gabriel once. "I'm sorry, Gabriel. I didn't mean to hurt you. But if you say things like that in public, I'm not going to be able to help you, either."

"It doesn't matter, Enrique, because I'm leaving."

Enrique still gripped him by his left shoulder. His breath in Gabriel's face was hot and reeked of mescal. "Dude, if you walk out that door, there's nothing I can do for you. Arturo wants us later on. You can't just decide that you have other plans."

"What if I wanted to leave with Natalya?"

"Anything you want to do with Natalya you can do right here," Enrique told him. "What, you think someone's going to arrest you because you have your dick out in public? We own the police, Gabriel. And Arturo owns the club. You leave, he'll know about it. You're gone longer than it takes to piss in the alley, he'll send people after you. One of them might be me."

Gabriel shrugged and pushed his big brother's hand off his silk shirt. "I'm sorry, Enrique, but I have to do this thing. I have no choice in the matter. I wish I could make you understand, but I can't, so I'm just going to ask you to trust me."

"I trust that you're committing suicide, and you won't let me stop you, that's what I trust."

"Think what you want, Enrique. When I'm done, I'll bring your truck back."

Enrique clapped his hands over his own ears. "Don't let me hear where you're going, Gabi."

Gabriel looked into his brother's eyes for a few seconds, wishing there was a way to explain, or something else he could say. But they could barely hear each other as it was, shouting at top volume, and he knew Enrique was right. If Arturo wanted him to do a job and he wasn't available, Arturo would take that as a treasonous act. The tigers would be well fed if they found him.

He turned away and headed for the door. It didn't matter. None of it mattered. Only that he got the truck and drove south, through the Mexican night, as fast as he could.

She waited for him, out there in the jungle.

Three weeks had passed since then. Gabriel had kept his appointment. Now he drove his brother's truck north, always north. The cab was crowded with two other men in it, the back weighted down so much that the front wheels didn't always find the purchase they should, especially on dirt and gravel roads.

He missed Enrique, and there were moments, when he woke up in the middle of the night by the side of the road, that he feared what would happen to him when his task was done.

But he had not regretted his decision for a moment.

13

After his visit to the Bowles place, Buck returned to the Laven-
der house and spent the rest of the day there, walking it inside
and out when the rain allowed, taking photographs and measurements. A forensics team finally showed up, and he vacated
long enough to let them do their work. Not hungry, he skipped
lunch.

The other deputies from the Elfrida office showed up, one
by one, to see the crime scene. He wasn't sure how much their
appearances had to do with professional curiosity, and how
much with morbid fascination, but he was in no mood to argue
with them.

Always, he was aware of the ticking watch on his wrist, the
hours slipping by. Lulu Lavender was out there somewhere,
possibly getting farther away every moment, possibly closer
to death. If there was something he could find here that would
point him in the right direction, he needed to look for it.

But the more he looked, the more he felt there was nothing
that would do the trick. No road map with a route handily
marked in yellow highlighter. No postcard saying "Wish you
were here."

He had talked to the various reporters who had shown up
and asked them to hold the story. He hadn't liked doing so.
The cynical part of him thought the whole idea was a smoke
screen. Maybe Ed just didn't want to have two high-profile
disappearances at once. The sheriff was an elected official, after all, and getting reelected was never far from his thoughts.

Of course, he didn't know if the probable abduction of a
mixed-race girl, of Hispanic and African-American descent,

would have the same grip on the television viewing public as that of a pretty blond white girl. The savage nature of the murders might help, but then again, blacks and Latinos died all the time in America without making the evening news.

Getting word out to the press sometimes helped in this kind of case. It brought in volunteers who could scour the surrounding countryside for clues. Scoot Brown and Carmela Lindo were on that, dressed in yellow slickers and rubber boots, walking the acreage of the Lavender place and the public lands beyond their fence. Publicity also brought tips, most of which were nonsense but had to be investigated anyway, wasting valuable person-hours. Sometimes a tip paid off, though, and as long as this case was shielded from the media, that wouldn't happen.

Raul Bermudez was back at the substation, where he had taken Lulu's personal computer. She had a Dell desktop system, and Raul, their resident techie, was sure he could break her passwords. Maybe an e-mail from an admirer, or a stalker, would help identify a suspect. Buck had searched Lulu's room for a diary, finding none. Donna Gonzales was cataloging what Lulu did own—a few photos, a case of CDs and books, jewelry, makeup. Her clothing. Clues could be anywhere, especially when you had no idea what you were looking for.

When it became apparent that the forensics team would be working late into the evening, Buck called home and told his wife Tammy that he wouldn't be there for dinner. "You need your strength," she said. "What are you doing?"

"I'm at a crime scene," Buck replied. "It's a bad one, Tammy. Tell you the truth, I don't think I'd want anything to eat anyway." Even though he had passed on lunch, he still didn't have the slightest appetite.

"Well, you drive careful when you do come home. I'll pray for you, Buck."

"You do that," he said. "While you're at it, pray for the Lavender family. They need it more than me."

"Well, I don't know who they are, but I'll do my level best," she promised. Tammy had unending faith in the power of prayer, notwithstanding the fact that most of her prayers went unanswered. She prayed every day that Buck wouldn't have an accident or die in the line of duty, and so far he had done neither. But she also prayed for bigger things, like an end to abortion across the globe, death to all terrorists, most members of the media, all homosexuals and assorted liberal figures who came into her crosshairs. Mostly Buck found her goals ridiculous and was just as glad that she didn't have the direct pipeline to the Lord that she wished for.

She was a good woman in a lot of ways: honest, hardworking, loving, kind to strangers and animals. She had taken most of the responsibility for raising Trey, their son, who had been killed six years before in the crossfire of a gang war in Phoenix when he'd gone to the wrong nightclub on the wrong night. As long as you didn't cross her fairly arbitrary lines of decency, at which point loving turned to hating in a heartbeat, she was fine. It was that streak—judgmental, intolerant, happy to use her religion as a cudgel instead of a crutch or a foundation for a decent life—that scared Buck. He found that he didn't mind working long hours, sometimes seven days a week. The times he'd tried to talk to her about her intolerance she had turned angry, accused him of trying to lead her away from God.

Which had not been his intent. But each time he tried, she seemed to turn more and more to the cornerstones of her faith: her Bible, a couple of TV evangelists, and some right-wing websites she had found that buttressed her more extreme viewpoints. He had, after several nights spent on a couch in their living room, decided that he considered peace at home more important than trying to interfere with prayers that had little effect anyway.

But watching the sun disappear in the west from the Lavenders' front yard, he wasn't sorry he was here instead of there.

When exhaustion claimed Buck and he finally climbed into bed and drew the covers over himself, Tammy rolled over to face him. "I prayed for you," she mumbled.

"Better you'd prayed for the missing girl," he said.

"But her family's been killed? She's better off dead."

"Why would you say that?"

"Dead she's in the arms of our Lord," Tammy said, sitting up in bed. "With her family, if they carried Jesus in their hearts." Buck had found her beautiful once, a long time ago. When he met her, she had long dark hair and dark eyes that flashed with mischief, sensuous lips that he loved to feel against his own. With her conversion to religious extremism, however, she seemed determined to erase everything any man would find desirable or sexy. She'd let her body go—she wasn't fat, just flabby, with no tone, no shape to speak of. To bed, she wore an ankle-length cotton housedress, buttoned almost to her chin, with plain white socks on her feet. The outfit had all the sex appeal of a hospital gown, except that it didn't gap open in back. She had taken to cutting her hair herself, and it looked it—about chin length, all the way around. She wore no makeup, and she cried constantly, usually about the world of sin and wretchedness she inhabited, which left her eyes bloodshot and her nose chapped and red. "I know I'd want to die if you were gone," she added.

He had often thought of leaving her. But then she said things like that, and he thought it was just selfish to divorce a spouse because she had found a new way to live that you didn't agree with. She was still the same woman, somewhere deep inside, the same Tammy who had loved laughter and children and puppies and sex and the wildflowers that bloomed twice a year, in wet years, after the winter rainy season and the summer monsoon.

It just seemed harder to find her now.

"She's still alive out there, and I'm sure she's terrified," Buck said. He didn't know that for a fact—and he still wasn't sure if she had done it all herself—but he dearly hoped it was the case.

"She's young, right? She'd most likely be in heaven if she had died too."

"You can't possibly—" Buck didn't end the sentence. Tammy *could* believe what she'd said. That was the whole problem. She had gone so far over the edge that she would rather see Lulu Lavender dead than rescued.

Buck couldn't agree with that, couldn't even accept that if God—the way Tammy thought of Him—existed, He would let a family be slaughtered like hers had been. Where was the sense in that? What purpose could it serve?

By the same token, he didn't hold the devil responsible either. Whoever had killed the Lavenders and taken Lulu was evil, but that evil lived within the murderer's heart, not someplace deep under the Earth's crust. No cloven hooves had marked the Arizona dirt that day, and the wounds Buck had seen had not been caused by a pitchfork.

Better people take responsibility for their own actions, Buck thought, *than try to pawn off their deeds on imaginary beings.*

Tammy rolled away again. He reached out, put his hand on her shoulder, but she shrugged it off. He would have liked to make love tonight, to try to salvage some bit of human closeness from what had been a horrific day. He knew she wouldn't have it, though. She wanted to less and less, it seemed. She had got it in her head that unless they were trying to have a baby—and they couldn't, no more after Trey the doctor had said—it was sinful, even if they were husband and wife. Once in a while he could convince her otherwise, but only through heroic effort, and he had to deal with the aftermath the next morning, when she knelt in prayer so long that her knees were rubbed raw, tears streaming down her face as if she had consigned herself, through that marital act, to eternal damnation.

He closed his eyes and tried to will sleep to embrace him in her stead.

Interlude: 1536

The wind soughing through the branches of pine trees mimicked the rumble and crash of distant surf. Years had passed since Alvar Nuñez Cabeza de Vaca had seen the ocean, and it would, he believed, be a lifetime before he would see it again. He had loved the sea until it turned on him. Even so, he found himself missing it.

Squatting out of the wind behind an outcropping of dun-colored rock, Alvar looked down the hill at the throng filling the valley. He had come to think of them as his people. Six hundred strong, they represented more than twenty different villages. They were savages whose only exposure to the true Faith was what he had been able to bring to them, most of them naked or else clad, as he was, only in the rawest skins, their faces and bodies painted or tattooed or scarred or adorned with bones, but they were kind and decent people who followed Alvar and his three companions willingly, even enthusiastically.

He rested on his haunches, observing his congregation. The sun had dropped behind the hills that walled off the valley a short time earlier, and in twilight's gloom the Indians gathered around fires. Some ate; others danced or shouted or sang. The Moor, Estevan—Alonso del Castillo's slave—no doubt was either making love to one of the Indian girls, or was about to, or possibly had just finished. Alvar didn't know if it was his exotic appearance, with his dark brown skin and tight black hair (But then, to the savages weren't they all exotic, pale skinned, hairy-chested and bearded?), or his easy laughter or his facility with languages, but the girls seemed unable to resist Estevan's *charms, and he unwilling to deny himself their attentions. Alvar suspected trouble would come of it, sooner or later.*

Probably sooner, because these past several days Estevan had changed his ways, paying attention to only one young lady. A remarkable beauty, to be sure, she had thick black hair draping down her back like an ebon waterfall and dark eyes that fairly glowed with an inner fire when she laughed (which, in Estevan's presence, she did often). But she was also the daughter of a shaman and betrothed to a young warrior, a tall, muscular specimen who wielded a spear as if he had been born holding it. Alvar didn't like the way the young man eyed Estevan, didn't like the way Estevan made no secret of his attraction to the girl, didn't like the way the girl responded whenever Estevan so much as glanced in her direction, and the way she had stopped paying the least mind to her intended.

If it came to trouble, Alvar would have to try to keep it confined to those two, Estevan and the young warrior. He had not survived shipwreck, slavery and solitude just to die under the spears and arrows of his followers, turned against him by the actions of one of his own.

Alvar turned his gaze to the east, where the moon had just begun to rise over the hills they had crossed yesterday. Was it ungodly to think of the Indians as his tribe, his congregation? He was no priest or holy man, just the simple treasurer of the ill-fated Narváez expedition. There was no earthly reason for strangers to flock to him over anyone else.

But they had. He liked to credit the force of his own personality, but in his honest moments he knew it was because he had the power to heal, and because he treated those he met with respect and decency. Surely God had bestowed the healing abilities on him as a means of saving his life for some future task. If not for the fact that he could lay hands on the ill and the injured and restore their health, Alvar Nuñez Cabeza de Vaca would have been killed long ago, in the Floridas or somewhere else along the way. Instead, he had survived, even prospered, if prosperity were counted in the number of people who called one friend or brother, or in skins, or in backloads of corn laid at one's feet.

The storm that had lashed the ships of the Narváez expedition had occurred in October of 1528, he remembered. He had tried to keep the calendar in his mind, tried to note the changing of the seasons, in case he ever found his way back to civilization and would need to report his adventures to the Crown. It was hard to do, though. They passed through arid country, cold in winter and hot in summer, but dry far more often than not, making spring and autumn hard to distinguish. And during the times he had been near starving, naked and alone in the wilderness, or kept in the bonds of slavery, his mind had not been working as it should and the days and weeks and months had blurred into one another. He believed that five years had passed, possibly more, since he had last seen any Christians other than Alonso del Castillo, Andrés Dorantes and Estevan.

The miracles that the good Lord worked through Alvar's hands had terrified him initially. On the first occasion, an Indian had been taken ill with horrible stomach cramps, vomiting and diarrhea wracking him to the point that death of thirst or starvation seemed imminent. Alvar had been brought into the man's presence by the Indian sorcerer into whose service he had been pressed. While the sorcerer blew on the sick man through a tube, chanting and clicking his tongue—all to no avail—Alvar had felt himself filled with the power of the Lord. He had tried to resist, fearing that Satan, not God, directed his hands. But he had been drawn to the patient's side, and his hands—quite out of his control by now—pressed down onto the sick man's stomach. Words he had never heard, much less uttered, escaped his lips, and blood flowed over his fingers even though the man's gut had been uninjured, his skin taut. Then something emerged into Alvar's waiting hands, a stone smaller than his fist, as smooth as a river rock, coated with blood. Reacting instinctively, Alvar hurled the stone into a nearby fire, where it sizzled like a ball of fat and vanished.

With its disappearance, the man's health returned. Almost instantly, he sat up—his stomach still smooth, skin unbroken, although coated with the blood that had washed over Alvar's hands—and smiled. Color flooded into his cheeks. When he spoke, a cheer went up from those gathered around. Within a few minutes, he strode around the village telling all who would listen how the slave had saved his life.

Alvar's master had been unable to keep him after that—and more, had immediately come to see Alvar as a peer rather than an inhuman beast. He had freed Alvar, who headed west, as he had always encouraged the others stranded in the Floridas with him to do. East would only take them to the same ocean they had come from, with Spain an impossible distance away. West and south, in Mexico, he would find Christians, he was sure. So he followed the sun, and God led him to his fellows, captives of the Anagados. He joined them, and on their second day together they managed to escape. Running for days, they finally found the Avavares, enemies of the Anagados, who happily took them in. When a fall injured one of the Indians and Alvar, again doing the Lord's bidding, healed his injury, the Indians excitedly spread the word to the peoples to their west.

In this way, the four reunited Christians made their way toward the sunset, word of Alvar's powers preceding them, the welcome they received growing at every stop. Villages offered everything they had to the Christians, knowing that when they brought the four travelers to the next village they would be repaid and more. No two tribes spoke the same language, but there were similarities from one tongue to the next, so they could understand one another and translate the next village's words.

There were moments when Alvar forgot his humility and thought of himself, looking upon those who followed (and, yes, worshipped) him, as their Lord and them as his flock. At those times, God the One and Only refused to smite him, so Alvar determined that he was being saved for some other purpose in days or years yet to come. When the temptation grew too strong, Alvar had to remove himself from the others, to remind himself that it had not been so very long since he had been naked and starving, wandering mindlessly through the wastelands of the Indies. He tried to make his plans at these times, uncorrupted by adulation and unswayed by his fellow Christians.

Now he worried about Estevan and the girl. He didn't be-lieve that the generosity of the Indians was without bounds, although he had yet to find them. If it came to a fight between the Moor and the Indian warrior, though—over a situation in which Estevan was clearly in the wrong—the Indians might easily rise up.

And yet when he saw Estevan and the girl together, he rec-ognized lust and more, and it became ever harder to imagine that the black would give her up without a struggle.

He would talk to the Moor, he decided. And to Estevan's master, Castillo. He would make them both see what could happen, if they were not careful. His mind made up—anyway, the wind sent icy fingers under his loincloth, and below, warm fires and prickly pear wine beckoned—he started down the hill. He dressed as the Indians did, barefoot, with an animal skin over his loins as his only attempt at modesty. He carried a spear with a stone tip lashed to it, which God willing he would never have to use against a human being.

When he reached the valley, what he found in the glow of the fire outside the shelter the Indians built, every night, for him to share with his comrades, shocked him. Estevan was not making love, after all, although he was with the girl again. In-stead, he had found a chunk of white stone that looked as pure as Italian marble. The girl sat cross-legged in the dirt, naked, arms folded almost demurely over her breasts, while Estevan chipped at the stone like a sculptor, using harder rocks as hammer and chisel.

"Now you're an artist, Estevanico?" Alvar asked him.

"Perhaps I always have been," Estevan replied with a grin. "But I never had such a subject before, or such a perfect stone to carve. It's as if she hides inside, just waiting for me to bring her out."

"Where did you come by it?"

"Here, in the camp. Like it was biding its time here until we came."

"And when we move on tomorrow, what then? Will you carry it on your back?"

"Señor Castillo has already taken care of that," Estevan

answered. "He is showing some of the Indians how to make wooden wheels. There are trees here tall enough to form planks from. By midmorning at the latest, I will have a cart, and a ramp to load her onto it. Many hands make the work go fast."

Alvar simply shrugged and went into the hut. Estevan had it all figured out, it seemed. He had an answer for everything, and he had charmed his own master into helping in his crazy scheme.

Alvar only hoped that it was a scheme they would all survive.

DAY TWO

1

The fact that Buck's sleep proved unsettled and restless didn't
change the time that his alarm went off. He rolled from bed,
glancing back at Tammy's stationary, blanketed mound. She
rose later and later these days, unlike earlier times when
she would already have been out milking and gathering eggs.
He thought the changes in her had started after Trey's death,
but maybe it had been more gradual than that and he just hadn't
noticed. She still hadn't moved by the time he had showered
and dressed, only the steady rise and fall of the blankets giving any proof of life.

His ranch, the Circle S, sprawled largely in the shadow of
the Mule Mountains, so daybreak took longer to hit than it did
for the rest of the valley. From the window over the sink,
though, as Buck ran water into a coffeepot, he saw Aurelio out
at the barn with the ranch's white Ford F-350. He left the pot
on the yellow-tiled counter and walked out through the kitchen
door.

Aurelio's age was something more than sixty, but he seemed
unsure himself, or unwilling to say if he did know. He had
worked for the ranch since Buck's father owned it, before it had
been split between Buck and his older sister. As if he knew even
before she announced it that she would sell her share and move
to Las Vegas with her dentist husband, Aurelio had offered to
work for Buck on his piece. Buck had taken all of twelve seconds before agreeing, and had never regretted his decision.

Aurelio wore a straw cowboy hat that had been crushed
and stained and stepped on, but was as much a part of him as
the apple-round cheeks that squeezed his eyes into narrow

slits and the white stubble that dusted his jaw like a light snowfall. A blue denim jacket provided a layer of warmth, but it would come off, Buck knew, as soon as the sun's presence was more than a few stray beams breaking through a pewter sky. Aurelio carried a bale of green hay toward the back of the pickup, walking with bowed legs on heel-worn work boots. When he saw Buck come out, he nodded and grinned.

"That pasture is pretty used up?" he said. His sentences often rose at the end like questions, but he didn't expect an answer. "I'm gonna move 'em over a little." In Arizona, a free-range state, Buck wasn't required to keep his cattle fenced at all. Anyone who didn't want Buck's herd or someone else's on his land had to fence them out. Buck preferred to keep them contained, however, and to fence off separate pastures so he had some control over where they grazed. The sixty-some animals had been confined in one pasture for a little more than a month and had denuded the grasses there. But the next pasture over hadn't been grazed all year, and although a drought had kept the state drier than usual for a decade, the grass had responded well to the summer monsoon, growing tall and thick. Aurelio didn't have to tell him his plans in any detail; the two men had worked together and discussed their strategy long enough to know what each other had in mind.

As much as Buck's cattle liked fresh grass, they were completely enamored of green hay. They would follow a truck bed full of it all the way to the Pacific Ocean if they could, so even working alone, Aurelio should be able to move them through the gate onto the next range. He might come back to the stable, a low brick building on the other side of a wood-fenced corral from the barn, to get a horse if he needed to chase down some stragglers, or to track down any calves who had wandered away from the herd and gotten snagged in mesquite or trapped in a deep wash. Whatever he had to do he would, and by the time Buck came home tonight the herd would have been successfully moved.

Like all ranchers, Buck had hoped that his son, Trey, would want to take over the ranch when he couldn't work it any longer, and he had steeled himself against the probability that

Trey would have other plans. That decision had been made by other forces: a stray bullet and bad timing. The fact that they would never even have the conversation broke Buck's heart every time he thought about it.

"Sounds good," he said simply.

"Oh, and that pregnant cow? I think she's about due."

"Cut her out and bring her down to the barn, then," Buck said. "Keep an eye on her. Most likely we'll be up all night again."

"They never want to calve during the day, that's for sure?"

"It's a plot. Keep us exhausted so they can take over the world someday."

"They already think they own it," Aurelio said, laughing. He would stick around. He had never married, and lived in a cabin on the far side of the stable, one of the ranch's original structures from the late 1890s, that he had retrofitted with insulation, electricity and running water. He had a satellite for his TV, a library card from the Copper Queen Library in Bisbee, and a couple of prostitutes down in Nogales he visited occasionally, and he didn't seem to want much else out of life.

Buck shared the laugh. "That's a fact."

Sitting at his desk with a white Superman mug of coffee steam-ing close at hand and the whistle of the wind outside, Buck read over the initial report from the forensics inspectors in Bisbee. The coffee was made from beans he bought over in Bisbee, French roast, strong and aromatic. Its smell relaxed him just as much as too many cups would wire him, and after a largely sleepless night he needed some of that wiring to keep him focused as he worked through the dense pages.

The report contained—unfortunately, he thought—no major surprises. The boys had been killed by their knife wounds, Hugh and Manuela by bullets fired from a .38. The report suggested that his earlier conclusion—that the boys had come first—was correct. The killer hadn't wanted to risk awakening the parents, so he had done the boys with the quiet weapon. By the time he reached the master bedroom, he was no longer worried about making noise—and they were more capable of fighting back effectively at close quarters—so he'd pulled the gun.

What about Lulu, though? Maybe he had started with her, binding her in some way so she wouldn't be a threat. Finished off the rest of her family, then drove away. Tire tracks the rain hadn't completely washed away belonged to a full-sized truck. Wrangler AT/S. The tracks had been compared to the Lavenders' truck and to known delivery vehicles, with no matches. Didn't mean it was the killer's—pickups were as common as houseflies around the region—but it was better than nothing.

If he had taken Lulu out first, then it indicated that she was the prime target. Buck had wondered about that anyway—why kill everyone except her, if the goal all along wasn't to take her alive? No one had survived to pay any ransom, not that the Lavenders would have been able to afford much anyway. He didn't want to think about the possibility of a sexual predator, but he had to consider it.

The footprints outside the house hadn't matched any of the family members either. But Scoot's photos weren't much good, since he hadn't put anything in the frame for size comparison. And the rain had hit before he'd made casts, so the prints were pretty much a dead end.

Unknown fingerprints had been found at various spots inside the house, but not necessarily in places the killer would have touched. Once they had a suspect in custody, the prints might help place him at the crime scene, but by themselves they meant nothing.

The report had come fast, less than twenty-four hours from the time the FI team had arrived at the scene. As Sheriff Gatlin had said, until they had a crime scene for the Lippincott kidnapping, the quadruple murder was Forensics' biggest priority. While Buck appreciated the speed, the uselessness of the sheaf of papers depressed him. He knew life was not like television, but he hadn't been able to keep from hoping that something in the report would point at a specific perpetrator.

Since that hadn't happened, he would have to do some real investigating. He still kind of liked the neighbor for it. New in town, relatively, and there hadn't been any major homicides on his road before he'd come. Plus he drove back and forth to school with Lulu on a semiregular basis. Maybe something had happened there, some teacher/student affair that had turned bad. Buck would have to find out a little more about him, and maybe check that shed behind his house.

2

"Oliver Bowles works for you?"

"That's correct," Franklin Hinckley said. "I chair the environmental sciences department here." Brightly lit by a bank of overhead fluorescents, Hinckley's office, from its gray speckled linoleum floor tiles to the visible edges of the bookcase, was virtually spotless. Posters and topographic maps covered two walls, and a bookcase, stuffed so full that some books lay sideways on top of the others, filled the third. The fourth was mostly window. Hinckley had stationed his desk in front of the window, facing the door, so that Buck sat in a visitor's chair with Hinckley practically silhouetted in front of him. Made it hard to read the man's face. Buck guessed it wasn't accidental.

"And what exactly does he teach?"

"Environmental Sciences 103," Hinckley said without looking it up. "Studies of Human Impact. Also a class on the natural history of the San Pedro River, which is one of his specialties."

"Two classes? That's it?"

"He's new," Hinckley replied. "He wanted some time to himself so he could work on a paper, or I guess maybe a book, about the San Pedro. So yes, at this point he's part-time faculty."

Buck nodded, in case Hinckley wanted to elaborate further. He seemed like the kind of man who, if Buck could find the right button, might say more than he had intended. Hinckley clammed up, though, so Buck asked another question. "Is he good?"

"Excuse me?"

"Is he good at his job? He a good teacher? However you

judge such things, I don't know, through student reviews or test scores or whatever."

Hinckley regarded Buck through the top half of his bifocals, as if taking a second look at him. The department head was a black man, almost sixty, Buck figured, and heavy. He had a cannonball of a head, with short hair trimmed close, gold-rimmed glasses and a winning smile that came and went as suddenly as the Sulphur Springs Valley winds. He had on a crisp blue Oxford shirt with a red and gold striped tie and navy pants. The matching jacket dangled from a standing coat rack near the door. A whiff of Bay Rum transported Buck to his boyhood, when his father would put on his only suit and knot an unfamiliar tie around his neck for a dance in town or a veteran's parade.

"As far as I can tell so far, yes, he is good," Hinckley said. "He knows his material. He communicates it effectively, and he engages his students. We are a community college, not a university, and not to put too fine a point on it, many of our students barely escaped high school by the skin of their teeth. Dr. Bowles's are not what are so affectionately termed dummy classes, and the material he presents could be challenging to some. Is challenging, in fact. Dr. Bowles seems capable of ensuring that they come out of the class understanding it. To my mind, that makes him a good teacher."

"He's a doctor?"

"He has a Ph.D., yes."

Buck inspected the toe of his own boot. Playing hick cop in hopes that the college professor would underestimate him. It had been known to happen. "Students like him?"

"We haven't had any complaints," Hinckley said. "His reviews are generally favorable."

"Any in particular who have a strong opinion one way or the other?"

"None that come to mind."

"Could I have a look at his personnel records?"

"Absolutely not," Hinckley said firmly. "Unless you have a warrant, of course."

"Any reason I should get a warrant?"

"You're trying to make me say something bad about one of my most recent hires," Hinckley said. "I don't care what has happened in his past, Dr. Bowles is a qualified person, knowledgeable about our region, and he has the ability to present science in such a way that students are excited about it."

"It's his future I'm concerned about," Buck said. "But the way you bring up his past, it sounds like maybe there's something there I should know about. Is there?"

Hinckley didn't answer. He had folded his arms over his massive chest. Buck wished he could see the man's eyes better.

"I'll find out," Buck said. "I'll go to the last place he worked, and the one before that. It'll take me more time, though, and time is the one thing I'm really short on right now, since a life may be on the line. So that'll piss me off. I would never threaten you, but you wouldn't want to have me around when I'm pissed off."

"I'm inclined to believe that," Hinckley said. "Since I don't especially want you around now, and apparently you aren't even pissed off yet."

"Nope, not yet. You can keep it that way."

"It's not a state secret, I suppose," Hinckley said. "Although I'm sure he would prefer it be treated like one."

"If it's not relevant to the case, I'll forget it the moment it hits my ears," Buck promised. "But if it is . . . let's not forget that a person's life might be at stake."

Hinckley blew out a breath, looking at the surface of his desk as if inspecting it for wayward dust motes. "There was some . . . trouble, at his old school, San Diego State University. An affair with a student."

"Is that still considered a bad thing?"

"It happens more often than I'd like to think about. Consenting adults spending time together, intellectually stimulating conversation. Things happen. But you know, in today's world, it's all about the appearance of propriety. Every school has regular sexual harassment workshops for faculty and staff, even for students. And the teacher/student relationship can be a powerful thing, with most of the power resting in the hands of the teacher. It's easy to see an affair as a powerful person subverting the will of a weaker one, making a consensual situation look like something else altogether."

Buck had hit the button. If Hinckley hadn't had an affair of his own, he'd at least been tempted.

"Do you know the details of Bowles's case?"

"I can't imagine why they'd be relevant. Anyway, all I know is that the young woman decided to end it, and to go public. Apparently it was a bit of a scandal for a while. Dr. Bowles is married, of course, as well as being years older than the student. The university had no choice but to let Dr. Bowles go, and by doing so they persuaded the young woman not to sue. The department chair at San Diego State is a longtime acquaintance of mine. He knew of Dr. Bowles's interest in the San Pedro and general expertise in the southeastern Arizona region, and suggested he might be a good fit here. I interviewed Dr. Bowles and agreed."

"And he hasn't had any affairs with any students here."

"Not to my knowledge."

"If he did?"

"I would not tolerate it. He would be terminated immediately. He knows that and has agreed to—if you'll excuse the vernacular—keep it in his pants."

"No whispers? Rumors?"

"Nothing that I've—"

Buck cut Hinckley off. "Do you know who Lulu Lavender is?"

Hinckley cleared his throat, tapped into place an already military-neat stack of papers. "She is one of his students. Apparently also a neighbor, who rides to and from school with Dr. Bowles from time to time."

"And that's okay? A young female student spending time alone with him in his car? How long is it to his place, thirty or forty minutes?"

"I have no reason to think there's any relationship there other than what I've already described," Hinckley said firmly. "He drives her to school. He is her teacher. When they get home, her family is there, and his wife is at his house. She knows about the arrangement and approves of it."

"But then, she stuck with him after the first affair."

"You say that as if it's a bad thing."

"Just commenting. I try not to judge people."

Hinckley laughed. "Isn't that precisely your job?"

"I'm a cop, not a judge or jury. I'm just trying to make sure I know what the relationship is between Bowles and the girl."

Even silhouetted against the window, when Hinckley tensed Buck could see it, could almost see the man's dark skin blanch. "Oh, Jesus," he said. "When you said someone's life might be at stake . . ."

"Lulu Lavender's family was slaughtered," Buck told him. "She's missing. Almost thirty hours at this point. The clock is running out for that girl, and I aim to find her."

"You don't think Oliver . . ."

"I don't know. I can't afford to disregard him, though. I'd appreciate it you don't tell him we talked. Or anyone else, for that matter."

"I simply can't believe he's capable of anything like that," Hinckley said. "He's not that kind of person."

"Thank you," Buck said. "I'll take that into consideration too. I'm not saying he's guilty, or even a suspect, at this point. Just what we call a person of interest."

"But more interest, after what I've told you."

Buck nodded his head. "More interest. That's a fact."

3

The news blackout had not, as of yet, had the effect that Ed Gatlin had hoped for. Driving back to the station, Buck wondered if it would discourage Lulu's abductor, and if so, how long it would take. And if the man—he was convinced a man had snatched her, if only because so few kidnappers of teen girls were female—would really let her go, or just kill her, when he gave up. From what little news he'd caught, the Tucson press and the national media hadn't let go of the Elayne Lippincott story long enough to even notice four dead people and a missing girl.

He had not been able to turn up any living relatives to inform of Lulu's disappearance. In itself that wasn't a bad thing, but relations could sometimes point an investigation in a direction that law enforcement hadn't considered. Hugh Lavender had been an only child, and his parents had both died in a car crash eight years earlier. His grandparents had long since passed away, and if there were any great-aunts or -uncles Buck hadn't found them yet. Manuela's family had lived here in the Valley, but her mother had died of emphysema in a Bisbee hospital a few years back, and her father a year later from a gunshot wound outside a bar in Douglas. An older brother had died in Vietnam. Manuela had brothers and sisters, but they were down in Oaxaca somewhere. Buck remembered her telling him that her father was the only one of their family who had made it to *el norte*.

As he drove, Buck watched the sides of the road, looking out at the fields greened up by the summer monsoon. Oliver Bowles drove this same road, with Lulu Lavender sitting in his passenger seat. What did they talk about on those rides? Did they ever pull off the road, take some lonely dirt trail, get friendly? If she didn't turn up soon, Buck would have to expand the search to include all the rural roads between school and home.

He still wanted a look inside that shed too. He didn't have probable cause for a warrant yet. Didn't mean he couldn't do it.

It would just have to be the hard way.

Elfrida was slightly less than twenty-five miles north of Douglas on Highway 191, which had been Highway 666 until Bible-thumpers like Buck's wife Tammy had forced the state to change it. The town called itself the Heart of the Valley, but the word "town" implied something a little grander than a visitor would see. Elfrida straddled both sides of the highway with a cluster of shops, gas stations, cafes and bars, and most of the residents lived scattered about on the surrounding rangeland.

The sheriff's substation there was in a barnlike building that also contained the Fire Department. Sheriff's offices in Bisbee, Douglas and Willcox were too far away to respond quickly to emergency calls in the center of the vast Sulphur Springs Valley. Cochise County was as big as Connecticut and Rhode Island combined, and the valley itself was thirty miles across at its widest point and a hundred miles long, anchored by Douglas at the border. Willcox dominated the north, where Interstate 10 passed through, but the valley continued up beyond that, eventually flowing into Aravaipa Canyon.

When he had been promoted to patrol lieutenant and transferred out to Elfrida, Buck didn't complain. He lived outside of Bisbee, on the northwestern edge of the Mule Mountains, but it wasn't a bad drive to work. He liked being able to see the Swisshelms and the Perillas, the Pedregosas and the Dragoons and the Chiricahuas and the Mules, just some of the mountain ranges hemming in the valley, which he could at this posting. And outside the immediate proximity of Ed Gatlin, he had more freedom to do his job the way he wanted to do it, without worrying so much about the crease in his trousers or the shine of his boots.

He pulled into the gravel parking area in front of the sub-station and killed the engine. Thirty-one hours. The girl had been missing for thirty-one hours, and what did he have?

Not a whole hell of a lot.

He walked inside. Raul Bermudez looked up from Lulu's computer, which crowded his desk along with his own. "Buck," he said, "have a look at this."

4

There is a TV in the cabin, and he turns it on. Lulu remains
blindfolded, but after telling her that no matter how much she
screams no one will be able to hear her, he removes the gag. She
tests it anyway, screaming until her throat aches and she gags,
bile burning the raw tissue there. Finally he storms over to her
and slaps her a couple of times, and she gives up. He wouldn't
make a mistake on something like that, something so basic.

She hopes that turning on the TV will be a mistake, however. He will realize how many people are looking for her,
how utterly he has screwed himself. Jace will be on, and Oliver
maybe, and other friends, pleading for her release. But he tunes
it to a twenty-four-hour news channel, and while she hears hour
after hour of commentary on Elayne Lippincott—and how, she
wonders, can these people find so many ways to say they know
nothing more now than they did yesterday?—her own name
never comes up. Lulu is pretty sure he killed her family, although she didn't see him do it, and no one mentions the four
dead people either. It's as if none of them ever existed. The
thought makes her weep, inconsolably, not that there is anyone trying to console her.

The air smells different here than it did at home. She can
make out pine and cedar. When they first came in there was a
musty odor, as if wherever they were had been closed up for a
time. That clued her in to the idea that they were someplace remote, not his regular home. When she explored the bits of floor
and wall that she could reach with her hands, she found knot-
holes. Walls of knotty pine and mountain trees and a cold night
convinced her that he had brought her to a mountain cabin.

But today, when she asks him what he means to do with her, he refuses to answer. He won't answer any question directly, not even a simple one like is it day outside or night, which she can answer herself, but throws at him as a test. Most of the time he ignores her, sitting in the other room with the TV on, or going outside, maybe going away altogether. Once he is silent for hours at a time, and she strains against the chains that hold her, tries to rip her blindfold off, but he has secured her in such a way that she can't do either. She screams again, after that, more from rage and frustration that any hope that she will be heard.

He comes back, and he gives Lulu a hamburger he must have bought someplace fairly distant. It is cold, and the grease has congealed in its wrapper, and he gives her a plastic bottle of water to wash it down with, and she thinks she has never had a finer meal in her life. Then he takes the bottle and the wrapper away from her, slaps her once, hard across the cheek and says, "When is she coming?"

"Who?" she asks.

"When is she coming?" he repeats.

"I don't know who you mean."

"When?" He slaps her again, harder. His hands are soft, the skin like a baby's, but still it stings when he whips one across her cheek. And of course she never sees the hand's approach, so each slap startles her anew.

It is almost a relief. She has wondered what he wants with her. Rape has come to mind, of course, but he doesn't seem interested in her that way. He hasn't touched any private parts, except in the brief initial struggle when they were both flailing at each other. He subdued her quickly, though, pressing something over her face that had caused her to pass out.

So she waited for something, a clue as to what he wanted, and the waiting had been terrible.

Now it is here. He wants information.

She would gladly give it to him, if only she could understand what it is he wants to learn.

5

"I'm sorry, Mr. Drexler," Hilario Machado said. "We just don't have any positions available for you right now." He smiled when he said it, like he'd been smiling ever since Barry had walked into his office after filling out an application on the computer terminal in the front of the store and then waiting on a metal bench for almost thirty minutes. The smile was nearly as slick as his hair, with its visible comb lines. He was a kid, not even thirty, Barry guessed, and a Mexican. And he got to make decisions about who would work at the largest store in the area, one of the biggest employers after the prison and the Border Patrol.

Barry pointed to a printout of his application, sitting ignored on Machado's desk. "I have retail," he said. "At the Redi-Market. And a letter of recommendation from my boss there."

"I understand that, Mr. Drexler," Machado said. "It's not that I doubt your qualifications; it's just that I don't have a job to give you."

"I heard you hired people my age."

"We do, when we have suitable openings. We just don't have any right now. Maybe in six months."

In six months Barry could default on his mortgage, which he only had two years left to pay on. It would have been paid off long before except that he and Clarice had refinanced twice, extending the term each time.

"He was a Mexican too," Barry said. "My last boss. I don't mind workin' for 'em. I can even speak it a little."

Machado's weasely grin faded, as if Barry had said something wrong. "I think you'd better go now, Mr. Drexler," he said. "Thank you for your interest in our company."

"Isn't there someone else I can talk to?" Barry pleaded.

"No, there's not. Good-bye, Mr. Drexler."

Barry snatched the letter of recommendation, in its own separate envelope, from the kid's desk. He might need the letter someplace else.

If there was, in fact, anyplace else to try.

Wal-Mart was in Douglas, not far from the Mexican border, on a strip dominated by fast-food restaurants. Pancho Villa had crossed into the United States around here, Barry had heard, often enough that the army had stationed hundreds of men in Douglas in the days before the First World War had required their attention elsewhere.

Looking at the faces that surrounded him in the parking lot as he walked back to his truck—olive-skinned, black-haired, mostly speaking Spanish—he thought maybe General Black Jack Pershing had won the battle, but Pancho Villa had won the war. As if to prove the point, dust kicked up by a sudden wind blew across the border from Agua Prieta and into his eyes.

Barry climbed back in the truck and drove the streets of Douglas's historic downtown. Most of the businesses here fronted onto G Avenue, although there were a few on Pan-American, the road that led up from the international border and connected with Highway 80, and more along Tenth Street. On G, many of the signs he saw were in Spanish, and most of the people Hispanic. Other shop windows were boarded up or simply vacant. A few businesses had English names—the Gadsden Hotel, the Grand restaurant, Southern Arizona Auto Company, where he had bought his truck nine years before, Strathcona Electric—but they were outnumbered by Spanish ones.

Douglas was the biggest city for fifty miles around on this side of the border. Agua Prieta was far larger—estimates ranged from sixty to seventy thousand people over there, while Douglas had closer to sixteen thousand. Bisbee, the county seat, was less than half that size. To get any bigger, one had to go all the way to Sierra Vista, third largest city in Arizona, on the other side of the San Pedro Valley.

And yet here in Douglas he barely felt like he was still in the United States. He'd lived in Arizona all his life, except for basic training in Georgia and a stint in Vietnam, and he had always known there was a strong Mexican presence in the state. But somehow, when he hadn't been looking, they seemed to have taken over.

Uneasily, he parked the truck on G and Twelfth and walked down the west side of the street as far as Seventh, then crossed and came back up the other side. The buildings were mostly brick and stone, built between the turn of the century and the 1920s, Douglas's boom years. The Phelps Dodge Company had located the smelter for their Bisbee copper mines here, precipitating early growth, and then the military had swelled the population during the war against Pancho Villa. Since then, the city had been in slow, steady decline, as if the high desert country hoped to reclaim it little by little.

The only HELP WANTED sign he saw was printed in Spanish, and it was in the window of a women's shoe store. He didn't bother going in. When he reached Tenth, he walked toward the east as far as the post office, then crossed and returned toward G, past the library and Bank of America (which, judging by its clientele, might have been the Bank of Mexico). Still nothing presented itself.

Frustrated, he got back into the truck and slammed the door. He could always refi the house again, but with only two years to go he had hoped to own it free and clear. Anyway, that would leave him with mortgage payments and no income until Social Security kicked in. That was still a few years off.

The other alternative was selling the place. But ranch property often sat unsold for years. Even if he did manage to sell, could he be sure of finding a more affordable place? Maybe a rented mobile home on a small lot somewhere, or a fixer-upper here in town, or up in Bisbee. Those were all question marks, uncertainties, and he had spent the last thirty years counting on living in his own place until the day he died.

Barry cranked the engine and peeled out of the parking

place beside the curb without even looking. A horn blared behind him, and he glared back over his shoulder at a Latino driving a brand-new fire engine red Ford truck. Barry gave his old GMC the gas and left the Ford behind.

6

"Tonight's guest is Joseph Dominick, who has revealed to authorities that he was secretly dating missing teen Elayne Lippincott of Arizona and that the night of her disappearance, she was supposed to sneak out of her house to meet him. Can I call you Joe?"

"I guess. Most people call me Joey."

"Joey it is, then. First things first, Joey. Why did it take you almost two weeks to come forward? Didn't it occur to you that the police would need to know that Elayne had left her family's house of her own accord?"

"I didn't, you know, want to get mixed up in it. On account, partly, that I had a girlfriend, and—"

"So you were cheating on this other girl with Elayne Lippincott. Did you tell the authorities that?"

"Yeah, I did. And now she won't even answer the phone when I call anymore."

"I don't blame her, but let's continue. You said that was part of why you held back this vital information. There's more?"

"Yeah, I mean, I don't know if she even left her house. She never showed up where we were supposed to meet, in the Target parking lot. If I knew for sure that she was on her way and someone grabbed her, then I'd have gone to the cops first thing, you can count on that, Larry. But since I didn't know, I figured I didn't have actual information, I only had a lack of information. And what good would that do?"

"I think you've learned that it's better to let the police make those calls, right?"

"Yeah, I guess it is."

"And why was she sneaking out? If you had a date, why didn't you just pick her up at her door?"

"Oh, her parents hate me."

"I can't imagine why."

"They just have this thing about me, I don't know. Like I'm not good enough for her or something. But she didn't let that stop her from seeing me, we always just had to sneak around."

"What about Elayne? Was she seeing anyone else, or are you the only cheater involved?"

"Elayne? No, just me."

"Why is that?"

"I told her I didn't want her fooling around with nobody else, you know? On account of I was going to help her with her modeling career."

"Are you in the business? A modeling agency, maybe? Advertising?"

"Me? No, I work at the Tune and Lube. But see, I have this kick-ass— Oh, can I say that on TV?"

"That's fine. They'll bleep it out if you say something you shouldn't."

"Okay, sorry. I have a good digital camera, so I was taking some pictures of her. And this buddy of mine knows a guy with this website."

"A modeling site, I presume?"

"Something like that, yeah. It's called Hot Local Bitches dot com, and it gets, like, thousands of hits a day, and you can vote for your favorite, and—"

"Did you love her, Joey? Were you in love with Elayne Lippincott?"

"I . . . I guess so, yeah. I mean, she was a fun girl. We had a lot of laughs. And, you know, you've seen her picture. Great body, nice hair, so I guess, yeah."

"Well, we're glad you've finally decided to talk to the authorities, whatever your reasons for holding back as long as you did. Thanks for being here with us."

"No problem, dude."

7

Buck wheeled a chair over next to Raul's desk and plopped into it, exhaustion weakening his legs. "Glad to," he said, glancing longingly through his open office door at his coffee cup, exiled on his desk. Any coffee left in it was cold, and the pot had been turned off. The mug bore the S-shield logo from Superman's costume, and had been given to him by a woman he'd arrested years before for running a meth lab out of her mobile home. She had endangered the life of her four-year-old daughter as well as her own, and a stint in the county prison had convinced her of that. When she got out, she brought Buck the mug as a thank-you gift. "If it means I can sit awhile. What've you got?"

"The girl had a blog," Raul said. "A weblog."

"I know what a blog is," Buck said. "I may be a redneck, but I'm not an ignorant one."

"I never called you a redneck," Raul said with a mischievous grin. He smoothed down his thick black mustache. He was slender, muscular and liked to think of himself as a sharp dresser, and maybe he was—Buck was redneck enough not to know Armani from Perry Ellis, and not ashamed to admit it. Today Raul wore his uniform, which he'd had tailored to fit better than most sheriff's officers'. Off-duty he favored suits and ties or, on particularly casual occasions, bright polo shirts with dress slacks. Always, he kept his hair neatly combed and his shave close, except for the mustache of which he was so proud. Buck knew he hoped to be a detective someday so he could dress nicely all the time.

"And I never called you a wetback," Buck said. "Now, what'd you find on the girl's fancy typewriter?"

It took Raul a second to realize Buck was kidding. When he did, he just shook his head. "Like I said, she had a blog. I've been reading the entries for the past couple of months, and it's pretty interesting."

"Girl's eighteen years old," Buck said. "What could she have to say that would be so fascinating?"

Raul raised an eyebrow. "To begin with, I think she's involved with an organization that provides assistance to UDAs," he said. He always used the acronym for undocumented aliens when referring to the illegal migrants, and hated it when Buck refused to. Raul had family on both sides of the border and was cognizant of the fact that some Mexicans believed that Latino law enforcement officers were ruled by self-hatred, so he tried to demonstrate Latino pride in whatever outward fashion he could. Buck made a point of always using some other term: illegals, wetbacks, *pollos*, taco-benders, tonks—a Border Patrol term that described the sound a migrant's head made when hit with a flashlight— just to tweak Raul. They had known each other long enough to be friendly enemies. "Bridges Not Borders. There are a few references—oblique, but clear enough, I think, to work-ing on behalf of folks who were robbed or lost or dehydrated on the trip."

"But she's—"

"I know. She's eighteen. Teenagers do have minds of their own, Buck, if you can remember that far back. And there's nothing yet to say that her parents weren't involved too."

"Keep reading, and let me know. That could be enough to get them killed, the way some people feel about illegals around here. Or if maybe they were hiding some on the property, or a *coyote* came over and there was a fight."

"I'll keep you posted," Raul promised. "But there's more. This is what I wanted to show you. These last few entries, on the night she died and the days before, she keeps talking about a dream she's been having. Like a recurring dream."

He swung the monitor around so Buck could read it, and pointed to the text in question. The night she died, Lulu had posted:

> The dream again. Getting tired of writing that. Only it's a little different each time, and this time it was clearer than ever. She's *coming*, and in this one I could actually see where on the border. It's like she's giving me a map so I can meet her. I know this spot. I could see stars and the moon in the sky, so if I wanted to put that much work into it I could probably figure out when. What I don't get is why she's telling me all this. Does she really expect me to be there to meet her? She's a figment, right? Dream stuff? She's got to be, because in my experience marble statues don't walk and talk. I think I even hear her name in the dream, but I'm not sure if that's what it is. Something like *Aztlán*.

"Pretty strange, huh?"

"You think it has something to do with her disappearance?" Buck asked.

"I don't know. It's mostly the timing—the night she disappears, she posts something like this. And before that, night after night for almost two weeks, she's writing about this dream. This statue girl, made of white stone, only her eyes open and her lips move and she says things, and all the time she's getting closer and closer to the border. Lulu even names places in Mexico that she's stopped on her way up."

"So she's got an active imagination, or she's taking drugs, or something like that."

"Buck, you know as well as I that Lulu Lavender was no doper. Imagination, maybe, but this is a little beyond that."

"So what, you think she's going crazy? Sudden onset of schizophrenia, she flips out, kills the family and runs away?"

"That's a possibility. I think maybe we should show this to a shrink, see what the verdict is."

"We can do that," Buck said.

Raul pursed his lips and stared at his fingernails, resting on the keyboard. Buck had the impression there was more he wanted to say, but he was hesitant to.

"What is it?" Buck prodded.

"Well, I did a little snooping around, Buck."

"That's kind of your job."

"I know. But what I found is . . . disturbing."

"Raul, I was inside that house. I knew those people. You want to talk about disturbing?"

"Okay, Buck. Here it is. I checked on a couple of those places in Mexico Lulu mentioned. Where the statue had been?"

"And?"

Raul tapped the keyboard quickly, and Lulu's blog vanished from the screen. In its place Buck saw a newspaper site from Durango, Mexico. *¿Milagro En El Zape?* the headline read. "I know you can read some Spanish, Buck. But because you *are* a redneck, it'll take all day, so I'll paraphrase. According to this story, a miracle occurred in a little town called El Zape last week. A flash flood threatened a small church in the center of town. But a statue of a young girl that no one had ever seen in the square before spoke to the flood, and it changed course, ran down a side street and out of town. A dozen witnesses saw it, the paper says."

"That's pretty strange," Buck admitted. "I don't know what it has to do with our case, but it's one for the record books, I guess."

"There's more," Raul said. The bantering mood of a few minutes ago was gone. He typed again, and once more the monitor changed, this time showing a news site from Ciudad Obregón. "This story," he explained, "is about something that happened in the town of Yapachic. Three bandits attacked and shot two women running a bodega, escaping with all the cash in the joint. Before they made it a block away, they were stopped by what witnesses claim was the statue of a girl. This statue blinded the three, allowing authorities to capture them. At the same time, apparently, the statue appeared inside the bodega and healed the wounds of the two women there. The women saved the bullets from their bodies as souvenirs."

"So this is, what, some kind of *Weekly World News* type website you're showing me?" Buck asked.

"These are respected newspapers, Buck. They report things most U.S. papers wouldn't touch, but that doesn't mean they're making it all up. There are two more similar stories too, from Bacanora and Moctezuma."

"I didn't say they were making anything up. I just don't see the connection. Maybe Lulu was reading these same newspapers, and the stories made their way into her dreams. Or she wasn't having dreams at all, and the whole thing is some kind of put-on."

"Sure, that's possible," Raul admitted. "But it would take a lot of effort. See, the news stories are time-stamped when they're posted online, usually in advance of the print edition's release. And Lulu's blog posts also show the time she posts them. And her dream posts, showing what she calls 'she' or 'the girl,' have always been posted at least twelve hours *before* the news stories have gone up."

Buck didn't answer right away. What could he say to that? That he didn't believe in miracles, UFOs, vampires or spirits? He didn't, but it looked like maybe there was a little more going on here than he could readily explain.

"I know it's crazy, Buck. I hesitated to even bring it up to you. But I thought you should see it for yourself. You're the senior officer here; you get to make the tough decisions. This is something you want to dig into more, let me know."

"This point, we can't really afford not to follow up on anything, however ridiculous it looks. I'm just not too sure where we go with it from here. Ed's not going to approve a trip to Mexico based on this, even if we thought there was something there. If I took him this, he'd have my badge."

"I understand that, Buck. I haven't told anyone else about it. We can keep it between us if that's what you want."

The space Ed had rented them had been a feed store once. A crew had gutted it and put in prefabricated cubicles, leaving only the front counter, where Donna Gonzales sat to answer the phone and talk to walk-ins. They didn't have any cells—prisoners had to be hauled up to Bisbee or down to Douglas.

Raul's cubicle was just past the counter on the left. After his came Carmela's, then Scoot's. Buck had an office at the back with a door that closed. They were still in Raul's, but Carmela and Scoot were in the field and Donna never listened in on the others.

"Let's keep it quiet for now," Buck suggested. He rose, peering over the edge of the cubicle to make sure no one had come in. "I'll poke around some, see if I can find a way it figures in. And if you come up with anything else online, let me know."

"I will, Buck."

Buck stopped himself before leaving Raul's side, as another thought came to him. "One more thing," he said. "Can we find out who was reading her blog? If that's how the killer found the Lavenders, maybe we can back our way into finding him."

"I'll check on that, Buck."

"Thanks," Buck said. He didn't know if it would get them anywhere, but at least it was an angle. "And Raul?" he added. "That's good work."

8

"The point," Oliver said, "is that the San Pedro is the only un-dammed river in Arizona. Now, there's a reason it hasn't been dammed—its flow has never been sufficient, or consistent enough, to generate electricity." He stood at the front of a lecture hall. More than half its seats were empty, and the students in the remaining ones had scattered themselves throughout the hall. Behind him, a slide of the San Pedro River filled a pull-down screen. "But it's still worth looking at, if only because there are no other free-flowing rivers in the state left to study. Cochise County, where we're standing, has the second greatest diversity of mammals in the world, after the Costa Rican rain forest, and much of that diversity centers around the San Pedro, as well as on sky islands like the Chiricahua Mountains. Birds too and insects, reptiles . . . it's an incredibly rich resource, and it's right here. But it's troubled. These last few years, as the growth of Sierra Vista and Fort Huachuca have drawn more and more water, the San Pedro's flow has been affected. At one time last year, for the first time in recorded history, its flow was at zero. Nonexistent. Keep in mind, this is the state's last un-dammed river, and even it's drying up. So what lessons can we take away from this?"

Oliver gazed out at the students. Blank expressions, a couple scribbling notes as if he had said anything in the last five minutes that should be new to them. Second row, third from the left, the seat that Lulu ordinarily took was empty.

Fatigue battered him as suddenly as a flash flood. He raised a hand to cut off any responses that might have come. "You know what?" he said. "We're done for now. I'm sorry, but there's something going on that I can't talk about and I just don't have the energy for this today. Read the first section— that's three chapters—of Bowden's *Killing the Hidden Waters*, and we'll talk about it next time. And keep this aphorism in mind: Turn off a light, and hear a river sigh."

He let the students file out as he packed up his slides and notes. No one seemed to mind the abbreviated class period. Thinking back on his own college years, Oliver knew that he would not have objected either. Love of learning sometimes took a backseat to love of leisure time.

When the lecture hall had emptied, he slung his leather briefcase over his shoulder and walked out, flipping off the lights as he left. Outside, he paused for a moment, wondering if he should inform Franklin Hinckley that he had dismissed the class early and would be skipping his office hours. He decided that Franklin would figure it out if he needed him. The wind chilled him, and he rolled down the sleeves of his blue denim shirt, buttoning them at the wrists.

In the Saab, he glanced at the empty passenger seat and slipped U2's *Joshua Tree* into the CD player. The only radio station he could pick up here with any consistency was KDAP, and while he liked Howard Henderson's voice on *The Trading Post* in the morning, he was not in the mood for country songs about liquor, loss and angels looking down from heaven. A peal of thunder accompanied the jangling guitars of the opening notes, and Oliver looked to the sky. The glowering thunderheads there reflected his emotional state.

9

Buck watched Oliver Bowles speed up Davis Road, too fast given the pounding storm, make a right onto the slippery muck of Larrimore Trail and approach the gate to his own property. Oliver noticed the sheriff's vehicle then, and drove more slowly to his garage. Buck had parked near the house but hadn't gone inside, and apparently Jeannie, if she was at home, had not heard his approach over the drumming of the rain on the house's aluminum roof. Buck still wanted a look inside that shed, still considered Oliver the likeliest suspect he'd run across so far. But what Raul had shown him online had raised serious doubts.

Stepping out of the garage, Oliver closed the door and started toward Buck. Buck left his vehicle at the same time, letting the rain pelt his hat and clothing. "To what do I owe the honor?" Oliver shouted over the racket.

Buck waited until they were within reasonable conversational range to answer. "Dr. Bowles, I'd like to get a look inside your shed," he said.

"And you can't wait until the rain stops?"

"I'm afraid not."

"You got a warrant?"

Saw that one coming a mile off, Buck thought. "No, sir. If you need me to get one then I'll call over to the office and have one of the other officers round up a judge. This is a small community, Dr. Bowles. We can always find us a sympathetic judge when we need one. I'll just sit there in my vehicle out of the rain until it gets here."

"I'd feel better if you had one."

"You have something to hide, Dr. Bowles?"

"Of course not." Oliver's face seemed open, honest, but it was hard to read with water running down it. He wore a knit tie, loose at the throat, with the collar button of his shirt open. The rain plastered the shirt to him; it did the same to Buck's uniform blouse, and he wanted to get under some shelter. "But I'd feel like we were playing by the rules."

"I'm all in favor of the rules too, Dr. Bowles. But under certain circumstances, they take a backseat to expediency, far as I'm concerned. I could have just looked before you came home."

"Why didn't you?"

"Because if I had, anything I found there wouldn't have been admissible as evidence."

Oliver smiled. "Just what is it you think I have out there?"

"Whatever you may have, sir, it's staying dry while we're getting soaked."

Oliver laughed at that. "Okay, help yourself. Take a look. Just one thing."

"What's that?"

"Stop calling me 'sir' and 'Dr. Bowles.' It makes me feel like I'm older than you." Oliver was thirty-eight; he judged that Buck Shelton was almost a decade his senior.

"I'm sure you're not," Buck replied. "But I'll tell you what. After I look inside, I'll decide what I'm going to call you."

"Fair enough." Oliver led him around the house and back toward the shed, about fifty feet away. New brush and grass had grown up in what appeared to have once been a worn-down walkway between the house and the shed, no doubt due to the winter rains and the summer monsoon. At his own place, Buck would have tried to keep it clear, but he didn't mind, as it gave him something to step on besides slick mud.

When they neared the door, he could see that it was unlocked. *Good sign,* he thought. If Oliver had parked the girl in there, he'd have secured it somehow.

Oliver flipped up the latch and pulled the steel door open, then stood out of the way. Buck shouldered past him, peering into the dim interior.

A lawnmower, a weedeater, a few gardening tools. Three cardboard boxes stacked up in one corner. A gasoline can. Spiderwebs.

"That what you expected to see?" Oliver asked.

"Pretty much. But I had to look; you understand that."

"Not really. You think I'd kidnap my own neighbor?"

"I don't know, Oliver. I do know you have a bit of a history of getting involved with students a lot younger than you. Beyond that, I don't know much about you at all."

Oliver eyed him with a stern expression. "You could have asked. I'd have told you."

"I did ask about your relationship with Lulu Lavender," Buck reminded him.

"And I told you about it. Everything about it."

"Maybe so," Buck said. "But I couldn't know that, could I? Until I checked it out for myself."

Oliver's intent gaze hadn't wavered. "You want a cup of coffee or tea, Lieutenant Shelton? Since you're soaked to the skin?"

"If it's quick," Buck said. "I think maybe I've wasted enough time here already."

Oliver didn't quite know why he'd invited the lieutenant in. The man had, after all, practically accused him of murder and kidnapping.

On the flip side, he seemed willing to admit that his suspicion had been mistaken. *Either that or he's trying to get me to drop my guard,* Oliver thought, *and reveal something. But there's nothing to reveal.*

"I take it the investigation's not going too well?" Oliver said when they sat down with their mugs at the pine kitchen table. Jeannie had come in to greet Buck, then gone back to what she was doing in another room.

"Could be better," Buck admitted. "I got to say, when I found out about your affair with a student back in California, I really thought maybe I was on the right track."

"Having an affair hardly makes someone a killer," Oliver said.

"I know that. But you know, you're in a new house in a new state with a new job. Might feel like you have more at stake, more to protect. And if you fell back into old habits . . ."

"Oh, I get it, Buck. I'm just saying, in this case that's not what happened. My saying it doesn't make me innocent, but I am, and I hope you believe that, because as long as you're wasting time investigating me, Lulu's real kidnapper is getting farther away."

"You might be right about that, Oliver." Buck drained his cup. "And I ought to be doing something about it, oughtn't I? I'll get out of your hair. Appreciate the hospitality."

"Anytime. Sorry I didn't have doughnuts."

Buck smiled. "Every civilian gets one doughnut joke," he said. He put his mug on the kitchen counter, next to the sink, and picked up his hat from the table. "Next time, I shoot you. Right in the gut."

"It's a deal," Oliver said. He walked Buck to the door, where the lieutenant shook his hand and headed out into the storm's aftermath.

11

Barry sat around his house for a while, but he couldn't get comfortable there. The place reminded him of Clarice. Her framed picture stood on the buffet, the look on her face mildly disapproving. The buffet contained dishes bought for them as wedding presents that he hadn't used since her death, but couldn't bring himself to get rid of. Over the couch hung an Indian-style wall hanging she had bought in Phoenix, a dream catcher that he pointed out wasn't really made by Indians and should be in the bedroom anyway, but that she had thought looked perfect over the sofa. Even the coiled cloth rug in the entryway, which she'd found at an antiques store up in Benson. These things made him think about everything he'd lost in his life and everything he stood to lose. After a couple of hours he stormed out, slammed the door behind him and climbed back up into the truck. He needed to get away, to be around other people, to get outside of his own head for a time.

After driving aimlessly for thirty minutes, he found himself parked on the gravel lot of the Rusty Spur Saloon, an adobe building standing by itself on a quarter-acre lot in McNeal. He couldn't remember the details of the drive. He had been churning over his anger at his boss and that fuck down at the Wal-Mart and all the Mexicans who had come to the United States to take jobs away from Americans, and next thing he knew he was spraying stones and water at the other trucks in the lot and coming to a shuddering halt.

The saloon had a tin roof and a heavy wooden door, standing open. A screen kept some of the bugs and most of the rain out. He could hear Toby Keith turned up loud. The inside was dark and cool, and Barry tugged open the screen door and walked through into a different world, leaving behind the monsoon and some of the heartache.

Barry ordered Miller in a bottle. The bar had six stools and three drinkers, each with an empty between him and the next guy. One booth stood empty, but it held at least six, and Barry would have felt bad taking that much space. So he sat down between two of the guys, nodded to both and started in on his beer.

By his third he was complaining about his employment situation to the guy on his right. They had started out just chatting casually, and he hadn't even noticed when the conversation took this turn. "Listen to me," he said when it occurred to him. "Running off at the mouth like this, telling you my troubles."

"Don't worry about it, man," the guy said. "Man drinks in a bar, he's got to know he'll hear a sad story or two. That's why we're here, ain't it? Support our brothers in their time of need?"

"That's downright Christian of you," Barry said.

"I do what I can." Lean and weathered, the guy wore jeans and worn boots and a Western-style tan work shirt with pearl snaps. His hair was brown, trimmed military-short. His most striking feature, Barry thought, was pale gray eyes that seemed to glow in the bar's dim interior, as if the guy had a candle inside his head. Barry couldn't begin to explain it, but he felt as drawn to those eyes as a moth to a lightbulb. He could trust a man with eyes like that. They would reveal any trace of dishonesty, would signal deception before it could happen.

"You want to go sit in the booth?" the guy said. "I'll buy you another and you can finish your story without worrying about anyone else hearing you."

Barry wondered for a second if the guy was trying to pick him up. He'd been with a few women besides Clarice, but not many—a couple of B-girls in Saigon, two others in high school before that and a couple of awkward encounters since she had passed away. He'd heard about men who went with men—you didn't reach adulthood these days without learning about such things—but he didn't think he'd ever met one. Not that he knew about, for sure. This guy looked plenty masculine, though, with a stringy muscularity, no trace of makeup or earrings or anything like that. His shirtsleeves were rolled up over tanned, corded forearms, and his shoulders were broad, and of course he had those eyes. Barry tipped back his bottle, drained it, set it down on the wooden bar top with a loud clunk. "Sure," he said. What he hadn't had was anything regular except his right hand, Vaseline and satellite TV since he'd lost Clarice, and he wondered if this guy made a move, that kind of move, would he be able to resist?

The guy ordered them both another beer and carried the two bottles over to the booth, the strong fingers of his right hand clutching both necks. Barry slid in, his jeans sticking once on the vinyl, and the other man sat across from him. He kept his hands above the top of the table, at least one on his bottle. "You were telling me about the guy at Wal-Mart," he prompted.

"Don't know what else there is to tell," Barry said. "He didn't quite laugh in my face, but I could tell he wanted to."

"Sure," the other man said. "He's got a job; all his people have their jobs. What's it to them if a white man can't afford groceries?"

"Exactly," Barry said. Maybe the guy wasn't interested in him in a physical way. That was better, anyway. He didn't know what to do with a man, that way, but he felt a closeness with this stranger that he hadn't known since Clarice's death. Like the two of them connected on some wavelength he hadn't been broadcasting on for years. "You hit it right on the head, buddy."

"I've been there too," the man said. "Hell, every white man in this bar, in this whole damn county, probably has."

"Got that right," Barry said. "I . . . I can't remember your name. I know you said it, but . . ."

"That's cool." The guy stuck his hand out for another shake. "I'm Carl Greenwell."

The name sounded vaguely familiar, but Barry couldn't place it. Carl kept him talking awhile longer, buying rounds as they went. Rings of bottle sweat ran together on the varnished tabletop, forming pools. When Barry's eighth or ninth Miller showed up, Carl grabbed the bottle. "Listen, Barry," he said, lowering his voice. "What would you think if I could show you a way that you could make a difference? You could fight back against the forces that are ruining this country?"

"Hell," Barry said, trying to tug his beer free of the other man's grip, "I'd say sign me up."

"That's what I was hoping you'd say. Why don't you bring that along and come with me?"

Barry saw no reason not to accompany Carl Greenwell. Outside, the rain had stopped. Rays from the late afternoon sun slanted beneath the clouds, giving a golden glow to a cloudburst over the Mule Mountains to the west. "What are you driving?" Carl asked.

Barry indicated his rust-pocked old GMC truck. Carl nodded and continued toward a gleaming black Expedition with tinted windows. The front passenger door opened, and a man got out, nodding once to Carl. "Give Joe your keys," Carl said. "He'll follow us with your truck."

Without hesitation, Barry fished the keys out of his pocket and gave them to the man who had climbed down from the dark SUV. Carl opened the rear doors of the Expedition, and Barry got in behind the driver, a man wearing a straw cowboy hat with a dark sweat stain around the base of the crown, mirrored sunglasses and a gray camo-patterned T-shirt. Carl sat beside him in the rear. "Let's go home, Marc," he said to the driver. "We have a lot of stuff to show Barry."

12

Vivian Stiles had been twenty-two and brilliant, a senior with her choice of graduate programs ahead of her, a consenting adult in anyone's book. She was sophisticated, worldly, and had amassed plenty of experience at life and sex. She had told Oliver that she'd been sexually active since before her sixteenth birthday, and when she described the number of lovers she'd had, of both genders, and some of the things she'd tried, he felt that if anything, she would be corrupting him and not the other way around.

Even so, he had not come on to her. She sat in his San Diego State classroom during lecture periods, dressed in college casual, cleavage revealed by low-cut tops or tanks or tight, skimpy numbers that laced up the front, snug-fitting jeans or shorts or tiny skirts that displayed miles of shapely leg. She visited him during office hours, at first to discuss issues relating to course work or grades, later just to pass the time. For a twenty-first-century college student, Vivian was remarkably articulate, and talking to her was more like conversing with a colleague than a student.

Gradually, their exchanges became more and more personal. She shared stories of her romantic history and seemed fascinated by Oliver's description of his nontraditional marriage, in which both partners occasionally had other lovers, with full spousal knowledge and consent. Vivian seemed fascinated by the arrangement and the fact that Oliver and Jeannie both thought it kept their marriage fresh and vital.

From that point, her interest in him seemed to change. Her

flirting grew more direct. It didn't take long for Oliver to realize that he could have her in a second, that all he had to do was lock his office door and she'd start tugging her clothes off. He was not, at the moment, involved with anyone besides his wife, but he wasn't looking for involvement, either, particularly not with a student.

But he couldn't deny the attraction he felt, mentally and sexually. Vivian had a remarkable figure, athletic but soft where it counted, curvaceous instead of cut. Cascading waves of auburn hair framed a face equal parts angelic and devilish, her green eyes heavy-lidded, her lips just slightly thinner than traditional beauty standards dictated, her jaw pronounced, as if defying him to deny her anything. He flirted back but gave no consideration to taking the next step, until the time he accompanied her to her off-campus apartment to pick up a birthday gift she'd promised him, and when the door was closed she shoved him against it, pressing her body against his. Her mouth sought his lips, his neck, his shoulders, and her hands moved across his back, his chest, his groin. He tried to protest, but not forcefully, and then he was hard, his own hands roaming to breasts and behind, tangling in her hair. She rolled her tight T-shirt off, unclasped her bra, and as his hands explored the swell of her breasts, she lowered to her knees and opened his pants, taking him in her hungry mouth.

The first time, she finished him that way. He wanted to reciprocate, but Vivian turned him down, assuring him that he would more than make it up later. By which she meant forty minutes later, when they had retreated to her bed, naked together, still learning the curves and corners and crannies of each other's body as the afternoon light slanted in between half-open blinds and dust swirled lazily in the air. He reached between her legs and found her moist and ready, and he began manipulating her with his fingers, but she pushed his head down. He kissed and licked a trail down the valley between her breasts, down her stomach, down, until with tongue and fingers he brought her to a shuddering, screaming orgasm. By then he was hard again, and she guided him inside her. Moving expertly, controlling his rhythm and bucking beneath him, she held him at the edge of orgasm for a long time, until he could hold off no more and exploded inside her.

The physical sensations she delivered to him were incredible. But after they were done, guilt warred with the pleasant afterglow. Oliver knew she was on the pill and got regular checkups for STDs, but he had taken no precautions of his own. And his arrangement with Jeannie required that they discuss prospective partners before anything happened. She would never have agreed to let him play with a student, knowing what it could do to his career. He had sworn not to get into such a situation for the same reason.

Yet here he was.

Having broken so many rules at once, he decided he couldn't tell Jeannie. The affair continued, Vivian demonstrating her experience and a definite attraction to high-risk behavior, going down on him in public or semipublic places: the beach, his office, an empty classroom, a campus parking lot. Once she took him into the back row of a quiet movie theater, hiked up her short skirt, undid his pants and straddled him. It turned out to be the shortest Merchant/Ivory film he had ever seen, or felt like it.

In private, she was just as inventive, wanting sex as often and in as much variety as she could get.

Finally, after very nearly getting caught in the act by a campus security guard, Oliver decided that it had to end. He couldn't risk his career and his marriage anymore, not even for such a stimulating and agreeable partner. He told her his decision over a quiet dinner at her apartment.

Vivian broke down. She not only wanted to continue the relationship, but she wanted to make it official, wanted him to leave Jeannie for her. Oliver refused. She threatened retaliation, swore that she would tell his wife.

Instead, she told Bob Crandall, his dean.

Worse, she was able to back up her charges with e-mails, photos and cards, all of which she had saved. Oliver was called in and informed that he had to resign immediately or be fired for having violated the school's policies in such a visible and egregious way.

That night, Oliver told Jeannie what he'd done.

The third scene in a row, after Vivian and Bob, almost turned out to be more than he could handle. He moved to a motel for a few weeks, seeing Jeannie only occasionally. He knew that his dishonesty had wounded her, and even if he had been less perceptive, she made no effort to hide it.

Not once during the days they were apart, however, did they end a day without saying "I love you" to each other.

A month after his resignation took effect, Jeannie agreed to stay with him. Bob Crandall helped get him in touch with Franklin Hinckley, and when the offer came through from Cochise College, they put their house up for sale and started to think of the future in positive terms, as the beginning of a new phase of life. They agreed to try monogamy for a change, and as far as Oliver knew both of them had lived up to the pledge.

But the past leaves its imprint on every human soul, and Oliver knew that he would carry the marks of his failure for the rest of his life. Buck Shelton had found out what he'd done, and it had made him a suspect in a multiple homicide and abduction. For all he knew, he was now suspected of the abduction of Elayne Lippincott as well. Oliver felt that the decisions he and Jeannie had made about their marriage were personal and private, and it offended him that anyone would equate extramarital intimacy with murder.

Jeannie came in shortly after Buck left and found Oliver still sitting at the table, cradling his empty mug between his hands. "What was all that about?" she asked.

"I think he talked to Bob Crandall," Oliver said. "Or Hinckley. Either way, he knows about . . . you know, about me and Vivian. And just naturally assumes that if I'd fuck a student once then I'd do it with an eighteen-year-old neighbor too. Which, since I'd be sure to be caught, means that I'd murder her family and hide her out in the shed."

"He can't be too serious about it," Jeannie said, "if he sat in here and drank coffee with you."

"I'm trying to figure out that part too. I can't decide if he really believed I was guilty and expected to find her in there, or was just going through the formalities. Maybe he thought that if I was relaxed enough I'd let something slip."

"Or maybe he knows you didn't do anything and wanted to make peace over coffee."

"Maybe that," Oliver agreed. "I just don't know."

"When he left, it didn't sound like he really suspected anything. At least to me, in the other room."

"I don't think he did, but I don't know him well enough to really read him. He might have planted a bug for all I know, hoping I'd confess to something after he left."

Jeannie leaned against the jamb with her arms folded over her chest, head cocked at an angle that reminded Oliver of Benji, the movie dog, regarding him for a long moment. "You didn't, did you? I mean, I know you're no killer, and I don't believe you would have sex with Lulu. But I'd like to hear you say it."

"Jeannie . . ." Oliver's first impulse was to feel insulted, to decry her lack of trust. Barely had the thought entered his mind than he reconsidered. She had every right to doubt. The hurt he had caused her with his lies, his deceptions, had never left her, for all that they had worked to put it behind them. "No. I didn't. I wouldn't. I hope you believe me."

She came to him then, put her arms around his back. "I do, Oliver," she said. "It's just . . . all this stuff, with Lulu and her family, so close by. It all has my head a little fucked up, that's all."

He squeezed her, feeling her comfortable warmth against him. "You're not alone there, sweetheart," he said. "Not at all."

13

Peggy Olsson got a weird vibe from her new guest. She was Sensitive, with a capital "S," and had learned to pay attention to her instincts. They rarely steered her wrong. Even back in high school, the night she had refused to get into Tony Corbett's Impala after the spring dance, it had been because she picked up a strange feeling from Tony. Twenty minutes later he had steered the Impala into an oncoming semi. Sadie Franks, who had taken the seat that would have been Peggy's, hadn't died in the accident, but to this day she had to roll around in a wheelchair that she operated with her mouth, so Peggy had to think she'd made the right choice.

Normally she closed the cabins down after Labor Day. There was just no percentage in keeping them open. During the summer, Arizona's desert heat drove flocks of tourists up the heights of the Mogollon Rim. But in autumn, tourists wanted to see color-changing deciduous trees, so the Rim's pine forests didn't suit. And skiers had no use for the Rim's sheer cliffs, which limited winter business. The springs and summers earned enough to meet Peggy's needs, and during the fall she hired Wes Colton to do maintenance work on the cabins, getting them ready for the winter and the following spring's guests.

The place was all that was left from an ill-considered marriage to that same Tony Corbett, who had recovered from the accident except for intense pain in his hips whenever the weather changed. His family had owned it for generations. Tony was an only child, and by the time he died in prison, victim of a mattress spring sharpened into a seven-inch shiv,

Peggy had grown closer to his parents than she'd ever been to him. They willed her the cabins, and she'd been running the place for more than twenty years now.

The man—he said his name was Dana Fortier, but she wasn't even sure that was true, since she'd called him Dana on the path a few days before and he hadn't even appeared to hear her—had seemed so desperate, and the money he'd offered so good, that she had broken her own rule and let him take a cabin. She had even given him the one he wanted, farthest from her place, closest to the Rim. She saw very little of him after that, mostly knew he was around because his truck would pass back and forth in front of her cabin with its curtained Gem camper shell on the back.

Still, that vibe.

Part of it, she believed, was due to his appearance. He had dark eyes that shifted around a lot, a prominent nose and a kind, slightly nervous smile, as if he waited in constant fear of how others would perceive him. His dark hair was thinning on top but thick on his arms and what she could see of his chest, curling up out of his open shirt collar. She suspected the fur continued down his stomach and on his back too—not a look that appealed to her, particularly, but she thought it created the effect of a harmless pet.

In addition to the visual strangeness, he smelled odd. Sweet, in a way, but not pleasant. The nearest she could come to describing it was imagining that someone had poured sugar into a carton of milk and then left it out in the sun all day.

There was more, she knew. When she tried to parse out just what it was, all that came to mind was a photograph she had seen, as a young girl, inside a book of wartime pictures that her father had kept on a high shelf in his den. One photo in particular had burned itself into her brain, and as a girl she had found herself drawn back to it again and again, when she had the house to herself, fascinating and repulsive at the same time. It showed a mass gravesite, she couldn't remember from which war, and bodies—some recent, some old enough that bones poked through papery flesh—being bulldozed into an open pit.

Peggy hadn't thought of that picture in years. But every

time she looked at Dana Fortier—or whoever he was—he reminded her of it. The whole experience of having him around forced her to look back, to dredge up memories long since left behind. She didn't find the process altogether unpleasant. Like any life, hers had had its share of hard times and sorrow, but she also had two younger sisters, both with families, whom she loved, and plenty of happy moments to look back on.

He was up to something back there. That, she decided, was what it came down to. He wanted secrecy, not just solitude. He wanted a place where he wouldn't be found out.

She couldn't have that. She didn't want anything illegal happening on her property. Determined to learn what it was, she waited in her cabin, working on needlepoint, until she heard his truck drive past again. Rushing to the window, she watched it head out to the Rim Road and away. Sitting down again, she waited another thirty minutes, then set the needlepoint aside, donned a leather jacket against the mountain chill and struck out through the trees. Avoiding the road and going cross-country, she could be at his cabin in ten minutes.

She would get to the bottom of this before another hour had passed.

Bridges Not Borders occupied a concrete block building that had once been a garage or a stable behind the home of Nellie Oberricht, the organization's founder. She owned five acres near the western edge of the Douglas city limits, about four miles from the border. A concrete floor had been poured and partially covered by rugs that Buck guessed had been hand-made in Mexico or maybe Guatemala. Posters adorned the walls, some showing Mexican artwork and crafts, others with simple declarations of the group's philosophy: "A PERSON CAN NEVER BE ILLEGAL." "HUMANITY IS NOT A CRIME." "BORDERS=PRISON BARS."

Buck had met Nellie a few times, even arrested her once. He had no problem with the work her group did as long as it didn't cross the lines of legality that had been drawn by the state. Which, he guessed, was the whole problem. Bridges Not Borders, like other humanitarian groups, provided aid for undocumented aliens. Sometimes that aid consisted of putting cases of water bottles out in the desert so that migrants wouldn't die of thirst. Other times they got more involved—driving migrants to doctors, hiding them—and those were the acts that crossed the line.

If the migrants didn't cross the line—meaning the border—in the first place, or only crossed it legally, none of these issues would exist. But they did come, hundreds of thousands every year, like an ocean lapping at the American shore. The Border Patrol apprehended many of them, processing them and returning them to the Mexican side. Others got through to jobs in Maine or Arkansas or Ohio or right here in Arizona.

Still others died en route. Hyperthermia in the summer, hypothermia in winter. They got lost in the deserts and mountains. Their guides abandoned them. Buck had seen too many dehydrated bodies in the desert, skin blackened and tight, whites of their eyes gone pink from burst blood vessels. Sometimes they tore their clothes off and the sun fried them lobster red. One he'd found had suffocated on dirt he had clawed from the desert floor in a deluded belief that he was drinking from a pond—the man's mouth had gaped open, and dry soil caked his lips and swollen tongue. With luck he found them before the coyotes did, before the insects had eaten out their eyeballs and bored through their scalps. He had sympathy for Nellie's point of view, but he wished Mexico would fix its own economy so its citizens would stop dying on his turf.

Buck knocked once on the open door, then entered. Nellie stood up from behind a desk piled high with documents, file folders, literature. In the middle of it he could see a computer and telephone, both overwhelmed by the sheer amount of paper.

"Always a pleasure to see you without handcuffs in your hand, Buck," she said. She was a tall woman, five-eleven he remembered from booking her. One forty-five, although she had maybe gained a pound or two since then, but it sat well on her. Her brown hair, streaked with silver, fell straight and reached almost to her waist, accentuating her height. Her smile appeared genuine, and Buck had always found it pleasant, as he did the deep, mellow tones of her voice.

"Hello, Nellie," he said. "You keepin' out of trouble?"

"Am I supposed to tell the truth, or make you happy?"

"Let's just pretend I didn't ask," he said.

She nodded, an action that set her acres of hair in undulating motion, and sat back behind the desk. A stack of newspapers and magazines filled the one white plastic chair for visitors. Nellie didn't offer to clear it, so Buck remained standing.

"But this isn't a social visit," she said. The smile had vanished from her handsome face, with just a hint of bemusement left in her emerald eyes.

"No, I'm afraid it's not, Nellie."

"We haven't done anything wrong, Buck," she said. "I

mean, I know you and I don't always agree on what's right and what's wrong, but I'm talking by your standards, not mine. I've placed some water lately, made some phone calls, even paid some visits across the border. Nothing more than that. It's been quiet, what with the rains and all."

"Nellie, you know Lulu Lavender?"

"Of course," Nellie said. The flash of spirit in her green eyes faded as she blinked. Nellie could read people as well as any lawman, Buck had always felt, and she saw bad news on the way. "What's happened, Buck?"

"Lulu's missing," he told her. "The rest of her family's been killed."

She was silent a moment, swallowing once, then blinking and looking away from Buck. Her left hand had curled into an awkward fist; her right gripped the edge of the desk so hard the knuckles whitened. After a moment she met his gaze again, as if she had taken that brief opportunity to work out how she felt. "God damn it," she said, her voice cold. "God damn. You don't know who did it, or you wouldn't be here."

"That's right, Nellie. I was hoping maybe you could point me in some direction or other."

"You've made a mistake, Buck. This is . . . I am outraged by this, I truly am. Lulu is a gentle soul, a wonderful girl with nothing but love in her heart. I can't begin to fathom why someone would wish her harm, or anyone else in her family for that matter."

"I can't either, Nellie. That's why I came here. In case there was something you could tell me. I don't mean to say that it was UDAs murdered those folks, but it's within the realm of possibility, right? Or maybe some *coyote*, upset with her for some reason? Could she have gotten mixed up in a drug deal?"

"Not Lulu," Nellie said with a certainty that Buck hoped was well founded. "Never."

"Can you know that for an absolute fact?" Buck pressed. "I'm not looking to tangle you up in anything, but I have to know. Were the Lavenders hiding anyone out at their place? Or guiding anyone, something like that?"

"Lulu didn't do that kind of thing," Nellie said. "She

staffed a table up at the Farmer's Market in Bisbee. She raised funds; she wrote letters to the newspapers. Things like that. I wouldn't even let her go out with me into the field yet. There's no way she would have encountered anyone like that."

"But people come here to the office."

"Family members, sure," Nellie replied. "Those who are here legally. No one without documents is brought to this office, ever."

"I'd like to believe you, Nellie."

"I guess it's your choice. Believe me or not."

Buck suspected that Nellie would lie to protect her organization and its charges. At the same time, she would take Lulu's disappearance seriously, and he believed she would do whatever she could to help.

"Guess I have no reason not to," he said. "But if anything comes to mind, or if you hear anything, let me know right away, okay?"

"Of course. If you can think of any other way I can help, just say the word. Can I ask what steps are being taken to find her?"

"We're doing everything we can," Buck answered, knowing that this time he was lying to her.

On his way back to his Yukon, he decided he would make it true.

15

"I need the Search and Rescue Team," Buck said. On his way back to his office, he'd called the main sheriff's office in Bisbee and got Irena Mendez, Sheriff Gatlin's assistant, on the line.

"Ed will have to authorize that," Irena said. "And he's in Sierra Vista giving a press conference."

"Irena, this Lavender girl has been missing for too long, and we've got nothing," Buck said. "There's no more time to wait. Just call 'em in and put it on me."

"Buck, Ed will have your ass for that."

Irena had a tendency to exaggerate, Buck knew. Ed would be pissed. He would rant and fume and threaten, but he would stop short of yanking Buck's badge. Still, he could make life miserable for a good long while.

"I'll take that chance, Irena," he assured her. "If there's a footprint, a hair, a skin cell anywhere near the Lavender ranch, I want it found." The Search and Rescue Team was composed of citizen volunteers, mostly locals with their own four-wheel-drive vehicles. They generally fanned out looking for lost hikers, wayward Alzheimer's patients, that sort of thing. Putting them to work searching for minuscule clues on a property as big as the Lavenders' was not typical, but Buck had run out of other ideas. His own officers had canvassed the property, but not as comprehensively as fifty or sixty people could.

Of course, he would no longer be able to keep the murders quiet, once all those volunteers found out about them. That would be something else for Sheriff Gatlin to be angry about.

But since he had gone this far, he figured he might as well take one more step off the cliff.

He gave the sheriff thirty minutes to finish his press conference, studying transcripts Raul had made of Lulu's blog while he waited, and then he dialed the cell phone of Gina Castaneda, a reporter from the NBC affiliate in Tucson. She answered on the second ring.

"Gina, it's Lieutenant Buck Shelton, from the Cochise County Sheriff's Office," he said.

"Buck, how are you?" Gina replied. They had met several times, usually on occasions when she hoped to use him to learn more than he or Sheriff Gatlin wanted to tell.

Not this time.

"I'll tell you the truth, Gina, I've been better."

"What's wrong?"

"Were you at the sheriff's press conference just now?"

"Yes, I'm headed back to Tucson," she said. "Why?"

Both of them on cell phones, then. Buck eyed the road ahead, familiar and straight, but a momentary lapse of attention could be enough time for a coyote or a cow to amble out onto the pavement. "I know it's an awful thing, that girl being missing," he said. "But I've got a situation down here that's just as bad, and it's not getting any attention at all."

"Tell me."

Buck took a deep breath. There would be no going back after this. "A family of four was murdered the other night, and a fifth, a teenage girl, is missing from the house."

"That's horrible!"

"It is," he agreed. "But the press is so wound up over Elayne Lippincott that no one's covering this crime. I need some exposure to help find this girl."

"Hang on a second, Buck."

The line went silent. Buck pictured Gina as he remembered her, with rich olive skin and intelligent dark eyes and shoulder-length hair with the sheen of black silk. Her features were sculpted, precise, as if a news director had designed the perfect on-air reporter. Her eyes were set well apart, her nose small and well shaped, her teeth white and even. The only thing that might have been considered a flaw, except Buck found it endearing, was that she had very full lips, the upper more so than the lower, in a reversal of the norm. More than once he had watched her on TV and wondered what it would be like to kiss those lips.

"Buck?" Her sudden return took him by surprise, almost as if she had known what he was thinking.

"Yeah, I'm here."

"We're turning around, heading your way. Can you meet us at the crime scene?"

Buck agreed, and gave her the address of the Lavender ranch.

When he hung up, he filled his lungs with air again, held it, blew it out.

He had leapt over the edge.

And Ed Gatlin would be waiting at the bottom.

16

Carl Greenwell's ranch sat almost right on the border, a few miles to the east of Douglas. There wasn't another real city for hundreds of miles in that direction, Barry knew. New Mexico's largest border crossing was the relatively small town of Columbus, making El Paso the next big city that way.

And in between, as Carl pointed out, flowed a tidal wave of human traffic, the never-ending surge of migrants and drugs.

Marc drove the Expedition along some of the ranch's dirt trails, with Barry pointing out sights along the way: a well, a windmill, a barn containing generating equipment. In an emergency, the ranch could be entirely self-sufficient, Carl explained, off the power grid and with its own water. They even had satellite phones and Internet access. Barry didn't quite get why Carl was so pleased by the fact that they could withstand a siege, but Carl claimed they could, and he returned to that theme time and again.

He showed Barry six buildings, two adobe houses that looked like they'd stood for a hundred years, the others more modern corrugated steel structures that Carl said were bunkhouses, storage buildings and the like. The steel buildings had been arranged in a semicircle around the two adobes, all set in a shallow valley and sharing a common gravel driveway. A wooden observation tower stood atop the highest of the surrounding hills. Marc tooted the Expedition's horn, and Barry saw someone in the tower wave back.

Tall fences topped with razor wire surrounded the entire property, more daunting by far than the border wall made from Vietnam-era landing mats. Barry had seen as they entered that two men carrying what looked like automatic rifles guarded the front gate.

"This looks like a fort," he commented when Marc stopped the SUV outside one of the adobes.

"Better," Carl said. "Because forts are owned by the government, and the American Pride Ranch is one hundred percent private property."

"I didn't see anything like cattle or sheep or any of that," Barry said.

"It's not that kind of ranch, Barry. Our products are freedom and security for the American people."

"I don't follow," Barry said.

"Come on inside," Carl offered. "I'll introduce you around and explain."

As Barry followed Carl in, Marc drove the Expedition toward one of the steel buildings. Before he reached it, someone inside began opening a big door. Barry could only see darkness inside. Joe had already parked Barry's GMC in the drive.

The larger of the two adobe buildings had two stories, topped by a flat roof. The walls were at least a foot thick, with deeply recessed windows, and inside heavy wooden beams crossed the ceiling and offered structural support.

The interior furnishings weren't stylistically in keeping with the building. An institutional-style green metal table with a dozen matching chairs occupied the center of the main room, flanked by steel filing cabinets in black, tan and gray. Scuffed and stained whitewashed walls went unadorned by artwork or anything else that would indicate people lived here. A rolling chalkboard/bulletin board had maps of the region thumbtacked to it. The place reminded Barry more of a nursing home or hospital waiting room than a ranch house.

In another room, a bit more comfortable than the first, people sat on threadbare, mismatched furniture. They were mostly men, Carl's age or younger, casually dressed and fit, with short hair. Barry noted a lot of camo pants and tattoos. Two women completed the group, about the same age as the men, also casual and muscular. A few people huddled around a TV; others played video games on yet another set; still others sat by themselves nursing bottled beers or canned sodas and reading books or playing quiet card games. If the other room had looked like something from a residential care facility, this one looked like the common room in a jail. Several people smoked, and the room stank like an overflowing ashtray.

"These are some of our guys," Carl told him. "Our heroes, I call 'em. Guys, this is Barry. Barry, gentlemen and ladies, has recently been fucked over twice, once by his Mexican boss and once by the personnel guy at Wal-Mart—another individual of the Mexican-American persuasion, I might add."

"That's fucked up," someone said.

"I thought Wal-Mart was a good American company," another added.

"Used to be," Carl replied. "Now they sell cheap foreign-made crap, and if you've been inside the one in Douglas lately you'd be lucky to have heard anyone speaking English. They pay for shit and they won't even hire decent folks like Barry here."

Carl turned to Barry and lowered his voice. "Not that I have anything against Mexicans." He pointed at two men, one sitting by the TV, the other under a floor lamp with a thick book on his lap. "Nestor and Raimundo are both Mexican," he said. "Nestor's from Juarez, and Raimundo, he's from . . . Where you from, Raimundo?"

"Detroit," Raimundo said. The room erupted in laughter.

"Mexican-American, whatever," Carl said. "Point is I got nothing against them."

"Hell, no," Raimundo agreed. He was the one watching TV. "Carl ain't no hater. Or if he is, he hates everyone just the same."

"Damn straight. I hate someone, it's because I got a good reason to. You can't judge people because of where they're from or what color their skin is, not in this world." Carl's gaze seemed to bore through Barry's eyes, right into his brain. "You got to give people a chance, trust that they'll do the right thing. Then if they don't, if they fail you, then you cut them loose or do whatever has to be done. Someone fucks you over, you have to deal with them in kind, right? But not because someone's Mexican or German or black or whatever."

Barry felt like he was being preached to, as if Carl were some kind of evangelical on a Sunday morning TV show he had accidentally flipped to while looking for sports scores. Everything the man said made sense—or was that the many beers, the unfamiliar surroundings, the empty stomach?—but why he made the effort remained a mystery. Carl had, for all intents and purposes, picked Barry up at the Rusty Spur. Bought him booze, brought him to the ranch, showed him around. In Barry's experience, someone only treated you like that if they wanted something. Since he didn't yet know what Carl wanted, he moved hesitantly, taking shallow breaths, not allowing himself to relax completely.

"I know a lot of good Mexican folks," he said, aware that it came off halfhearted after Carl's articulate sermon.

"Listen, I've dragged you all over the place without offering you anything," Carl said, abruptly changing the subject. "You want another beer? Something stronger?"

"I could maybe use a Coke," Barry said, aware that he had reached his limit and wanting to hang on to some semblance of control. "Or maybe some coffee?"

Carl flashed a warm, reassuring smile. "Good idea," he said.

Fifteen minutes later, Barry and Carl sat at the big institutional table. Four of the others had joined them, including Nestor from Juarez, Bob Worthy, Hank Elbert and Connie McKay, one of the two women, who sat close to Barry. She had short brown hair that hugged her scalp, hanging just about to chin level, a narrow, pinched face and brown eyes. Firm breasts bulged a plain orange T-shirt tucked into snug jeans. Barry had seen Bob Worthy before, tall and gangly with black hair tied back in a short ponytail, and after several minutes he remembered that the guy worked at the gas station where he often filled his truck. Hank Elbert, short, swarthy and muscular, was new to him.

Carl held court, sitting at the table's head, and the others sat like students gathered around their teacher. "The thing is," he said, "the little guy can't compete against the giant corporation, and he can't compete against the government. Both of those entities are only out for themselves, to increase their own wealth and power, and the average American gets smashed in the middle, like the cream in an Oreo cookie."

"But that's the free enterprise system at work, right?" Connie asked. "Isn't that, like, the fucking American way?"

"It used to be," Carl answered quickly. "But it's been corrupted. There was a social compact that existed. You'd go to work for a company like GM or Bethlehem Steel, and you'd do your job eight hours a day for thirty years, with a couple weeks a year for vacation. In return you'd be paid a fair wage, and then when you retired, you'd get a guaranteed pension, along with your Social Security. Somewhere along the way, that social compact got thrown out the window. Now you got guys like Barry here, working at a country market instead of for a big corporation, because any corporation in this part of the country has moved to Mexico. And if they have a branch here at all, they're hiring Mexicans and Asians and Pakistanis or what-have-you instead of someone like Barry. And they've given up on the pension idea, defaulted on their promises, and left hardworking Americans in the lurch."

Bob Worthy's cigarette, forgotten on the lip of an ashtray, burned a long tail of ash, its smoke inscribing silent curlicues above the table. Barry nodded, thinking of his brother Stu's situation, retired without a pension. No one spoke as Carl took a breath and continued.

"It's all because unchecked immigration has swollen our population with too many people willing to work for too little money and benefits. Look at who's having the most babies these days. Hispanics, blacks and Asians, not whites. They come here and then they reproduce, and their kids take our jobs and reproduce again, and before you know it, who's being squeezed out? The corporations put their bottom lines ahead of their responsibility to the country that gave them everything, and they hire people willing to work part-time for shit wages and forget about benefits. The government doesn't mind because they still rake in their tax dollars every which way. And what's the result? Massive white unemployment, people trying to get by on Social Security and collecting aluminum cans by the highway, an exploding population of meth-heads and car thieves, hopelessness and heartache."

He stopped. Barry didn't think he'd ever seen anyone say so much so fast. He thought the man made sense, but his head spun despite the strong coffee, and he figured he'd have to think it over for a bit.

Barry felt pressure against the outside of his thigh as Connie leaned into him, reaching for a bowl of sugar packets. She had a cup of coffee too, which had gone neglected during Carl's tirade. As Barry glanced at her, she met his gaze, smiling. He glanced quickly away, then back. She hadn't moved, eyes on him, lips curled in a private grin, upper leg pressing against his. "He's something, ain't he?" she said quietly, meant just for Barry.

"Can't deny that," Barry said. He felt nervous, as if this woman might be coming on to him. *But earlier,* he thought, *you believed Carl was. You're not so handsome as all that. Don't go thinking you are.*

In truth, since Clarice had passed he had only been with two women. One had been a drunken nighttime fumbling in her car outside the Rusty Spur, with a woman whose name he hadn't even been able to remember when he'd run into her at Safeway two weeks later. The other, more satisfying but also pricier, had been with a working girl up in Phoenix. Working woman, more like. She had been in her forties, still young as far as Barry was concerned, with a model's lean figure and bottle-blond hair, but she knew how to make a man feel like he'd been through the wringer, in the good way.

He didn't think Connie really was interested—she was just being friendly, the same way that Carl had been. This was an amiable group. It didn't seem like a real ranch, and Barry hadn't decided what to make of it, although he was developing an idea.

He knew that groups of self-styled Border Patrol types, amateur militias, watched the borders to keep out illegal immigrants. They had become particularly well known when they organized as "minutemen" and brought in volunteers from around the country. Even before that, and certainly since, there had been smaller groups, each staking out a portion of the border to watch. Barry suspected that's what the American Pride Ranch really was. The armed guards at the gate had tipped him off first, and since then nothing had happened to change his mind.

He didn't have a problem with it. He didn't know why they had let him inside—did they want him to join their group? He couldn't see why. His military experience was a long time back.

But he did know, as he sat at the table surrounded by people he had never met before this night, embraced in unfamiliar warmth, that he had not felt this appreciated in a very long time.

17

He is an odd-looking man. She realizes this only today, when the blindfold slips enough for her to get a good view of him. In fact, everything about him is odd, Lulu thinks. He speaks to her only in precise, formal diction, using few contractions, never stammering or hemming. Even when his sentences contain only a single word, they are clear and that word is carefully chosen. At the same time, he almost never responds to her, even when she asks a direct question. It's as if he doesn't hear her, or chooses not to, like a puppy ignoring its name when it's called. He can be looking right at her with his strangely hooded eyes, and she will speak and he will not even register that he is being spoken to. Sometimes she loses patience and screams right in his face, but unless he has initiated conversation he refuses to respond.

He is not a large man, although she can't tell exactly how tall—it's hard to judge from her position on the floor with her hands tied. He's wiry, and appears to be stronger than his build would indicate. His chest seems almost concave instead of convex, for instance, and his arms are thin, not muscular. But he has no problem lifting Lulu when he wants to move her. Like his arms, his fingers are long and tapered but lacking in definition, with seemingly no knuckles at all.

His hair is dark and wispy, like that of a desiccated corpse after a few years in the grave. The skin of his face is pale, dry, parchmentlike, and flakes off his scalp, his forehead and his prominent nose. Veins show blue beneath it. Protruding from that thin hair like a misshapen balloon is that bulbous, peeling brow, split across the middle by a deep crevasse. Shaded by

his brow are those almost black eyes. His mouth is wide, with
thin lips so red they look lipsticked. Below that his chin tapers
to a scrawny neck with an Adam's apple nearly the size of a
Granny Smith jutting out of a thatch of black fur.

He wears clothes, Lulu believes, chosen off the rack at dis-
count stores. They don't fit him well, because nothing would
unless it was custom made to his odd proportions.

Just now, he's away from the cabin. He left once and returned with groceries—he's a bad cook, leaning heavily toward canned soups, beans and meat, even for breakfast, but he
keeps her fed and keeps plastic bottles of water for her—or
fast food, or other supplies; sometimes she can't tell why he
has left.

The fact that he has begun to stock up on supplies makes
her think he intends to keep her here for some time.

What seems like once every hour or so, he asks the same
question, the same thing he's been asking since he brought her
here.

"When is she coming?"

"I don't know who you mean," Lulu says.

"When is she coming?"

"Who?"

"The white girl. When is the white girl coming?"

After this happened a few times, Lulu figured out who he
meant. Still, she hasn't let on to him that she knows, continues
to play ignorant. At first she might have told him, but not now.
Now she has had time to reconsider that idea. As long as he
wants something from her, she judges, he will keep her alive.
When he has the information he wants, then he will kill her
like she believes he did the rest of her family.

He has been gone for almost an hour this time. For the first
thirty or forty minutes, Lulu was afraid to move. She's already
sore from sitting for however many hours it's been—she can almost lie down to sleep, but the chains hold her arms above her.
Her shoulders are screaming with pain, her legs and ass chafed
from sitting. More than anything, she wants to stand, to walk, to
move around. He hates it when she tries, though, except for
three times when he led her to the cabin's bathroom and stood

over her while she, blindfolded, did her business. This is an improvement over the first night and morning, when he expected her to do it where she sat, in a metal bowl like a dog dish.

She relaxes somewhat when he doesn't come back for so long. She works the blindfold against her shoulder, pushing it up so she can see a tiny wedge of her surroundings. She is in a room that is probably a bedroom. He always leaves the door open, and she can see into the kitchen and a little bit of a big front room, where he often lets the TV play all day long. From her place on the floor she can't see anything out the bedroom window except the upper branches of nearby trees, but the kitchen door has a four-paned window she can see through. Still, there's nothing out there to look at except more trees.

The cabin is a mess. He hasn't thrown anything away—she guessed that, from the smells, but now confirms her hunch. Food wrappers, empty cans, newspapers he's read are all strewn around the floor. You'd think it would take a week to make that much trash, she thinks. It's like there's something broken in him, something that has never really learned how to be human.

The floor and walls are both of knotty pine, unpainted. Most of the furniture, what little there is of it, is the same. The chain that holds her in place is looped around a radiator pipe that comes out of the wall and attached to shackles clasping her wrists. The radiator hasn't been turned on, and it got cold during the night, but he tossed her a thin wool blanket with which to cover herself when he heard her teeth clacking together. The pipe is solid—she has tried yanking against it, and though the chain rattles, the pipe always holds firm.

Now that he's been gone for a while, she tries again. This time she can see what she's doing, see that the pipe's weakest point is probably a welded joint a few inches down from where the wall pipe meets the first coil of radiator. She maneuvers the chain to that point and yanks as hard as she can, throwing all of her weight away from the wall and radiator.

It doesn't give a centimeter. Her muscles howl in pain, the jarring shock of her effort like slicing into them with a dull knife.

She blinks back tears, then decides what the fuck and lets

them flow. Great wet sobs burst from her chest. Tears roll
down her face and plop onto the floor, and she knows she's going to have to pee, crying always does it, but what can she do
about that? It won't be the first time since he took her that she
has done it in her pants, and probably not the last either.

She's just getting control of her breathing again when she
hears a noise outside the cabin. At first she tenses, afraid that
it's him, returning at last. He'll go into his usual routine, asking about the white girl, and he'll get mad when she refuses to
tell him, and he'll slap her.

But the front door doesn't open. Lulu hears the sound of
something, or someone, moving around the cabin. Leaves
rustling, branches snapping. A stray dog, maybe, or depending
on how far out in the wilderness they are, maybe a bear. Definitely not him—he moves quietly, like a ghost.

Lulu's attention is drawn to the kitchen door by the noises
outside, and as she watches a face appears in the window. It's
a woman, older, white, with red hair and big blue eyes. Lulu
has never seen her. The woman peers in through the window
cautiously, as if she knows she's trespassing, pressing her
hands against the glass to cut the glare. But then she sees Lulu
and her mouth falls open, eyes going wide. One hand drops to
her mouth as if she's afraid she might scream.

She shouts something through the glass and Lulu thinks
she's saying, "Are you all right? Do you need help?"

Lulu doesn't know whether to nod or shake her head, since
the two questions are contradictory. But the gag is gone so she
cries, "Help me, please! Get me out of here!"

The woman tugs at the door, yanks at it, but can't get it
open. "Try the front!" Lulu shouts. "Hurry!"

The woman hears and understands. She nods. "I'll be right
there!" she calls. Lulu hears the sounds as she runs around the
cabin, hears the rattle of the front door, also locked.

Then for a long moment, silence. Did she give up? Maybe
she went for help, to call the police. But no, after another few
seconds there's another sound at the door. A key rasping in the
lock. The woman has a key, or she fetched it from someplace.
Maybe this is her cabin and he's only renting or borrowing it.

The door swings open with a squeak and footsteps clomp across the wooden floor, and the first thing Lulu sees when she comes into view is the red hair, catching a stray shaft of sunlight from a window so that it blazes like flame. But there's something wrong, it's entering at a strange angle, and Lulu realizes that the woman is being tossed inside, not walking in. And he follows her, an expression of fury on that strange and horrible face.

"I'm sorry, I'm so sorry," the woman says. Her voice is deep, gravelly, and her figure is lush, Lulu sees as she sits up on the cabin floor, and with that pretty face this woman was a knockout in her younger days—even now in her sixties maybe she's a looker—and Lulu thinks that finally she's going to see him do what she's been dreading. Sexualpredator—the two words have merged together in the modern vocabulary, and so far he hasn't expressed any sexual urges whatsoever, but maybe just because Lulu is too young for him, and now that he has this older woman, this poor woman whose mistake was trying to rescue Lulu, he'll let it out.

He reaches for the woman. His mouth is a thin line, his dark eyes cruel. "Mister," the woman says, "you'd better let us both go or there's going to be trouble, I already called the—"

Cops, she would have said, or police, or sheriff. But she doesn't get the word out before his strong hands reach her head, one of those knuckle-less hands twining in her hair and the other grabbing her chin, and he brings his knee behind her back, she's still sitting on the floor, and he twists. The woman gets out a scream, but it's cut off by a loud snap, and then her body slumps, the air fills with the smells of her body voiding into her pants, and he releases her. She collapses to the floor. He has, Lulu knows, just killed again, right in front of her.

He closes the door now. Turns that horrible gaze on Lulu.

"When is she coming?"

18

By the time Gina Castaneda's van arrived, trucks and SUVs had started to clog the narrow dirt lane that led past the Bowles place to the Lavender ranch. The van had to weave its way between the parked vehicles. When Buck saw it coming, he pulled Humberto Rojas, one of the volunteers, aside. "Make sure everyone has a flashlight," he said. "And some water. They're going to be on their feet a long time."

Humberto hurried to pass the word, freeing Buck to greet Gina. He did so with a friendly handshake when she stepped from the van. She returned it, adding a warm smile, then excused herself while she consulted with her cameraman. Buck watched them examine the grounds, check out the exterior of the house. Finally she situated the man so that the gathered search party members would form a background, lit by the last golden rays of the setting sun.

That settled, she turned her full attention to Buck, and the effect was like having a laser beamed at him. "This is where they lived?" she asked. She held a little leather-bound notebook and a pen, and jotted notes as they talked.

"That's right."

"And they were murdered inside the house?"

"Four of them were," Buck said. "Hugh Lavender, his wife, Manuela, and their boys Kevin and Neal. Like I said, the fifth, Lulu, is missing. She's eighteen. We think she was taken by whoever killed the rest of the family. These people behind us are here to scour the area for any clues that we might have missed initially. There's anything out there, they'll turn it up."

"But you don't think they'll find the missing girl?"

"Why do you say that?"

"Because you called me, Buck. If you thought these people would find her, you'd be just as happy to keep the media out of it. You need more eyeballs on the problem."

He gave her a grin. "I guess people in the media aren't as dumb as folks say they are."

A furrow marked her brow for a second, then vanished as she got the joke. She laughed and touched Buck's arm. "Gee, thanks for your support," she said. "Nice to know I'm appreciated."

"Oh, you are," Buck said, lowering his voice a notch. In his left hand, he held a framed picture of Lulu at the County Fair with one of her market hogs. It had been taken two years before when she was with the 4-H, but she still looked more or less the same. "You're exactly right too. The more people looking for her, the better at this point."

Gina studied the photo. "That's her? How long has she been missing?"

Buck didn't have to think about his answer. "Somewhere over thirty-six hours," he said. "Every hour that goes by, she's in greater danger. I want this girl found."

"Well, let's get to it," Gina said. "I'll put you on camera and you can make your case."

Buck should have known he'd end up on the screen, but he hadn't really thought things through that far. Too late to get out of it now. Old Ed would really have something to fume about when this aired.

Gina rehearsed her opening a couple of times. Buck, nervous, barely heard her. It wasn't until she was holding the microphone before her and he caught a slightly different, crisper inflection in her voice that he realized they were shooting a take.

"Tragedy shook the rural community of Elfrida, in Cochise County, yesterday, when it was learned that Hugh Lavender, his wife, Manuela, and sons Kevin and Neal had been murdered during the night, and eighteen-year-old daughter Lulu has apparently been kidnapped from the family home. I'm here with Lieutenant Buck Shelton of the Cochise County Sheriff's Office, the detective in charge of the investigation.

Lieutenant, in the background we can see people preparing to search the property. Can you tell us about that?"

She held the microphone toward Buck, who cleared his throat before responding. "Well, umm, they're volunteers with our Search and Rescue Team. We've covered the property before, but not with so many people. If there's any clue to her whereabouts, we'll find it with all this help."

Gina held the photo toward the camera, and the cameraman zoomed in on it. "Here's a photo of Lulu Lavender. As soon as we're back in the studio we'll get this up on our website, but in the meantime, Lieutenant, if anyone sees this girl, what should they do?"

"They should call 911 or their local law enforcement personnel," Buck answered. "I'd really appreciate it if everyone could keep their eyes open for her. Lulu has suffered enough, and we need to get her home safely."

"I'm sure our viewers will do what they can, Lieutenant Shelton. And I know that Lulu Lavender has a dedicated champion working day and night toward her safe return."

The cameraman lowered his camera and Gina dropped the mic at the same moment, practiced and professional. "Thank you, Buck," she said. "I appreciate the call, and I really hope this helps."

"Can't hurt," Buck said. He knew, however, that Ed Gatlin would disagree with that assessment.

Watching Gina get back into the van and drive away, Buck felt a fervent desire to leave town with her.

19

Oliver tried to focus on a paper about the San Pedro River's contribution to migratory bird routes, but though he had done the research, he couldn't seem to get the words to flow from his brain to his fingers. This was what he had looked forward to the most, trying to turn the humiliation of being fired into a positive. With his real estate–swollen savings account, he could teach part-time and put some serious effort into writing. He had in mind a book about the San Pedro combining the latest scientific data with the natural history and human history, all the way back to the Coronado expedition, which had followed the river's path into what had become the United States, in search of legendary cities of gold.

But he kept thinking about Lulu, and Lieutenant Shelton's certainty that he had her locked up in the shed—a certainty that seemed to have originated in his distaste for the decisions Oliver and Jeannie had made about their marriage. *Yes, I took those decisions a step too far,* he thought, *when I slept with a student. But is that the part Shelton objected to? Or simply the idea that I would fuck someone to whom I wasn't married?* No good way to tell, he knew, short of asking the lawman, and that wasn't a conversation he wanted to have.

Finally, he shut down the computer, convinced that nothing good would come of his efforts today. He walked into the kitchen, poured a glass of iced tea. As he stood there, absent-mindedly sipping from it, Jeannie came in. "Heard all the racket?" she asked.

"No," he said. "Guess I was in my own world. What racket?"

"Something's going on at the Lavenders'," she reported. "A bunch of trucks have been going by for the last hour or so."

"Wow," Oliver said, surprised that he'd been so oblivious. "I wonder what's up."

"No clue," Jeannie said. "I've been working, but when I heard the noise I peeked out the window. There are a lot of lights down there, but that's all I know."

Curiosity overcame Oliver's desire to avoid Buck Shelton. "Guess I'll go check it out," he said. "If I get arrested, call my lawyer."

"You don't have a lawyer," she reminded him.

"You're right. Find me one, and then call. Spare no expense, as long as it's cheap."

Jeannie laughed. "Okay," she said. "But try to stay out of trouble."

"No guarantees," Oliver said on his way out the door.

The evening was warm, with the fresh, slightly musty smell of the high desert after a rain. Spadefoots, desert toads that lived underground and only emerged when the rain had pounded on the earth with enough force to rouse them, sang out their mating cries with a sound like hundreds of mutant ducks. A few clouds remained in the sky, and in the spaces between, stars glittered by the millions. He knew that as the night wore on, the starscape would only become more and more impressive.

From his gate to the Lavenders' was almost half a mile of dirt road, and Oliver enjoyed the crunch of the hard-packed earth beneath his boots, the rhythm of his arms and legs. Since early adulthood, hiking the West had been one of his abiding pleasures. This hardly qualified as a hike, but it still beat sitting in his home office or standing before a classroom. He listened to the calls of the spadefoots and the resounding buzz of cicadas, locusts and their giant cousins the horse lubbers, until the scattered voices and rustling brush from the Lavenders' ranch drowned them out.

Jeannie was right; a lot of trucks had passed by their house. They were parked all along the road, most of the way to the Bowles's gate. Around the Lavenders' ranch house, Oliver

could make out people with flashlights, spreading away from
the house. A search party of some kind, he assumed. Maybe it
meant there was some new lead. He didn't hold out much
hope that they'd ever find Lulu alive—not after what had been
done to the rest of the family—but he couldn't bring himself
to imagine her any other way.

At the house he found a kind of mini command center.
Buck Shelton sat in his white Yukon, surrounded by the staticky crackle of walkie-talkies. Buck held one in his hands, another resting on the seat beside him, and the vehicle's radio
squawked as well. He acknowledged Oliver with a raised eyebrow, and Oliver waited until the detective had issued a stream
of commands into one device after another.

"What's up?" Buck asked when he had lowered the last
walkie-talkie.

"I was going to ask you," Oliver said. "We saw all the
trucks going by."

"That's our volunteer Search and Rescue Team," Buck
said. "They're locals who take time out to help us when we've
got to find someone."

"So you think Lulu is still here on the property?"

Buck shook his head. "I think there might be a clue somewhere that we missed," he admitted. "Maybe she was hauled
out in a vehicle, but maybe not. At this point I can't afford to
dismiss any possibilities, no matter how remote."

"So this is a long shot."

"It definitely is. You just missed a TV truck—my mug will
be on the air tonight asking for help finding her. The news-
woman promised to try to get the story onto the network feed,
so it'd go out nationwide instead of just southern Arizona. I'd
keep away from the TV if I were you, unless you like horror
shows."

"That'd be good," Oliver said, dismissing the self-
deprecating comment. Buck Shelton looked tired. Oliver
didn't know the man well, but didn't remember him having
such dark, heavy bags under his eyes the first time they'd met.
Even his manner was less alert than it had been earlier. "Since
by now she could be anywhere."

"Could be." Buck gazed out at the searchers beyond. After a long moment, his attention returned to Oliver. "Can you do something for me?" he asked.

"I can try," Oliver said. "As long as it doesn't involve confessing to any crimes I didn't do."

"Not that," Buck said, smiling for a change. He reached into the vehicle and brought out a file folder full of white paper. "Lulu had a blog," he said. "One of my guys went through and printed all the entries, and I've been going through 'em. Mostly the recent ones, but even back a ways."

"You think it has something to do with what happened?" Oliver asked.

"Like I said, I can't afford to dismiss anything. And it just might. She wasn't stupid enough to put her address or phone number online, but if you read her blog carefully enough you could maybe figure out where she lived. She wrote about some of the landmarks, the view from her room, the fact that there were only your two properties on her road, that sort of thing."

"Seems like a supremely bad idea."

"Lulu's a smart girl but she's still just a teenager," Buck said with a weary sigh. "She doesn't always make the most sensible decisions."

"I suppose that's true of all of us."

Buck regarded Oliver closely, as if he had just revealed something significant. "What?" Oliver said. "You never made a mistake?"

A smile crinkled the corners of the lawman's eyes. "I wouldn't go that far."

"So what is it you want me to do?" Oliver asked.

The lieutenant blinked, as if he had forgotten all about his request, and the papers in his hands. "That're the thing," he said. "There're some things in here that I don't get, and maybe it's just because I'm not well enough educated. I wonder if you could take a look at it for me, and see if you can't make some sense out of it."

"What is it?"

"In the last few days before she disappeared, Lulu wrote about these dreams she was having," Buck said. "Strange dreams, you ask me, about this white statue of a girl, traveling north through Mexico, performing miracles at just about every stop."

"Does sound a little strange," Oliver agreed.

"Thing is, my guy Raul, who reads Spanish better than me, checked on some Mexican newspapers online. According to those, the miracles were happening, in the towns she named, just the way she described. And before you ask the next question, she posted her entries *before* the newspapers posted their stories."

Oliver felt a tickle at the back of his neck, like an ant crawling up him. He rubbed at it but found nothing there. "There's no independent verification of these so-called miracles? No confirmation of what's in the newspapers?"

"Not yet. Raul's making some phone calls down there. What were you thinking?"

"Well, without knowing what Lulu's involved in, it's hard to know anything for sure. But it seems possible that the newspaper sites are taking information from her blog, then making up stories to fit. Why? I don't know. Maybe it's some kind of code. She wasn't involved in drug trafficking or anything like that?"

"First thing I think of around here when something terrible happens is meth," Buck said. "It's the drug of choice for rural communities, and it's a slow-motion disaster in the making, a plague."

Oliver paid attention to the news, and he had heard the same thing. He had never sensed that Lulu used, and she'd certainly never mentioned it, but he had to ask.

"As close to the border as we are," Buck continued, "I also have to guess that cocaine might be involved, or marijuana. The drug trade with Mexico contributes more to their economy than oil, tourism and Mexicans here sending money home combined. It's huge business and it hits this area hard. I haven't seen any indication that Lulu, or any of the Lavenders, are involved with the drug community, though. No paraphernalia in the house, no drugs either. Everyone I talk to says she was clean and sober. So I have to think it's not that.

"But there is something else. Lulu is a volunteer for a humanitarian group offering aid to illegals. So even if it's not drug-related, it's still possible that it has to do with border crossing. Code telling when certain areas will be free of Border Patrol, something like that, maybe."

"How would she know that?"

"I don't have any idea. Don't see how she could. I'm just offering ideas, because I don't like the first one I had."

"Which was?"

Buck shifted his gaze to his dashboard. "Which was that she really was just describing dreams. And the dreams were of things that were happening, but that she couldn't have any way of knowing were."

That tickle again.

Oliver didn't believe in anything supernatural. He claimed to keep an open mind about such things, willing to be convinced by hard evidence, but so far nothing he had seen or heard about fell into that category. He had only heard Buck Shelton's description of Lulu Lavender's blog—far from evidentiary in any way—but the whole idea creeped him out.

"What is it you want me to do, exactly?" he asked, dreading the answer. "Miracles are definitely outside my field of expertise."

"Mine too," Buck admitted. "What I was hoping you might be able to contribute was academic. You teach at a college; you were at a big university before that. Maybe along the way you've met someone who could tell us what this statue is all about, if anything. I mean, I don't even know if it's real or not, but maybe it has some kind of history, right?"

"Could be," Oliver said.

Buck drew a paper-clipped stack of papers from the folder. "These pages are the ones that refer to the statue," he said. "You can have these copies, and just let me know if you learn anything."

Oliver took the pages, feeling as if he'd been trapped into something he hadn't meant to agree to. *No turning back now,* he thought. *Trapped or not, I have to at least make an effort.*

"Thanks, Dr. Bowles. Oliver. I really appreciate this."

"Hey, if it might help find Lulu, I'm happy to do it," Oliver said. "Happy" might have been too strong a word, but he was willing. That was the main thing. He would do anything he could for Lulu.

20

Buck didn't get home to the Circle S until after ten. When he got inside, he found Tammy sitting at her computer, posting on a religious message board. She gave him a dry peck on the cheek and shut down. He had sat down to reheated steak, potatoes and corn in the kitchen, at a table crowded with the materials for the rag dolls she was making for her church rummage sale (Buck always thought of it as *her* church, even though he attended occasionally) when she joined him. Her hair was loose, her housedress baggy. He could hardly remember a time when she had paid attention to the way she looked, except when she dressed for church.

"How was your day?" she asked him, drawing out a chair and sitting across from him at the table.

"Shitty," he said, knowing that it was the wrong thing to say, that he was baiting her.

"Hawthorn!" she said, going for the unused first name, as she did when he offended her or pissed her off. "What a thing to say."

"I'm sorry, Tam. But you asked. That poor Lavender girl is still missing. I called out the Search and Rescue Team and went to the press. Now Ed Gatlin is going to be riding my ass and I've still got nothing."

"Well, you can pray for her in church on Sunday," Tammy suggested.

"I doubt that I'll be in church Sunday."

She looked like she'd been swatted in the ass with a two-by-four. It wasn't like he never skipped church. Lately, he been skipping more than he attended. "How can you not go to church, Buck? If you want to find this girl—"

"It's precisely because I want to find her that I need to be out there looking for her, and not sitting in a nice building with pretty windows asking for help that's not going to come."

"I'm surprised at you, Buck. Truly. How can you even think that way? As if the Lord would turn His back on some-one in need."

"Tammy, He already turned His back on Lulu Lavender and her family. He let her get kidnapped, let her family get killed. If that's how God does things, I don't want any part of it. And don't give me that business about working in mysteri-ous ways, because I got enough mystery in my life right now."

Tammy sat across from him, her mouth working but no sound coming out. He wasn't sure why he had chosen now to turn their difference of opinion into a battle, but he had done it. Probably the frustrations of the Lavender case, which he di-rected at his wife and her God because he had no place better to put it. Not fair, he knew. It had been imminent for some time, though. Probably just as well to get it out in the open.

"Do you honestly feel that way?" she asked. Her forehead had rippled like corrugated cardboard. She had pressed her hands flat against the table so hard that her fingers showed white.

"I do, Tammy. I know it's hard for you to hear, but that's what I believe."

"Well, I . . . I don't quite know what to say, I guess. I'll pray for you. But beyond that . . ."

"You don't need to say anything, Tammy. I guess we have some stuff to talk about, but maybe not just now."

She nodded vigorously, her hair flopping around her face as she did. "We certainly seem to, Buck," she said, standing abruptly. "I pray that the Lord sees fit to burn some sense into you, because if He doesn't I fear for your immortal soul."

Without another word, or even eye contact, she rushed from the kitchen. "And I guess I'll be sleeping in the living room tonight," Buck said to himself, watching her shapeless form go out the door.

As it happened, he didn't get much sleep. He poured himself a shot of Jack Daniel's, a rare vice to which he felt entitled, and sat in his big leather chair to mull over his day. He left one light burning, a floor lamp, which he sometimes used to read by. He hoped the Jack would help him sleep, but he didn't intend to drink enough to guarantee that result.

He guessed he should have known it was coming. His father had also combined ranching with the law, and it hadn't worked out that well for him either. Dwayne Shelton had been a city cop in Sierra Vista back in the days when it was a sleepy little army town called Fry, established mainly to serve Fort Huachuca's needs. From the stories he told, it seemed that many of his professional difficulties came about because the army had its own police force, and they wanted to be the ones to handle infractions involving soldiers. Which, as it turned out, were most of the town's crimes in those days. Dwayne's status as a veteran had earned him no breaks with the military police.

But the sixties turned into the seventies, and the nation's appetite for drugs kept increasing, pot but also heroin, cocaine and the rest. Southern Arizona became a convenient entry point for much of it, which meant that suddenly the old man's life turned a lot more interesting. Of course, the fledgling DEA caught many of the drug cases, and Customs turned up some drugs that smugglers tried to bring across. But plenty made it over, which led to increased levels of crime in Fry as well, as the occasional dealer or smuggler arrest.

During this time, Buck remembered, his folks' marriage seemed to catch on a snag. They had always seemed perfectly matched, meant for each other as far as he could tell. But the more hours his dad put in on the job, the more arrests he made, the less he was willing, or able, to tell his wife. The two essentially stopped talking. This all happened around the time that the cash started flowing more freely than it had before. Dad explained it away by saying he'd been picking up a lot of overtime hours, which certainly seemed true. But he expanded the ranch and bought a new sports car and upgraded his wardrobe, and no one believed it was just overtime money paying for everything.

The marriage finally ended, and Buck and his mother moved out of the house into an apartment in town. Buck spent weekends at the ranch except when his dad's job got in the way. It didn't last, however, because less than a month later Buck's father took three 9mm slugs in the back of the head. His body was found halfway to Tombstone, near the long-abandoned mining town of Fairbank.

The money dried up then, as did the enmity between his parents. Suddenly Buck's mom seemed to forget that she'd moved out on the old man, and she returned to the ranch for an extended mourning period. Buck, as the man of the house, had gotten a job and started contributing what he could to the family coffers.

When he told his mother he was joining the CCSO, she cried for the first time since his father's funeral.

She died well before he made lieutenant.

Knowing he came from the seed of a dirty cop made Buck determined to keep his career on the up-and-up. This turned out not to be a problem, as no one offered to throw huge amounts of cash his way anyhow. He decided early on that he would not be one of those cops who let the suspicion and free-dom and power and fear that came with wearing a badge and a gun destroy his family and warp his values.

He had married young, to a "nice" girl his mother would have appreciated. Buck appreciated her too, in those days. She wasn't so nice that they couldn't have a good time to-gether, in and out of the bedroom. He'd met her on a case, when she was working at a convenience store that had be-come a target for holdup artists. On his third trip to the store he'd asked her out. On the six-month anniversary of their first date he'd proposed.

And yet here he was, back in the living room, sipping Jack Daniel's straight up as outside the stars wheeled overhead, dragging the night toward morning.

21

"Ken, another day ends with no word on the whereabouts of the missing Elayne Lippincott. The young would-be model has been missing now for more than thirteen days, and authorities are beginning, privately, to admit that they fear the worst, although Cochise County Sheriff Ed Gatlin still insists that he remains optimistic.

"Elayne Lippincot's parents have increased the reward they've offered for her safe return, to half a million dollars. Speaking through Jim Jennings, their attorney, the Lippincotts say money has no meaning without their daughter, so they'll mortgage the family estate to come up with the reward money, if that's what it takes. The increased reward spurred a new flood of calls to the sheriff's office's dedicated tip line, and Sheriff Gatlin says every available deputy is working those leads.

"In other area news, the sheriff's office has revealed that four people were slain, and a teenage girl kidnapped, in the rural community of Elfrida late yesterday morning. We're putting a picture of eighteen-year-old Lulu Lavender on the screen next to the picture of Elayne Lippincott, and asking anyone with any information as to the whereabouts of either of these young women to call the sheriff's office or 911.

"Up next, Ken has a story on Tucson's growing bat problem. Stay tuned for that."

22

Across the county, in their ranch house under the shadows of
the Swisshelm Mountains, Jeannie Bowles wasn't sleeping
either.

Oliver had come back from visiting the Lavender place in
a strange mood. Quiet, reflective, with something clearly on
his mind. At first he wouldn't talk about it. She prodded and
poked, but he retreated deeper into himself, so she left him
alone and went back to her own business. She had been re-
searching livestock and native plants, hoping to turn their few
acres into something that could help support them instead of
simply taking up space.

Later, he had emerged from his office with a printout in his
hands. "I'm making a quick trip back to San Diego," he announced.

"Really? Why?"

"Lieutenant Shelton asked me for a favor," Oliver said.

"What kind of favor?"

"Lulu kept a blog," he explained. "There's some pretty
strange stuff in it, and he thought maybe someone in the academic community could shed some light on it. Now that I've
read it over, I think Stan Gilfredson might be just the guy."

"And you can't call him up, talk to him over the phone?"

"Sure, I could," Oliver agreed. "And he'd have what interest in helping me, exactly? It's not like we were ever particularly close, and after . . . what happened . . . I'm not sure he'd
even return my call."

Vivian Stiles, she remembered, had been a favorite student
of Stan's. Vivian hadn't necessarily been harmed in any way

by her affair with Oliver, but she had felt used, manipulated by his position of authority. Probably she had been. Stan Gilfredson had been one of the professors who had confronted Oliver personally after the news started to spread, and Jeannie suspected there were still strained feelings between them.

"Then what's being there in person going to accomplish?" she asked.

Oliver shrugged. "I'm hoping that if I'm standing in his office he'll at least hear me out. Once he sees what I've got, I'm counting on his professional curiosity to bring him on board."

"Are you planning to see anyone else while you're there?"

"I may run into some people on campus," Oliver said. "No one in particular, though."

He let it go at that. Now, standing by the window watching moonlight etch the peaks of the Pedregosas, Jeannie realized that what bothered her was the possibility that he would see Vivian. She understood how unlikely that was—Vivian had made it clear after Oliver broke it off that there would be no going back.

Jeannie rubbed her bare arms. The nights here turned cool, even in summer, and the window glass was cold to the touch. She'd been trying to sleep in cotton shorts and a tank top, but finally her restlessness had gotten the better of her. She got out of bed, poured herself a glass of water and went into the living room to try to sort out what she felt.

Jealousy was not, she had always believed, part of her makeup. She didn't believe that people should, or could, own others. If two people loved each other, as she and Oliver did, then having intimate relations with others wouldn't threaten their marriage. The important thing was not who slept with who but that Oliver always came back to Jeannie, and she to him, often with new and interesting variations to introduce.

Sex was great, especially with Oliver. But it was fun with others too. Variety, that old spice of life, only made it more interesting.

So where did that reaction to the possibility that he might see Vivian come from? It was especially strange since the chance that he would want to, or that Vivian would, was slim to none.

Maybe, she thought, it was because Vivian had been a violation of their agreed upon rules. She'd been too young, and a student besides. And that affair, with its broken rules, had threatened their livelihoods, uprooted them, changed the direction Jeannie had believed their life together was headed.

She had grown up in the Northeast, daughter of a philosophy professor—the head of his department—and a successful attorney. Her parents had been liberal, politically active, generous with time and money. Her childhood home had vine-covered brick walls and a steady stream of intelligent visitors who engaged her in their wide-ranging conversations. She had ready access to books, played with expensive dolls and Steiff teddy bears and Stave puzzles, went Christmas shopping in Manhattan and saw Broadway shows and vacationed on the Vineyard.

Life had taken her to Europe and eventually to California, where she met Oliver. She had stayed, willingly. But even though it was on the opposite coast, somehow she had always believed that they would have a life like her family's. Instead, they were childless—her body's statement, apparently, about her life goals—and living in rural Arizona instead of a coastal center of academia. She loved it here, more than she had expected. That didn't mean it wasn't a huge adjustment, though. Anytime life's plans were turned upside down, anxiety followed. That, she convinced herself, was all her sleepless night meant. Vivian was a symptom of her unease, not the cause. Aggravated, no doubt, by the murder of the Lavenders, just down the road. But if Oliver wanted to go back to California— particularly if it could help find Lulu—then he absolutely should do so.

She would be fine here, Jeannie decided, for the day or two he'd be gone.

Interlude: 1536

From five hundred and eighty men, the expedition of Pámfilo de Narváez had been reduced to four hundred, then forty, and finally four. They had wandered lands without roads, without visible paths, following ancient traces that their Indian hosts knew deep in their hearts, needing no signpost or marker to indicate. They had visited villages where starvation and sickness were common, where the three Spaniards and the Moor had to heal and heal, hour after hour, villages in which they could barely walk because the people who had nothing wanted no more from life than to touch them, even though their skin was burned and dried by the sun, their hair and beards unkempt, tangled, their bodies naked as the Indians among whom they tried to pass. They had also traveled into towns made from blocks of dried mud, with permanent houses and cultivated fields. In these wealthier towns people could spare time and effort for art, and so they were given jewelry and blankets and pottery. And they did not lack for people to carry what they were given, because the number of Indians who followed them had swollen beyond counting, into the thousands.

These were pleasant villages and the people were kind and hardworking. European peasants tended to be mistrustful of strangers, while these welcomed their visitors with gifts and smiles and dances. They offered their crafts, what food they had, their wives and daughters and sisters—offers which, surprisingly, Estevan refused, because he still lay only with the one girl, whose name was Akta, or something like it. He continued his sculpture, as well, and Alvar was surprised to see

that, although the black man had never sculpted before, he
had a gift for it, working away like a man possessed. The
strange white stone they had found took on her likeness, a little more each day, and in skill Estevan seemed to match the
greatest of the Roman sculptors (although in fact, Alvar knew,
he might have misremembered their statues; memories of Europe had grown hazy, as if that part of his life, albeit the
largest part, had happened to someone else, an accomplished
storyteller, and he had only seen Sevilla and Ravenna and
Cádiz and Madrid and his home in Jérez in his mind's eye,
through pictures planted there by the speaker's words).

At times, Alvar worried that Estevan had been possessed,
so steadily did he work on his sculpture, creating such beautiful art. He had often feared, over these months, that there
would be a price to pay for using un-Christian magic, for
opening their souls to forces they could neither understand
nor control. God had created the Heavens and the Earth, but
the people they lived among did not recognize Alvar's God,
and yet he had seen more miracles here than he ever had in
Europe. Estevan had stopped healing, saying that he needed
his energies for his sculpture, and Alvar could not help but
wonder exactly what role native magics played in its creation.

The Indians gladly hauled the crude wagon Andrés and
Alonso had told them how to build. Estevan left the block of
stone in the back of the wagon, rather than removing it each
time he wanted to work. He climbed in back with it, and using
his stone tools (which he kept having to replace, as they wore
out against the white rock) he chipped and molded and
formed. The girl, Akta, seemed endlessly patient, posing for
him with her mischievous grin. Perhaps she took some per-
verse pleasure in covering her breasts before him, when ordinarily she went about with them exposed. Perhaps she simply
enjoyed being looked at and knowing that Estevan created an
image of her which would last, unchanging, for many years
after she had aged and died.

Her young man, her betrothed, however, did not look upon
her continued involvement with the Moor as happily. His
name, Alvar had learned, was something like Ukuka. Alvar

saw him watching Akta and Estevan from a distance, his arms
folded over his chest, chin up, eyes narrowed to angry slits. Alvar lived in fear that the young man would explode one day,
that his anger would get the better of him and he would lash
out.

The night it finally happened was a dark one with a bare
sliver of a moon rising late over the eastern mountains. They
had crossed through a pass between two taller ranges several
days before, then traveled south through a wide, flat valley
filled with lush grasses and yucca plants holding their spikes
in the air like the spears of triumphant Christian warriors.
They stopped for the night in a grassy meadow where enormous trees grew along the banks of large pools of water, fed,
Alvar guessed, by underground springs. Water had been
scarce for most of the trip, and the Indians could barely contain themselves long enough to ask the Christians to bless the
ponds before they leapt in, splashing and drinking and even
fornicating in watery bliss.

Later, they spread out among the trees and set up their
tents and shelters, building fires from fallen branches. The Indians who bore Estevan's wagon that day—what would they
give to have a horse? Alvar wondered—had left it off by itself,
at the base of a rocky rise. Alvar guessed they had put it there
intentionally, so that Estevan and Akta could find some privacy for their evening's activities, which Alvar knew often began with art but ended with copulation.

Outside the circles of light cast by the fires, the grassy
fields were dark, moonlight barely sufficient to silver the tips
of the grasses Alvar walked through. He had left the compan-
ionship of his fellow Spaniards as well as the Indians—whom
God loved but who became wearisome with their constant
pleas for healing and for Alvar and his fellows to bless their
food and drink and nearly every activity—in quest of quiet
contemplation.

As he walked through the tall grass, however, he caught a
glimpse of Ukuka, stealing toward the secluded outcropping
behind which Alvar knew Estevan and Akta had gone. At first,
he thought to call out to the Indian, but thinking better of that

impulse, he decided to follow, to see what Ukuka might do. In days and years to come he would regret that decision.

Ukuka wasted no time. Alvar guessed, later, that his mind had been made up and he had been looking for the right opportunity to act. Alvar waited until Ukuka would not see him before following the Indian behind the rocks. He had barely reached them when he heard Akta cry out in surprise and alarm.

At that Alvar hurried his pace, scrambling up and over the rocks that separated him from the open space where the wagon had been left. He had just cleared the top of the outcropping when he heard Estevan shouting. In the dim light, for a moment Alvar wasn't sure he truly saw what he thought he did, but in seconds he realized that his worst fear had come true.

Ukuka had twined Akta's long hair in his fingers. As Alvar watched, unable to help, Ukuka threw his weight from his right leg to his left, swiveling at the hip. Pulled off-balance, her mouth open in agonized terror, Akta stumbled toward him. Ukuka kept twisting, and her ankles caught each other. She fell, and with him tugging, her head slammed into the side of the wagon. Alvar heard a sickening crack, and blood spurted into the wagon, spraying onto the ribs and breast of the white statue. Ukuka slammed her head down again. When it hit the wagon this time, her muscles went slack. More blood sprayed the air, the wagon and the statue.

Estevan had watched the whole thing as if frozen in place. When Akta's limp body fell to the grass, he was released from the spell that bound him and he lunged at Ukuka. The Indian was tall and muscular, but still off-balance from killing Akta, and Estevan drove into him, spurred by fury. Alvar scrambled down the rocks, lost his footing, and fell sprawling into the tall grass. When he pushed himself to his knees, Ukuka's lifeless body drooped in Estevan's hands, the Moor's hands around the Indian's throat.

Estevan dropped Ukuka on the ground beside Akta. His dark eyes were swollen with tears, which left silver traces down his cheeks. "Alvar, I . . ."

"I saw how it happened, Estevanico," Alvar said. He

lurched to his feet unsteadily, as if the earth had tilted beneath him. "But I fear the Indians will not believe us. They know you wanted the girl, who was pledged to another."

"And they know I had her," Estevan protested, his forehead creased, lower lip trembling.

"Not under God," Alvar pointed out. "In sin, not in holy covenant. Which you could never have, as long as Ukuka lived."

"But Alvar . . ."

"There is nothing for it, Estevan. Much has happened on this long journey of which we may never speak. If we told the truth about our healing magics to other Christians, we would be burned as witches. This is but one more secret we must keep until the day we die, from the Indians as well as our fellows."

"The bodies . . . ?"

"We'll bury them under these rocks," Alvar suggested. "Tomorrow we move on from here, so they don't have to stay hidden for long. When it is noticed that Akta and Ukuka are both missing, we'll speculate that they ran away together."

Estevan's head swung around toward his sculpture. "My statue?"

"You will abandon it, out of your sorrow that she did not tell you she meant to run off with her lover."

"Her blood is all over it!"

"Is it?" Alvar asked. "Where?"

Estevan took a faltering step toward the wagon, then another. He stopped, gripping its side in quaking hands. "Alvar, it was! I saw it."

"I saw it too, Estevanico. But I see it no longer."

"How . . ."

"This is a strange land we cross, my friend. I have stopped asking 'how' when I see miracles in it. I fear the answers."

"Alvar, wise father, how can we—"

Alvar didn't let him finish. "We have much to do, Estevan, and precious little time to get it done." He bent to the nearest of the rocks lying on the ground, wrapped his fingers around it and tossed it to one side. "Best we get to work."

The two of them labored through the night, mostly in silence. In the morning, the absence of Akta and Ukuka was noted, and Akta's father surmised just what Alvar had hoped. Alvar backed his theory, as did others. Within an hour it was accepted as fact. Estevan didn't have to pretend to his grief—the tears everyone saw in his eyes were real. He left wagon and statue where they were, without a look back.

Alvar did not know—would never know—that the spot on which the wagon had come to a rest that night, and on which the wagon was abandoned by the procession, was on top of the line that would be drawn across the continent, hundreds of years hence, to mark the boundary between what was Mexico and what would become the state of Arizona.

To him it was just another square of earth that had to be left behind to get to where he wanted to go: back into the embrace of Mother Spain, of king and country and God.

DAY THREE

1

Buck chased his light breakfast with three cups of strong cof-
fee, hoping the caffeine would replace the sleep he hadn't
been able to get. Before he was out of the house, he had a call
from Ed Gatlin's office instructing him to report there before
continuing on to Elfrida. This was unusual in itself—it being
Saturday, the call was more than just unusual, it was downright unique in Buck's experience. The sheriff had been working weekends for these last couple of weeks because of the
national focus on the Elayne Lippincott disappearance, but for
the most part that work had been limited to making TV appearances and being available for interviews.

Depending on what route he chose, Bisbee could be between Buck's place and his office out in Elfrida, so it wasn't
too out-of-the-way to drop in. He took Highway 80 south,
through the Mule Pass tunnel. Bisbee clung to the hills on his
left. Past old Bisbee, he swung around the huge Lavender Pit
mine, remnant of Bisbee's mining heyday, and around the
traffic circle out toward Douglas for a couple of miles, until
the turnoff for the Cochise County Justice Complex. Not yet
on duty, he played a Flying Burrito Brothers CD as he drove,
sometimes singing along. He was a country boy through and
through, he figured, but the sixties had happened even out in
the sticks, and his taste for folk-rock and country-rock had
never left him.

At the justice complex, he parked in the lot and walked inside through tinted glass doors. The reception area was quieter
than on weekdays, but Buck nodded hello to a few folks on his
way back to the sheriff's office.

Ed waited for him behind an expansive wooden desk free of paperwork. A closed laptop and a telephone had been pushed to the far right, and a mound of file folders looked precarious on a credenza behind the sheriff. The United States and Arizona flags stood in one corner, poles crossed, next to a glass-fronted display case containing trophies, commendations and awards along with a couple of antique pistols. One, Ed had told him, had belonged to John Slaughter, who had been sheriff of Cochise County in the late 1880s and had owned a ranch near the border, outside Douglas, that was now a museum.

Ed's vulture-like head was hairless except for a bushy salt-and-pepper mustache and thick eyebrows. He put both eyebrows and 'stache into play, helping to express his unhappiness. "You fucked me," he said before Buck had even settled into a visitor's chair. "You fucked me, you fucked this department and you fucked your own investigation."

"The investigation, Ed, was already pretty fucked, you may recall. We're fresh out of leads, and if going public might generate some then I had to do it."

Ed's elbows rested on his desktop, sleeves neatly buttoned. His meaty hands wrung each other like he wanted to squeeze all the moisture out of them. His uniform shirt bit into his thick, veiny neck, but he kept it crisp and his tie neatly knotted, and he looked every inch the law enforcement professional, as if he expected a camera crew from CNN at any moment. His blunt-featured face had a wide mouth and oddly feminine eyes. Usually florid, now it verged toward eggplant, as if he'd spent his whole morning working himself into a rage while he waited for Buck.

Ed took a deep breath, as if willing himself to be patient. "It almost sounds, Buck, like you've become . . . confused . . . about who's the sheriff here. You aren't confused, are you?"

"Not at all, Ed," Buck said. He tried on a smile, attempting to defuse the tension in the office without making Ed think he didn't take the situation seriously. "But you said yourself it's my investigation, right?"

"It is," Ed said. "And if you've guaranteed that little girl is

killed, it's on your head. But it's my department, and as you
may or may not be aware, we've got a lot of media scrutiny on
us right now. A fucking ton of it."

"I'm aware."

"Presumably, then, you're also aware that press contacts
are supposed to be run through this office."

"I'm aware." Buck said again.

"And yet you chose to disregard that rule."

"I know you're very busy, Ed. I know what you're going
through. And I was desperate. If there's a way to find Lulu
Lavender, I want to do it. I took a calculated risk that a little
regional coverage might turn up a lead that I couldn't find any
other way, and I didn't want to have to take you away from the
Lippincott case to do it. Obviously, I miscalculated. If you
want my badge over it, just say the word."

Ed regarded him carefully, his right eyebrow arching up
like a furry tent roof, as if considering it. "That can wait," he
said finally. "If you killed the girl, you can bet your ass I'll
have your badge. But if somehow you accidentally managed
not to, you might be able to keep it."

Thanks for the vote of confidence, Buck thought. Remembering that he didn't want to piss off Ed Gatlin any more than
he already had, he kept his mouth shut and simply nodded.

After another few minutes of being dressed down, Buck
got back out to his Yukon. He peeled out of the lot and continued east on 80, turning off at Double Adobe Road, where the
drop into the vast Sulphur Springs Valley began just past High
Lonesome Road. The day's clouds hadn't started to build yet,
and the sky was a deep, clear blue. Halfway down the valley,
someone drove over a dirt road, and in the still air the dust
plume hung suspended for at least a mile. Over it, a trio of
buzzards inscribed lazy circles in the sky.

Buck's favorite entrance into the valley was from just below Tombstone. There Davis Road wound through some of
the area's finest ranchland before uncoiling into an arrow-
straight eight-mile stretch that dropped steadily until it reached
the valley floor, where the straight line continued, level now,
for another seven miles before it started curving again, back

toward the mountains on the eastern edge. Larrimore Trail was there, and that was where he believed the truth about Lulu's disappearance had to be found.

On the way into Bisbee, Buck had mulled over how to tell Gina that he wasn't happy with the previous night's broadcast. She had kept the story focused on Elayne Lippincott, adding Lulu only as an afterthought. That had not been his intention when he'd fed her the information. He had hoped to put Lulu Lavender on at least equal footing with the Lippincott girl. Elayne's family had not, after all, been murdered. So far no evidence showed that anyone had died in that case. In spite of his decades of law enforcement experience, Buck liked to think the best about people. He wanted to believe that the media wouldn't choose to ignore the deaths of four people simply because they were black and Latino. Maybe once, but not in the twenty-first century.

His conversation with Ed, however, had made it clear that complaining about it would be professional suicide. Ed had been a cop once, but now he was a politician and he played a different game than Buck. He was the boss, though, and he made the rules, which Buck had already broken in public. Ed wouldn't allow that to happen many more times.

Which raised a question. Buck had heard that people needed to try to keep the number of major stressors in their lives to a minimum at any given time. If you're moving, don't change jobs. If you're moving and changing jobs, don't adopt a child or get a divorce. Too much at once resulted in depression, sometimes suicide.

So if his marriage was falling apart, which seemed a distinct possibility, could he risk getting fired?

Maybe that wasn't even the right question. If he determined that it was necessary to the investigation—if it seemed the only way to find Lulu—he would go back to the press, and keep going, until he had turned it into the same kind of media attraction that the Lippincott case had become.

Which made the real questions: Could he keep the marriage together through it all? And if not, what else he could do to mitigate the damage to his life?

He felt a little ashamed of worrying about his own problems with Lulu still out there somewhere, no doubt terrified and praying for rescue. Regardless of what happened with Ed and with Tammy, nothing could happen to Buck that would come close to her ordeal.

Thinking along those lines brought another realization. Buck pulled the Yukon over to the grassy shoulder and executed a three-point turn. He had just passed through Bisbee, but now he headed back that way.

The one time he had talked to Jace Barwick, Lulu's boyfriend, had been by telephone, on the day she had disappeared. Jace had been broken up, genuinely distraught. Buck had met plenty of liars in his years wearing a badge, and he believed that Jace was not pretending.

But a couple of days had gone by. Jace was, no doubt, still in shock. Buck had new information—not much, but a little—and maybe the elapsed time would have allowed Jace to consider things a bit more carefully. He glanced at his watch—not even nine yet. Jace was only twenty, so chances were good that he'd wake the boy up. Sometimes catching a person off-guard like that worked out well, he knew. He didn't doubt Jace's honesty, but even so, it wouldn't hurt to get him at a vulnerable moment. You never knew what someone might recall at a time like that.

2

He did, in fact, wake Jace up.

The young man lived in an old mining cottage off Tomb-stone Canyon, painted purple with metallic gold trim. It had been painted at least a quarter century before, maybe longer, and time and weather had aged it so that it didn't stand out from the other houses around it as much as it might have. It had a tin roof, which Buck had seen from the highway, so rusted and corroded that he was surprised it kept out the rain at all. The forty-six-step climb from the street had winded Buck, leaving him red in the face and hoping Jace wasn't the kind of kid who ran when he saw a badge.

The front door of the cottage had been painted orange, also faded now. It didn't look too bad with the purple, but con-trasted horribly with the metallic gold trim around it. Buck could have done without the stars and moon too—decals ap-plied probably around the time the building was painted but peeling and flaking except where they were gone altogether, leaving behind discolored spots in the orange, vaguely shaped like celestial objects.

Bisbee had once been the biggest city between St. Louis and San Francisco, when the Copper Queen mine had been produc-ing like mad. Miners had thrown structures all over its steep slopes, especially up Tombstone Canyon from downtown. Some were grand homes; most were considerably smaller and less impressive. In the 1970s, after the mines started to fail and the miners abandoned the town, Bisbee's economy collapsed. Hip-pies and artists moved in to take advantage of the cheap real es-tate. This home, Buck figured, could probably have been had for a thousand dollars or less. The paint job had no doubt happened during that period.

He rapped on the ugly door, his right hand resting on the butt of his service weapon. No one answered so he pounded again, louder. The door rattled, and he worried briefly that he would knock it down. This time, however, he heard movement behind it. He waited another couple of minutes, and then the handle turned and the door swung open. A young man stood inside in red and black plaid boxer shorts, scratching his pale chest. His hair was thick and dark brown, his eyes puffy with sleep, and his mouth hung open as if closing it was just more trouble than he could manage. "Crap," he said.

"You Jace Barwick?"

"Yeah—oh, are you the guy who's looking for Lulu?"

"That's right, Jace. Were you expecting someone else?"

"No, it's just . . . Cops don't visit often, you know, and the couple times they have it wasn't to collect for disadvantaged children."

"You've had some run-ins with the law?"

Jace shrugged. He stopped scratching his chest but moved his hand around behind his back and started in on another spot. "Hasn't everybody?"

"Not necessarily," Buck replied.

Jace gave another wiggle of his shoulders. "Lulu and I are involved with various political causes," he said. "Sometimes the cops don't like it." He blinked a couple of times, as if consciousness had just started to catch up with his body. "Sorry, you want to come in?"

He stepped away from the door and Buck followed him inside. The cottage was one big room, its floor made of tongue-and-groove planks painted deep blue. A freestanding kitchen counter separated off an area containing a sink, a small refrigerator plastered with stickers of cartoon characters and what must have been rock bands Buck had never heard of, and a hotplate on a tile counter. Pots and plates had been piled on the counter behind the hotplate. On the wooden freestanding unit were plastic tumblers, stacked upside down on top of one another, and a couple of ceramic mugs.

Jace slept on the other side of the room. A mattress with a tangle of bedding lay on the floor below a window that was open about four inches. No curtains blocked the window; sunlight blasted through, nearly obscuring the view to the next peak, the next couple of miner's cabins similarly occupied by non-miners. Nearby stood a wooden wardrobe with no doors that served as Jace's closet. Clothes hung inside, surprisingly neatly considering the rest of the place. Beside that a low bookcase had two shelves actually devoted to books and two others holding underwear, socks, T-shirts and the like. The room reeked of incense in spite of the open window. *Guess all the hippies haven't gone yet,* Buck thought.

"You want some tea?" Jace asked.

Buck looked around for someplace to sit. Against the white plaster wall by the door, to which some of the same posters he'd seen in Lulu's room had been stapled, leaned two webbed lawn chairs, folded shut. Next to them stood a TEAC stereo system with a glowing red power light and yellow digital display. No sound came from it. Probably, Buck thought, Jace had fallen asleep listening to a CD. Beside that, sitting on the floor with cords and cables snaking all around it, Buck saw a desktop computer system, turned off. He gestured toward the lawn chairs. "May I?"

"Go ahead," Jace said.

The yellow and aqua chair unfolded with a raspy squeal, and Buck settled tenuously into it, hoping the frayed ribbon webbing would bear his weight. "No thanks on the tea," he said. "I'm good."

"Mind if I make some?"

"It's your place." The chair groaned when Buck shifted, but it held. "Lulu spend much time here?"

"Once in a while," Jace answered. He moved behind the counter and ran some water into a copper-bottomed saucepan, then put it on one of the burners. "She's a good girl, you know. Her parents like me well enough—liked me, I guess, now. But they still prefer her to sleep at home, even though they know we've been, what's the phrase? Sexually active."

"Can't say I blame them for that."

From beneath the counter, on the side Buck couldn't see, Jace pulled a box of tea bags. He chose one and placed it inside a mug, paper tag hanging out, then leaned against the counter waiting for the water to boil. "You have any idea where she is yet?"

"I was hoping maybe something had occurred to you," Buck said. "Or that maybe you'd heard from her."

"Not a thing," Jace admitted. "I don't mind telling you I've been worried, though. Practically tearing my hair out, not sleeping well. I just want her to be okay, you know?"

"I know, Jace. And I'm sorry to say that my investigation isn't bearing fruit yet. That's why I'm here—I figure there must be more I can find out about Lulu, something that'll point me in the right direction. So I thought, who better to learn from?"

Jace shrugged. So far it was his most useful skill. "I don't know what to tell you. I don't know anyone who'd want to hurt her."

"You said the two of you are involved in various causes," Buck reminded him. "Some of which attract the attention of law enforcement. Can you tell me about those?"

"She's not really too involved in that sort of thing, except through me," Jace said. He pinched his tea bag out of the mug and set it on the counter. "Except Bridges Not Borders, which is more her deal than mine. I mean, she'll come up to Bisbee for a peace march or something, and sometimes pass out flyers or petitions down in Douglas, but she's not part of the committee, doesn't go to meetings or anything like that. With school and all she's got plenty to do."

"I'm sure that's true."

"So I don't see how her disappearance could be related to any of that. I guess maybe if she crossed the wrong people while working for Bridges Not Borders, some of those Minutemen or something . . . Have you looked into that?"

"Not yet," Buck admitted. Nellie Oberricht had assured him that Lulu was never put into a position where she would encounter such people. He had thought at the time that she was telling the truth, but truth wasn't always objective. If Lulu had

been out in the community posting notices and circulating petitions, she might well have run across people who took a different view of things than she did. When it came to immigration
issues there were almost as many opinions as there were people
to hold them, and anyone who claimed they knew the absolute
solution to the problem was lying, delusional or both.

"Are you going to?"

"Yes," Buck assured him. "I'll be looking at everything
and everyone until I find her. I was just hoping you could narrow the field a little for me."

Jace peered into his mug as if the answer could be read in
the tea leaves—except that they, of course, had been confined
in the bag and removed. "I wish I could come up with a magic
answer for you," he said.

"You and me both, son," Buck said. "You and me both."

3

Lulu can't escape the stink of the dead woman.

Then again, she hasn't been allowed to shower since he took her, and she still wears shorts that she has peed in several times, so the dead woman is probably glad she can't smell Lulu. He hasn't bothered to move the body, but just leaves it on the floor where it fell, among the litter from fast-food meals and frozen dinners and the soft drink cans. Lulu doesn't know if he's leaving it there to torture her, or if now that the woman is dead she is beneath his notice, just like Lulu's questions and complaints are beneath his notice. He seems to live in his own interior world, she thinks, paying little attention to anything outside it except when he specifically wants something.

She has figured out what he wants. Not how he knows he can get it from her—that she doesn't understand at all. But what it is, she is pretty sure of.

He wants to know when and where *she* will cross the border. The white girl, whose name might be something like Aztlán, and then again, might not.

The trouble is, even if she wanted to tell him, she can't. She doesn't know herself. She knows only that she will know—that when it is time, she will be granted the knowledge, maybe in a dream or some other way. It isn't like she has a printed itinerary or anything. All she knows is what she has seen in her dreams. The white girl is coming, Lulu is supposed to meet her, and after that . . .

After that, she doesn't know. The dreams never go past the moment of meeting. Even then, they're . . . well, they're

dreams. Vague, obscure, contradictory, changing in her mind
even while she tries to get their details straight, to remember
them. She remembers reading about Freud, about a study in
which people were supposed to transcribe someone telling
them about a dream three times in the first few minutes after
waking up, and how the details of the dream would be different each time, but in the teller's head she would be describing
the same dream. It's just that the brain can't cling to the first
set of memories because the second and then the third set
override them. So even if she had been given a date, a time, a
place, she would have no guarantee that what she remembered
was the right date or time or place as it had been offered.

But she can't explain that to him. He doesn't want to hear
anything except the answer to his question. And if the answer
is "I don't know" or "I can't tell you" or anything along those
lines, it earns her another slap from those butter-soft hands.

And now, apparently, Lulu has earned herself a companion, a dead woman on the floor in the doorway to her room—
the bedroom in which she has been kept, which she has come
to think of as hers, as if she could or would want to possess
any part of this cabin, or this experience. He'd tied the blindfold on tighter, and she can hear him walk to the doorway now
and again, where he pauses, presumably checking to make
sure she hasn't messed with it again.

She hasn't, because she knows what she would see, if she
could see, and she chooses not to. But there's no mistaking the
reek of her, the spoiled meat smell that gradually overcame
the smell of the bodily wastes she evacuated into her pants
when he snapped her neck. It has a sweet underscent but the
predominant odor is sharp and nasty, filling the room, filling
her nose, inhabiting, she suspects, her own skin cells and the
fibers of her clothing so that she will never be completely free
of it again.

If he leaves the woman there, it will only get worse. Already she can hear the buzz of insects on the body, flies, and
several times during the night and morning the flies have left
the woman's body and landed on Lulu, causing her to awaken
and swat them away. She has already had to contend with a

few spiders and is desperately afraid one of them will be a black widow, or else a centipede will get inside and bite her, or maybe a tarantula. Most bites would not cause death, which would, at this point, be a welcome relief, but they would cause intense pain, agony, and she would not, she is sure, be allowed to seek medical attention or to treat the bites in any way.

All her life, Lulu has collected hugs the way her friend Sasha collects horse figurines. To pass the time and to try to ignore the dead woman, in her mind she makes a list of the people whose hugs she misses the most. Mom, Dad and the boys top the list, of course, and those are hugs she doesn't believe she'll ever have again. Grandpa Lavender gave great hugs too, but he's been gone for years now. Jace, of course. Becka, wiry and strong, is one of her favorite girl-huggers. Oliver Bowles is stingy with his, probably because he's a teacher and all, but she's had a couple and liked them. Paul, her first real boyfriend, during her senior year at high school in Elfrida, when they used to go up D Hill outside Douglas to make out. Some of the best have been hugs from complete strangers, at peace marches or at the Farmer's Market—the kind where someone just agrees so intensely with what she's doing that he or she spontaneously open his or her arms.

Will she ever add another hug to the collection? Magic 8-Ball says "not looking good."

Footsteps come toward her doorway, interrupting her list-making. An exaggerated pause, and then another one sounds, as if he has stepped awkwardly over the woman's body. *At least she's an inconvenience to him that way,* Lulu thinks, with some degree of satisfaction. The footsteps continue, straight toward her.

Lulu waits, mouth closed, willing herself to be relaxed, casual. *He's not going to hurt you too much,* she tells herself. *He doesn't want you to die, because then he'll never find out what he wants to know.*

"When is she coming?" he asks.

"I don't know."

He slaps her, across the left cheek. The blow stings.

"When?"

"How many times do I have to tell you, I don't know!"

He slaps her again, with the other hand. Her right cheek starts to burn.

"Do you want to end up like her? I know you know she's still there. She tried to rescue you, and I had to kill her. I don't enjoy killing, particularly, it's just something that has to be done sometimes."

"Like the way you killed my family?"

"It had to be done. Because I needed you to be able to tell me when she's coming."

"And I can't do that."

He slaps her again. Lulu tastes blood. *Will he ever figure out that the slaps hurt but they're not having the effect he wants?*

"You will tell me," he says. "You don't want to end up like her, alone on the floor of a cabin somewhere with the bugs picking at you. Do you want to see her eyeballs? They've started in on those but haven't finished yet; it's really quite fascinating. I can take off your blindfold if you'd like to see that."

"No, thanks," Lulu says. He's probably bluffing, she figures. There's nothing to see from where she is, chained on the floor. Nothing that would help her escape. Which means the reason he wants her blindfolded is that he doesn't want her looking at him. That's fine with her—from the few glimpses she's had, she finds him hideously ugly. She would rather look at the partially consumed eyeballs of a dead woman than at his face. "Look, I can't tell you when she's coming, or even where, because I just don't know. So you might as well let me go. Either that or fucking kill me already."

She braces for a slap that doesn't come. *Is he thinking it over? Will the time come,* she wonders, *that he'll realize I'm* never *going to tell him? Will he kill me then, or let me go?*

She shakes her head, even though she knows he won't understand why and there is no one else to see. *He'll never let me go.*

I either escape or I die here. There are no other choices.

4

He considered himself an artist of death. His talents were le-gion, and killing—in creative, masterful ways appropriate to the gravity of the subject itself—was only one of them. Another talent was knowing what might happen, what should happen, and which path of those available he needed to take to ensure the right result. Yet another was being able to nudge people along, when necessary, to get what he wanted from them.

But with Lulu Lavender around, he felt like a novice at all of it.

He should have known the redheaded woman—Peggy Olsson, his landlady—would come snooping, and he should have put some artistry into her death, not simply snapped her neck like a barbarian. For that matter, he should have put more effort into the deaths of the rest of the Lavender family. Killing two with a knife and two with a gun? Where did one locate the aesthetic in that?

According to his grandmother's version of family legend, when he was born a cloud of angry blackflies preceded him from his mother's womb. His aunt (both women had raised him together, after his mother's death in childbirth) always insisted the flies emerged from his mother's mouth as she breathed her last. What they agreed on about the flies was that they foretold his gifts, his talents, in a real and unforgettable way (although at least one of them, if not both, had obviously forgotten some of the details). He had never believed either one—both women were imaginative and prone to hysteria—and he had made early examples of his art from them, apprentice pieces he understood, but he had only been eleven years old at the time, still learning by anyone's standards.

After they were done, he stayed in the house with their bodies for three weeks before anyone discovered them. During his time alone he taught himself about anatomy and pored through their books and journals and grimoires, the best of which he stashed among his own possessions so that when he was moved into foster care, they wouldn't be sold along with the rest of the old women's things.

His life had been spent in similar pursuits—honing his craft, practicing his talents, learning ways to improve himself. He had stumbled upon his first references to the white girl, but having become aware of her, he had made her a focus of his attentions. Now he was close, so close, to possessing her. While he still wasn't sure what her origins were, or even exactly what she was, the effect that she promised—ever more power, so that the proximity of someone like damned Lulu (shackled and blindfolded, mewling like a lost kitten half the time) would never again limit his abilities—made her worth the long search and the desperate measures he had taken along the way.

The trouble with magic was that, while one could discover certain secrets by experimentation, by trial and error, specific objects like magical artifacts had to be discovered by being told about them or reading about them. Which meant someone else had to know about them first. In the case of the white girl, he had learned from a man who called himself Kale, a Hawaiian variant of Charles (although the man didn't appear to have a drop of Hawaiian blood in him), who had himself learned about it from Silliam, a mage who had written about the girl before his early, violent death. He and Kale had not been friends, but they had been peers, had shared information from time to time. Kale had recognized as soon as he'd spilled what he knew about the white girl that he should have kept silent. Probably he had never believed she would surface again anyway, so talking about her didn't matter.

Kale had been wrong. Now she came, casting her long shadow once more across the earth. She had been born of magic, forged in blood, and if the legends were true, she could restore to her people that which had been lost. That had been her intended function, and the shaman whose creature she was had knowingly, willfully sacrificed his own daughter so that it might one day come to pass. On the other hand, she could be used almost like a battery, generating power untold to any who knew how to claim it. He believed himself to be among the latter, and he had every intention of doing just that.

He crossed to the cabin's front door and turned the knob, pulled it open. Fresh pine-laden air wafted over him, the breeze skritching trash across the hardwood floor behind him. Shafts of sunlight transformed the pine branches into delicate lace-work; smaller trees and shrubs lurked in the shadows of the tall ones like members of an entourage waiting for their chance to overthrow their betters. Birds darted from shadow to sunlight and back. A gray squirrel spiraled up a nearby trunk.

Nature for its own sake held no interest for him. Nature as a means to power, however, held a great deal. Power was the thing that drove him, the only thing.

As he stood in the doorway, though, he realized why he had been drawn to the door. His talents weren't completely disrupted by Lulu's presence, after all. A distant rumble coalesced into the sound of an approaching truck's engine. He opened his senses more, sent a tendril of wonder across the gap, through the trees, searching for the truck.

The connection was hesitant, broken, like an FM radio signal in a long tunnel, but sufficient. The truck's driver was named Wes Colton, and he did repair work on Peggy Olsson's cabins. She had called and asked him to come and look at some leaky roofs, and after putting her off for a few days— she was hot, even at her age, and with a kinky imagination, but she didn't pay all that well and a guy could put more food on the table with cash than with pussy—he was on his way to do as she had asked.

He would have to keep an eye on old Wes. It wouldn't do to have him getting suspicious, wondering where Peggy had gone. It especially wouldn't do to have Wes calling the police. Not when he was so close.

He closed the door again and sat down on a rocker made of bent branches to plan his response. As much as he would enjoy killing old Wes (already, a vision of flaying him alive with pine branches, inside one of the empty cabins, passed through his mind like a comforting memory), he thought in this case it might be better to hit the road again. He wasn't getting anywhere with Lulu here, and he was so far removed from the main event that he started to fear he would miss it altogether.

That was it, then. By the time Wes figured out Peggy Olsson wasn't planning to throw another hump at him, he and Lulu would be on their way home.

5

Barry had heard about people waking up with someone's mouth on their cock—mostly in men's stroke magazines, although he figured there had to be some basis in reality—but he had never imagined it would happen to him. Then again, he never would have expected some of the things that had happened last night. Connie McKay had kept up her flirting late into the evening. When Barry suggested it was time for him to head home, she and Carl had both pressed him to stay. "There's always an extra bed here for a good American," Carl had said. Barry, tired and still a little buzzed, had finally agreed, and Connie offered to show him the spare bed.

Turned out, the "spare" bed was her own. And she didn't plan to give it up. Before Barry could object, she worked his zipper down and reached into his pants. Barry thought there was something unseemly about the whole thing—he had only just met her, after all, and there were all those people in the house. But he couldn't deny the effect she had on him. He was hard in no time, moaning and bucking under her ministrations.

Then she pushed him onto the bed and peeled off her own clothing. Her breasts were small and round, with hard nipples poking out at him. She explained a slight sag by saying that she almost never wore a bra, preferring the feel of men's hands to cotton, silk or lace. Her stomach bulged and her ass was a little flat, but even with these minor flaws she was the sexiest woman Barry had ever seen naked for free. And the only one who had acted like she thought something similar of him.

That first time, she used her mouth and hands and vagina and ass, finishing him with her mouth again. Every time he

thought he couldn't hold back any longer, she sensed it and
stopped what she was doing, squeezing the base of his shaft
until the feeling passed. He felt like some kind of love god, a
porn star who could go and go. Clarice had never known any
tricks like that.

So when he woke up with her mouth on him once more,
left hand squeezing his balls and the right one stroking the
shaft between mouth and fist, he was pleasantly surprised but
not as astonished as he might have been. She had already
demonstrated her skills and her willingness to use them.

This time, she didn't try to prolong it. By the time he was
fully awake and aware, he was shuddering through his orgasm. Connie kept her mouth clamped over him for a minute
more, squeezing out every last drop, then gently released him.
When she looked up into his eyes, she was smiling broadly.
"Breakfast of champions," she said.

"That was . . . unexpected," Barry said. "Great, but . . ."

"I'm glad you liked it," Connie said. "I wanted to do something special for you. I'm just glad you slept naked last night."

He hadn't had much choice, since he hadn't come over in-
tending to spend the night. Carl had found him a new toothbrush
he could use, but no one had volunteered any nightclothes. Not
that Connie had left him with enough energy to dress if he'd
wanted to. "So am I."

Connie sat up, turning to put her feet on the floor. "Carl
wanted to see you when you got up," she said.

"Oh, okay." He thought it was odd that she had already
talked to Carl. But then, he was the one who had been sound
asleep. She might have been up for hours. Connie dressed
quickly and efficiently, tossing him some flirtatious smiles,
but there was no further playful interaction. *Just as well,* Barry
thought, *or I'd be too sore to pee.*

He met Carl at the big dining table, where coffee had been
set out along with biscuits and gravy in a big stainless pan.
Carl urged him to fill a plate, and they took those and their
coffee outside, to a shaded ramada at the back of the house.
Here they sat down on cushioned wrought iron chairs, setting
their mugs on the matching white table. They sat in silence for

a time, and then Carl indicated the field of tall grass stretching out toward the south, stalks swaying in a faint breeze as if waving a morning greeting. "That's mostly blue grama," Carl said.

"Blue what?"

"The grass. Blue grama. It's a native grass, what a lot of this region used to be covered with, before humans came and brought livestock to graze it all away."

"You really love this country, don't you?" Barry asked.

"Bet your sweet ass." Carl raised his mug for another sip, gazing off at the grass. He put it back on the tabletop with a chuckle. "That Connie, she's something, isn't she?"

The sudden topic change took Barry by surprise. *How much does Carl know?* he wondered. "I'd say so," he answered, guessing that was noncommittal enough.

"She work you pretty hard?" Carl asked. "Once she gets going, she doesn't always like to stop."

"I kind of gathered that," Barry said, uncomfortable with the conversation's direction.

"She likes you, though," Carl said. "She told me this morning."

"I kind of like her too," Barry admitted.

"That's good," Carl said. He shifted in his seat, so he faced Barry instead of the open fields. "We all like you here, Barry." A grin flashed across his face, then was gone. "Not the way Connie does. But you're good people, you know, and I think you'd fit in well here if you want to."

"I appreciate that," Barry said.

"Do you know what it is we do here?

"Near as I can see, you're a, what would you call it? A border protection group."

"Good a name as any," Carl said. "We've been called a lot worse. Militia, paramilitary outfit, bunch of idiots with guns."

"Well, I have to say I approve of what you do. Too many illegals crossing around here."

"Not just here. Everywhere. Millions, and more every year. The economy down there just keeps getting worse, and as long as there's money to be made here, even illegally, they'll keep coming. The government keeps pretending the problem doesn't exist, and there's not much any of us can do about Mexico's economy. So the only way to make an impact is to defend the border, and that's what we do."

"Someone's got to."

"I'd like you to consider joining us," Carl said. "It's a volunteer thing; we can't really pay you. We do provide room and board for some of the guys, but since you've got your own place, you'd probably just want to stay put there. We can feed you, though, maybe help out with other things from time to time, as we can. That is, you know, if you're interested."

Barry sat there, speechless, for a couple of minutes. Every time he phrased a response in his head, he thought of something else and forgot what he wanted to say in the first place. He'd had the same experience at job interviews—so intent on answering correctly that he felt detached from his own brain and couldn't answer at all.

"You don't have to make up your mind right now," Carl said. "In fact, I'd like it if you take some time, think it over. It's not the kind of thing you should just jump into."

Barry nodded. He understood the wisdom of Carl's words. He had been on the verge of jumping at the offer, but on Carl's advice he held off. He couldn't remember the last time a person, or an organization, had wanted him like these people did. Maybe running into Carl at the Rusty Spur had been accidental, but the man had apparently seen something in him. He had started trying to woo Barry—that's what it was, almost like a romance—on the spot. Then Connie had upped the stakes, making it resemble a romance that much more. To hear the way Carl talked, she had slept with him and maybe others of the men here, maybe all of them.

Then again, a woman didn't learn the things she knew without a little experience. Since he was the most recent beneficiary of that experience, he didn't think he ought to complain about it.

"Best offer I've had in some time," he said after a while. "Only one, come to think of it, but still. If you think I've got anything to offer, I'd be proud to throw in with you."

Carl's smile beamed at him like a spotlight. "I'm glad to hear it, Barry. I don't think you'll regret it."

"I should keep looking for a job," Barry hedged. "If I find something, I might have to rethink it, but till I do I got nothing better to do with my time."

"Of course," Carl said. "Like I told you, it's all volunteer. Some folks put in a lot of time, some not so much. Whatever feels right to you."

"We can kind of play it by ear or whatever?"

"That'd be great, Barry." Carl finished off his coffee with a big gulp and put the mug down hard on the wrought-iron table. "I'm gonna let the others know."

He scooted his chair back, scooped up his mug and plate and headed back into the building. Barry remained where he was. The ramada was warm and pleasant, the aroma of the grass sweet, the songs of the birds who hopped from the ramada's roof, to a yucca stalk, to the ground and back, relaxing. He had no place better to go for the moment, and he wasn't up to another round with Connie. He spread his feet out on the ramada's brick floor, tilting his mug forward and back, watching the liquid inside swirl around with a tiny insect floating on top. He had felt like that—dizzy and without an anchor—until last night.

For the first time in a long while, he thought that maybe he had a purpose again.

6

Raul reached him by radio before he made it into the valley, and by the time Buck pulled up to the intersection of Double Adobe Road and Highway 191, Raul waited at the corner in his cruiser. Buck brought the Yukon to a bouncing halt beside Raul's car and thumbed down the window.

Raul approached the vehicle with a manila envelope in his hand. "What's up?" Buck asked him.

"I didn't want you to get all the way up to Elfrida just to turn around again," Raul said. "We got a possible hit on a visitor to Lulu's blog."

"And it's down in Douglas?"

"Looks that way," Raul said. "There's a warrant in the envelope too."

"You've been busy."

"We have time not to be?"

"Reckon not," Buck said.

"Anyway, Lulu's blog didn't get a lot of readers, and most who did check it out were friends of hers. Fortunately she had a tracker on it that recorded who her visitors were. I've been on the phone with ISPs last night and this morning, and was able to identify the most common ones. They turn out to be people like Jace Barwick, Paul Templeton, Becka Benedetti—friends of hers that we've already interviewed. But there was one IP address that hit her blog on a daily basis, sometimes twice daily, up until the day she disappeared."

"But she wasn't posting after that."

"Which nobody knew until they checked," Raul pointed out. "You told Jace that morning, but even he checked back a couple of times after that, like he couldn't bring himself to believe it. But this one user was checking it religiously until that day."

"As if he knew she wouldn't be posting anymore," Buck said, nodding as Raul's meaning sunk in.

"Exactly."

"So who is it?"

"That's what you need to find out," Raul said. "At least, I figured you'd want to. I can do it if you'd rather."

"You're losing me here, Raul."

"I was able to identify the computer that's been visiting Lulu's blog, but not the person. It's down in Douglas, at the Geronimo! Internet Cafe."

"There on Tenth?"

"Yeah, near San Antonio, I think. Kind of across from Sonic and down a little."

"I'll go down," Buck said.

"Figured so. There's a list in here of all the exact dates and times the computer—actually two different machines in the same place—was used to access her blog. I don't know if they can track who the user was at those times, but in case they can, that's why you've got the warrant."

"I'm on it," Buck said. "Thanks, Raul."

"*De nada.*" Raul left the package with Buck and returned to his car.

Buck watched him pull out, then put the Yukon into gear. Instead of turning left up 191 toward Elfrida, he turned right and sped down past the airport and prison complex and into Douglas. He had to slow as he entered town, but he still made it to Geronimo! in less than twenty minutes.

The Internet cafe shared an old brick building with an insurance agency. A small storefront window didn't let much light in, and the cafe's sign, hand-painted on weathered plywood, didn't impress. A floodlight had been mounted on the wall over it, shining down on the sign at night. Buck believed the nights to be their busiest time, but he had never seen more than one or two vehicles parked in the paved lot out front.

At the moment he saw only one, a red pickup that looked as if it had been driven over from Japan across the ocean's floor; stained, weathered, with the rear window glass shattered and huge rust spots everywhere. He parked next to it, not too close in case whatever it had was contagious, and went inside.

Geronimo! smelled like the Internet access, not the coffee, drew what business it did have. The stink of burned coffee left on a warmer hit Buck before he got the steel-framed glass door open. Maybe they made a pot in the morning and left it brewing all day, he guessed. With any luck they made a fresh pot at night, when there might be a customer to imbibe it. A bell dangling on a piece of string from the inside door pull rang when he went in.

"Right with you!" a voice called from a doorway behind the sales counter. Young, male and casual, all of which Buck had expected. The counter looked like it had come with the space, as if maybe a retail store had occupied it before. On a flat cabinet against the back wall stood a two-burner hotplate, with a metal coffeepot cooking on one burner. He couldn't see where the coffee was actually brewed, and guessed it was in the back room.

Along the wall opposite the sales counter stood eight wooden folding tables with computers on top of them. Each table had a rolling office chair in front of it. The computers were turned on; screen savers showed on the screens, some pinging and bonging as they worked. One computer was an Apple and the rest off-brand PCs. Cables snaked along the floor behind them, and at the back of the room on another table a printer waited for anyone to send it a file.

Less than a minute passed before the proprietor emerged from the back room. "Help you?" he asked.

"You the owner?"

"Owner, manager, CFO, janitor," the man said. He was thin but with a paunchy gut. His blond hair was short, crew cut style, and what Buck guessed were Celtic symbols had been tattooed on his neck and arms. "You need a computer, or is this official business?"

"It's official," Buck told him. "There's a young lady missing. It's possible that her abductor used one of these computers to stalk her online. If you have a logbook or something—"

"Shit," the man said. "I knew that was a danger—so many creeps out there these days. That's why I installed those." He ticked his eyes toward the ceiling. Buck followed his gaze. Cameras had been mounted at all four corners of the room, pointing in, and a fifth one, about a third of the way back, pointed toward the front door and window. "Well, that and getting broken into once just about put me out of business. Figured if it happened again, I wanted to know the bastard who did it."

"Do you keep the tapes?" Buck asked him, heartened by the presence of the cameras. He would owe Raul a beer if this panned out. Hell, a case. "If I give you some dates and times, can you show me who was using specific computers at those times?"

The guy eyed him, squinting suspiciously. "I could," he said. "Seems like maybe there are privacy issues involved, though."

Buck fished the warrant from the envelope he carried. "Like I said, a girl's life might be at stake. If that's not good enough for you, I got a warrant too."

The guy's head began to bob. "Sure, sure," he said. He didn't even glance at the warrant. Privacy, Buck guessed, only went so far. "That's cool. I got tapes going back two weeks, then I reuse them. They're in back. You got those times?"

Buck put Raul's list of IP addresses and the dates and times they had accessed Lulu's blog on the counter. "These machines," he said, pointing. "These times. I need to know who was using them, and pictures would be great."

The man studied the list for a moment. "Yeah, okay, got it. Got it." He bent over and pulled a wire-bound student's notebook from beneath the counter, then flipped pages. Each page had a date inked on top and names, check-in and check-out times written beneath it in different hands. He stopped at the most recent date on which Raul had found that one of his computers was used to visit the blog—the day before the murders at the Lavender house.

"Says here that Michael Blaine used that machine that day," the guy said.

"Do you know him?"

"Can't place him."

"You can't have so many customers that you can't remember them for a couple of days, can you?"

"Well, A: I'm not here every day and every night; I have an employee who might have been here then. And B . . . well, I can't remember what B was going to be, but there was something."

"Check the next date."

The man flipped the page. "Someone named Phil Henrick."

"You don't know him either?"

The guy shrugged. "Sounds a little familiar, maybe."

Buck had him check through the rest of the times on Raul's list. Each one had a different male name written down. The man couldn't remember any of the customers. "Get the tapes," Buck said.

The guy shrugged again and went into the back room. Buck hoped the tapes were more useful than the logbook, in which people apparently wrote down their own names and times. "Can you also pull credit card receipts and match them up to these names?" he called.

"Most people pay cash," the guy replied. "But I can look through my files and see what I got."

"Please do." Buck's patience waned more with every hour that passed. He wanted to be looking for Lulu. If this idea bore fruit, he would be thrilled, but he began to fear it would turn out to be another dead end.

Five minutes later, the guy returned with an armload of black VHS tapes. Labels had been handwritten on masking tape and stuck to the sides. "Here they are," he said. "Each tape is time-stamped, so what you've got here are all four cameras for the times and dates you specified." He put the tapes down on the counter, then tore a page from the back of the spiral notebook. Clicking a pen, he drew a rough map of the shop and labeled the computers A through H. "The IP addresses you gave me correspond to F and G," he said, "so those are the machines you want to keep an eye on."

"Thanks," Buck said. He folded the map and tucked it into

a pocket, then gathered up the tapes. "I'll get these back to you when I'm done with them, unless they become evidence."

"Whatever," the guy said. "They're cheap these days."

Buck had the station's TV brought into his office and hooked a VCR up to it. The camera quality at Geronimo! left a lot to be desired, and the images were black-and-white, but as he fast-forwarded looking for the correct times he saw people— mostly male—moving in comical fast motion to the computers, working for a while, then disappearing. A couple of them spent hours at the same machines. Then he reached the first time he needed, 12:33 P.M. on the day before Lulu's disappearance. He pressed PLAY, slowing the tape.

A man came into view, sitting down before computer G. He was dark and wiry, wearing a loose, dirty polo shirt and jeans. When he leaned over the keyboard, the shirt rode up at the waist, revealing dark back hair. He combed his hair over a balding spot on the back of his head.

Buck ejected the tape and found another for the same time, hoping for a better angle on the guy's face. Again he had to speed through the hours until he reached the right time. There was the guy again. He sucked on his cheeks while he looked at the machine, and his thick bushy brows wriggled about on his face like nervous caterpillars. Buck stopped the tape, ejected it. He didn't have the technology here, but he could send the tapes up to Bisbee and have printouts made from them.

When he found the same guy on computer F at the next time Raul had identified, Buck sat back in his desk chair, folded his hands over his stomach and smiled. "I don't know who you are, mister," he said. "But I will. And I'll put your ass in jail for a long, long time."

7

Leaning against the passenger door of the blue Toyota, Gabriel
tried to snooze, but Clemente Bueno's thick bulk kept bumping into him. Finally, he drifted off, only to awake a few miles
farther up the road, his eyes glued half-shut, mouth tasting
coppery and foul. A pressure against his ribs (in his sleep it
had been Natalya's breasts, wrapped in that loose black mesh)
turned out to be Clemente's pudgy arm.

Clemente was barely five feet tall, with a farmer's stocky
build and short legs, which meant that whenever he wasn't
taking his turn behind the wheel he sat in the middle, legs
straddling the gearshift, the earthy reek that wafted up from
his armpits offending the other two men equally. Clemente's
face was dark, his eyes slanted, his lips and nose as thick as
his accent. He had grown up in a household where Spanish
was not spoken, he had explained, and he hadn't heard the
language until his teens. He still spoke with a thick Indian accent, and when Gabriel sprinkled his sentences with English
or borderland Spanglish, Clemente always looked a little confused, as if he didn't quite understand. He looked to Gabriel
like pureblood Indian, and maybe he was. He seemed never to
take off his straw cowboy hat, despite the fact that it regularly
banged into both of the other men in the small truck cab.

Driving the truck was Rafael Camacho, the third member
of their little band. Rafael was a native Spanish speaker and a
poor man, possibly poorer than Clemente. The belt that held
up his ill-fitting black pants was made from a section of a
car's seat belt, tied instead of buckled in front. His striped
T-shirt, orange and red and black, had a woman's capped

sleeves. His face was emaciated, his hair looked as if he'd cut it with a rusty knife and no mirror. Scars trailed up his arms like thick pink worms. Gabriel was afraid he was sick, and he didn't want to be anywhere near the man, but the decision was out of his hands. Rafael and Clemente had both been Called, the same as him.

Gabriel never had learned, and had come to accept that he never would, how she got in the truck in the first place. He had driven it to a remote jungle clearing in Oaxaca, following directions he didn't understand how he knew, and in that clearing he had met Clemente and Rafael. They were just as ignorant as he about why they had all come. They had slept in the clearing that night, and in the morning a statue had been in the truck's bed that hadn't been there before. They had snugged a dark green plastic tarpaulin over it with thick hemp rope and bungee cords and started north. In various towns along the way he had heard rumors that the statue left the truck to perform miracles, but whenever they looked, there she remained, underneath her tarp.

At the edge of a town (no sign identified it, and Gabriel hadn't looked at a map in days) Rafael pulled the truck into a CITGO station and stopped at the pump. "We need gas," he said. "And I need to shit." He said this last with a wide smile that showed rotten teeth and gaping pink holes, as he always did when he was able to stop at a place with indoor plumbing. He had never lived in a house with a toilet, he explained, and as a result he took great joy from using other people's whenever he could.

How did I end up with these losers? Gabriel wondered. A glance into the truck's bed reminded him. Since he sat against the door, he had to fill the tank. That was the rule, and the fact that Clemente always rode in the middle didn't enter into it, since neither Gabriel nor Rafael wanted to sit there.

He worked the door latch and climbed out, stretching, feeling his bones pop, glad at least to be in the relatively fresh air and away from the smells of Clemente, who stank of the farm, and Rafael, whose odor was more understated but unhealthy. Gabriel had been using extra cologne, stashed with a couple changes of clothes in a bag lashed in the back under the tarp, so he could combat their aromas with one of his own.

He glanced nervously across the street at the *lavandería* and into the gas station's single service bay, so crowded with used tires and equipment a car couldn't be driven into it. Piñatas dangled from beams above the opening: a purple Barney, an orange Pikachu, Buzz Lightyear, Spider-Man, a stiff-necked yellow giraffe with green polka dots. Gabriel had hoped their course would take them through Chihuahua, maybe—anyplace except right back through Sonora. He had not called Enrique since taking his truck, or Carolina, for that matter, but he had a feeling if anyone from the Sonora Cartel saw and recognized him, Arturo's big cats would be spitting out chunks of him before the day was out.

No one paid them any attention now, though. An old man crossed the street at an angle, holding a plastic grocery bag by its handles. A woman in an upstairs apartment glanced their way as she piled bedding on the windowsill to air out. The guy working the gas station's cash register eyed them to make sure they didn't bolt without paying, but he didn't seem to take any special note, and Gabriel didn't recognize him.

Gabriel topped off the tank, closed it up and then got back into the truck, in the driver's seat. Let Clemente's elbow dig into Rafael for a while. He was awake now, he might as well drive.

"You ever been there?" Clemente asked as he slid onto the bench seat.

"Where?"

"Across the line? *El Norte?*"

"Sure," Gabriel said. "Plenty of times. I have relatives in El Paso."

"To work, though?"

"No," Gabriel said. It was a lie—he had crossed over once, in his late teens, and picked lettuce for a season. He hated it and never went back illegally. "You?"

"Sure," Clemente said. "Every fall for six years. I had a grower who would always hire me, but after the last couple times I got deported, I stopped going back. Next to last time, we had this *coyote* who was supposed to get us to Phoenix, but he got lost and we almost died in the desert. Time after that I got there, but *la migra* swept the fields on my third day and sent me back. I was out five hundred dollars, U.S., that time, and for what? That's when I gave up. It's just not worth it."

Gabriel agreed. There were plenty of better ways to make money, he had learned. *Norteamericanos* wanted the cheap labor Mexicans provided, but didn't want to pay the price of having Mexicans living among them. They would, however, pay any price for drugs. The Sonora cartel didn't even have to have its own supplies—they made bank from Colombians and Guatemalans just for the privilege of transporting their loads through Sonora and across the border. When they did run their own dope, the money was even better. They could pay a farmer a few hundred dollars for some coca leaf, process it, ship a few kilos across the line, and in Chicago or New York or L.A. sell the kilo, ounce by ounce, for almost two hundred thousand.

Gabriel didn't see that kind of money, of course. There were many links on the chain, and he was still near the bottom. But Enrique had explained the profit potential of their business, and it only took one look around Arturo's estate to know that there was virtually no limit to what they could all earn.

And he had given that up for what? To drive around in a stolen pickup with her, a cargo that he didn't even understand, making his way north. If they did cross the border—he was more and more sure they would—they would have to do it in the truck or else carry the statue, which none of them wanted to do.

He did all of it because he had seen a vision and heard a name. Aztlán. Arturo would never understand that, and neither would Carolina. When this came to an end—if it did—he would have to move on, maybe into the north or maybe to Baja, where nobody knew him. Not Sonora or Juarez—he wouldn't live a week in either place.

Rafael finally came back from the toilet, that stupid, gap-toothed grin on his skinny face. Gabriel cranked the engine as

Rafael sauntered across the tarmac, and he had the truck in motion before the man had closed his door.

He had started this, and he would see it through. But more and more he wondered what it really meant, and whether he had made the right choice by getting involved with it.

8

When Buck got to Nellie Oberricht's ranch, she was not in the
Bridges Not Borders office out back. He knocked on the door
of her ranch house, and when no one answered that, he stood
in her dirt driveway for a few minutes, scanning in every direction, hand over his brow to shade his eyes. South and west,
clouds piled on themselves, white and lumpy on top like dirt
rolled under the fingertips, gray and threatening beneath. Shadows streaked down from them, broken by fainter streaks of
sunlight. A couple of hours, he guessed, until the rains hit.

Finally, he spotted her off to the east of the former stable or
garage, on her knees, tugging on a strand of broken barbed
wire. She wore leather gloves and a long-sleeved pink shirt,
open over a T-shirt, it looked like, and blue jeans. A straw
hat—a lady's gardening hat, not the cowboy hats practically
ubiquitous in ranch country—shaded her head. A few miles
beyond her, a dust devil whirled, pale tan against the blue sil-
houette (brown and green only where the sun chose to spotlight it) of a mountain range down in Mexico.

He didn't call out, but watched as Nellie twisted a length of
wire around the barbed wire, then twisted its other end around
the stretch of barbed wire to which the first section had been
connected until it had been cut, or broke. When she had the
repair done and tilted her hat back with one gloved hand, he
called and waved.

Still on her knees, Nellie returned the wave. She gathered
her tools into a bucket, put one hand on the nearby fencepost
to steady herself and lurched to her feet. Carrying the bucket,

she cut across a field toward Buck, leaving a wake like an ocean liner's in the grass.

"Do you have any news about Lulu?" she asked when she was near enough to be heard.

"I wish I did."

"It's so rare that I get two visits from you in the space of a week, Buck. What's the occasion this time?"

"I wanted to pick your brain a little, if that's all right."

"Let me put this stuff down," she said, shaking the pail with a loud rattle. "Then we can walk around and talk, if you like. I'll be inside all afternoon, so I'd like to get some sun while it's here."

"Sure," Buck said. "That'll be fine."

He followed her to the back of the building in which she kept her office. This side clearly showed that it had, in fact, been a stable—the Dutch doors of the stalls remained, although she only opened a regular door and went in just far enough to put her tools and gloves on a shelf. Tall sunflowers stood against the wall, their broad yellow heads blocking the Dutch doors, making it obvious that horses no longer used them.

"What progress have you made, Buck?" she asked when she emerged again.

"Not enough, I'm afraid."

"Isn't time usually a factor in cases like this?"

"I'm not precisely sure what a case like this is," Buck said. "It's not exactly a kidnapping, in the usual sense. There hasn't been a ransom demand or anything like that. But yes, time is a factor in any case, especially when someone's life may be in danger."

Nellie looked sideways at him as she led him down a foot-path that ran behind the stable and her house. "I'm not accus-ing you of anything," she said. "I'm sure you're doing what you can."

"I'm trying my best," he assured her. "I just wish I had more to go on."

"What can I do to help?"

He reached into his shirt pocket and brought out a small

print he'd had made of the man from the Geronimo! surveillance tapes. "You know this guy?"

Nellie took the picture, examined it closely. "I've never seen him," she said. "He gives me the willies, though. Who is he?"

"That's what I'm trying to find out," Buck said.

"Do you think he's the one?"

"It's possible. I just don't know."

"Well, if a picture can carry vibrations, that one does, Buck. And they're not good ones."

Buck put the photo away, not wanting to let on to Nellie how much he agreed with her. "I know you said Lulu is never put into a position where she would have much interaction with illegal aliens."

"That's right."

"But how many hours a week did she volunteer with your group?"

"Probably about twenty," Nellie said without hesitating.

"Leaving her plenty of time to do other things."

"Mostly classes and homework, to hear her tell it."

"Her boyfriend says she was also involved with some of his causes. Said she used to circulate petitions, put up posters around town, that kind of thing."

"I suppose that's true," Nellie said. Just beyond her house, the land dropped away into a sloping field full of wildflowers. Tall Arizona prickly poppies, white-petaled with egg yolk centers, towered over purple and red and yellow and blue blossoms. She caught him looking at the display. "Beautiful, isn't it?"

"It surely is."

"One thing we can thank the monsoon for. Along with water to live on, of course. I try to come out here whenever I get tired of the afternoons inside, listening to the thunder and feeling sorry for myself."

"Can't blame you, Nellie," Buck said.

"So your point is, she could have encountered someone while engaged in these other activities. Someone who might want to hurt her, for whatever reason."

"I got the impression she didn't exactly make a secret of her politics," Buck said. "Someone could have seen her at the

Bridges Not Borders table at the Farmer's Market, maybe, then run into her again while she was out with a petition or something."

"You're not talking about migrants here."

"Doesn't seem like they'd have much reason to complain about her views."

"Not really. But then . . ."

"I was thinking more like Minuteman types. Vigilante border watchers."

"There's no shortage of those," Nellie said. "The American Border Patrol, Arizonans for Border Control, Border Guardians, the Minutemen Civil Defense Corps, Minuteman of One of Arizona, even a new one called Mothers Against Illegal Aliens. Oh, and another fairly recent one is American Pride, right here in Douglas. I don't know much about them yet. Some days you can't throw a rock around the border area without hitting one of those groups."

"Any you can think of who might be especially violent?"

Nellie stopped, chewed on her lower lip. Her gaze was distant, off into the stratosphere somewhere. "Peter Endicott was convicted of pistol-whipping a migrant," she said. "But there's some doubt as to whether he actually did it, and since he's in jail in Texas, he obviously didn't take Lulu. Some of the others . . . it's hard to say. If they've committed violent acts, they haven't been caught at it, for the most part. But they surround themselves with guns, they live these paramilitary lifestyles, they patrol the border as if they were real law enforcement officers, even though many of them have had no military or law enforcement experience at all. Living that way, violence is never far from the surface, and I wouldn't be surprised to hear that one of them, or even a whole group, had gone over the edge."

"I need more than that, Nellie. If I'm going to look at these guys I need to know where to start."

She rested her hand on his arm, lightly, surprising him with its casual intimacy. His own wife hadn't touched him like that in longer than he cared to remember. "I wish I could help, Buck. If I had the slightest idea where to send you, I would.

But I can't really keep track of all those groups, you know? I'm a little busy trying to make sure those who do come over don't get brutalized by them or anyone else, and don't die of thirst or exposure out in the desert. The more the state talks about absurd ideas like building a big wall between us and Mexico, the more time I have to spend writing letters and talking to the press and the legislature to try to stop it. Has everybody forgotten Reagan already?"

Buck didn't follow. "What does Reagan have to do with it?"

Nellie lowered her voice and mimed speaking into a microphone. " 'Mr. Gorbachev, tear down this wall!' The Berlin Wall became a symbol of oppression, and tearing it down was the ultimate act of freedom. Have we already turned from the country that championed freedom into one that wants to surround itself with its own walls? Doesn't that just make us into one big prison?"

Buck didn't think she sought an answer, so he didn't try to provide one. He didn't have any to give. He agreed that the wall idea sounded like a pointless waste of taxpayer dollars. On the other hand, one reason the immigration problem had got so out of hand in Arizona was that Texas and California had clamped down with walls of their own.

"Anyway," Nellie continued, saving Buck from having to respond, "do the people advocating a wall even realize what the financial impact of Mexican migrants is on us?"

"You mean from school costs, hospitals, that kind of thing?"

"I'm talking about the positive financial impact," Nellie said, her voice raised in agitation. Her cheeks had flushed, and her head bobbed as she spoke, setting her long hair aflutter. "I don't have the articles in my pocket, but I can show them to you in the office. It's been estimated that undocumented workers cost us about fifty-five grand each for a lifetime of menial labor. But against that you have to stack the reduced cost of goods, like fruit and vegetables and chicken, and so on, that are unrealistically inexpensive because of the cheap labor they provide. Then you add in the fact that many, many of them don't get paid in cash anymore. They're paid by check, and taxes are withheld from those checks. If they don't file,

that full withholding remains with the government. Some use
phony Social Security numbers—they'll never get back what
was withheld or collect benefits. Undocumented workers buy
groceries, sundries, clothing, gas, and they pay sales taxes on
those things. They pay rent, heat their homes, pay for power
and water, maybe cable TV. I've seen a reasonable estimate
that they add three hundred billion dollars a year to our gross
domestic product. Of what they do get paid, some of it is sent
back to family in Mexico, but even these remittances generate
funds for U.S. banks and financial service companies."

"So you're saying they're a net positive for us?"

"From an economic perspective, a huge positive. They
could build a wall tomorrow and deport every noncitizen
worker. You know what would happen? Our crops would rot in
the fields. Those that did make it to market would cost four
times as much. Same with our meats and beverages. Dishes
would pile up on restaurant tables, with no one to bus them.
Those same politicians might find it hard to get their houses
cleaned, and if they get fed up at home, they're not going to be
able to get a clean room in a hotel. There's a huge economy
that operates largely through the labor of undocumented
workers, and if they were gone, not only would that economy
dry up overnight, but that part of the mainstream economy
that is fueled by their spending would as well. A billion dollars for a wall wouldn't look like such a great deal then, would
it? We'd be better off decriminalizing the border, allowing
Mexicans to come here legally to work, and putting our resources toward keeping out the real criminals, drug dealers
and terrorists."

"I don't think I've ever heard those statistics," Buck admitted. He didn't exactly feel dumb, faced with her barrage of
facts, but he couldn't deny that she was better informed than
he was.

Looking at her, he noticed something else. Not only had
her cheeks flushed, but her lips were moist and parted, her
green eyes wide and liquid. It was almost as if ranting about
an issue about which she cared so deeply was an erotic experience for her. Watching her as she sucked in deep breaths,

causing her chest to swell with each inhalation, was surely one for him.

He looked away quickly, into the distance. That dust devil was long gone. High winds had spread out some of the clouds so that they looked like tread marks on the sky, but others, bunched and glowering, came behind them. He couldn't understand exactly why he was having such thoughts about Nellie, whom he had known for years, without ever being attracted to her in the least.

He had to get out of here.

"Thanks for the insight, Nellie," he said, aware even as he did how thin it sounded. "If you think of any border watch types you suspect might have violent tendencies, or would have had some occasion to run across Lulu, let me know, okay?"

"I'll do that, Buck." She examined the ground beneath her feet, as if she had realized how uncomfortable she'd made him. They shared a couple of meaningless words, and he headed back to his truck, determined to make some actual progress on this case before the afternoon rain came.

9

Oliver Bowles sat at a table screened from the ocean breeze by
a thick wall of Plexiglas. A few hundred feet down, the waves
splashing up against the La Jolla coastline threw shards of
sunlight like sparks from a welding torch. At mid-afternoon,
lunchtime should have been over, but the patio was crowded
with diners and drinkers enjoying the view and the balmy air.
A family with two young children had the table next to Oliver's;
a towheaded boy in a Teenage Mutant Ninja Turtles shirt
(*They never go away,* Oliver thought, *or they do but then they
always come back.*) kept bumping Oliver's table, sloshing his
Sprite, as he darted back and forth from his own table to the
transparent wall to watch seals heaving up onto the beach at
the Cove. The kid bumped the table yet again, and his eyes
met Oliver's, a shy and repentant look on his face.

"Cowabunga, dude," Oliver said with a smile.

The kid brightened, clapped a hand over his mouth and
dashed back to his table, where he whispered the tale of
the old man who knew turtle-speak into his mother's ear. She
laughed and raised her glass toward Oliver, who returned the
gesture with his own.

Stan Gilfredson had agreed to meet Oliver in the Ocean
Terrace Bistro at George's at the Cove, which seemed like a
more comfortable place to get together than on campus. As
Oliver waited, sipping his Sprite and putting off the waiter, a
college-aged kid in a white shirt, black tie and black shorts, he
wondered if Stan was dodging him after all.

When twenty-five minutes had passed with no sign of him,
Oliver fished his cell phone from the inside pocket of his navy

blue blazer, which he had draped over the back of his chair. He flipped it open and was scrolling for Stan's office number when a shadow passed over the table. Oliver looked up into Stan's unsmiling face.

"Thanks for coming, Stan," he said. Stan tugged back one of the black metal chairs and sat down, blinking into the sun. In his mid-fifties, he had long, fine red hair that had mostly gone silver and a ruddy complexion. He wore a white shirt, sweat-stained below the armpits and straining to reach across the bulk of his vast stomach. It was open at the neck and rolled over a belt that held up wrinkled khakis. Stan had never been known for sartorial elegance, but his mind was quick and held within its gray folds incredible stores of knowledge. He had published two books and dozens of papers on Latin American anthropology.

"Sorry I'm late," he said as he settled his bulk into the chair. The arms were on the tight side for him, but he managed. "Traffic."

"I know what you mean," Oliver said. "I rented a car at the airport, and by the time I hit the Ardath exit I realized how much I love it where I'm living now. Out there, if there are three cars at any given intersection it's a major event. Coming into La Jolla, remembering how horrible it can get on that stretch, I thought my head would explode."

The waiter swept in, and Stan ordered a salad and a Coke without consulting the menu. The waiter nodded his assent and vanished again.

"I'm only here because you said somebody's life might be at stake," Stan said. He still had not smiled. His expression seemed fixed on general disapproval, indicated by a wrinkling of the forehead and a grim frown on his thick lips. "I hope you were being honest with me."

"Absolutely," Oliver replied. "I'm actually here because our local sheriff—well, the lieutenant who's investigating the case—asked me to try to find out some information about some things the missing girl wrote in her blog."

"Who is she?"

"Her name is Lulu. Lulu Lavender, melodiously enough.

She lives down the road from Jeannie and me, and she's one of my students. Whoever took her killed the rest of her family, her parents and little brothers."

Stan gave a brief nod. "A student? You're not . . . ?"

"No," Oliver said firmly. "Nothing like that."

"All right." Stan stared off toward the water for a few long moments. "And this local yokel thinks there might be something in her blog that can help find her?"

"It's pretty strange stuff," Oliver said. He had printouts in a briefcase underneath his chair. Before he got them out, though, he briefly described what Buck Shelton had told him about the incidents Lulu had described being reported as fact—after she had written about them—in Mexican newspapers.

As he talked, he saw Stan's expression finally soften a little. He had hoped the man's intellectual curiosity would overwhelm everything he felt about Oliver. When he was done, Oliver took a sip of his Sprite. Stan's salad had come and sat, ignored, while Oliver spoke.

"That's all very hard to believe," Stan said.

"Tell me about it. Lieutenant Shelton gave me printouts from the Mexican news sites, so if you can read Spanish, you can compare them."

"My Spanish is fine."

Oliver bent forward at the waist and grabbed the handle of his leather briefcase. Pulling it into his lap, he worked the clasps. When he saw the papers inside, printouts of Lulu's blog, he was reminded of how much he missed his student's laugh, her sharp, inquisitive mind. He tried to speak, but his voice caught, and he downed a big swallow of his drink to clear it.

"Sorry," he said after a moment. He passed over the sheaf of papers. "Here's her blog."

Stan's thick fingers closed over the printouts, and without comment, he laid them on the table next to his plate. He worked on his salad as he scanned them. He took about fifteen minutes, flipping page after page, eyes scrolling rapidly down each one. When he reached the end, he stacked them neatly, lining up the edges, and put them back on the table.

"I can tell you a couple of things, right off," he said. "Some of it will need a little research, but not all of it."

"Okay. What's it mean? Do you know what the 'white girl' is?"

"No idea," Stan said. "That's one of the areas that will require some further investigation."

"What about that name, or word? Aztlán?"

"That's an easy one, and something you could have Googled instead of having to fly out here to ask me."

"I did," Oliver admitted. "But I'm the earth sciences guy, remember? There were a lot of different links with different meanings, so I wanted your take on what it is and how it relates here."

"The traditional definition of Aztlán is that it's the place from which the Aztecs came to the surface of Earth," Stan explained. "They traveled from underground, through Chicomostoc, the seven caves, and came out in Aztlán in the Aztec year 1 *Tecpatl*, roughly corresponding to AD 1168. From there they migrated south into Mexico, where they were when Europeans came. That's one take on it. Anthropologically speaking, it makes sense in that the migration of the human race began in Africa, sweeping up through Asia and into Europe and down into Australia. From Asia we crossed the Bering Strait, or the land bridge that existed there at the time, into what would become Alaska, and then came south along the west coast, or just off it in boats, into Mexico and on into the rest of Central and South America. Since the Aztecs had no cultural memory of the whole journey, they settled on a mythical starting point. Complicating this was that they were not the first settlers in the region, but a group who came from the north into the region already inhabited by the Toltecs, with their civilization of great antiquity."

"Is there a physical place that corresponds to it?" Oliver asked.

"That depends upon whom you ask. Different scholars locate it at different spots in northern Mexico, possibly on the coast or an island on a long-gone inland sea. More recent folk traditions place Aztlán in the United States—it is a place, these traditions insist, that belonged to Mexico before the United States annexed the west and southwest and took it away. Again, there is a reasonable basis for this interpretation, as there are linguistic links between the Aztecs and western Indian tribes like the Pima, Yaqui, Hopi, Paiute, Shoshone and a few others."

He stopped talking long enough to fork another chunk of salad into his mouth. "One more thing you should know about Aztlán," he said when he had swallowed it, wiping his mouth with a napkin as he spoke. "Not only did the Aztecs—and by extension, the indigenous Mexican people as we know them—believe that they came from Aztlán, but they were certain that one day they would return. They would reclaim Aztlán, their traditional birthplace, and occupy it forever."

The meaning of his words took a few seconds to dawn on Oliver. "Which would be a problem for the U.S., if Aztlán is somewhere within our borders."

"Indeed it would." Stan looked almost amused by the idea. "People think immigration is out of hand now. There have already been calls for Mexico to re-annex California, Arizona, New Mexico and Texas, and parts of Nevada, Utah and Colorado."

"Surely they don't think they could attack us with their army."

"They don't need to. The Hispanic population of the border states is booming. To those who give credit to this theory, the whole migration thing is part of it—people coming north so they'll be in place when the takeover happens. The theory—and I'm not saying I agree this is happening, but if you're inclined in such directions you can certainly imagine it—is that they will win all the state offices in the four border states. It's already widely believed that the borderline is just a figment dividing two Mexican populations—it didn't exist, after all, until the Gadsden Purchase in 1854—and that when the Hispanics have control of those states the line will shift, with Aztlán being the name given to the new border territories."

"So if there's some connection between this miracle-performing 'white girl' and a return to Aztlán . . ."

"More likely it's just some strange dreams your student's been having, after coming across the story of Aztlán, or maybe some of the controversy about the border state annexation, in one of her other courses."

"Sure," Oliver agreed. "I'd go along with that, if not for two things. The seeming miracles reported in the Mexican press—"

"Not always the most reliable source—"

"Combined with the fact that someone really did kill her family and kidnap her," Oliver finished. "To me, that's the really relevant part. I don't know if the dreams and this Aztlán business are related to it, but by sheer proximity—that's what she was thinking about, and blogging about, in the days just before the incident—it seems that there might be a link."

Stan tapped the papers again. "It could be. I'm certainly not saying there's not. I would point out one other thing, and then I should go—I have a late class this afternoon."

"What is it?"

"She mentions some other names, in passing. Names she isn't familiar with, she says."

"Right," Oliver said. "I don't remember what they were."

"Alvar, Estevanico, Alonso. Those are all members of the Cabeza de Vaca party. You've heard that story?"

"Good old 'head of the cow.' Refresh me on the details?" The waiter buzzed by like a bee around a flower, and Oliver waved him away. Stan regarded his now-empty salad plate mournfully, as if he would not have objected to another course, but he went on.

"A Spanish expedition was destroyed by hurricanes off the coast of Florida in 1527. The men took refuge on rafts, which were separated in heavy seas. Alvar Nuñez Cabeza de Vaca wound up alone and was captured by local Indians who kept him as a slave. Showing some magical healing abilities, he was released and managed to hook up with three other members of the expedition, Alonso del Castillo, Andrés Dorantes and Estevan, Dorantes' Moorish slave. Together, healing as they went, they crossed Texas, finally meeting other Spaniards again in Mexico, eight years later. They were the first Europeans—and African—to visit the American Southwest.

Really, the first to travel through any of what would become the continental United States."

"So in addition to learning about Aztlán, she was exposed to Cabeza de Vaca. And she didn't remember hearing about any of it, except as names in a dream."

"Is she a good student?"

"One of my best," Oliver said.

"So that's a pretty unlikely scenario. Another explanation might be that, for reasons of her own, she didn't want to describe, in her blog, how she knew about these concepts. It's more romantic if they're just ideas that present themselves in dreams."

"Lulu's generally levelheaded. That doesn't sound like her."

"A lot of young ladies are both levelheaded and romantically inclined," Stan said.

"That's certainly true. I wouldn't say Lulu is without imagination. But I think she's scrupulously honest—maybe to a fault, as you'll see in some of her blog entries. I just don't see her as someone who would hide or disguise knowledge she had earned as vague images that came to her dreams. When you tack on the rest of what we know, I can't help feeling like there's something there."

Stan chuckled. He still had not smiled, and his dry laugh lacked genuine humor. "You're supposed to be the science guy. I'm the anthropologist. I'm the one who is supposed to believe in magic."

"Do you?" Oliver asked him. His throat was parched, he realized. He looked about for the waiter, wanting him to return after all, but couldn't locate him.

"I believe there are forces that operate in the universe that you and your hard sciences comrades have not explained to my satisfaction," Stan said. "Mexico is full of magic, if you listen to its people. Look at the folktales. Look at the literature of Latin America. Is it a coincidence that 'magic realism' is so omnipresent? Look at the paintings of Diego Rivera and Frida Kahlo, not to mention lesser-known folk artists. Magical occurrences are daily events, according to them. Are they wrong?"

"You don't think most of that stems from superstitious

people trying to explain complicated natural phenomena using the vocabulary available to them? Then writers and artists adopting that native vocabulary in a metaphorical way?"

"Certainly that's one way to look at it," Stan said. "On the other hand, I have a friend outside Ensenada who had testicular cancer. He's an American citizen. He went to half a dozen oncologists here, Scripps, Sharp, you name it. They beat it back and it returned, more advanced than it had been. He was not a happy man, my friend. Losing both his balls was looking like his *best* hope, and that's not my definition of the best of anything. Finally, in desperation, he turned—on the advice of one of his oncologists, and only with a great deal of pressure from me and some other friends—to a *brujo*. You know what that is?"

"A witch doctor."

Stan shrugged, nodding. "More or less. A shaman, a witch doctor, a magical healer. Like Cabeza de Vaca, I suppose. Anyway, this *brujo* didn't cut him open, didn't make him ingest anything, but he massaged my friend's testicles to the point, my friend said, that he was starting to think the *brujo* just got his jollies that way. After about ten minutes of that, he rolled something between his fingers and showed it to my friend. It looked, he said, like a tiny dart, with a point on one side and featherlike extensions on the other. The *brujo* claimed that he had removed it from my friend's testicles and, further, that it had been placed there because my friend had been cursed. He had taken it out, but unless my friend did something about the curse, it would return."

"This is starting to sound like a horror movie," Oliver said. "Aren't these people supposed to be gypsies?"

Without even acknowledging the comment, Stan continued. "Without making a long story unbearable, my friend had, in fact, made an enemy of a shaman in a tribe deeper in the interior. He traveled, free of pain for the first time, back to that shaman and made peace with him—which involved, if I recall correctly, the transfer of a couple thousand dollars. But when he came back to his doctors here in the States, the cancer was gone. As if it had never existed."

"I suppose if you believe something strongly enough—"

"I never said my friend believed anything," Stan said. "He was as agnostic about magic as you are. He is not an academic, certainly no fuzzy-headed anthropologist. He's a real estate speculator. Remember, he sought out Western medicine—scientific medicine. He had to be convinced to try this *brujo* as a last resort. The other option was cutting off his balls. He didn't believe in it, but he didn't have much choice."

"So you don't think there was a psychological component to the cure."

"I know there was not," Stan said with certainty. "I don't think psychology can erase cancer. My friend still has both testicles—and uses them frequently, with a variety of lovely young *chicas*, he claims. He believes in magic now, I can tell you that. But he didn't at the time."

Stan put his hands on the table, his right resting on the stack of paper, his left on the tablecloth, and was silent. Oliver considered a number of objections or arguments, discarding each as inadequate before he gave voice to it. He was left with nothing to say.

Finally, Stan cleared his throat. "I really need to get to class," he said, glancing at the sun, which had lowered toward the distant horizon line. "I'll read these more thoroughly, and call or e-mail if I come up with anything else that might help."

"I really appreciate that, Stan," Oliver said.

"I'm not doing it for you."

"I understand that. But Lulu needs all the help she can get, and right away."

Stan pushed his chair back, pressed his pudgy hands against its arms and hoisted himself out of it. His face was red, and a raspy exhalation escaped his lips, and Oliver hoped he didn't have a heart attack before he had a chance to look at the printouts. Without any parting formalities, Stan exited the restaurant, leaving Oliver at the table. The families had left; only one couple, deep in romantic bliss and paying him no attention whatsoever, remained on the patio with him.

The waiter returned, took Oliver's credit card and came back a couple of minutes later with a receipt to be signed.

Oliver signed it, then left the patio, descended the staircase and found himself on Prospect Street, amid high-end galleries, clothing shops and restaurants. Expensive cars crowded the street: Mercedes, BMW, Jaguar, Hummer, Range Rover, an old Ford Pinto with surfboards sticking out the back providing contrast. Families of tourists in shorts or swimsuits, carrying boogie boards and blankets, skin reddened by the sun, walked alongside businesspeople and wealthy retirees.

Somehow, none of what he saw seemed real to him. Not as real, at any rate, as the image of a shaman squatting in the desert, shaking a copper-headed rattle and letting a poisonous snake slither up his arm.

10

Buck was driving up the valley, from Nellie's ranch near the bor-
der to the sheriff's substation in Elfrida, when the first heavy
raindrops splatted against his windshield. Within moments,
rain pounded the roof and washed over the street before him,
as if the sky itself wept at the hopelessness of the search for
Lulu Lavender.

As soon as the metaphor occurred to him, Buck laughed at
the pomposity of it. Lulu was someplace under the same
sky—if it gave a shit, it could point down with a massive,
cloud-formed finger and show him where. The squall matched
his mood, that was all.

He hadn't eaten lunch, so he cruised past the station and on
up to Baker's Haus, where he picked up a turkey and ham
sandwich to go and a bag of cookies for the staff. Fifteen minutes later, he walked into the station, a white paper bag in each
hand. He had barely cleared the doorway before Raul was on
his feet, coming toward him with papers in his hand. "You'll
want to see this," Raul said.

"What is it?"

"DNA report from the lab," Raul replied. "They got a hit
on skin cells from under Kevin Lavender's fingernails."

"Are you shitting me?" Buck asked, his spirits elevated.

"That's what the report says," Raul answered. Buck took
the papers from Raul's hand and dropped into the nearest
chair. "Guy was in the system once, in Oklahoma," Raul continued. "Almost a decade ago. But you've got a photo, a name,
an address, fingerprints, the works. Even better, the prints
match a couple found in the Lavender house."

Buck only half-listened to Raul, intent on reading for himself what the man was trying to tell him. He had summed it up, though. The epithelials, as the report put it, belonged to a man named Henry Schaffer, and his fingerprints had been found on a light switch and the bathroom faucet in the Lavenders' home. He was thirty-one years old, with a last known address in El Paso, Texas. Having just come from Nellie's, Buck couldn't help wondering if the fact that Henry Schaffer had lived in a border town had any bearing on the case.

He looked at the photo that had come in with the report, a booking photo from Lawton, Oklahoma. Mug shots were rarely flattering, and this one held true to that rule. Even then, at twenty-two, his hairline had been receding, his smooth forehead shining under the camera's flash. A heavy, beetled brow shielded small dark eyes that glared off to the subject's right, as if unwilling to look directly into the lens, or attracted to something out of view. His nose bulged toward the camera, accentuated by the wide-angle lens used. Beneath it, dark lips were slightly parted, showing uneven teeth. Buck couldn't put his finger on exactly why, but he got an unpleasant sensation from the photo, as if Henry Schaffer had been making a half-hearted effort to disguise utter contempt for the whole process and the people who had brought him into it.

Kind of like Nellie and her vibrations, he thought.

Almost exactly like that, because Henry Schaffer and the man in the Geronimo! tapes were undeniably one and the same. Buck couldn't suppress a smile as he continued reading.

Schaffer had been charged, and convicted, of aggravated assault. There had been an encounter in a liquor store late at night; he and another customer had exchanged words, and then, when the other man turned his back, Henry had smashed a bottle of cheap California Chardonnay against his head. He had served eighteen months, during which he'd been involved in a couple of prison altercations. Nobody had died in any of the fights Buck could connect to Henry Schaffer, but the man—albeit only five foot nine, 152 pounds—seemed perfectly willing to respond with violence to any provocation, and maybe to none at all. Blood had been taken for medical reasons during his incarceration, which had provided the DNA sample finally matched by the lab in Bisbee.

"Donna!" he called abruptly. Donna Gonzales came around a corner, her uniform crisp and pressed. He pushed the photo toward her. "Get copies of this out to everyone you can think of. DPS, all the PDs in the county, every sheriff's office in the state, Border Patrol. If anyone has seen this guy I want to know about it."

"I'm on it, Lieutenant," she said. She snatched up the photo and hurried away, leaving behind only traces of a flowery perfume.

"And Donna!" he called after her. Her footfalls stopped, turned around, and she hove into view again. He held up the bag with the cookies. "Make sure everyone who wants a cookie gets one. Including me. I'll be in my office."

This time when Donna left, he did too, bound for his own office. He would be on the phone for quite a while, he guessed.

Maybe he'd get a chance to nibble on that sandwich while he was on hold.

His first call was to Ed Gatlin's office in Bisbee. Instead of the sheriff, he got Irena Mendez. "He can't come to the phone, Buck," she said. "Haven't you heard the news?"

"I've been a little busy, Irena."

"Do you have a TV down there? You might want to turn it on."

Buck hung up the phone with a sigh. He had what could be the first real break in the Lavender case, and Ed was doing another press conference? He wished Elayne Lippincott had never disappeared—not for her sake but for his own.

"Donna!" he shouted one more time. "Turn on the TV. Apparently Sheriff Gatlin's getting some more airtime!"

". . . indication points to suicide, and—"

"Does that mean there is no foul play suspected, Sheriff?"

"We haven't ruled anything out, but at this point it appears that Victor Lippincott's fatal wound was self-inflicted."

"If this is determined to have been the result of foul play, would you assume that it's connected with the disappearance of his daughter Elayne?"

"You're asking me to engage in hypothetical reasoning, ma'am. I wouldn't be much of a law enforcement professional if I did that."

"But with Elayne still missing, isn't it possible that—"

"Anything is possible. And like I said, I'm ruling out nothing. For now, though, we're not making any such connections. I'm keeping an open mind and looking at the facts as they're presented, not trying to prove one hypothesis or another."

"Can you say how Mrs. Lippincott is taking it?"

"How would you expect her to take it? Her daughter has been missing for two weeks, and now her husband has apparently taken his own life. Bea Lippincott is under a doctor's care, under sedation, and that's all I'll say about her right now."

"Just to clarify, Sheriff, you don't think there's a definitive connection—you don't think that someone has it in for the Lippincott family and has turned his attention from Elayne to Victor Lippincott?"

"There are no indications at this time that that's the case, no. Once again, we'll look at every scenario, however likely or unlikely, until we know the truth."

"Did Victor Lippincott leave a note?"

"We haven't found a note anywhere in the house, which means that everything is just speculation at this point in time. Speaking of time, I'm afraid that's all the questions I have time for right now. You'll all be informed of any further developments in this case."

12

Lulu's head throbs, as if someone has built a highway on it and
eighteen-wheelers roll over it every few seconds. She is back
in the truck again. A filthy rag has been shoved in her mouth
and secured there with duct tape wrapped around her head—
every time she moves it (which makes the throbbing that
much worse, so she avoids it when possible), she can feel it
yank on the hairs stuck underneath. What she can't avoid is
the motion of the truck, which seems to have no shock ab-
sorbers at all. Every bump or seam or uneven patch of road
jostles or shakes or vibrates her, and the pain makes her want
to throw up, but she knows if she does, she'll choke on it,
and she doesn't want to die here, in the back of his truck,
trussed up like a steer on rodeo day. Thunder and a staccato
drumming overhead make her think they're driving through
a storm.

She doesn't remember much about getting into the truck.
He came to her, but she was still blindfolded and didn't know
until he shoved it in her face that he was holding a piece of
cloth soaked with something, chloroform or ether or whatever
it was he had used on her the first time, back home. Knowing
what to expect this time, she tried to hold her breath, and then
feigned unconsciousness. But she had inhaled enough of the
stuff that genuine unconsciousness engulfed her just the same.

When Lulu woke up, she was in the truck, where she has
remained. She has no idea what time it is, or how long she was
out. At some point she passed into a sleep state and dreamed,
and in the dreams she saw the white girl again. The white girl
didn't speak to her, but she acted as if she wanted to. Now that

she is awake again, Lulu tries to remember the details—not what happened in the dream but what the dream *told* her.

Because she is pretty sure she knows now where the white girl wants her to be, and when. It would help if she knew for sure what day it was, or what time, since for all she knows she is supposed to be at the meeting place right this minute. She doesn't think the white girl would ask her to do something completely beyond her control, but she's never been in this situation before—she doubts if anybody has—so she really doesn't know for sure.

Lulu has always known she needed to get away from him. He'll never let her go alive. He hasn't even promised that he would, if she told him what he wanted to know, and she is not naive enough to believe he would live up to such a promise if he made it.

Now, in addition to her own survival, she has another reason to want to escape. The white girl is counting on her. Why, she has no idea.

But Lulu has every intention of coming through for her if she can.

13

"Barry!"

He started, letting out a surprised grunt and blinked away sleep. He had dozed off in a chair in the common room while some of the other guys watched Fox News. In a dream, he had been in a hotel room, one fancier by far than any he had seen in person, like something from a movie about rich people, and he had just entered and was waiting for Clarice to come in. She had just been in the hallway with him, holding a big brass key and counting off the numbers on the doors they passed. But she didn't come in and she didn't come in and she didn't come in, and he was just realizing that she wasn't going to when someone shook his shoulder and woke him up.

Connie's face swam into partial focus, too close to his to make out clearly. "Barry, wake up," she said, her tone urgent. Her eyes were wide and alert, her lips parted, her expression one of utmost solemnity. *She's not waking me up for a poke,* he thought, disappointed by the realization.

"What's up?"

"There something we have to do," she said.

"What?"

"Come on," she said. She released his shoulder and clutched at his hand, catching three fingers. She let those go, grabbed again, and this time closed her whole hand around his. Some time had passed, he realized. The news had ended and a reality show played, and the people sitting around the set were different than the ones who had been there.

She pulled on his right hand at the same time that he used his left to push off from the big, soft chair in which he had fallen asleep. When he was on his feet at last, the world started to clarify. Connie wore a long-sleeved red T-shirt and black jeans over Western boots. In her left hand she carried a black nylon gym bag, zippered shut. Outside the windows, rain hammered the bare earth and lightning strobed the darkness.

As she hurried down the hall, Connie looked over her shoulder at his clothes: a plain white undershirt, blue jeans and boots. "Do you have another shirt here?" she asked. "Something darker?"

"I haven't been home," he said, following along after her. "There's a flannel shirt in my truck. I think it's green and blue plaid. Why?"

"Put it on," she said. It sounded like an order. "I'll tell you why on the way."

Barry didn't feel much better informed than he had been when he was sound asleep. *On the way where?* Connie charged forward like she was late for the mall on the day after Thanksgiving, and he struggled to keep up. "What about a hat?" she asked.

"That's in the truck too," he said.

"Good." She tugged open the front door. A ferocious wind blew rain inside, but Connie seemed not to notice. She bowed her head only slightly as she stepped out into the downpour. Barry braced himself for the cold shock of it. As they ran for his truck, parked across the broad gravel area from the door, stinging drops whipped his face and soaked his shirt to the skin.

"You have the keys?" She had to shout to be heard over the wailing wind. A lightning bolt illuminated her for a split second, standing beside the truck's door, hunched against the weather, brown hair plastered to her skull. Raindrops tracked down her face like tears, but Barry could not imagine anything that would make Connie cry.

He patted his right front jeans pocket. He kept his keys there, hooked to his belt loop by a length of silver chain. Drawing them out, he pushed past Connie and unlocked the truck. She tossed the gym bag in, climbed in behind the wheel, then slid across the bench seat. He followed. He seemed to be doing a lot of that tonight.

Once he had settled in behind the wheel, he closed his door and took the hat and shirt that Connie offered, putting them on without question or comment. When he finished, she nodded toward the ignition. Barry shoved in the key, unwilling to hide his growing unhappiness with her behavior, her imperious attitude, the fact that she happily issued commands and assumed they would be obeyed without question.

She sat and waited, arms crossed over her chest, while he turned the key, gunned the engine. "We going somewhere?" he asked.

"Drive," she said. "I'll tell you where to turn."

"What's all this about, Connie?" he asked, driving anyway. He reached forward and cranked up the heater.

"We have to do something," she said. "For Carl. It's important."

"Why isn't he here?" Barry asked. "He didn't tell me anything about it."

"He's a busy man. He told me; I'm telling you. I speak for Carl, don't worry about that."

"Just seems strange, us rushin' off like this. It's dark, it's raining—"

"I didn't take you as the kind of guy who fucking complains all the time."

I'm not, Barry wanted to say. He held his tongue, knowing that to object would just prove her point. He drove in silence, turning where Connie directed him. The truck's headlights cut a ragged cone through the storm-dark night; its windshield wipers banged an uneven percussion in counterpoint to the rain's steady barrage. They headed toward Douglas, along Highway 80.

After a few minutes, she put a hand on his thigh and squeezed gently. "I'm sorry, baby," she said, making her voice a purr. "I didn't mean to sound harsh. It's just that I didn't want to talk about this inside, where the others could hear. This is something Carl asked us to do, and he wants it kept quiet."

"He didn't ask me," Barry said. His words were curt, and he didn't bother to disguise the grumpiness he felt. Clarice had done the same thing to him sometimes—assuming he would just do as she said without telling him why, or what her intentions were, and his response had generally been the same: anger that simmered under the surface until it finally boiled over in a shouting argument that could last for hours, or days. Connie couldn't know that, of course, and in almost every other way she was the complete opposite of Clarice.

"He knew you'd listen to me," Connie said. "He knows we have a . . . a special bond."

"That what you call it?" Barry wished he could keep the edge out of his voice, but he didn't know how to bring it under control. Was it something more than just anger? He didn't know that either, but suspected (from a tickle under his arms, a dryness in his mouth, a liquid churning in his gut) that fear might play some part in it as well.

"Barry, honey, I'm trying to explain it to you, okay? It wasn't the kind of thing he could just come out with. And he didn't want to talk about it at the ranch, like I said. Turn up here."

They had passed through the intersection of 80 and Pan-American, where the highway hooked west and eventually northwest toward Bisbee and continued past the Motor Vehicles Division and an abandoned auto dealership. He didn't know the name of the street he did turn on, and through the rain and dark he couldn't make out the sign. The road led north between tall grasses and spiked balls of yucca with stalks that reached toward the sky as if trying to spear the thundering clouds. Lights burned in the windows of trailer homes set back from the road.

"Are you gonna tell me what this is all about?"

"I said I would. Slow down and watch for a dirt road on the right."

He did as she said, wishing she would get to the point already. They neared the dirt road, its terminus barely an opening in the high grass, with a couple of mailboxes on wooden posts canting drunkenly in the soaked earth. "That one?"

"That's it," she said. "Kill the headlights."

"What's goin' on, Connie? I mean, what the fuck—"

"Just do it!" she snapped. Barry complied. With the moon hidden by storm clouds, he could barely see to negotiate the turn. He made it slowly, feeling the truck slip as its tires tried to find purchase in the rain-slick mud.

Beside him, Connie shifted and raised the gym bag from the floor onto her lap. The sound of its zipper seemed loud in the quiet truck, even against the background din of the monsoon. He glanced over, afraid to take his eyes off the narrow dirt trail for long, but the bag's interior was as dark as a cave, as dark as he was beginning to fear her heart was.

As she drew something from the bag, a flash of lightning glinted off dark steel. "What the fuck?" he said again.

"If you want to be precise, it's a Government Model .38 Colt Super," she answered. "It's twenty years old if it's a day, but they built them like tanks back then. It's been fired and cleaned recently, and it's absolutely pristine. And untraceable."

Barry stopped the truck. He didn't intend to drive another inch until she had explained what they were up to.

"You know we're in a war here, right?" she asked.

"I thought the war was in Iraq."

"Not that one, although having a border like a sponge makes us vulnerable to terrorists too. I'm talking about the war to defend our border, Barry. The war to save America for Americans. How many illegals do you think cross the border every day?"

"I don't know, a few thousand?"

"That's on the low side," Connie said. "Last year the Border Patrol sent back half a million, just from Arizona. That doesn't include all the ones they missed, of course, or the other states along the border. We're being invaded. They're doing it slowly, without an army, but they're doing it. They've almost taken over Arizona and New Mexico. If we don't start fighting back, they will."

"So what, you brought me out here so you can shoot at illegals?"

"You're still thinking too small, Barry." She pressed the

gun into his hands. He didn't want it, tried to refuse it, but she kept up the pressure until it was either open his palms and accept it or have his fingers crushed. He hadn't held a gun in years, had never been much of a hunter. Vietnam had eliminated any desire to see bullets tearing flesh, smashing bone. "See that house?"

Barry followed her pointing finger. A short distance up the dirt road was the place she meant, a manufactured home sitting on a small fenced lot, surrounded by empty fields of grass and sunflowers and thistle. Three windows were illuminated, that he could see, and a floodlight over the door shone down on a forest green wooden staircase attached to the front. Wind drove raindrops through the floodlight's cone at a slant. "What about it?"

"That's where Hilario Machado lives," Connie said. "You remember who that is?"

Barry had to search his memory. It seemed like ages ago, but it had only been, what, yesterday? Day before?

"Guy from Wal-Mart."

"The guy who wouldn't hire you, but hires his own kind. Wal-Mart used to be a symbol of America, Barry, but that store draws people over here from across the border. Sometimes they just come to shop, but then maybe they see it as the Promised Land, and they sneak back in just so they can live in the same country as it. Or so they can get jobs there."

"What about him?" Barry asked. He was afraid he already knew, though. The niggling fear that had dried his throat and upset his stomach and made his skin itch blossomed into a full-bodied thing that threatened to leave his limbs shaking and helpless, his gut spewing.

"He's alone in there," Connie said. "He's not married, has no family in this country. He sends some money to his father in Mexico, but his mother's dead, and he's insured. It's not like anyone will suffer. Not even him—that Colt would stop a bull in its tracks."

"You want me to . . . You want me to shoot him?"

"Carl wants you to kill him," Connie said, finally putting words to it.

"Why?"

"It's a fucking war, Barry. He's the enemy. More than that, he's a symbol, just like that Wal-Mart is. You know you wanted to do it when he turned you down. Now you can. No witnesses, no danger of being caught, no harm to any other living soul. But the statement it'll make—that's what makes it important, Barry. That's what makes it necessary. We have to let them know that they can't take our country away from us."

It was crazy. *She* was crazy, and so was Carl, so were the whole lot of them. Killing the poor sap wouldn't send any kind of statement.

Except Barry didn't know anything about politics. He had heard some of the people at the ranch arguing about immigration issues and other things, the war, the economy, terrorism. Every one of them seemed smarter than him, better informed. They watched Fox News while he fell asleep. No, he wasn't to be trusted on such things; he was too dumb and ignorant.

Anyway, Connie sat close to him in the truck, and it was like they were in a cocoon together, with all the rain and the lightning and the politics outside. Her legs pressed against his and her hand touched his thigh again, fingernails stroking, stroking, and her breath felt hot on his neck, and his blood pounded like the rain on the roof, rushing to his groin, thundering in his ears. She was a woman of the world, one who had been around and done all sorts of things, and Carl was some kind of genius, and he was just a dumb hick who didn't know a good thing when it slapped him in the face or woke him up with her mouth.

"It's loaded?"

"Ready to go."

He started to grab for the door handle, but she moved faster, taking his face in both hands, pressing her lips against his, her tongue moving through them and into his mouth, probing. Then she released him, and at the same time his hand found the handle and pulled it. The door fell open and he dropped to the muddy road, shutting it.

Barry slogged through mud that sucked at his feet toward the little house, about forty yards away. The wind-whipped rain stung, and his clothes, just beginning to dry, were soaked again, chafing where they rubbed against his skin. A fence about three feet tall surrounded the house, with a gate halfway down the gravel drive. He worked the gate, let it close on its springs with a bang. He thought something moved inside, a shadow against one of the walls he could see through a window. He kept going, up the wooden steps, stomping hard to loosen some of the mud that had adhered to his boots. Before he could even knock on the door, it opened, spilling yellow light out onto the little landing made by the top stair.

"Yes?" Hilario Machado said. "You—"

Barry raised the weapon, its barrel less than a foot from the shining head with its precise comb lines, and squeezed the trigger like they had taught him back in basic, so many lifetimes ago. A clap of thunder almost drowned out the boom of the gun, and he wondered if it had gone off at all or had maybe misfired, but lightning and the yellow light from inside showed him that Hilario Machado tumbled backward, blood spraying like black paint, up and back. From where he stood outside, Barry waited until Machado had hit the floor, jerking and quaking, and fired two more times, each bullet slamming into Machado's yellow short-sleeved shirt and causing another reflex jerk. Then Machado stopped moving, and Barry, still gripping the weapon in his right hand, jumped off the top step and ran back toward the truck that hunkered in the darkness on the muddy road, toward Connie and Carl and a new life unlike any he had ever known, the life of someone who has murdered another human being.

14

Police work could be the most frustrating job in the world, Buck thought, but then once in a great while it turned out to have a certain elegance, when everything came together like the steps in a ballet.

He drove through the punishing monsoon, north up Highway 191, with Raul Bermudez at his side. Scoot Brown and Carmela Lindo followed in another vehicle. Ed hadn't been willing to reassign any of the officers working the suddenly more complicated Lippincott case, but six officers from the Willcox office would join them at the scene.

"Busy night," Raul observed. "I can't believe you hooked this all up so fast."

"It just happened," Buck said. "I started making calls, trying to follow up on what happened to Henry Schaffer after he got out back in Oklahoma. I got lucky and found a cop in Lawton who not only remembered Schaffer, but had a CI who was friends with him, so he was able to keep tabs on the guy even after his probation was up. Schaffer didn't stick around Oklahoma, but he wanted someone to know where he'd gone, so he told his buddy, the CI, that he was moving to Arizona."

Buck swerved around a coyote carcass, its blood running toward the edge of the road along with the rainwater. A gully alongside the highway roared with water that would overrun its banks at some low point and send a flash flood across the highway, unless it hit a wash first that directed it off into the desert. "When he landed here, he changed his name, got a driver's license under the new identity, Dana Fortier. Turns out that a Dana Fortier got a fix-it ticket a few weeks back, outside

Willcox, for a busted taillight. He gave an address in Dos
Cabezas. I got hold of the officer who wrote him up, and he
confirmed the pictures we have of Henry Schaffer. Same guy.
The place in Dos Cabezas is pretty isolated, up a dirt road off
186, toward the hills. Perfect place to stash Lulu."

"Lucky break," Raul said.

"Sometimes that's what the job's all about. If we didn't
have luck we'd be totally screwed."

Raul laughed. "Got that right," he said.

During the day, or even on a clear night with a good moon,
Buck knew, a person driving on 186 could look up and see the
two vaguely head-shaped lumps on the mountain that gave
Dos Cabezas its name. The town was largely a ghost town
now, a few inhabited dwellings mixed in with the remains of
adobe buildings from a mining boom that had gone bust most
of a century before. In the dark you could drive right through
it and never know it had been there.

It was just about an hour from Elfrida, past the turnoff for
the Chiricahua National Monument. While things seemed to
have fallen together quickly, it had been after nine before
Buck had confirmation on the Dana Fortier/Henry Schaffer
connection and the address, and another hour had passed while
he worked out the logistics with Willcox, keeping Bisbee in
the loop as he did. Fortunately they'd been able to rouse a judge
and get a warrant during that same period. He had called
Tammy, who had sounded neither surprised nor disappointed
to hear that he would probably be out all night. He was himself both surprised and disappointed by that fact.

She had also told him that Aurelio had said the pregnant
cow was in labor, and he'd be staying with her in the barn tonight. Buck knew that cows didn't necessarily calve in the
middle of the night, but he had spent enough long hours in
late-night barns, or out in the fields, observing and assisting,
that it seemed to him that it was their preference. He liked to
be present for births and regretted that he would miss this one.
In his mind's eye he could see her sides (white with brown
markings) contracting. She would lie down on the hay as the
contractions worsened. A membrane, like a water balloon full

of blood, would issue from her, then she'd get up and it would tear, and the next contraction would expel a thick stream of amniotic fluid, releasing a stink that could knock a grown man back on his heels. Finally, another bubble, this one the birth sac, would present. Buck would be able to see the calf's hind hooves inside. Cows took no Lamaze classes, but she would know without being told that she had to push. If the calf got stuck, or presented improperly, Buck would know it soon, and he'd break out the calf puller, but that hadn't been necessary as often as it had when Buck was a kid himself. He chuckled at the memory.

"What?" Raul asked.

"Bad joke I thought of," Buck said. "Rancher humor."

"Like 'You might be a redneck if . . .'?"

"Not quite."

"Lay it on me, bossman."

"You asked for it. Okay, kid visiting his rancher grandpa, from the city. Grandpa's got a cow ready to calf, and the kid, who's a real pest with all his questions, wants to watch. Grandpa worries, because he'll have to concentrate on the cow, but finally agrees. The process takes a long time, calf is turned wrong, rancher has to latch on to one of its legs with a calf puller and tug. When it's all over, he turns to the kid, who has been wide-eyed and silent the whole time. 'Okay, Johnny,' he says, 'you got any questions?' 'Just one,' Johnny says. 'How fast was it running when it hit her?'"

Raul laughed politely, and Buck told him about the pregnant cow and why he would rather be home tonight, except for the possibility of finding Lulu. Either way made for a long day.

He had asked Donna to brew a pot of strong coffee, and the four of them—even though Scoot and Carmela had just come on duty a couple of hours before—had shared it, then poured the remainder into a red steel thermos. Donna would stay in Elfrida to coordinate from there and to make sure that the heart of the valley wasn't left completely unprotected, but she had the coffeepot and could always make more.

Buck stayed in touch with the Willcox unit by radio, and both groups closed on the sleepy town at about the same time, shortly after midnight. The rain had not let up, and Buck's hands and shoulders ached from fighting the wheel, struggling against wind and water and tension. Sweat gathered under the Kevlar vest he wore beneath his uniform shirt. Excitement and something that might have been hope plucked at his nerves like a fiddler at an Elks Club dance.

The town of Dos Cabezas sat high enough in the foothills that the landscape looked like the mountainside had dropped off in jagged chunks and the houses had been built around them. Lights here and there indicated where occupied structures were. NO TRESPASSING signs decorated the properties close to the road, as if to warn off ghost town devotees who might mistake an inhabited home for an abandoned one. The effect from the road was to make the town look singularly unfriendly, an impression the wind and weather did little to correct.

High Springs Trail came up suddenly, after a hilly curve. One of the old adobes sagged at the corner of High Springs and 186, its eroded blocks jumbled around most of a single upright wall as if in miniature impersonation of the landscape. Raul pointed out the road sign, and Buck braked hard, skidding into the turn. "Thanks," he said. "Almost missed it."

"I knew it should be right around here," Raul said. Buck had MapQuested the address before they left Elfrida, and Raul had been holding the printout in his lap, examining it now and again with a flashlight. "Almost a mile up here. Nine-point-three tenths."

"Got to figure he probably won't have a welcome sign out."

"I wouldn't think so."

Buck glanced into his rearview and saw that Scoot's vehicle had made the turn behind him. He radioed his Willcox contact, Patrol Lieutenant Randy Cummings. "Randy," he said when they had connected. "We're on High Springs."

"I'm almost there," Randy replied amid a wash of static. "Want to hang on and wait for us?"

"Roger that," Buck said. He reported the plan to Scoot, and they both shut down their engines and lights. Less than five minutes had passed when two more sets of headlights turned off 186, from the north, and jounced up High Springs. Buck picked up the radio again. "That you, Randy?"

"If you're blocking the road in front of me, yes."

"I didn't figure it would get a lot of traffic tonight."

"Probably a safe bet. Ready to roll?"

Buck responded by gunning the ignition and switching his lights back on. "Rollin', rollin', rollin'," he said.

"Rawhide!" Randy finished with a laugh. He was older than Buck, in his mid-fifties, and Buck knew he was a huge fan of old TV and movie Westerns. Willcox was the home of Rex Allen, who had starred in both kinds, and every year for Rex Allen Days, Randy and some of his friends dressed up in B-movie cowboy finery and rode in the parade.

"You got a plan?" Randy asked him.

"I figure we knock on the door, say it's a candygram."

Randy laughed again. " 'Mongo like candy,' " he quoted.

"You got it. When he opens up, we identify ourselves, toss the warrant in his face, go in and find Lulu."

"You know the girl, Buck?"

"I know her."

"That's good. You do the shouting, then, and we'll hope she's someplace where she can hear your voice."

Buck didn't reply. The road was rugged, climbing over rocks and dipping into washes filled with swiftly flowing water, and he had negotiated it fine, but now he'd come around a bend and there was the place they were looking for. He stopped, killed the lights. "Bingo," he said into the radio. "Lights out, boys and girls. Let's move in dark and quiet."

The cabin was built almost up against the side of the mountain, which sloped up and away at a steep angle. Sycamores and twisted ash trees surrounded it, almost screening it from the road. A mailbox on a stone post stood at the road with the house number painted on it, and up close to the house, half-covered by a blue tarp that the wind had blown partly off, sat a dark pickup truck. The base of the house was made of stone, with wood starting above the lower edge of the windows. It was dark, but a yellow bug light burned in a little alcove over the front door. Buck couldn't see behind the house—the trees and the mountainside and the house conspired to completely obscure everything beyond the cabin.

Without lights, he pulled slowly up to within a couple hundred feet of the place. There he shut off the Yukon. Behind him, the other four vehicles also stopped. Everyone climbed out into the lashing rain and wind and huddled beside Buck's SUV for a quick conference. They agreed that Randy's team would fan out behind the cabin, while Buck and Raul went in the front door. Scoot and Carmela would remain under cover in front, in case anyone came out the windows.

The approach settled, Buck switched on a Maglite and drew his service weapon. He walked toward the cabin, playing the light on the path ahead. The tarp snapped in the wind, and somewhere around the house an unseen shutter banged irregularly, like the reports of pellet rifles at a shooting gallery. Buck wished he could hear noises from inside the cabin, but at least the sound of his approach would be masked by the weather.

Training the light on the rear of the truck, he saw a broken left taillight.

She's in there, he thought. *Hang on, Lulu, we're coming for you.*

15

Jeannie tried to watch TV, but the wind blew too ferociously and the satellite signal kept fritzing in and out. She finally gave up and turned on a Miles Davis CD, then put on an oversized Mickey Mouse T-shirt, climbed into bed, pulled the covers up over her legs and tried to read. The CD helped, but it didn't completely drown out the wind, which whistled and howled. Horror movie wind, it was, ghost story wind. She tried to tell herself she was being silly, but she was sorry that Oliver had gone to San Diego today. With the murders up the road still fresh in her thoughts, slasher flick sound effects were not conducive to relaxation.

Oliver had called from San Diego to say that his flight had been delayed because of weather in Tucson. Whenever he did land, he'd have a two-hour drive home. No closer airport could handle large planes—he could have flown into Sierra Vista, only an hour away, for another couple hundred dollars, but if a big commercial jetliner couldn't get into Tucson, what chance would a little prop job have of landing there?

Three years before they bought the house, a Sulphur Springs Valley wind had wrenched off the roof; the upside was that the house had a brand-new roof, but Jeannie feared that it could happen again on a night like this. Sitting in bed with Barbara Kingsolver's *The Bean Trees* propped against her thighs (she had become accustomed to the idea that she would be living in the Southwest—the real Southwest, not California—for a good long while, and that region, with its tripartite Indian, Spanish and Anglo heritage, was so different from her Northeastern roots that she wanted to understand it better), she uttered a loud "Fuck!" when the power went out. By the time she located her bookmark and slid it into place, flipped back the blankets and turned her legs off the bed, the lights had come on again, flickered twice and then stayed on. The digital clock on her nightstand and the one on the VCR beneath the bedroom TV blinked triple zeroes at her.

She froze on the edge of the mattress. "Stay on, stay on, stay on," she whispered.

The power gods obeyed. The CD had stopped, but the lights kept shining. Jeannie blew out a breath and put her feet on the floor anyway. She had to go around the house and fix all the clocks, and make sure nothing had stayed on that shouldn't have.

Jeannie had just made it into the living room when she heard a pounding on the front door. She let out an inadvertent shriek and clutched her shirt collar, bunching Mickey's ears into her fist. For a brief moment she tried to convince herself that it was only the wind banging something against the house, but then it happened again, louder and more insistent.

She didn't expect anyone but Oliver, and he wouldn't be home for hours yet—would maybe just be landing about now. Should she keep quiet and hope that the visitor outside would move on? But she had stepped into the living room, where four feet past the door a window, blinds wide open, looked out toward the covered walkway and the front yard. The unknown caller had only to take a couple of steps to see her.

Instead of trying to hide, Jeannie crossed to the door and leaned toward the peephole she had installed right after they moved in. At first she couldn't focus on the person on the other side, who was not only sopped to the skin but moving rapidly, maybe stepping from foot to foot, trying to warm up. She saw plastered-down black hair and slender, dark, bare shoulders. When she finally did recognize her nighttime visitor, at first she didn't believe what she saw.

She rattled the doorknob, but it wouldn't turn. She had locked the knob with the thumb latch, so she twisted that and tried again. As she yanked the door open, the soaked girl outside practically fell into her arms. "Lulu!" Jeannie shouted. "Oh my God, Lulu!"

Lulu pressed herself against Jeannie, soaking through her Mickey T in seconds. Jeannie wrapped her arms around Lulu, drawing the weeping girl inside, shoving the door closed with her left foot. Lulu's back and shoulders wrenched with each gasping sob, so that Jeannie felt like she was trying to contain a large, anxious puppy. "Lulu, Lulu," she kept saying, lowering her voice, trying to be comforting. "It's okay now, Lulu. It's okay," she said, knowing that it really wasn't, that even though Lulu was here with her now, the girl's family would never be with her again.

Moving Lulu across the floor so that they could sit down on the sofa, Jeannie noticed that Lulu's feet tracked mud and blood over the carpet. "You're bleeding!" she said. "Are you okay?"

"I . . . I . . ." was all Lulu could manage.

Jeannie made her stand on her own for long enough to look her over. She wore a pink cotton tank top, stained and soaked through, and red silk boxers with SpongeBob SquarePants on them. Her arms and legs had been scratched and cut, and her filthy bare feet bled as if she had walked across ground glass to get here.

"You're hurt," Jeannie said. "We should get you to the hospital."

Lulu shook her head, her wet hair streaming out to its full length, shedding droplets over the couch, window and coffee table. "No," she said, able to form words for the first time since coming inside. "No time for that."

"Did he . . . ?" She left the question unasked, not sure how to phrase it. Lulu seemed to know what she meant.

"No. He didn't hurt me that way."

Jeannie didn't want to see her standing there in pain, shivering and bleeding. "You need a hot shower," she said. "I'll put some water on to boil while you're in and then we'll have tea and you can tell me what happened."

Lulu nodded at this suggestion. "Cops?"

"Right, we should call the lieutenant. What was that guy's name? He and Oliver are becoming buddies, it seems." She remembered tucking his business card into the front of the phone book. Retrieving it and lifting the phone to her ear, she glanced back at Lulu. "Oliver's out; he'll be back sometime tonight."

"O-okay." Now that Lulu was more still, Jeannie could see that her lips were dry and split, her cheek bruised, her left eye purpled and swollen.

"Crap!" Jeannie said, pressing buttons and listening to the phone. "It's dead. Must be the storm." Cell service wasn't an option at the house.

"Unless it's . . . it's him," Lulu said. Her eyes welled with tears again.

Jeannie didn't have to ask who she meant. "Come on," she said. "Let's get you in the shower. You're safe here; he can't get to you anymore."

"My . . . my family's dead, aren't they?"

Jeannie bit down hard on her lower lip. "Yes. I'm sorry, Lulu. They are."

Another nod, and Lulu looked at the stained carpet as if assessing the damage her feet had done. "I figured."

Jeannie led Lulu (who took tiny steps, as if she were a hundred years old) to the bathroom, took a couple of plush towels from the linen closet and started the water for her. She made it as hot as she could stand and figured that would work for Lulu. As the bathroom steamed up, she gave the girl another brief hug and then left her to her solitary ministrations, sure that the shower would give her a chance to mourn in peace and privacy.

Closing the door behind herself, she headed back to the living room to try the telephone again.

16

Oliver's cell phone rang as he crossed the San Pedro River heading into the little Mormon-settled town of St. David on Highway 80, trying to peer through the darkness at the river. It was impossible to see, of course, a dozen or so feet beneath the roadway, unlit by moon or stars. But with the strength of this monsoon it was certainly down there, flowing south to north, a fact with which he liked to confuse his students until the realization dawned on them that rivers paid no attention to the artificial designations of cartographers and simply moved, like all water, downhill. The San Pedro River—like millions of people, it seemed—flowed from Mexico into Arizona. And like the tide of immigration, it had never been dammed. The river had dried up briefly, during times of drought and over-use, but it always returned, flowing ever northward toward its own future.

He had finally landed around eleven-thirty, a little more than an hour before. He had left his car in short-term parking, since he'd only been gone for the day, and the Tucson airport was still small enough that twenty minutes after disembarking he had been on the road. The rain had let up in Tucson, but here, off Interstate 10 between Benson and Tombstone (O.K. CORRAL GUNFIGHT DAILY! the sign read, with a picture of Kurt Russell in Earp garb; he wondered sometimes if tourists marveled at the actor's resemblance to what they assumed was the historical Wyatt), he had already caught up to it. Lightning silhouetted gargantuan cottonwood trees standing beside the road.

He pawed at his blazer, found the phone, its screen glowing

blue in the dark car as if imitating the lightning outside. *Jeannie,* he thought. He had tried calling as soon as he landed, but the call had gone to voice mail. Another attempt, from Benson, had met with the same result.

But it wasn't Jeannie. It was a number he didn't recognize, with an 858 area code. San Diego. "Hello?"

"Oliver, it's Stan."

"Stan," Oliver repeated, surprised. He had almost reached St. David proper, where the speed limit would drop to thirty-five for about three minutes, then would jump back up to fifty. Shortly thereafter he would be out of cell range again. "Thanks again for this afternoon."

"Sorry for calling so late."

"No problem, I'm still driving home. If I lose you, it's because I'm in the middle of nowhere."

"I've been doing a little research into your situation," Stan said. "And I've learned some things . . . Well, I honestly don't know how to interpret them. So I thought I should tell you and let you see if you can make sense of it."

"So far I haven't been very good at making sense of any of this," Oliver said. "But I'll give it my best shot. What'd you come up with?"

"The thing is, Oliver, I think it's all of a piece."

"I'm not following, Stan. What do you mean?"

"The 'white girl' your blogger talks about, the miracle statue. I think it ties into the Cabeza de Vaca story."

Oliver steered with his left hand, fighting the temptation, in his excitement, to press down harder on the accelerator. The windshield wipers kept up their steady sweeps across the glass. "How do you mean?"

"The authoritative version of their ordeal is de Vaca's own account, in his '*relacion,*' the story he put down in writing for the king of Spain. But Andrés Dorantes had his own version of events. He didn't write it down, but told it to interested parties, and eventually, after his death and de Vaca's, it was written down and privately published in Spain. Much of what he told was told to him by his slave, Estevan—including secrets Estevan had sworn to Cabeza de Vaca that he would never reveal."

"I'm with you," Oliver said. He hoped the man would get to the point before he left town and lost the signal.

"According to Estevan's tale—and this part, de Vaca didn't put into his version—they did a lot more healing than de Vaca admitted to, and none of them really thought their Christian God was behind their powers. De Vaca had become the slave of an Indian shaman and had learned magic from him, and the rest of it, according to Estevan anyway, just seemed to come naturally, flowing from de Vaca into the rest of them. Especially Estevan. Of course, Estevan was dead by the time Dorantes revealed any of this, killed at the pueblos on the Marcos de Niza expedition. And Dorantes—not wanting to be burned at the stake—claimed that the magic had affected everyone but him. Point is, somewhere along the way, Estevan fell in love with a girl, a shaman's daughter, and started sculpting her. He told Dorantes that his love was so strong that he put his magic into every bit of effort, that he had never been a sculptor but with magic guiding his hand, even working with the crudest of tools, the statue was coming out more beautiful and lifelike than the master sculptors of Renaissance Europe could have done."

"And you think that's the white girl Lulu wrote about?"

"It could be," Stan replied. "Especially considering what happened next."

"What's that?"

"The girl had another lover—I guess she was betrothed—and he confronted her and Estevan as they tried to put the finishing touches on the sculpture. There was a fight, and she was killed, her last life's blood splashing the statue. Estevan abandoned it then, afraid of what her blood might do to it."

"This is all kind of out there, Stan." Oliver had gone through the town, passed the brightly lit Express Stop and was on the dark stretch leading almost due south. The speed limit was back up to fifty and he struggled to hold it there.

"I thought I had convinced you that you need to give in to magical thinking to understand this stuff," Stan reminded him.

"Right, sorry, go on."

"They left the statue where she died, after burying her

body and the man's, whom Estevan killed. I do think this is your girl's statue.

"Word of it has spread throughout the magical community—and yes, before you ask, there is one, and I'm not talking about David Copperfield and Lance Burton. I'm talking about serious magic users, the underground occult. The statue—missing for at least three centuries—is reputed to be an extremely potent artifact, capable of endowing its possessor with incredible powers. Except nobody knows for sure because like I said, for several hundred years no one has known where it's been. Lately, according to my sources—and before you ask, don't—there's been a bit of a buzz around it, suggesting that maybe it's resurfacing. Its return is somehow supposed to herald the rediscovery or reclamation of Aztlán—I told you it all tied together. They call her *La Niña Blanca*. This is something that people would literally kill to get their hands on."

Oliver thought about the Lavender family, dead in their little ranch house, and missing Lulu. "Okay, Stan. Thanks for all this. It's way more than I could have dreamed of."

"You got me intrigued," Stan said. "And now that I've made a few inquiries, I guess I'm involved in some way too. Let's hope I'm wrong and the damn thing stays missing."

"Sounds good to me." Stan was starting to break up, and Oliver knew the call had to come to an end. Just in case, he pulled off the road outside the Holy Trinity Monastery. The rain sounded louder when the car was still.

"One more thing," Stan said. "Nobody knows what the de Vaca party's route was precisely. Most current scholars think they went directly into Mexico from Texas, and never got into New Mexico, much less Arizona. Hallenbeck, though, who wrote one of the first definitive histories of the adventure, believed that they did make it into Arizona. Not only that, but according to Hallenbeck's figuring, they passed right by where you live, through the Sulphur Springs Valley and into Mexico near Douglas. I don't know what connection that has to anything, but thought you should know it."

"I owe you a big one," Oliver said. "Let me know if there's ever anything I can do for you, Stan."

"Just don't bone any more students, Oliver. That's good enough for me."

"You don't need to worry on that score." Oliver checked his mirror, but the road was as empty as it had been since Benson. As he pulled back onto Highway 80, he thanked Stan again and ended the call. Before he put the phone away, he tried Jeannie again. No one answered. Just in case, he tried Lieutenant Shelton, with the same result. *Where is everyone?* he wondered.

The speed limit was still fifty, but he sped up to sixty-five, so that when it jumped to sixty-five in a few minutes he could accelerate to eighty without the change being too abrupt.

17

At the door, Buck swallowed and dropped his flashlight back into its sling on his duty belt. Raul, holding a tactical entry ram in both hands, gave him a single sharp nod. Buck pounded on the solid wooden door hard enough to rattle it in its frame. "Cochise County sheriffs!" he shouted, backing away two steps and putting both hands on his .40-caliber Beretta. He held it high enough to fire over Raul's shoulder if it came to that.

No answer came from within. "Take it down," Buck said. Raul nodded again and swung the ram from the shoulders, slamming it into the door just above the lock. The frame splintered under the blow, the door swinging into darkness. Raul tossed the ram to his right so it wouldn't be in the way and clawed his weapon from its holster.

A half second of silence followed, maybe less. Then the darkness bloomed with fire and thunder, as if the sky's crash of light and sound had somehow transported itself into the little cabin. Buck almost had enough time to blink before hot knives darted into his face and neck and thudded against his chest. *Buckshot*, he thought as he threw himself backward, twisting in midair, breaking his fall with his left hand so he didn't drop the gun in his right, and then, as his elbows folded and his knees touched down and his stomach and finally his chin landed in the mud beyond the cabin door, in that moment when time seemed to stand still, he thought, *Buck shot,* and even managed a brief smile.

And then he remembered Raul, who had gone in first.

"Raul!" he shouted.

Raul had gone down, flat on his back, hands splayed out to
his sides.

In the dim light the blood pooling behind his head—what
remained of his head—looked black with silver highlights.
Raindrops rippled the pool.

From around back came the sounds of people shouting,
running. "Don't go inside!" Buck cried. "It's booby trapped!"

He knelt beside Raul, grabbed a wrist, felt for a pulse. He
couldn't bring himself to touch the neck, where one might
have been easier to find, because there just wasn't much neck
there. Flaps of shredded skin joined shoulders and chin.
Raul's face was hamburger, one eye gone entirely and the other
oozing white.

He found no pulse, no life.

Already he was thinking of whom he'd have to notify. Raul
wasn't married, but he dated a woman who worked at the
Gadsden. Anna something, Buck thought. He would have to
find her and let her know. And then there were Raul's parents,
his brother and two sisters and their families. Uncle Raul was
a favorite with the kids.

"Buck."

Randy Cummings stood beside him, touched his shoulder.

"He's gone, Randy."

"I can see that."

"Bastard set a booby trap in there. Shotgun, connected to
the door. Soon as it opened up, the gun went off, and Raul
took the worst of it."

"You're hit too," Randy said.

"I'm fine. She's not in there, is she?"

"We haven't entered yet."

"I'm pretty sure the front door is clear now. Just use plenty
of light and be careful. If she's in there, we have to find her,
but I don't think she is. I think this was nothing but a trap."

"We'll check, Buck. You've got to get to a hospital though."

"I have to get down to Douglas, tell Raul's family what
happened." He blinked hard, swallowed. "It's on me. I should
never have let him go in first."

"He knew the score," Randy said. It sounded heartless, but

it was just Randy's way: direct and honest. He squeezed Buck's shoulder as if to hoist him back to his feet. "Come on, Buck. Carmela or Scoot can drive you. We'll take this place apart board by board. Anything's here, we'll find it."

"The fucker set us up," Buck said. He steadied himself against Randy's stable form and rose slowly, feeling suddenly ancient and infirm. "Over the span of years and in different states, all for this. All so he could take out a cop. What kind of human being is he?"

"You sure he is one?"

"On the way back we would have argued about what music to listen to. He would have wanted Ricky Martin or Christina Aguilera or Selena, some Latin pop star, and I would have said, I hate that Mex shit, you might as well listen to *corridos* about drug dealers and dead dogs or something."

Randy draped an arm around Buck's shoulders, trying to steer him away from Raul. "You're in shock, Buck. We have to get you out of the storm."

"Of course I'm in shock, some murdering motherfuck just killed my friend."

"We'll find him, Buck. He couldn't have done all this without leaving some traces. We'll find him, and he will pay."

"You'd better find him before I do, Randy," Buck said. "Roy Rogers and Hopalong Cassidy never killed the bad guys, right? They just shot the guns from their hands and then knocked them out cold."

"That's the way it usually went," Randy said.

"You'd better find him because if I do, I will kill him. No matter what. I will kill him."

"Come on, Buck." Arm over Buck's shoulders, Randy walked him toward the Yukon. "I'm going to keep Carmela here with me. Scoot'll drive you down to Douglas. Hospital first, promise me."

"Hospital first."

Randy led him to the passenger side, opened the door, helped Buck into the seat. Tenderly, as if assisting a child, he fastened Buck's seat belt. "I'll get Scoot," Randy said, and then he ran back into the night and the rain.

Interlude: 1536

The first time he saw men on horseback, after his years in the wilderness, Alvar thought they were centaurs or some other miraculous beasts. They rode toward him from far off in the distance, over a flat, barren plain. Heat shimmered off the dirt, adding to the sense of unreality, as if they came through a veil of some kind. Behind them the plume of dust they kicked up lingered in the still air like low brown clouds.

Alvar had been so immersed in the realms of magic that the simple explanation—they were Spaniards, and they rode horses—didn't occur to him until Estevan shouted out. "We are saved!" the Moor called. He turned to Alvar, walking a dozen paces behind with eleven Indians behind him (Alonso del Castillo and Andrés Dorantes had stayed in a largely abandoned village ten leagues back, too exhausted to continue), and Alvar could see that, parched as they all were, tears had formed in the man's eyes. "By the grace of the good Lord our God, those must be Christians!" Estevan said.

It was true that the Indians they had lived among and traveled with these many years did not ride horses. They could learn to, he supposed. They had demonstrated that they were not the subhuman beings other Spanish adventurers had claimed. Even Alvar's paternal grandfather, Pedro de Vera Mendoza, conqueror of the Canary Islands, had staffed his household with conquered Guanche slaves that the old man described as inarticulate, unintelligent and incapable of holding on to thoughts that weren't beaten into them. Alvar and his companions had found the opposite to be true; the Indians they had befriended had different experiences and beliefs, but they were just as able and quick-witted as any European.

"If it is true, Estevanico," Alvar whispered while they were still alone, "and they are Christians, not another word of our ungodly doings must ever pass our lips."

Estevan squeezed his lips together with two slender fingers. Alvar could see in his eyes that the Moor agreed. He only hoped the man could be trusted.

He had suspected they neared civilization, and believed they had long since crossed into Mexico. Days ago, in an impoverished village where the ancient natives (there were no children, and few men or women of an age to fight or labor) had surrounded them and spent an hour touching their flesh, baked by years in the sun but, even so, pale and hairy by comparison, fingering their hair and beards, feeling the rags they wore about their loins, Alonso had become separated from the others, and at one point had let out a cry of alarm.

Alvar, Andrés and Estevan had broken free of the crowd and joined him at once. Alonso pointed at one of the village's warriors, a man with short dark hair that he undoubtedly cropped with one of their stone tools, a round belly and a grin that revealed only a dozen or so teeth. Alvar found nothing especially strange about the man on first examination. The villages they had passed through in recent weeks had been poorer than the permanent adobe settlements they had seen before, the number of healthy adults fewer, but except for his health and age this man did not seem especially noteworthy.

"Ahh!" Estevan said. He saw whatever it was that had made Alonso cry out, and he moved closer to the warrior, almost hesitantly, pointing at the man's chest.

The warrior wore a narrow strip of leather around his neck and, suspended from that, a sort of amulet. Alvar realized, once he examined it, that the thing was a buckle from a sword belt. A horseshoe nail had been stitched to it with a bit of thread.

These people had precious little, not even much corn to offer their guests, and they had neither swords nor belts nor buckles, neither horses nor shoes nor nails.

Those things could only have come from a European.

Alvar brushed past Estevan, grabbing the amulet in his fist. "Where did you get these?" he demanded. "How did you come by them?"

An interpreter who had accompanied them from the last village came forward and translated Alvar's questions. When the warrior spoke, the interpreter, a tall, lanky fellow with one eye and a horrible scar where the other had been, said, "From heaven."

"You did not go to heaven after it," Alvar insisted. "Who brought them from there for you? From whom do you have these things?"

The warrior pointed to the south and west, and spoke again. "There is a river," the translator said. "He says that bearded men such as yourselves came to the river while he and some friends hunted there." He turned back to the warrior, who continued his tale. "He says that the bearded men rode on the backs of beasts and carried spears twice as long as a man is tall, and long knives, and wore clothing over their entire bodies and over their heads."

"Armored Spaniards, with lances and swords," Andrés said, his voice fraught with wonder.

"He says there was a fight. They stabbed two of his friends with the long spears, but he hid across the river until they had gone. When he went to see his friends, he saw that the bearded strangers had left these gifts for him in the sand."

"No doubt one's belt was broken in the scuffle," Alonso said. "And a horse threw a nail."

"Where did the men go?" Alvar asked.

"Back across the river and toward the sea," the interpreter said after relaying the question.

"We must go the same way," Alvar said. "Those are our people, and we must be reunited with them."

The interpreter translated that, although Alvar had not meant him to, and the warrior's eyes bugged with fear. He backed away from the Spaniards, shouting something to his fellows, and the rest of the villagers kept their distance after that. Alvar and his companions didn't even sleep in the village that night, but kept going and camped several leagues away.

After that, the villages they encountered were mostly abandoned, fertile fields bearing crops left to rot. What natives they saw had taken to the mountains, hiding. They said that bearded men had invaded and burned their villages, taken their children and any women and men able to work.

Slavers, Alvar understood.

Over the next few days, most of the Indians who had followed them for so long, village to village, week by week, turned back. Everyone knew what it had taken Alvar days to comprehend: Spaniards were raiding up from Mexico City, enslaving the natives and leading them away, killing any who dared to defend their lives and their homes.

Alvar knew that they had to catch up to the Christians, slavers or no. He had demanded a quickening of their pace, which had worn out Andrés and Alonso, and then had continued on ahead with Estevan and a handful of the Indians who remained steadfast. Now they would meet, for the first time in years, people of their own kind.

Coming out of the wavering air, the four riders reined up before Alvar and Estevan and peered at them with confused expressions. "I am a Christian," Alvar explained. The words felt strange in his mouth. "I am a Spaniard!"

"You don't look like one to me," one of the riders replied. "Don't look like anything I've ever seen. A hairy-legged Indian with a beard, perhaps."

"My name is Alvar Nuñez Cabeza de Vaca," Alvar said. "I was the treasurer for the expedition of Pámfilo de Narváez, lost in the Floridas. My companion is Estevan, a Moor, the property of Andrés Dorantes, also with that expedition. Dorantes and Alonso del Castillo, also Spaniards and Christians from the Narváez expedition, wait for us ten leagues or so behind, too weak to continue."

"Even if I believed all that you say," the rider who had spoken before answered, "what would you have me do?"

"My Spanish may sound odd because I have not been using it much these last years," Alvar said. "But have you known an Indian who could speak it as well? We are countrymen, and fellow Christians, and I insist that you take me to your captain.

*He will send men and horses back to fetch our companions,
Castillo and Dorantes."*

*The riders spoke quietly among themselves, so that Alvar
could not overhear. He knew they would go along with his request. But he did not like the way they eyed his Indian companions, whom they no doubt saw as nothing more than other
potential slaves.*

*He had worried for many months, if not years, that when
he finally met Christians again, he would fall out with them
over his use of magic during his time among the Indians. Now
he knew, without a moment's doubt, that he had been wrong
all that time. They would still fall out, but it would be over the
treatment of the Indians, whom the Spaniards valued only as
wealth, as property, and whom Alvar viewed as friends and
fellow humans put on Earth by God. He wondered how
strained relations would become with those Spaniards he
would encounter.*

*Alvar and Estevan had feared burning at the stake. That
was not to be Alvar's fate, or Estevan's, but Alvar would never
successfully rejoin Spanish civilization. After several years
and other adventures he would find himself in chains and then
banished to Africa, and although the king would annul the
sentence and he would die in honor, he would never again feel
at home in Europe. Estevan would die in the north, on the expedition of Fray Marcos de Niza in search of the seven cities
of Cíbola.*

*Alvar went to his grave believing that neither of them men-
tioned the white girl again, as long as they lived.*

He was wrong.

DAY FOUR

1

"Barry. I need you to come in here for a minute, buddy."

Barry walked through a darkened doorway. Inside a room he hadn't seen before, Carl Greenwell sat at a table, bathed in the blue glow of a small TV with no signal. "What's up?"

"Look at this here," Carl said. "It's a DVD I just had burned. You know what that means?"

Barry wasn't up on technology—he'd had trouble with the relatively simple application process at Wal-Mart—but he got the general idea. "Sure."

Carl fingered a slender remote control. "See, Connie shot some digital video footage earlier tonight. I thought you should take a look at it."

"Connie did?"

"That's right."

"Of what?"

"Just watch." Carl thumbed a button on the remote. The TV screen flickered, a black horizontal line broke the picture and scrolled out of the way, then Barry was looking at a small house on a dark night, with a light over the door and lights in the windows. A figure climbed some steps to the door, silhouetted. The door opened. A bright flash, and whoever had opened the door fell away while the first figure turned his face to the camera for the first time, the light from overhead catching him for just an instant.

"Look familiar?" Carl asked.

"That's me!" Barry hadn't been offered a chair, and he felt like the room was tilting away from him. He grabbed at the edge of the table. "Connie filmed *that*?"

"So it seems."

"Why? Why would she do that?"

Carl pressed the STOP button. "Because I asked her to."

"You? You set me up?"

Carl shook his head slowly. "Barry, you know we're doing important work here, right?"

"Sure, but—"

"Truth is, I knew as soon as I started talking to you in that bar that you were the guy I needed for a truly delicate job. But I had to make sure you'd go through with it. I couldn't know, not that fast, what the depth of your commitment to our cause would be. I admit I used you, in a way, in order to guarantee that you'd follow through when the time came. Thing is, the time is coming sooner than I expected. It's coming tonight, and I need to know that you'll do what I ask you to. I need to know that you'll be able to pull the trigger when I say so, not just when Connie does. Make sense?"

Barry scooted a chair away from the table without asking permission, and sat down in it. Six feet on the ground felt more secure than just his own two. "In a way, I guess. But you could have just asked me."

"Barry, I couldn't take that chance. Not with something like this. And there just wasn't time to take it any slower."

"What is it you're gonna want me to do, Carl?" Barry asked, biting back his fury. "What's so important you had me kill a guy for no reason?"

"There was every reason for it, Barry. You know what the reasons were. He had to die, and you had to be the one to take him out. I did you a favor there, and if you don't see it now, you will in the long run. As for later tonight, it'll be the same kind of deal. Like I said, I need you to be able to pull a trigger for me. The people here at the ranch are good people, and their hearts are in the right place, but they can't be my trigger-man."

"Why not? Why not them, Carl, instead of me?"

"Many reasons, Barry. They're known associates of mine. I

know it's hard to believe, but some of them wouldn't cross that line for me, for our cause. I believed you would, and I was right. Anyway, I couldn't even ask them, because if the law—and make no mistake, although justice is on our side, the law isn't always—if the law questioned them, I couldn't risk having them know anything. But there would be no reason for anyone to question you about me, because you're not a known part of our group."

Barry sat for a moment, his hands pressing down on the tabletop as if it could keep the room from spinning. What Carl said made sense, in a way. If not for the fact that he had tricked Barry into killing the Wal-Mart guy, he would have had no problem with the logic. The only question remaining was, did sound logic overrule whatever problems Barry had with murder?

He didn't like the way Carl just stared at him with those luminous eyes, a half smile like the *Mona Lisa*'s on his handsome face. He was waiting for Barry to make up his mind, to commit all the way to some act that he had to guess was worse than the one he had already performed tonight.

Still smiling, Carl tapped the remote. "I know you're a good man, Barry, with a good heart. I know you love your country."

"Course I do."

"It it'll make things easier, I'll just remind you that this is digital video. It's not the only copy. With a couple of taps on a keyboard I could put this out on the Internet for the whole world to see."

"But you wouldn't . . ."

"Not if you're the man I think you are. I'm just protecting my own interests, Barry. Just protecting the rights of patriots to fight for their country."

That was it, then. Barry was stuck in the middle. If he refused to help Carl—refused to pull another trigger on this worst of all nights—he would go to jail for the rest of his life or get the needle for murder. But if he murdered again, he might go free.

Didn't seem to be a difficult choice at all, when he looked at it that way.

Barry released the table and brought his hands up to the sides of his head, as if he could hide from God and Carl and everything else. "I'm with you, Carl," he said. "I'm in."

2

They stopped for dinner at Las Humaderas on Calle 3 in Agua Prieta, just a couple of blocks below the Port of Entry into the U.S., and he believed she was sending them straight across. Maybe she would be able to magic up some paperwork for Clemente and Rafael and maybe a fake bill of lading to explain her own presence in the back. He didn't mind; in fact, Las Humaderas was nothing special, but he had met Carolina in A.P. and that was where their first date had been, and for reasons he couldn't quite explain he felt drawn back to it tonight.

The other two men happily let Gabriel pay, as he had been paying all the way up the interior. He didn't mind too much. Having decided that this whole thing was worth the trouble— and he had to think that, after this much time and effort, to have doubts would have driven him toward suicide—he figured it made sense that the only one of the three who had any money at all ought to be the one who spent it. By morning they'd be across the line, and he had a feeling, with no more basis than any of the other feelings that had brought them this far, that it would all be over soon.

All three of them were nervous. They knew they would cross the line tonight, and who knew how that would go? What if they were turned back at the Port of Entry? They couldn't jump the fence or slip through a cut in it, not with the truck and the statue in back. There had been drug tunnels from A.P. into Douglas in the past, but if there were any that hadn't been found out, Gabriel didn't know where to find them.

Which meant they would have to drive out of town, into the desert, and look for a place they could drive the truck across.

Thinking about this challenge during dinner, he had stayed quiet while Rafael and Clemente joked and laughed—neither, he believed, had ever been inside a restaurant even as nice as the mundane Las Humaderas. Gabriel maybe had a little too much tequila, but when they came out into the night, he still felt together, in control.

He felt that way right up until he saw Ignacio Bernal, one of Arturo's lieutenants, staring at him from across the street. In the yellow glow of brightly painted hotel wall, Ignacio stood with a woman—a whore, most likely, with a short skirt and fishnet stockings, bra straps showing under her skimpy top, her black hair teased out and her makeup heavily applied. Ignacio turned quickly when he spotted Gabriel looking at him, and tried to duck behind the woman. She tottered on her spike heels and had to grab Ignacio's arm for balance. Ignacio wore a Western-styled dark blue shirt with gold stripes, designer jeans, ostrich boots—his usual uniform, so even just seeing the sleeve the whore held on to gave him away. He had left the shirt untucked to hide the gun no doubt stuck in his waistband.

"What up?" Rafael asked him.

"Never mind, let's get out of here." They'd parked the truck around the corner on Avenida 2, as close a spot as they had been able to find. They weren't worried about the statue— she had shown that she could take care of herself. Gabriel grabbed on to both men, as if the tequila had just caught up to him, and tugged them toward the corner, his face turned toward the wall. He didn't want Ignacio to know for certain that he'd been seen. It would be best if Ignacio never knew for sure that he had seen Gabriel at all.

The sidewalk rose up near the corner, as if a root from some long forgotten tree had grown underneath it and buckled the concrete. Clemente tripped where two slabs joined unevenly, and Gabriel had to release Rafael to catch the big man. He got a grip under Clemente's arm and hauled him to his feet. By the time they reached the corner and Gabriel risked a glance back toward the bar entrance where Ignacio had been, he had already left.

Calling Arturo, Gabriel guessed. Arturo would have offered a reward, and Ignacio, never mind that they had shared blow together off the belly of a Las Vegas stripper in the back of Puerto Peñasco's El Principal Club, had gone to make the call that would earn him the cash.

"Come on!" Gabriel said. Clemente really was drunk. He stumbled again, but kept his footing. Gabriel would have thought the skinny one, Rafael, would show the effects first, but except for a stupid grin on his ugly face—Rafael's usual expression—he didn't seem intoxicated in the least. "We need to get out of here!"

"What's the hurry, *mi amigo*?" Rafael asked.

"You don't want to know," Gabriel said. Agua Prieta looked like a sleepy town, but it was a major transit point for Arturo's product. The man had a small army here, and Gabriel didn't look forward to a reunion.

He practically had to squeeze Clemente into his center seat and then shove Rafael in beside him. "I want to drive!" Rafael complained as Gabriel slammed his door.

Gabriel ran around to the driver's side and slid behind the wheel. "I'm driving."

"He's driving," Clemente said. He stifled a yawn. "I'm going to sleep now."

Gabriel twisted the key and grinned when the engine caught. A few blocks, that was all they needed to cover, and they would be out of town. Just a few blocks.

We can do that, he thought. I *can do that.*

3

Lulu stays in the shower until the hot water runs out. As it turns
tepid, she cranks the faucet knobs, draws back the shower curtain (green, with yellow daisies) and finds two thick towels left
folded on the toilet seat cover. The towels are also green, but a
dark green, like pine needles, instead of the lime green of the
shower curtain. Green seems to be a theme of this bathroom.
She knows Jeannie has remodeled it since moving here, strip-
ping the wood of the sink cabinet and staining it a dark forest
green, doing the same to the wood framing the mirror over the
sink. The walls have been painted a sage green that Jeannie
loves, and small, framed pastoral watercolors in complemen-
tary tones are hung on them. Standing in the tub, drying her
long hair and luxuriating in the thick softness of the towels,
Lulu understands why she went to the trouble. The room con-
nects to the outdoors, echoing a color that she is sure would be
visible through the window, in daylight. It's a pleasant, calm-
ing hue. Jeannie believes that surrounding herself with beauty
will keep the world's bad things at bay. There was a time that
Lulu might have agreed with her, but that time is past.

All she is doing, examining the bathroom in such detail, is
delaying the inevitable.

She has to face Jeannie, and Jeannie's questions. She will
have to face the police. She will have to face the fact that at
eighteen, she has suddenly become a victim, an orphan.

Tears threaten to fill her eyes again, and she fights them
back, steels herself against sorrow and fear and all the other
destructive emotions that might throw her off-balance, break
her resolve. Taking her time, she dries herself thoroughly.

Jeannie has put a sweatshirt, a pair of faded jeans and some cotton underwear on the counter beside the sink. Lulu swims in the sweatshirt and has to roll up the cuffs of the jeans several times, but Jeannie's slim waist is close enough to her size that she doesn't need a belt to hold them up. Jeannie has also left out a box of bandages, and Lulu applies them to the worst of the cuts on her feet. Borrowing a hairbrush and a tube of deodorant, she makes herself look semipresentable, even though she feels like she is rolling on knife blades.

Trying on a smile in the mirror (it feels forced, unfamiliar) she opens the door into the hallway and follows the light into the living room. Jeannie sits on her sofa with a steaming mug between her hands. A tray on the wooden coffee table holds another mug and a plate of cookies. Mesquite logs blaze in a kiva-style fireplace, scenting the air with a pleasantly smoky aroma. "Is this okay?" Jeannie asks when she emerges. "Do you need something more substantial to eat?"

"I don't think I could eat right now," Lulu says. "Thanks for the shower, though, and that tea will really hit the spot."

"I think you should drink it quick," Jeannie says, indicating a soft chair with a tick of her eyes. "I've been trying the phone, but it's still not working, and I think we need to go into McNeal and call the sheriff from there."

"Just . . . not quite yet?" Lulu answers.

"When you're ready," Jeannie says. "Sooner is better, though."

"I understand, Jeannie. Thanks."

"Can you talk about what happened? Did you escape, or did whoever had you let you go?"

"I don't mind talking about that part," Lulu says. Part of her wishes that she could have seen his face when he looked in the back of the truck and realized she had gotten away. "He kept me someplace far from here, like in a mountain cabin. But early today he decided we needed to come back here— I'm not sure why—and he drugged me and put me in his truck. I was always kept bound and blindfolded, but for the trip he tied me with rope instead of the shackles and chains that I had at the cabin."

"Who is he?" Jeannie asks.

"I have no idea. Not, like, one of your more talkative guys,
I know that much. Anyway, I didn't inhale whatever it was he
tried to dope me with, and it didn't knock me out for very
long. Made me feel sick as shit, but didn't keep me unconscious like it did that first night. So as he drove, I bounced
around in the back and worked on loosening the ropes. I guess
he wasn't a Boy Scout or anything, because I managed to get
free of them, and then I could take the blindfold off and look
around. I kept the ropes wrapped around me so whenever he
looked in back he thought, like, I was still tied up, and I kept
the blindfold over my head for the same reason. The worst
part was leaving the gag in my mouth, but he had taped that on
with duct tape and I knew if I took it off I'd never get it back
on right."

"Oh my God, Lulu! That sounds awful."

Lulu picks up a cookie—chocolate chip—and breaks off
an edge. She takes that tiny piece and snaps it again, then puts
one of the chunks in her mouth. "That's an understatement,
but it's in the right direction. The whole thing was just . . . I
don't have enough words for shitty to tell you. But today I felt
better than I had before, because I felt like I was getting somewhere. I had to find the right moment to make my break, when
he wouldn't see me and just catch me again."

"Weren't you scared?" Jeannie asks. She tucks her legs under herself. Lulu notices for the first time that Jeannie has
changed out of the Mickey Mouse T-shirt and put on a navy
sweater, blue jeans and fuzzy purple socks.

"I've been scared ever since the night he came to my
house," Lulu says. "Nonstop scared. I just kept thinking about
how much I wanted to see you guys, and Jace, and how maybe
I never would. . . . Tonight was the first time that I felt like
maybe I could do something to change my situation. Anyway,
I kept on sneaking peeks out the windows, trying to spot familiar landmarks. Finally I did, and then I got nervous all over
again, afraid that the closer I got to home, the more cautious
he'd be.

"I could tell we were driving through McNeal on 191. At

that market near the intersection with Davis Road, he stopped for gas. I played dead, laying absolutely still like I was still out cold. I guess the rope and blindfold and everything still looked convincing, because he went inside the shop to use the bathroom. As soon as I heard the front door close, I watched, praying. I could see the bathroom area, and when he went in, I opened the back, jumped out and ran for it."

"You ran all the way here from McNeal?" Jeannie asks, evidently astonished.

"Turns out it's not quite as far if you, like, keep away from the roads," Lulu says. What would it serve to tell Jeannie about how the wet grass sliced into her bare legs, the mesquite thorns ripped her flesh, the unseen stones shredded the bottoms of her feet, the mud tried to suck her down, the cold wind and rain punished her; or about the aching in her lungs that she had to run though, the terror that knifed into her every time headlights swept by on the road? Her friend feels bad enough for her already, and she doesn't want to make that worse. "I cut across fields. In the dark, even if he noticed I was gone right away, he couldn't have found me."

"You were taking a big chance, though."

"Not as big as staying with him would have been. He would never have let me go alive, I know that for a fact."

"Why didn't you just go to the nearest house and call the police?" Jeannie asks. To Lulu, her expression looks curious, not judgmental.

"He's . . . I don't know how to describe him. He's scary, and I think he knows things that . . . that he has no way to really know. Like he's psychic or something. I know it sounds crazy, Jeannie, but there's something about him that's different and strange, and I was afraid if I stopped anywhere close by, he'd find me right away, and maybe kill whoever tried to protect me."

Jeannie sips from her mug, her eyes watching Lulu from over the rim.

"I know," Lulu says, "so now you're thinking, like, thanks for leading him here. I just didn't know where else to go. I knew in my heart that there was . . . that Mommy and Dad and

the boys . . ." She presses her knees together, digs at her eyes
with the balls of her thumbs. If she starts to cry now, she
might never stop. "Anyway," she says after a while. "Now you
know why I'm not so anxious to go back toward McNeal. He's
out there someplace, looking for me."

"I understand, Lulu. Believe me, I've been terrified for
you, so I know you've got to be just about frantic. But we can't
stay here. Maybe we can go toward Douglas, at least far
enough to pick up a signal on my cell phone."

Lulu likes that idea better. At the back of her mind, like a
partially remembered fantasy, the white girl tugs at her, reminding her that she has to get down to the border. Douglas is
the right direction; McNeal isn't. She doesn't want to tell
Jeannie about that whole business, however. Not only would it
be too hard to explain, but doing so might endanger Jeannie, if
he found out somehow that she knew. "Okay," she says. "Let's
head for Douglas."

Jeannie leaves to find Lulu shoes and socks. Since Lulu's
feet are two sizes smaller, she returns with three pairs of socks
and some white sneakers with red and white laces. Lulu pulls
on the two pairs of white athletic socks—the plush cotton cra-
dles her wounded feet gently—and as she slips on the pink
anklets over those, she glances out the window and sees headlights bouncing through the front gate.

"Oh God, Jeannie!" she shouts. "Oh God, he's here!"

4

Although at first blush it seemed as if the world had turned
against him, in fact, the night wasn't all bad. The cop's death
had given him an almost erotic thrill at the instant that it happened, though he was miles away. During his travels he had
set up similar little surprises all across the country. Every now
and then he allowed himself to be arrested for some minor
transgression so that one or another of his addresses would
wind up in the system. Making sure that cops everywhere had
access to his information—as much as he wanted them to
have, at any rate—was time-consuming and maybe slightly
dangerous, but as long as it paid benefits like this—random,
unexpected thrills of delight—then all that effort was worth-
while.

Still, he had to keep track of Lulu Lavender. Tonight, he
was more and more convinced, was the night. The white girl
would cross the border, and he would meet her and take her
power for his own. Without meaning to, Lulu would lead him
to her. She would never have voluntarily taken him, he had
decided. But she thought she had escaped. As if he couldn't
even control his own bladder and had to use gas station bath-
rooms. She had struck out into the tempestuous night, never
dreaming that she would guide him exactly where he wanted
to go.

Lulu had proven more of a challenge than he'd ever expected, to be sure. She didn't know the extent of her own powers and abilities, but the white girl wouldn't have chosen her if
she weren't suitable. Maybe she was a descendant of the original model; he would never know for sure. He only knew that

he had underestimated her, at first, but he wouldn't anymore. She could be formidable.

She could also be just the ticket he needed to the future he wanted and deserved.

That was his plan, anyway. And no matter what her potential might be, *he* had long since passed the potential stage.

Before the sun rose again, he would have moved beyond his own current stage as well, into uncharted territory, knowing strength that no other human being ever had.

And Lulu, whether she knew it or not, would take him there.

5

Oliver didn't break any speed records, except his own—given
the weather and visibility, or lack thereof, trying to would
have been close to suicidal, and while anxiety nagged at him,
he had not lost all reason—but he drove faster than was entirely safe, sloshing through those "Do Not Enter When
Flooded" dips even when the water came up to the green Subaru's floorboards, and as his tires shimmied through the mud
into his own driveway, an hour and ten minutes after talking
with Stan, he was surprised to see so many lights on inside the
house.

The rain had tapered off here, but it had come down long
and hard enough to leave the driveway soupy. He parked as
close as he could to the house and dashed to the overhang,
leaving his briefcase in the car for now. He had tried calling
Jeannie off and on, whenever he had cell service, and had not
been able to get through. What had happened in the only other
house on their road alone would have been enough to send
him rushing home. *Be okay be okay be okay,* he thought as he
drove. The scariest time of his life had been in the weeks after
the whole Vivian affair blew up, when he hadn't known for
sure if Jeannie would stay or go. That fear had begun to fade
when she agreed to move to Arizona with him, but it had never
vanished completely.

That fear was totally eclipsed by his worry tonight, unable
to reach her by phone.

Added to that, however, was his concern over what Stan
had told him about Lulu's blog. When not driving one-handed
trying to reach Jeannie, he tried to reach Buck Shelton, with

the same lack of success. Had his overwhelming impulse not been to get home and make sure Jeannie was all right, he would have detoured to Elfrida and stopped by the sheriff's office there.

The front door was locked. That was new—until the mass murder down the road, they had only occasionally remembered to lock their doors at night. So far out of town, so isolated, the danger of break-ins seemed distant compared to what it had been in Southern California. Oliver dug into his pocket, brought out keys. On the third try his shaking hands managed to get the correct one into the lock. He turned it, twisted the knob and shoved open the door. "Jeannie!"

In the living room, Jeannie and Lulu stood (Lulu in ill-fitting clothes Oliver knew to be his wife's) pointing kitchen knives at him.

Laughing, Oliver figured, would be the worst possible response he could have.

At the same time, it was the one that erupted from him first.

"You two are terrifying!" he said when he could speak. "I'm glad I belong here."

"Oliver!" Jeannie shouted. "Do you find something amusing about us?"

He pocketed the keys and went to her, wrapping his arms around her unyielding frame. "No," he said. "Well, a little. Mostly I'm just relieved, you know? That you're okay, and Lulu . . ." He released Jeannie and turned to the younger girl, who launched herself against him. He caught her, squeezing tightly. "Lulu, I'm so glad to see you! Are you okay?"

"I am now, Oliver," she said. "I was so scared, but Jeannie took good care of me and now you're here and I know everything will be all right."

"We thought you were the creep who kidnapped her," Jeannie explained. A blush had crept up her neck and pinked her cheeks, and she twined her fingers together the way she did when she was embarrassed. Oliver hoped she didn't slice herself open on the knife she still held.

"I was working around to that." He released Lulu from the

hug but held on to her slender arms. "So you got away from him? He isn't in custody?"

"Or even, you know, dead," Lulu said. "Which, to be honest, would have been my first choice."

"Have you called Buck?"

"The phone's been dead," Jeannie said. "The storm—"

"Or you hope it's the storm," Oliver said. "And not him."

"We thought of that too," Jeannie said. "But then you showed up."

"I think we should get out of here," he urged. "We can go up to Elfrida, or—"

"No!" Lulu said, emphatic. "We can't go that way!"

"That's the direction he was last time she saw him," Jeannie explained.

"Okay, down into Douglas then. There's a sheriff's office there, and the Douglas police."

"That's fine," Lulu said, glancing away from him. He caught the motion and knew it meant something, although he didn't know what.

"On the way," he said, "you can tell me what you know about the statue of the white girl, and how it ties into Cabeza de Vaca, and what it's all got to do with you."

"It sounds like you know more than me," Lulu said. "Maybe you should do the explaining."

"Maybe I should. I have a feeling we both have a lot to tell each other."

With Lulu in the backseat and Jeannie next to him in the front, Oliver drove again, even though it felt like he had been driving all night. He told them about what Stan Gilfredson had said, all about the white girl, the statue carved by Estevan of the Cabeza de Vaca expedition, the commonplace acceptance of magic in Mexico. In return, Lulu told him what she had already described to Jeannie—and more, he suspected, from Jeannie's responses to details like the fact that the guy had killed a woman who tried to help her, and left her body in the same room she was kept in—of her captivity and escape.

As surprising as that was, it paled in comparison to the next thing she said. "We don't have time to go to the police, Oliver. We need to get down to the border."

"The border?"

"Yes," Lulu said. "She's almost there. I have to meet her."

He tried to see her eyes in the rearview mirror, wondering if she was in shock from her experience, or having some sort of psychotic episode. She leaned against the seat back, however, and he couldn't make out her eyes in the shadows. "Are you sure?" he asked.

"*Yes,*" Lulu said. Her tone made a declaration of urgency. "We have to get there now. We might already be too late."

"Do you know where?"

"*Oliver,*" Jeannie said.

"There's stuff going on here we don't understand," Oliver said. "I think we have to assume she knows what she's talking about."

"But we have to tell the sheriff that she's okay," Jeannie reminded him.

"We could tell Buck on the phone, if he'd ever answer. Keep trying him, and if we don't get him in the next couple of minutes, just call 911."

"When we hit Fifteenth Street, go left," Lulu said from in back. "Toward New Mexico. She's coming east of town."

She spoke with absolute certitude, and Oliver wasn't inclined to doubt her. While Jeannie kept trying Buck, he followed Lulu's directions, turning away from town instead of toward it.

He hoped he wasn't making a huge mistake.

6

A Klaxon that Barry had never noticed sounded throughout the ranch complex. Carl's followers responded like firefighters. No one swore at the deafening din. Instead, businesslike, a bit tense, they all stubbed out smokes and abandoned drinks, hurrying to their barracks. They returned to the big common room just minutes later clad in camos, strapping on gun belts. It felt, Barry thought, more like a military operation than the military had been, in the hellish stew of Vietnam.

Whatever Carl had been talking about earlier, the night's big event, he guessed it had arrived.

He didn't have camos to change into, or a room to do it in, except for Connie's. And he hadn't seen her since she had brought him back to the ranch after he'd killed the Mexican guy. After a few minutes, however, she showed up in the common room with everyone else. She had put on an olive-drab ribbed top with a high neck and long, tight sleeves, and camo fatigue pants like the others. On her feet she wore heavy black work boots. A webbed belt around her hips held a black holster with a flap; steel showed under the flap, but Barry couldn't tell if it was the gun he had used.

Noticing his stare, she tossed him a friendly smile. He didn't return it, couldn't think of anything he might want to say to her. Especially here, now, with her flanked by her comrades, everyone armed. *And me just a sucker, I guess, getting used by people smarter than me.*

Carl entered then, before the moment got any more awkward. "Fall out, people!" he shouted, sounding then just like Barry's old DI from Parris Island. "Trucks are waiting in front!"

The assemblage shouted a "Hoo hah!" and ran in formation out of the room, down the hall toward the door. When they were gone, only Carl remained.

"You ready for this, Barry?" Carl asked with a warm smile. He touched Barry's upper arm. "This is the real thing, bud."

"Ready as I'm gonna be, I guess."

"That's good. Come on, then," Carl said. "You're riding with me and Connie."

"Okay."

Carl led him toward the same black Expedition in which he had first visited the ranch. Marc, as usual, sat behind the wheel. An olive-drab T-shirt hugged his muscular arms. Connie had already settled in back. Carl motioned Barry in beside her, then slid in and closed the door. "Go," he said.

Without a word, Marc complied.

As the SUV jounced along a primitive road toward the border, Carl leaned toward Barry. "You know what I told you back there?"

Barry nodded. "Wasn't that long ago."

"Now that we're out here, I can let you in on a little more."

"What's that?"

"Have you ever heard of a succubus?"

Barry tried to scan his memory for the word. "No," he said, glancing at Connie. She just smiled and stroked his arm. "What is it?"

"Never mind," Carl said. "That's not exactly what she is anyway, but there's no closer word in English. Thing is, everything we've been telling you, about the threat from Mexican migrants, is true. But there's more that we haven't told you. It'll be hard to believe, but hopefully by now you know you can trust us."

"I ain't sure what to trust anymore," Barry admitted.

"You can trust Carl," Connie whispered. Hearing her say the words, so close to his ear he could feel her warm breath, he wanted to trust her. He couldn't, in fact, remember why he shouldn't.

"It's all true, like I said, but it's even worse than we told you. There's something happening tonight, like I mentioned, and if it doesn't go the way we want it to, it could open the door to America losing all of Arizona to the Mexicans. Other states too. What would the good old USA look like without California, Texas and everything in between?"

"What are you talkin' about?" Barry asked. "They got an army or something comin' this way?"

"They don't need an army," Carl replied. "They have magic."

Barry wasn't sure he'd heard correctly. "They have what?"

"I know what it sounds like," Carl said. "Believe me. It sounds fucking nuts. But you know, I can't sugarcoat it for you. You've seen and done things these last few days you'd never have believed, so this shouldn't be that much harder to credit."

"But . . ." Barry didn't know what else to say. Carl was right; it sounded crazy. At the same time, Connie rubbed his arm and her hot breath blew on his neck and they rolled along with a small army of their own headed toward the border, so what should he think? Every thought he had was crowded out by the next one that landed right beside it, and he couldn't get a grasp on any of them, trying to was like fishing for minnows with greased hands.

"And I'm a magician too," Carl added.

"I haven't seen you do any tricks."

"Are you sure? You never wondered how I found you at that bar, or why you came with me, or why you stayed?"

Actually, he had wondered about those things. He had convinced himself that it was all happenstance, the right two people bumping into each other at the right time. *Maybe not, though.* Maybe Carl spoke the truth now. It was just too hard to know for sure. Too hard to know anything for sure. Believing Carl and Connie felt like the easiest thing to do.

He decided not to fight it. "Okay, I guess you're right."

"Reason I'm telling you this, Barry, I want to be absolutely clear. When we're out there, you do what I say. No hesitation, no questions, no doubts, okay?"

"I guess."

"Not good enough."

"Okay, Carl. I'll do what you say."

Carl chuckled dryly. "Actually, it's not like you could do otherwise at this point if you wanted to. You will do what you're told—it's just you'll be more efficient about it if you don't try to fight against it. You hesitate, you could be killed out there. We all could. You, Connie, me, everyone. It comes down to you doing what you're told; I want to know you'll do it."

"Doesn't sound like I have a choice," Barry said.

"Not so much," Carl said. "When you put it like that, not so much choice at all."

7

Scoot Brown drove through the night, nervous, his fingers tap-
ping on the steering wheel in a pattern that Buck eventually
came to realize must be from video game play. Buck looked
away from his long, slender fingers at the rest of him: skinny,
from the shoulders up he was all neck and nose, with a bulbous Adam's apple and a beak to match. Scoot noticed he was
being watched and swallowed anxiously. "You call your wife
yet?"

"Shit," Buck said, remembering. "I turned off my cell before we made the entry back there, and in all the excitement,
you know, with Raul and being Cheneyed and all, I forgot to
turn it back on."

He had not called Tammy, and didn't know that he wanted
to. She often fell back on the cliché about how the Lord
worked in mysterious ways. If she had been praying for his
safety, could her prayers have put Raul in front of him at the
doorway? Had Raul taken a load meant for him? He didn't
want to dignify that theory by worrying about it.

Instead, he retrieved his phone and turned it on. By the
time it powered up, it had started ringing. The display told
him that the caller was Gina Castaneda. He pressed the button
to answer. "Gina?"

"Buck, thank God. I'm sorry to call so late; I hope I'm not
waking you or anything."

"No. What's going on?"

"I'm probably on your shit list, huh? I really did want to do
a bigger story on your missing girl, but my producer wouldn't

let me. He thinks the Lippincott girl is what everyone's interested in."

"What I figured." He didn't want to be short with her, but at the moment he had other things on his mind.

"The reason I'm bothering you now, Buck, I'm trying to confirm a rumor we're hearing. I'll tell you up front, Sheriff Gatlin's office won't comment yet. I don't need you to go on the record, just to let me know if it's worth trying to chase this down."

"I've been busy with my own case, Gina. Haven't really heard much about the Lippincott one, but I'll help if I can. What's your rumor?"

"That Vic Lippincott really did leave a note," Gina said. "Or if not a note, then financial records—I've heard it both ways. Either way, what it amounts to is that Lippincott was laundering money for a Mexican drug cartel through his bank. I guess the implication is that something went haywire and Elayne got snatched as a result. All this time he must have been trying to negotiate some kind of deal, but I'm guessing it didn't go. Maybe they showed him what happened to her, I don't know. But he killed himself rather than face what he'd done."

Buck gave a low whistle. "I haven't heard any of that, Gina. Like I said, I've had quite a night going myself." He ran through the night in his head, trying to see if he could tell her anything. He couldn't, though; except for losing one of his best officers and having to squeeze buckshot out of his own face on the ride down the valley, he was pretty much back where he'd started.

"I've got it from two sources, but like I said, nothing official. I also have a source inside the bank who confirms that there's something funky about some of their records. Word is the FBI is coming in to go through it all. I don't have to tell you what it would mean for a local news organization to beat out the big networks on this, Buck."

"Makes sense," Buck said. "I wish I could help you, Gina, but—"

His phone made a double beep, telling him another call was coming in. "I should take this, Gina. I get anything solid, I'll let you know." He disconnected and answered the other call. "Buck Shelton."

"Lieutenant, thank God I finally got you. It's Jeannie Bowles."

"My phone's been off, Jeannie. What can I do for you?"

"We have Lulu," she said.

He thought he'd heard correctly, but needed to make sure. A flash of lightning illuminated Scoot's anxious face, gaze fixed on the road ahead. "Say that again?"

"Lulu escaped and came to our house," Jeannie said. "She's fine. Physically, I mean."

"She's there now?"

"No, we're on our way down to the border. It's complicated."

Complicated? Sounded damn near impossible to Buck. "You can't do that," he said. "She's got to get medical attention. I've got to— Can I talk to her?"

"Sure, hang—"

Buck heard Oliver say something, then the man's voice came over the phone. "Buck, it's Oliver. I'm glad you're back in contact. This whole thing has gotten just a little strange."

"A little? Your wife tells me you're taking Lulu to Mexico."

"Not to Mexico, just to the border."

"The Port of Entry in Douglas?"

"No," Oliver said. "East of town."

Buck wished that *Star Trek*'s transporter was reality so he could teleport through the phone and throttle somebody. "Mind telling me why?"

"Lulu insists. It's all part of what I'm talking about, part of the strangeness. I don't think trying to explain over the phone is going to work. Can you meet us down there?"

"If you think you're taking Lulu Lavender anywhere near the border without me crawling up your ass, you're powerfully mistaken, Oliver."

"Wouldn't have it any other way, Buck."

"Meantime, unless you're worried about roaming minutes or something, why don't you try explaining anyway?"

He heard a loud sigh. "I assume you're sitting down?"

"I'll be on my ass until you see me walking toward you," Buck said. "So start talking."

8

Instead of going to the border crossing, Gabriel piloted the Toy-ota truck out of town, heading east. The turns seemed to be plotted in his head, like a map that hovered just in front of the windshield. The streets were dark out here, black with water that ran across them in sheets. Although the rain had let up, he kept the wipers going to bat away the spray that blew up onto the glass.

For the first couple of minutes he thought he had left Ignacio—or whichever of Arturo's soldiers drove a dark blue Lexus SUV—far behind. But as he skidded around corners and gunned down the straightaways, he caught sight of head-lights behind them. Sometimes they fell back, but then they charged on. After a couple of fast turns they were still there, and he knew it was no coincidence.

"They're chasing us," he said.

"Who is?" Rafael asked.

Clemente woke mid-snore, gave a snort and coughed wetly. "What?"

"Some people who work for the man I used to work for." He wrenched the wheel to the left, swerving around a mangy dog that had stepped suddenly into the street and spraying a plume of muddy water onto a steel fence. "He's pissed at me."

"What will he do?"

"To me? I don't want to know. It won't be pleasant, and it'll end up with vultures picking my bones clean out in the desert somewhere. He doesn't know you two, so you might get away with a clean shot to the back of the head."

Rafael swore softly while Clemente said something Gabriel

couldn't understand, probably in whatever Indian tongue was his native language. Gabriel knew the only thing keeping him alive was the statue in back, showing him the turns he had to take before they came up. If he'd had to try to find his own way out of the city, he would certainly have run into a dead end by now, or turned into traffic, or had his way blocked by a truck or slow-moving tractor or cart. Instead, each road he came to was open before him, with small exceptions like the dog he had so narrowly missed.

They had left downtown A.P. behind and passed through a suburban neighborhood. Large, luxurious homes stood cheek by jowl with tiny ones, and on one large lot a half-finished mansion stood like a corpse with half its skin flayed off. Mexico's economy was fucked, Gabriel believed, and as long as the cartels ruled the courts and the police and huge swaths of the government, as long as a tiny percentage owned most of the nation's wealth and hid from their own countrymen inside walled compounds, it would likely remain that way. He had just hoped to get a piece of it while he could, and then he'd given up that dream for a new one in which transporting a statue could somehow help all his people.

Those headlights rose up behind again, the Lexus's better tires and four-wheel drive finding purchase that the old Toyota couldn't on the wet road. He tried to squeeze more speed out of it, stomping on the accelerator, lifting his butt from the seat and leaning forward as if riding a balky mule. Gabriel thought he heard a shot, but it might have been thunder; the muzzle flash in his mirror could have been distant lightning.

Then another, unmistakable because a bullet slammed into the truck. *Probably hit the tailgate,* Gabriel thought, but he couldn't be sure. He heard the impact, felt it like ice on an exposed dental nerve.

"They shot at us!" Rafael said. Gabriel believed the stupid grin had finally vanished from his face, but in the dark it was hard to tell.

"Yes," Gabriel said. He clenched his teeth and twisted the wheel sharply left, launching the truck into another skid-sliding turn. Unrolling the window, he fished the nine-mil from his shoulder holster. To aim at the Lexus, he had to hold the gun across his chest and out the window, since the statue in back would block any shots through the rear window. He got off one shot, but then the truck lurched over an uneven spot in the road and the gun flew from his hand. He swore and rolled the window back up.

The map that he saw in his mind's eye changed, confusing him for a moment. He had thought he'd stay on this road, twisty as it was, until he was past the residential neighborhood. Instead, the map directed him to do the impossible: to drive through a ramshackle trailer/shed combination. "Crazy," he said.

"What?" Clemente asked.

"This." Gabriel had no interest in arguing with the lady in back of the truck. If she wanted to smash into someone's home, that was her privilege. He waited, holding his breath, until the time came. Another shot sounded, this one missing. Finally, he made another hard left, leaving the road, lurching over a yard of broken concrete and loose gravel.

"Aieee!" Clemente shouted, grabbing at Gabriel's arm. Gabriel shook the man's grip loose—the last thing he needed just now was the fool pulling him off course. He corrected slightly. The trailer, once white with a brown slash across it, but now sun-faded, weathered and dirty, rose up immediately ahead of them. Then his lights picked up what the map in his head hadn't shown clearly—a gap between the trailer and the wooden shed, maybe six feet wide. A single board slanted from the shed to the trailer, connecting the two. Another minute correction. He could thread the needle, but he couldn't miss the board. At seventy, he plowed through it, splintering wood against the top of his windshield. Then he rocketed through the gap and out the other side, onto another muddy road. The map told him to turn right, and he did.

Behind them, the shed—apparently held up by the board linking it to the trailer—collapsed into the gap, just as the Lexus tried to fit through. The driver of the Lexus must have instinctively twitched his wheel to the right, because Gabriel heard an impact and actually saw the trailer shudder on its blocks when the SUV hit it.

Gabriel heaved a great sigh. His internal map showed the border not too far away now, and with Arturo's soldiers out of action there shouldn't be anything preventing him from making it there.

Then he glanced up and saw the two full-sized pickup trucks barreling his way.

9

"Stop!"

Oliver punched down on the brake pedal, and the Outback came to a skidding halt. Lulu had called out in the proverbial middle of nowhere. Through clouds that had thinned and parted in spots, an edge of moon shone onto a rugged, boulder-strewn landscape of spiky yucca plants, tangled mesquites, shorter shrubs and grass. Geronimo Trail was dirt—mud now—and barely wide enough for two vehicles to pass each other without scraping sides. Oliver hoped the car didn't sink into the muck while they were stopped here.

"Where are we, Lulu?" Jeannie asked.

"I have no idea. All I know is this is where she wants me to be. Or as close as we can get on the road, anyway."

"So what?" Oliver asked. "We get out and walk?"

Lulu opened her door. The dome light came on, and in its glow he could see that she no longer looked afraid, or sad, or lost, all of which she had when he found her in his house. Instead, her gaze was steady, her forehead wrinkled in the middle above her nose, and she worried at her lower lip with her teeth. Her long hair had been tied back in a ponytail that had flopped onto her left shoulder. He found the expression familiar, and realized that it was the one she wore in class when she felt particularly sure of an answer or easily whipped though an exam. Confidence, determination, drive—these played across her face, replacing those other, less helpful emotions. "I'm walking," she said. "You guys don't have to come."

"Of course I'm coming," Oliver said quickly, unwilling to let her out of his sight now that she had come home. "You can stay with the car, Jeannie, to tell Buck which way we went when he gets here."

He and Jeannie had been together long enough that when she gave him her sidelong you-must-be-kidding look, he didn't have to ask for translation. "Tell him yourself," she said. "Leave a pile of rocks or carve notches in the trees or something. Just don't imagine you're leaving me alone in this car out here, because if you do, honey, you're only fooling yourself."

There remained, Oliver knew, a killer on the loose, who presumably wanted to find Lulu again. Oliver didn't think they had been followed—and if the killer had known she was at the Bowles house, he would probably have made his move before they took off.

Unless, he thought as a tickle ran up the back of his neck, *whatever it is that Lulu thinks is drawing her here is what he's really interested in.*

Lulu perched on the edge of the seat, her legs hanging out, anxious to go. Moths, drawn by the dome light, flitted excitedly around the ceiling. "If we're going, we should go," Oliver said.

Lulu didn't hesitate another second. She jumped into the mud and slammed her door. Jeannie's gaze caught Oliver's for a moment, but this time he couldn't begin to read it. When she turned away, he felt rebuked, as if there were something he should have said or done but failed to. Then they were both out of the car, and he slipped across the road and into the desert on the other side, following the women.

Lulu seemed to know where she was going, although she didn't explain how. She struck off cross-country, then found a wide, sandy wash with three-foot banks, leading vaguely southeast, and took that. A trickle of water ran along the wash's bottom. Oliver knew there was a risk that the trickle could become, with very little notice, a torrential flash flood. As long as the banks were low, they could scramble out when it came, but if the wash led into the rocks or cut deeper into the earth, he would have to recommend that they hike alongside it, just in case. Plenty of potential existed for a bad outcome to this night's adventure—he didn't want to add the avoidable *drowning in a flash flood* to the list.

Without the rain, the night seemed quiet. The wind rasped through branches and leaves, and he heard the occasional flutter of a bird, startled by their approach, even thunder crackling off to the north and east. But in the car in the rain for so long he had become accustomed to the steady percussion, and without it the air felt still even though it patently was not.

"Where are we going?" he asked after they had walked for a while.

"I don't know," Lulu said. "I'm just going where she says. And before you say I'm nuts, I know it sounds crazy. I can't explain *how* I know what she wants. I just do."

"Well, we're following you," Oliver pointed out. "So even if we were inclined to cast aspersions on your mental health, we wouldn't have much ground to stand on."

"And what ground there is is soaking through my Reeboks," Jeannie said. *At least she wore jeans and sneakers,* Oliver thought. He hadn't changed since his trip, and still had on dress slacks and shirt, his navy blazer and three-hundred-dollar leather Mephisto shoes, all of which were being torn by thorns and caked in mud.

He thought it best not to mention his sartorial distress. Instead he said, "We must be getting close to the border."

"Seems like it," Jeannie agreed.

A steep hill loomed in the west, blocking the moon-marbled sky in that direction. Farther south Oliver could see the shadowed outlines of others, but the wash led into a broad valley that sloped gently south, with the larger hills only at its edges. He guessed he was looking straight into Mexico—the far mountains were definitely over the line, and the one to his left probably straddled it. Here, the water had mostly soaked in or run off; hard, pebbled earth crunched under his shoes.

Ahead, Lulu stopped. She stood tense, poised, as if listening to something. *Voices in her head,* Oliver thought. But after a few seconds he heard it too—the growl of motors, coming toward them. Coming fast. And something else, that at this distance sounded almost like coughs. *Is that gunfire?*

"We'd better get down!" he said. He pushed past Jeannie,

grabbed Lulu's arm. "Lulu! Let's take cover until we know what's going on here!"

"But . . ."

He dragged her back to Jeannie, then took her arm as well. "Behind that mesquite," he said, pointing with his chin. "Let's just hunker down there and see what's what."

They went along with him, and the three of them took cover behind the spreading, twisted branches of a big, old mesquite. Anyone who trained a light right on it would see them, but he hoped it would provide sufficient cover otherwise.

They huddled there while the engine sounds grew louder, sometimes whisked away by gusts of wind blowing from the east, clacking the branches and swishing the grass, but when the gusts died the noise returned, more distinct than before. In another few minutes, three sets of headlights hove into view. Oliver didn't think they were on a road; the beams lanced up into the sky, then down, right and then left, like the skis of an acrobatic skier twisting and turning in midair. The first set was a good distance ahead of the two others. Bright flashes of light came from the rear vehicles, accompanied by more of those coughing sounds.

"Someone's being chased," Jeannie said.

"By somebody with guns," Oliver said. "This is not good at all. Are you sure this is where you're supposed to be, Lulu? Those could be drug smugglers, being chased by the *federales* or something."

"I thought the *federales* worked for the smugglers," Lulu replied. "More likely the local police being chased by *federales*. Or *coyotes* being chased by all of them."

"Either way, they've got guns and they're using them. I think we should get out of here while we can."

"You guys go," Lulu said. "I have to stay here."

"We don't go anywhere without you," Oliver said. "So just put that out of your head right now."

He felt Jeannie's gaze on him but still couldn't read it. Was she surprised at him? Angry? Impressed? It could have been any of those, or all at once. He kept his own eyes locked on Lulu, trying to discern if she was thinking this through clearly.

If she was in shock, hallucinating, he wanted to know it now while they could still hope to get away.

On the other hand, the fact that the three vehicles continued roaring up the Mexican high desert plain toward them indicated that *something* was happening here, or would be soon. Maybe not a good something, but something just the same.

As they came closer, he saw, etched in the headlight beams of the first vehicle, a tall barbed-wire fence. The vehicle—a pickup truck, he could make out now—kept coming, straight toward it. Without seeming to slow, it tore into the fence, then through it. It advanced what looked like a few more feet, then came to a sudden stop next to a bulky rock outcropping, the headlights dying at the same time as the engine, as if it had undergone a massive systems failure.

Behind it, the same thing happened to the other two trucks. The wind died for a few seconds, and Oliver heard squeaking doors, slams, shouts and the cracks of gunfire, louder than before.

"Any of those the white girl you're looking for, Lulu?" Oliver asked.

Her lips were parted, her eyes wide and liquid, and in the moonlight her cheeks looked flushed. "I don't know," she said, her voice a breath, the merest hint of a whisper. "I just don't know." She paused. She couldn't look away from the trucks. "I think I have to get closer."

That, Oliver thought, *is just about as bad as an idea can be.*

10

At Buck's insistence, Scoot Brown flipped on lights and siren and leaned on the accelerator, racing down 191 at more than a hundred, spraying sheets of water off the side of the highway. Buck had only gone as fast on this road once before, when an armed robber in a stolen car had led law enforcement on a high-speed chase that eventually involved twelve vehicles. The chase had ended on a wide curve when the guy just hadn't been able to keep his car on the road and flipped into a rancher's field, startling the shit, quite literally, out of a handful of cows that had been peacefully grazing there.

This time, because of the hour and the weather, traffic was light. The few vehicles they did encounter pulled over at their approach. Scoot cast a longing glance at the Elfrida station as they raced past, but didn't mention the bathroom inside or the fact that Buck had been on duty since morning, was wounded and bleeding from the face, and could probably use some medical attention. Buck didn't like the fact that informing Raul's family and girlfriend would be delayed, but Raul was gone and Lulu, for the moment, still lived. He wanted to make sure it stayed that way.

Where 191 hit Highway 80, beside the Motor Vehicles Division, Scoot hung a screeching, high-speed left, barely maintaining control over the SUV. "Easy, son," Buck said. "Won't do anybody any good if we're dead when we get there."

Scoot nodded and kept driving, through the red light at Pan American and into town, following the directions Oliver had given Buck. They passed through Douglas on Fifteenth Street, then stayed on it when it became Geronimo Trail, a rutted dirt

road that ran toward the Perilla Mountains that abutted the
borderline. Their headlights swept over barbed wire and rolling
pastureland, then the barbed wire fell behind them and the
landscape took on a rougher, untamed aspect. "We ain't going
to Mexico, are we, Buck?" Scoot asked.

"Not that I know of," Buck answered. "But Bowles has
been out of signal range on his cell for a while now, so I figure
we'll either stop when we see his car or when we hit the Gulf
of Mexico."

Scoot glanced over nervously. "That's a joke, right?"

"It's a joke, Scoot. We'll know if we reach the border, and
we won't cross the line. That'd be illegal."

Scoot looked like he was going to say something else, but
he swallowed it back and focused on keeping the Yukon on the
road. After another fifteen minutes or so, a green Subaru
appeared in their headlight beams.

"That's it!" Buck said. "Pull in behind it."

"Looks empty," Scoot observed.

"They've gotta be somewhere around." Before Scoot had
stopped the Yukon on the edge of the narrow road, Buck
opened his door and stepped into the muck. When the engine
noise stopped and the wind slackened, he heard a sound from
the south like someone raggedly ripping a giant sheet of aluminum foil.

"What's that?" Scoot asked.

"Small arms fire," Buck said. "Sounds like full auto."

"This guy Bowles own a machine gun?"

"Far as I know he doesn't even own a cap gun," Buck said.
"I think he's one of those pacifist types."

"Someone's shooting an automatic weapon at him, it's
gonna take a big peace symbol to keep him safe."

"We're the cops," Buck reminded him. "That's our job. Call
for backup."

He snatched the Remington 12-gauge from the vehicle,
clicked on his Maglite and ran toward the noise. A couple
minutes later he spotted Scoot behind him, his own flashlight
beam bobbing and dipping.

After ten minutes at full gallop, his face burning from the

wind, lungs ragged, legs thrashed by the brush, Buck reached
a point at which he could see the muzzle flashes from the
guns. He stopped short, thumbed off his flashlight and raised
a warning arm to Scoot. When the deputy pulled up alongside
him, Buck pressed down on his shoulder and they both lowered to a crouch.

"Can you tell what's going on?" Scoot asked.

Buck had been in the process of trying to determine just
that.

Fortunately the thinning clouds allowed more moonlight to
limn the scene. The gunfire came from people who had taken
up positions behind two trucks, and seemed to be directed toward a third truck a hundred yards or so ahead of the first two.
At this distance, Buck couldn't tell who any of the people involved were. He only hoped that Lulu and the Bowles couple
were not the targets.

"Let's move up," he whispered. "Stay low and keep your
light off until we're close enough to do some good."

"Right," Scoot agreed. Buck caught a quiver in his voice.
He didn't blame the kid. He was scared too, scared and in
pain. Each spot where the shot had entered his flesh burned
again, as if someone poked at him with a burning incense
stick. He dug some loose Advil tablets from his pocket and
dry-swallowed them, then started forward, hunched over. He
kept his right index finger pressed against the cold steel trigger guard of the Remington, ready to slip it inside if he
needed to.

He hoped it wouldn't be necessary, but more and more it
looked like that hope would be in vain.

11

The trucks rumbled down the graded all-weather Border Road, slowing about every fifty yards to let soldiers out, two at a time. They carried long guns and moved with military precision, taking up positions across the road from the tall border fence made from Vietnam-era landing mat. Whatever else Carl might have been—and at this point Barry recognized that could be a long list of things—he seemed to be a good drill instructor, or at least a skilled noncom. His men were efficient and did as they were told, neither of which had always been true back in Vietnam.

The black Expedition had joined the line behind the two trucks. The farther from the ranch they got, the worse the road became. The landing mat fence fell away and only seven-string barbed wire, cut or pushed down in spots, marked the boundary line. Every now and then Carl leaned out his open window and shouted "Hold the line!" to the soldiers, who responded with thumbs-up signs or grim-faced nods. To Barry it looked like they all knew they would potentially face combat tonight, like this was much more than a drill.

He wondered how much they knew about the things Carl had told him earlier, about magic and whatnot. He realized that he was having a hard time keeping a grasp on it himself; it slipped out of his mind like water through cupped hands no matter how hard he tried to hang on to it.

Finally, after the trucks had emptied their passengers and returned to the ranch, Marc brought the Expedition to a halt. Connie and Carl opened their doors at the same time and slid outside into the wind and rain, which had lessened to a mere sprinkle. Carl opened the back and pulled out three automatic rifles. He handed one to Connie and put one in Barry's hands. "M-16A2," he said. "You know how to use it, right?"

"Lot different from the last gun I fired," Barry said. "Think I can figure it out though." The weapon was lightweight, shaped like a dagger, wide at the buttstock and tapering to the muzzle, except where the handguard stuck out. He turned it in his hands, pointing it toward the ground, and wrapped his trigger finger around the guard. "Looks like a nice weapon."

"Three-second bursts in semi-auto," Carl said. "Thirty rounds in the magazine. That should be adequate for our needs."

Since Barry didn't know what their needs might entail, he simply nodded.

Marc took a fourth weapon from the back and closed the door. "What we're doing here, Barry," Carl said, "is setting up a perimeter. In this case, the perimeter line is the border. Anyone crosses it gets to deal with us. We aren't law enforcement and we don't have the power to arrest, and the weapons are, of course, strictly for self-defense. But if I'm right—and I think I am—then we'll be needing them tonight."

Even with his fatigues, Marc wore his straw cowboy hat and his mirrored sunglasses. He held an unlit cigarette between his lips and clenched it with his teeth when he smiled. "Surely do hope so," he said. "Been a long time since I shot anything smarter than a whitetail. Deer's got good ears and a decent sniffer, but it don't pose much of an intellectual challenge, you get my drift."

"Can you see with those on?" Barry asked him. "At night, I mean? Pretty dark out here."

"Got us here, didn't I?"

He'd followed the taillights of the truck in front of him most of the way out, but Barry didn't think he ought to press a man so anxious to shoot someone.

They hadn't been there for more than a few minutes when they heard the staccato burst of automatic gunfire. Carl thumbed a radio he carried on his belt. "All units!" he said. "Are any of you involved in that?"

A few staticky negatives came back to him. Many had heard

it, but none of the American Pride soldiers were part of it. "Keep out of it," Carl ordered. "Repeat, do not engage. I'll check it out. Everybody else hang back and wait for my signal."

He tossed Barry a grin. "Ready for some action?"

The sound of gunfire had turned Barry's bowels to liquid, and he clenched so he didn't lose control of them. "Sure," he said, even though he had not meant to. He had wanted to argue, to try to find a way out of this, but he couldn't bring himself to speak the words. "Sure," he said again.

"That's good, because I think this is what we've been waiting for." Heading east, toward the gunfire, Carl led the way, followed by Barry, with Connie and Marc bringing up the rear. Every fiber of Barry's brain told him he should be running the other way, even if he had to train his gun on his companions to escape, because there could be no good outcome to this. His muscles refused to respond, carrying him along after Carl as if that man, not he, controlled them.

A quick dash brought them to the top of a rise where they could look down into a wide valley slanting toward the south. The gunfight was happening down there, where three trucks were grouped, two in one spot and one by itself. It almost seemed as if Carl had known where the fight would be and had chosen that place for himself, letting his soldiers take the stretches of border where nothing was happening.

Carl squatted at the top of the rise, where the brush would hide them from anyone below. "There she is," Carl said.

"She?" Barry asked.

"That's right," Carl said. He didn't offer to elaborate further.

"Looks like the people in the back there are doing all the shooting," Marc observed.

"They'll stop when their targets are dead," Carl replied. "Then we can move in."

"We're not gonna help those people?" Barry asked. "They're stuck there, bein' attacked."

"They're no friends of ours," Carl said. "They're Mexicans, same as the ones shooting at 'em. Let 'em waste their own ammo on each other. What I want isn't going to be hurt by a few bullets."

"Unless they blow the gas tank," Connie said. "That could hurt her, maybe."

Carl spat into the dirt. "Could be," he said. "Damn it. I guess we do have to move in." He pointed to a big mesquite, its gnarled branches waving in the wind. "When we get to that mesquite, I figure we'll be in range. That looks like about two hundred yards, maybe two-twenty, from those two big trucks. Let's stay low and dark till we get there, then light those moth-erfuckers up."

Connie nodded. Marc, grinning again, chewed on the unlit smoke. "Works for me," he said.

Barry didn't respond, but he was pretty sure his input wasn't needed or wanted. Carl started down the hill. On their own volition, Barry's legs followed him.

12

Jeannie clutched Oliver's hand so tightly he thought he would lose circulation to his fingers. He didn't urge her to release it, however, because he wanted to hold on to her just as much. Lulu crouched beside him, so close that he could feel her breathing, the swelling of her torso when she inhaled bringing her back into contact with his arm, the cool air when she exhaled moving her back away.

They watched a massacre. Whoever had been in the first truck didn't seem to be armed, but the people in the other two peppered it with enough bullets to kill a brigade. In the dark it was hard to be sure, but he didn't think he'd seen anyone alive around the front truck for some time—occasional motion was probably just the bullets twitching plants. Those that didn't hit the brush *chunked* into the truck like a louder, more destructive version of the night's monsoon rain. A burnt smell—gun smoke, Oliver guessed—wafted their way on the wind.

"I think she's in there," Lulu said, her voice a raspy whisper.

"I hope you're talking about the statue, Lulu, because there's no one alive in there," Oliver answered.

"No, in the back, I think she's in the back."

The truck's open bed was the part that faced the gunmen. "There's definitely no one alive back there."

"But I need to get closer," Lulu said. "She needs me."

He grabbed her arm, more roughly than he had to. "It's suicide, Lulu. Maybe if those guys in the other trucks leave we can check it out. Until then we stay right here."

"I was supposed to meet her right when she crossed over," Lulu argued. "Not sit back and watch her from a distance."

"If she needs you, she needs you alive, honey," Jeannie said. "Just wait until the shooting's over." Oliver squeezed his wife's hand, glad for her sensible presence beside him.

Lulu shifted her weight and Oliver held her arm tighter, afraid she would bolt. "Just be patient," he said.

She pulled a little, but didn't yank her arm from his grip. She turned to him, mouth opening as if to speak.

A burst of gunfire from a new source silenced her.

This time, the shooting came from over Oliver's right shoulder, between them and the border, a little farther away from the trucks. For a change, it was directed toward the men with the guns. On the two trucks grouped together, window glass shattered and steel shredded. One of the men there screamed and threw up his arms, his weapon flipping into the air and out of sight in the darkness.

Other men, taking shelter on the far side of the trucks, returned fire. They still didn't shoot directly at Oliver, Jeannie and Lulu, but their fire angled more in that direction than it had before. A few inches' change of the guns might spray lead right toward them.

"Stay low," Oliver said. "This tree isn't much cover, but it's all we've got."

"Who do you think that is?" Jeannie asked, with a jerk of her head toward the newcomers.

"I'd like to think it's Buck and his crew," Oliver replied. "But there's no guarantee of that."

"They're using military hardware, but that's not law enforcement," another voice said. It sounded male, and close behind them. Oliver released Jeannie and Lulu and spun around, nearly losing his balance and falling into the thorny mesquite.

"Oh God!" Lulu said. A sob almost eclipsed her words.

"Who—?" Jeannie asked.

A man stood casually behind them, as if people weren't shooting each other in the dark. He looked short, slight, with a prominent nose, a shiny, bulging forehead, and a weak chin. Dark hair was parted to one side. He wore a dark-colored polo shirt and jeans that looked like they'd been ironed, and his arms and chest were hairy, tufts of it curling up from the open neck of his shirt.

"It's him!" Lulu said.

"The one who—" Oliver began.

"Lulu and I are old friends," the man said. "I've missed you, Lulu. You led me on quite a chase."

Oliver wished he had one of the guns with which everybody else around here seemed to be equipped. He didn't know how the guy had found them—he must have followed from their house—but he wanted the man dead before he could threaten or harm Lulu any more. "You just walk away from here," he said, "and I won't kill you. But if you bother this girl again, I will, and don't think I can't."

"Everybody *can*," the man said. He smiled, jamming his hands into the pockets of his crisp jeans. "*Can* is not the hard part. *Will* is the hard part, and while it may sound contradictory, the fact is that most people never do it, and most of the ones who do only do it once, by accident or out of rage. But the others—the ones who do it because they *want* to, because they have the will—often find that only the first one is truly difficult. You have not had that first, and I do not think you have the will to start now."

"There's always that rage thing you mentioned."

"Yes," the man said. "And your fists are clenched, your teeth gritted in such a manly way, your face flushed. All good indicators of rage. If you were going to kill me, though, you'd already have made your move."

"You haven't threatened her yet," Oliver reminded him. He didn't like the quickie psychoanalysis the guy had thrown down, especially since it seemed unfortunately accurate. Already the urge to jump the man, to knock him to the ground and pummel him to death with a rock, had begun to pass.

"There's rage, and then there's calculation," Jeannie said. "Turn around and get out of here before you find out which one I'm all about."

The man shifted toward Jeannie, his left hand coming out

of the pocket and rubbing his furry right arm. "Oh, yes. I can see that you might actually do it. Or try, anyway."

"Count on it," Jeannie said. Oliver had never heard her sound so cold.

"I'm afraid that Lulu and I have unfinished business, though," the man said. He inclined his head ever so slightly toward the first truck. "Down there."

"She's not going anywhere," Oliver said.

"I have to, Oliver," Lulu said, her voice quivering. "He's right. She's waiting for me there."

13

"The fuck?" Scoot Brown asked.

"Got me there," Buck said. "Busy night at the border."

He and Scoot had worked their way within about fifty yards of the front truck, the one that had been taking all the fire at first. He couldn't see how many dead there were—they had fallen into the tall grass and brush—but no one moved there anymore. In a way he was relieved. If the gunmen got back in the other two trucks and drove back into Mexico, then he'd have some unsolved homicides on his hands, but not a firefight.

Before they could, though, someone else started shooting, from off to Buck's right. Whoever the newcomers were, they fired at the men with the guns, at the back two trucks. The gunmen shifted their attention to the newcomers, and the gun battle that had looked to be winding down heated up again.

He and Scoot watched from behind a creosote bush about five feet tall and the same across. When people started shooting at them, its spindly branches would offer no protection at all. "Get on your belly," he told Scoot. "Keep your weapon up and pointed at those trucks, just in case they shoot. I'll take those guys up the hill."

Scoot did as he was told, flattening himself on the ground, his sidearm held in both hands, elbows in the mud supporting it. Buck crouched, readying the shotgun. He brought his finger inside the guard, resting it lightly on the trigger. "Cochise County sheriffs!" he shouted as loud as he could manage. "Everybody cease fire!"

The shooting continued. Buck waited a few seconds, then

repeated his warning. This time he punctuated it with a shot into the air. When its boom faded, he added, "Drop those weapons!"

He threw himself down as the first answering slugs zipped through the creosote bush where he'd been standing. Scoot returned fire toward the trucks. "Guys're good," he said.

The shooters coming down off the western rise kept firing at the trucks, and after a few seconds the ones there returned their attention to them. Buck saw one of them go down, then heard a wail of pain from the trucks. It looked like there were still three working their way off the hillside, and they kept up their barrage against the trucks, aided by Scoot's .45 rounds.

Where the hell is the Border Patrol? he thought. *Where the hell are the* federales? He should've called for backup from Douglas as soon as Oliver told him where they were headed, but getting to Lulu had been his only priority. *And where the hell is she?*

In another minute, the worst of it seemed to be over. The men at the trucks were all down—wounded or dead, he guessed. At any rate, they had stopped firing. The ones who had come over the hill had never fired at him or Scoot, confining their fire to the shooters at the trucks. Maybe they *were* BP, after all.

The sudden silence startled him. His ears still rang from the gunfire, but otherwise the night was still, even the wind giving up. In the east the sky had turned gray, a glint over the hills indicating that the sun would rise soon.

"Come on," Buck said. Scoot forced himself up out of the mud that caked his entire front. "Let's see just who the hell those people are."

He and Scoot walked toward them as they came toward the trucks. He saw uniforms, camo. Were they Guard troops? Marines?

"Buck," Scoot said.

"What?"

Scoot pointed. From behind a big mesquite stepped four more people. In the growing light he recognized three of them as Oliver and Jeannie Bowles and Lulu Lavender. "That the girl?" Scoot asked.

"That's her."

It took a minute to place the fourth one, a man. Buck had never seen him in person, but as he stared at the guy, he remembered the videos from Geronimo! Internet Cafe and the picture he'd been sent of Henry Schaffer, aka Dana Fortier.

The man whose booby trap had killed Raul. The man who he believed had kidnapped Lulu and killed her family.

On instinct, he raised the barrel of the shotgun. He couldn't fire, though. From this range he'd spray all four of them.

"That man in the back?" he whispered to Scoot. "In the polo shirt. That's Schaffer, the guy whose cabin we went to tonight."

"Where Raul . . . ?"

"That's right. If he tries anything at all, kill him."

"Be my pleasure," Scoot said.

Buck realized that he was walking stiff-legged, suddenly nervous about the coming confrontation. Even though it seemed the shooters at the trucks were out of play, he believed the real trouble had just begun.

The paths of the three groups intersected at the front truck, a little blue Toyota with as many holes in it as a colander. In the bed, partially covered by a shredded green tarp, stood something white.

Each group stopped about twenty feet away from the truck. Three bodies lay close to it, riddled with bullets. They were all male, and looked Mexican. The other two trucks had stopped on the far side of the border, but this one had torn right through the fence, barely making it into the United States before it had stopped.

This close, in the glow of dawn, Buck saw that the people from the hill were not Border Patrol or National Guard. Two could have been soldiers, a man and a woman, both fit and wearing military-style garb without insignia, but the third was an older man who looked like a rancher. Buck was sure he'd seen the guy around but couldn't place him.

He turned his attention toward the other group. "Lulu," he said. "You okay?"

She sniffled. She looked like she'd been crying. "I'm okay," she said.

"That the guy?"

"That's him," Oliver said.

"I've got my own beef with you," Buck said, catching Henry Schaffer's gaze. "You're under arrest for the murder of Raul Bermudez."

"First things first, Lieutenant," Schaffer said.

"Meaning what?"

"Our business here is far from done."

Lulu broke away from her group and walked to the back of the truck. Her motions were almost trancelike, as if she moved through some invisible, viscous liquid. Nobody moved to stop her. At the truck, she peeled away what remained of the green tarp. The truck's cab blocked Buck's view, so he stepped closer, trying to keep a clear line between himself and Schaffer.

What she had uncovered was a statue of a girl, carved from some gleaming white stone. It looked as clean and bright as if it had been finished yesterday. Buck remembered the story Oliver had outlined for him. The statue had to be the "white girl" from Lulu's blog. "It's you, isn't it?" Lulu said.

Henry Schaffer stepped out from behind Oliver and Jeannie. He had his hands in his pockets and he sauntered toward the truck like a man taking a Sunday stroll.

"That's far enough, Michael," the man who looked like a soldier said. He pointed his automatic rifle at the man Buck knew as Henry Schaffer and Dana Fortier. "But then, that's probably not the name you're using these days, is it?"

"Are you still Kale?" Henry asked. "Or is it some other variant of Charles?"

"It's Carl. I'm happy with my identity; I don't need to change it every ten minutes."

"I take it you men know each other?" Buck interrupted.

"Oh, forever," Henry said. "Or does it just seem that way, Carl?"

"Long enough," the one called Carl said. "I guess I shouldn't be surprised to find you here. A little outgunned, however. And definitely outclassed."

The old guy with the two soldiers looked just as confused as Buck felt, his head whipping back and forth between the two men as if he had unexpectedly found himself at a tennis match.

"Outgunned, maybe," Henry said. "I think outclassed is an exaggeration." He gestured toward Lulu, who caressed the white statue, ignoring everything else. She looked like a sleep-walker. "After all, I am the one who brought her."

"Maybe there's something to be said for delegation, for letting others do the dirty work. Anyway, I could have sworn you found her hiding behind a tree," Carl said.

Henry's calm demeanor slipped for a moment. "You have no idea what I've been through with her in the last week."

"The last week doesn't matter," Carl said. "Only what happens now matters. And you don't get to spill her blood on the statue, because you're just out for yourself. I'm the one who recognized the very real threat she poses."

"You think because you believe your cause is pure, you get to win?" Henry asked, scoffing. "The world doesn't work that way. Need I remind you that if either of us takes possession of that statue, her own desires mean nothing? So for all your high-handedness, you and I have the exact same goal in mind—excepting, of course, which of us benefits most from the girl."

"Hold on, both of you," Buck said. He wasn't sure who to point the gun at, but the soldiers, armed themselves, seemed like the more imminent threat, so he settled on them. "Any more blood gets spilled around here, it'll be me doing the spilling."

"You don't know what you're—" Carl began. He cut himself off with a wave of his hand. "Barry, just shoot them. Everyone but the girl."

Barry—the old guy—raised his M-16, his eyes widening in terror, like he couldn't believe what he was about to do. His finger tightened on the trigger. Buck didn't wait for him to squeeze it, but twitched the Remington toward him and fired. The charge hit the old guy in the upper chest, neck and face, tearing skin and cutting bone, sending a spray of blood and brain into the air behind him. Buck pumped another shell into the chamber.

Instead of falling, Barry kept bringing his rifle up into position. He squeezed off a burst. One of the bullets struck Scoot, blowing him backward to the ground. Another slammed into Buck like a punch from a sledgehammer. He went down, firing his second shell. This one hit Barry too, or what was left of him. After the second shot, not much remained of Barry from the chest up. Still, as he finally fell, he kept squeezing the trigger of the automatic. Its muzzle flash competed for brightness with the sun, which had just pushed up over the eastern hills.

Through blurred eyes, Buck saw Oliver Bowles push Jeannie down and throw himself on top of her. Biting back agony, he pushed the shotgun away and clawed his .45 from its holster. There was no one he could shoot, though—the two men had rushed to Lulu's side. Wounded, shaky, Buck couldn't be sure he wouldn't hit Lulu, and he couldn't take that chance. The female soldier stood to one side, watching, but she held her gun at her side as if she knew it wouldn't do any good. He could shoot her, he supposed, but it wouldn't accomplish anything except making him feel better.

Watching the two men, Buck was pretty sure he had started to hallucinate. Their outlines seemed to shift and change: human one moment, something else the next, the lines and edges strobing so fast the eye couldn't follow. They didn't exactly fight, but they stared at each other, and they both trembled with effort. It looked to Buck like two men arm wrestling without touching each other, all their power and focus put instead into mental combat of some kind.

"Hell, I can kill her," the woman said. She shrugged. Buck tried to level his .45 at her just in case she raised it.

"No!" Carl said. "It has to be a man. It has to be me!"

"Not a chance," Henry said. "I earned it. I found her."

"Earning has nothing to do with it," Carl replied, his voice strained with effort. "It's about power; you should know that by now." He leaned forward sharply, lunging without moving his hands toward his opponent. Whatever he did worked, though, knocking the other man to the ground. Henry struggled to rise, but Carl raised his hands and made a pushing motion, and—six feet away—his foe flattened as if a great weight smashed down on him. Blood bubbled from Henry Schaffer's mouth, then geysered up, drenching him and the mud around him, and he was still.

Carl tossed a wan smile to the soldier woman and reached for Lulu. From somewhere he had drawn a knife, slender-bladed, shining in the sun's first rays.

No time left. Buck raised his sidearm, aimed with eyes that could barely see. Squeezed the trigger three times.

The bullets flew true. Buck saw the impacts against the man's body, saw dust puff from his shirt. No blood blossomed there, and though Carl grimaced, he didn't fall or stop what he was doing.

He had Lulu's arm in one hand and he shoved her up against the statue. With the other, he brought the knife to her throat. Buck wanted to shoot again, but his hands trembled, weak. He could barely lift the gun and she was too close. . . .

Oliver's body flashed across Buck's field of view, charging into the man with the knife. He surprised Carl, and they both went down, landing in a low mesquite. Thorns tore at their clothes and skin as they wrestled, Carl trying to get the knife into Oliver and Oliver fighting to knock it from Carl's grip. From the corner of his eye, Buck saw the soldier woman lifting her M-16 toward them, and he managed to squeeze off one more shot. It hit her in the temple and blew out the top of her head, and she crumpled in a heap.

"Buck." Scoot had crawled up behind him. His face was pale and drawn. "Fuckin' body armor, huh?"

"Yeah," Buck said, glad they hadn't stopped to change after their assault on the cabin. The bullet hadn't penetrated the Kevlar, although the pain was intense and he thought he'd cracked a rib. Apparently Scoot's armor had stopped the slugs he'd taken too. "Can you walk?"

"I think maybe."

"Kill that bastard," Buck said. "The one in the camo, who Oliver's fighting with."

For the second time that morning, Scoot said, "Be my pleasure." He lurched unsteadily to his feet and walked toward the
struggling men.

Buck caught Jeannie's gaze as she looked on, imploring.
There was nothing left he could do except hope Scoot could
kill Carl without hurting Oliver—and before Carl killed
Oliver himself. He seemed to have the upper hand—kept getting his knife hand free and slicing at Oliver with it. To his
credit, Oliver, whom Buck had believed to be a pacifist, was
able to keep Carl down on the ground with him, and away
from Lulu.

Catching sight of her, Buck felt a momentary sense of dis-
belief snag him like a thorn. Her skin seemed to have turned
white—not quite a radiance, but almost as if she had been
dusted by marble from the statue. For a second he thought it
was moonlight reflecting off the sheen of her skin, but the
moon had been dipping toward the horizon and ducked behind
a cloud.

Scoot staggered up to the two men, past Lulu, who still
leaned on the white statue, and shoved the barrel of his service
weapon up against the back of Carl's head. Carl tried to jerk
his head out of the way, but all he succeeded in doing was
moving it so that if the bullet passed through, it wouldn't
strike Oliver. At the last moment, Lulu released the statue and
spun around, putting her hands on Scoot's shoulders. The
same white near-radiance that pearled Lulu's skin spread to
Scoot just as he pulled the trigger.

The bullet did pass through Carl's head, with a spray of
gore and skull fragments. Carl's body briefly went limp, but
then he rolled off Oliver and sliced at Scoot with the long
knife. With Lulu gripping his shoulders, Scoot fired again,
then twice more. All head shots, at close range.

Finally, Carl stopped moving. Scoot lost his balance, sitting down hard next to Oliver. Oliver struggled to his feet,
looking at Carl, at Lulu. He extended a hand to Scoot, helping
him back up, then turned to Lulu. He wrapped his arms
around the girl, who was crying now, really weeping, the
pearlescence gone, as if whatever spell had been binding her

to the statue was broken at last. Jeannie joined them, and Buck watched the three of them hugging one another, holding one another tightly, three people who loved one another.

If there's any magic there, he thought, *it's the good kind.*

14

Even after dumping the contents of a plastic gas can from one of the trucks stopped across the border all around the statue, it took most of the second clip in the woman's M-16 to hit the right combination of gasoline and spark—and Buck worried that he was a bit too close to the action, but he really didn't have the stamina to do it from farther back, where he'd have to aim more carefully—but when it worked, it worked. An explosion scorched his face, sent a gout of flame like a fiery jellyfish into the sky and lifted the truck off the ground. Buck dropped the gun and curled into a ball, his arms flung over his head. Bits of burning tire and white-hot sheet metal and, most satisfying, chunks of clean white rock that had once been carved into the shape of a girl who bore a remarkable resemblance to Lulu Lavender crashed to the ground all around him, but nothing bigger than one hubcap actually hit him.

Lulu had objected, wailing and trying to put herself between him and the truck. She still wanted to save the white girl, still thought there was some reason—some good reason—that the white girl wanted to meet her at the borderline. Oliver and Jeannie tried to convince her that whatever the white girl had in mind (if such a term could be used at all), it wasn't for anything healthy or clean, and the white girl couldn't be allowed to have her way. As they talked, they maneuvered Lulu out of the way and up the gentle slope, toward the road.

When debris had stopped raining down, Buck forced himself to his feet and walked up to where the others had stopped. The sun was out in full force, the only clouds a few wispy high

ones that wouldn't hold enough water to release it. Buck
looked back once at the torn fence with the two trucks on the
other side of it. Near where the truck had broken through, a
black plastic garbage bag fluttered on the wire as if a barb had
snagged a migrant's shadow when he crossed over.

"You suppose we'll ever know who the guys in those other
trucks were?" he asked when he reached the group.

"Looked like drug dealers to me," Scoot said. He had
walked up and looked them over, peering about anxiously as he
did, in case Mexican authorities came out of the bushes. "Fancy
clothes, expensive jewelry, those nice four-by-four trucks. They
had Mac-10s, what they killed them other Mexicans with."

"The ones who drove the statue up," Oliver said, "I wonder
who they were."

"We'll try to identify them," Buck promised. He had
moved the bodies away before blowing up their Toyota
pickup. Other men and a couple of women in camo gear had
shown up a while ago and identified Carl Greenwell, Connie
McKay and Marc Craig, whose body had been found on the
hillside. No one seemed to know the last name of the guy
Buck had obliterated, Barry something. They said they were
from the American Pride Ranch, which Buck recognized as
one of the border watch groups Nellie had mentioned, and that
Carl was the leader of their group and owner of the ranch.
They were solemn, and when Buck said the bodies would be
released as soon as the investigation was finished, they agreed
and went on their way. He figured they had broken all kinds of
laws, running military-style maneuvers on the border with
their automatic weapons, but he had enough on his plate at the
moment without worrying about them.

Lulu's nose was red from crying, her eyes puffy, and some
vomit still flecked her lips from throwing up after Carl had
been killed and she was released from whatever trance she'd
been under. "I . . . I can't help feeling like this is my fault,"
she said. "All these people—"

"It's not," Jeannie interrupted. She took Lulu in her arms
again. "Maybe it all centered on you in some way—that statue
did look an awful lot like you. But that doesn't mean you did

anything wrong, or you could have done anything to stop what happened. You're the victim here, baby, not the cause."

"Jeannie's right," Oliver said. Jeannie released Lulu and took his hand, holding it in both of hers. The love they shared was palpable, Buck thought, envious. "You've been through a horrible ordeal, Lulu. We'll do whatever we can to help you get past it. And to start with, we're not going to let you blame yourself."

She blinked away tears and smiled at them, showing her teeth, then turned and beamed it at Buck as well. He felt bathed in a warm light. *Something special about that girl,* he thought. *Can't deny that.*

Like Oliver said, she'll have a lot to get over. The murder of her family, her own kidnapping, everything she witnessed this morning.

He had a hunch she would be fine.

Rest of us'll have nightmares for a long time to come, but she'll get through it okay. Resilience of youth, and all that.

He glanced at Oliver and Jeannie again, leaning into each other, supporting each other. They'd never been through anything like this, but they'd be okay too, he believed, as long as they had that bond.

"Thanks," Lulu said, aiming that smile all around. "Thanks to all of you. I . . . I don't know . . . Ah, damn, I'm gonna cry again. Shut up."

Buck stifled a yawn. He wanted to sleep, wanted to lie down beside Tammy and feel her comforting, yielding flesh, like he had in the old days. But God, the paperwork that waited for him back at his office. Raul. All this.

For once, he was glad the press had the Lippincotts to obsess over. Sirens neared, and Ed Gatlin would have to hear about what had happened here—some of it, not counting the parts that Buck couldn't begin to explain in any way that wouldn't wind up with him on some psychiatrist's couch for the next three years. With any luck, the media, and the rest of the world, never would hear about it either.

Buck sure as hell wouldn't be telling Gina Castaneda about it.

15

Before they leave the scene, Lulu stops, turns, taking one last look behind. The flames have died down, and amid the twisted, blackened steel she thinks she can make out the bed of the truck, or something like it, hard anyway, and ridged.

That's the truck bed, she believes, that carried the white girl to her, across space and time, up the underside of the continent, for a meeting that ended before it really began.

And now, after all these years and all these miles, the white girl is in pieces, little chunks, few of them bigger than her fist.

She saved one, tucking it in her pocket when no one was looking. She puts her hand on the outside of the pocket now, feeling its shape, pressing on it so that the jagged side bites through the borrowed jeans, into her thigh.

Lulu has no idea why she took it, why she thinks it might be worth having.

No idea. . . .